Anna

Patricia Dixon

For my mum.
Thank you for everything, always and forever.

CHAPTER 1

I can clearly remember the first time I saw a funeral cortege. I was six years old. It was a summer's day and the weather uncomfortably humid. Pungent fumes from the traffic which buzzed up and down the high street burned my nostrils while we waited for our bus in amiable silence, watching the cars and lorries pass us by. The other people at the stop were chatting about the weather or gossiping but up to that point everything was quite normal, that is until I saw the coffin. The traffic had come to a full stop whilst the lights changed and right there, directly in front of me was the biggest, blackest car I had ever seen. Inside the car contained what looked like a wooden box and surrounding it an assortment of beautiful flowers and right in the centre, large white letters. I spelled out the word in my head. It said 'MUM'.

I looked up at my own mother who appeared to be staring at her shoes and asked her what was in the box. She didn't answer so I asked again, a little louder this time, also enquiring why the flower word inside the big car said 'MUM'. Ever impatient and prone to flying off the handle she told me to be quiet and stop looking, it was rude to stare. Not to be diverted, I asked innocently why it was rude to stare. I think in a desperate effort to shut me up she hissed a reply.

'Because someone's mother has died and *she* is in the box!'

I can feel now the harshness of those words as they hit me, like a slap, sucking the wind from my lungs as I stared in wide-eyed shock. I ignored the warning and turned quickly, focusing on the car. With whatever intuition I possessed at six, I realised with utter horror that not only was a dead person a few feet away from me, but it was also a dead mum. I couldn't move.

1

As the car started to move away, another black car crawled by in its wake. Inside, the people were dressed in black, squashed together, all staring straight ahead. Just as it drew level with me the woman sitting nearest the window turned and I caught her eye. I remember that she wasn't crying but looked incredibly sad. I couldn't move or tear my eyes away and it seemed as though everything was happening in slow motion. Our eyes locked, the sad lady's and mine. I was transfixed. The moment before the car moved out of sight she did the strangest thing, she smiled at me and despite my fear I smiled back. I have never forgotten that day, the sad lady or her smile. It wasn't a happy smile like when you receive a gift or set eyes on someone you love, it was the saddest smile I have ever seen in my life.

Today, it feels like it was only a heartbeat ago and I remember so clearly being that little girl on a hot, sunny afternoon, sat at the bus stop. And maybe I know why the sad lady smiled. Was she touched by my innocence, glad that I wasn't feeling her pain? Perhaps she was wishing for the impossible, to be transported back to a time when the chore of the day wasn't to face death in the face, when she had no concept of loss and lived in a world free from sadness and the awful emptiness that accompanies grief.

Now as I look out of the window of the big black funeral car I am travelling in, I wonder if people are furtively looking in on me. Are they wondering why I'm not holding a handkerchief to my sobbing mouth or wiping eyes which are leaking tears of despair?

It is actually the first time I have travelled to a funeral in one of these limousines. When my father died I was deemed too young, at eight, to attend the service. Instead I stayed at home and watched from behind drawn curtains as my dad and the black cars drove slowly away.

I hated my mother when she told me I couldn't go and kicked up an almighty fuss, especially as my older brother, who at thirteen had appointed himself the man of the house, was to be included. They tried to make me feel important by saying I had to help Mrs Wilson from next door put sandwiches and cake on plates for the wake. It didn't work and I seethed all day at the unfairness of it all.

Ironically, in my innocence, I had no idea that a time would come when the last place on earth I would wish to be is inside a funeral car. This vehicle, this journey, means you have suffered loss on a very intimate level. Maybe they should have let me go, to help me understand what seemed like a secret process and by saying goodbye to my dad the curse would have been lifted. Since then, whenever I have attended a funeral it has been in my own car.

I glance to my right and see my parents-in-law. They are sitting close together, hands clutched tightly in silent dignity and contemplation, staring into the distance. In front of me are my three precious children, not children anymore – young adults. I'm glad that for now I can only see the back of their heads, as to witness the sadness in their eyes tears open my heart. Melanie, my youngest, is resting her head on her brother's shoulder, and sitting next to Sam is my eldest son, Joe. All three are lost in their own worlds. I have no idea what they are thinking or feeling but as is the norm for funeral car passengers, they look straight ahead.

I don't want to disappoint any furtive onlookers so I purposely break the mourner-mould and continue to look out of the window. I'm wearing dark glasses so if I was crying, no one would see and as I'm not, no one will know. I need this time to make last minute preparations in my head, steel myself for the rest of the day and remind my heart not to give up.

As we drive through the iron gates and into the cemetery I can see the church in the distance. Thankfully, this isn't where we were married. I couldn't bear to say goodbye to my husband there, under these circumstances. Not in a place with happy memories or where we promised to love each other forever, parting only in death. How far away that day seemed, so distant that it caused us no concern, like it would never happen to us.

The sun is behind the ever-looming church, casting it under a dark shadow. My stomach knots, my palms are cold but strangely damp and I can't feel my lips because they are numb. The car sweeps around in a circular motion bringing us to the chapel doors and before a sea of people, all respectfully dressed and accessorised by sad, mournful faces. As the car draws slowly to a stop I realise that I'll have to get out first because everyone, especially the children, will be waiting for my lead. This is it, I tell myself. I've held everything together for weeks, months really, and rehearsed this day over and over in my mind. Be dignified, Anna. This is your final role as Matthew's wife. Don't mess it up.

I step out of the car and am welcomed with kind, reassuring words by the vicar. His strong hands fold around mine; they are warm and I know he is attempting to calm me. I am aware that everyone around is silent; the only noise is that of whatever the vicar is saying. I'm trying to listen but cannot concentrate because even now, in the middle of all this I have only one thought in my mind. It has plagued me for days and kept me awake at night. All I can think is… are you here?

Are you somewhere in the crowd, standing in the shadows or mingling with friends, family and colleagues, hoping not to be seen? Are you watching me, scrutinising my actions, my clothes, gauging my depth of sadness? Will you be judging me on how many tears I cry, be moved by the words in the eulogy? Or maybe you won't like the songs I have chosen and think you know better. Will you speak to me or identify yourself in some subtle way? Will I know you? Will you be young or middle-aged?

Maybe I'm wrong and you decided to stay away, preferring to remember how things were, not wanting to witness the distress of our loved ones or more likely, you just didn't have the nerve to face all this. I thank the vicar for his kindness and as he walks away I quickly scan the crowd and search, my squinting eyes unseen from behind sunglasses. Somewhere, amongst that jumble of people, looking at me, there is only one face I want to find.

I have no idea who she is or what she looks like. She may be here, the other woman, the person who has made all this a sham, a pretence. Because of her I cannot mourn properly a man whom I thought I knew, the man I promised to love forever and who promised to love me back. I believed in him and our marriage, never imagining he would let me down. The tears still refuse to fall for someone who betrayed me and loved another. I have been robbed of that simple emotion.

The mourners will see me today as a brave wife, battling through her husband's funeral, holding things together for the sake of the children. If only they knew that the man for whom they have gathered, to pay their respects, deserves none because he cheated on his wife. They have no idea of the turmoil inside me right now. A vicious disease, borne of anger, hurt and a million unanswered questions constantly eating away at me, eroding my memories and my life.

If you are out there, my husband's lover, quietly observing me from somewhere within the crowd then I dare you, step out of the shadows and make yourself known. Come over and shake my hand and let me look into your eyes. But mark my words, I've had plenty of time to prepare, and even if I'm not ready for all of this, I'm ready for you.

CHAPTER 2

Anna turned away from the mourners to meet the second car carrying close family. Her brother Philip, their mother Enid, cousin Naomi, best friend Jeannie, plus Dennis, Matthew's business partner and loyal friend, and his wife, Mary. As they stepped from the car Anna immediately spotted the murderous look on Phil's face and the reason for this became clear when Anna clapped eyes on her mother. To complement her hideous outfit it now looked as though she'd been punched in the face (always a possibility where Enid was concerned) either that or she'd developed some kind of facial allergic reaction. Above her top lip was a large, angry red rash which seemed to be spreading right up her nose.

The minute her mother was within earshot Anna hissed, 'For God's sake, Mum, what've you done now?'

Jeannie, spotting tension in the air, quickly intervened and explained that as they entered the cemetery Enid decided to touch up her lipstick. Unfortunately, not only was it deep crimson, her favourite, but she had also forgotten her compact so leant forward to apply it using the rear-view mirror. Due to incredibly bad timing it coincided with the driver hitting a speed bump, the offending lipstick then slipped and smeared her entire top lip, finishing off wedged up her nose. Jeannie had spent the rest of the journey frantically rubbing Enid's face in an attempt at damage limitation but her skin was now stained and as a result she looked a sight. Exasperated and completely lost for any words, sympathetic or otherwise, Anna left Enid in the hands of more patient others and went to check on the children.

They were huddled together next to the limousine, looking around nervously, taking in the crowd of mourners, unsure and uncomfortable in the glare of so many onlookers no matter how well meaning they were. Any tears that Anna had shed in the past week or so had not been for her loss, but the terrible effect the death of their father had on the children. It took every ounce of strength she had remaining not to break down right there and then as a huge tidal wave of emotion, reserved only for them, threatened to engulf her.

Joe, despite his tanned skin, looked tense and drawn and was doing his utmost to be strong and support his younger siblings. Joe was the serious, studious son and she knew he felt a certain amount of responsibility to take on the mantle as head of their family. It was a role he was unprepared for, and not what Anna expected from him. His backpacking adventure in New Zealand had come to an end and so had his carefree days. This was something she intended to deal with once today was over.

Sam, the light-hearted, independent, easy-going son was also putting on a brave face. The joker of the family, he had a wicked sense of humour and since joining the army at eighteen had matured quickly. Having spent the past two years away from home and in the company of his older and more experienced colleagues, he'd grown up in many ways. Yet despite all that, Anna sensed that he was overwhelmed by today and no amount of training, drills or routine could have prepared him for his father's funeral.

Finally, Anna's gaze rested on her daughter, Melanie, who breezed through life effortlessly, never seeming to have a care in the world, making friends, enjoying her youth and almost ready to leave the nest for university. With her usual confidence she appeared to be dealing best with her grief but Anna suspected that being there, the night the police came with news of Matthew's accident, had a lot to do with it. The initial shock and trauma of the event, the tears of disbelief and the sheer raw emotion she witnessed in Mel that evening probably meant she'd got the worst out of her system and now, the funeral was simply about saying goodbye to her dad.

Having spotted Enid's face, Anna saw Mel whisper something into Sam's ear and when he turned and saw his grandmother, both had to control another bout of nervous giggles. Earlier in the day, as close family began arriving at the house before the funeral, tension was ever mounting, and a black cloud of anxiety and apprehension began to envelop the lounge. Sam, who was sitting next to his sister, looked uncomfortable in his suit, pulling irritably at the collar of his white shirt as Melanie fussed with her dress, trying to avoid creases. Anna was in the kitchen making yet another cup of tea, glad of having something to do, despite her shaking hands which betrayed her outwardly calm appearance. She was carrying the tea into the lounge when Enid arrived, hearing the shrill sound of her mother's voice before her attention was drawn to the vision from hell that was her funeral outfit.

'Good God in heaven! Mum, what are you wearing?'

The words came forth from Anna's mouth before she had time to consider them as there, in all her glory, stood Enid. She was resplendent in a black velvet dress, far too tight and low-cut for women of a certain age and, as in her mother's case, endowed with a very ample bosom. This was distastefully accessorised with pearls, a gaudy fascinator trimmed with black feathers and a polka dot veil and worse, her silver dancing shoes. Enid looked truly frightful. To add insult to injury, topping off the whole ensemble, around her shoulders and draped in all its beady-eyed, scratchy-clawed, moth-eaten glory, was Aunty Elsie's beloved fox fur.

The offending heirloom had been involved in a long, drawn-out tug of war between mother and aunt for decades. Enid insisted that Elsie had gifted it to her and was the ultimate Indian giver. Elsie, however, was adamant that it was only on loan. It then mysteriously disappeared during her move to the care home where Elsie now resided. Today, of all days, the mystery was finally solved and the culprit identified, a revelation which left Anna lost for words and momentarily stunned into horrified silence.

Jolted straight back into reality by the guffaws and hysterical laughter emanating from Sam and Mel who were incapable at this point of any self control, Anna, recognising nervous laughter bordering on hysteria when she saw it, banished both of them to the kitchen. She was soon rescued by Joe who was watching from a safe distance, apparently more flowers had arrived so, passing Enid whilst averting her eyes from the frocky horror, Anna could only manage to whisper.

'Mother, you look bloody ridiculous!'

***

The service ran like clockwork, not that Anna could remember much of it; she didn't listen to the eulogy as there was no need. She knew exactly what it would say owing to the fact that she had given all the information to the vicar when he called to make arrangements. He had been kind and understanding even though he had never met Anna or Matthew, but this didn't seem to diminish his concern or desire to get things just right. It was through gritted teeth that she gave him a rundown of Matthew's saintly life (omitting his indiscretion) which he was now imparting on the rapt congregation.

In that special voice that vicars save for solemn occasions, he droned on about where Matthew went to school then on to how he and Anna had first met, waiting for their respective friends outside the Odeon. She was eighteen and Matthew was twenty-two. They were married in their local church eighteen months later (conveniently before the bump that was Joe began to show) and then on to how Matthew and his best friend Dennis joined forces to buy the small haulage firm from their boss when he retired.

Dennis, a few years older than Matthew, was the yard foreman and had taken him under his wing. They became great friends. Matthew borrowed money from his father and both men remortgaged their homes then worked all the hours God sent to build the successful company it was today.

The vicar moved seamlessly on, explaining that the births of Samuel and Melanie soon followed, who Matthew was admired by, his hobbies, his achievements, and so it went on and on. Dennis gave an emotional speech about his best friend, some of which caught Anna's attention. He described a loving father and husband who adored his family and wife, all the usual platitudes, but as the well meant words spilled out, Anna thought sourly that Dennis had been made a fool of too. He didn't know the truth.

Aware of restrained sobbing and sniffs from people all around her, Anna glanced anxiously at her sons to her side. Both had tears in their eyes or rolling quietly down their cheeks but were somehow managing to control their grief. At the point in the service where the vicar mentioned that Matthew was a lifelong Portsmouth F.C. supporter, as were both his sons, Joe's hand momentarily grasped Anna's. Feeling his pain, she wrapped her fingers around his and squeezed as much strength into him as she could muster, then the moment passed and his hand relaxed before returning to his own silent thoughts.

Melanie was on Anna's right, leaning against her shoulder, holding her hand and quietly dabbing away tears with the other. It was then that Anna noticed someone just behind her was really sobbing, so she turned quickly, realising it was Jeannie who, from her very swollen eyes and the tissue covering her mouth, was having trouble containing her emotions. It touched Anna's heart. Jeannie had known Matthew for as long as she had and having spent much of their adult years in each other's company, would miss him too.

During the whole service, Anna had to fight an incredible urge to turn around so she could look along every single pew and check each face. She imagined Matthew's lover, her jealous eyes boring into the back of the widow's head, watching and comparing every action and scrutinising each word of the eulogy. Anna felt incredibly self-conscious and slightly inferior in the presence of her invisible rival, if that's what you could call her.

At forty-two, Anna was frequently told she looked younger, the credit for which was always taken by Enid and her good genes. She'd always been slim, but in recent years the creep of pre-middle-age inches were gathering in all the wrong places so Anna was even more cautious of what she ate and exercised regularly. The result, she looked good in what she wore and had somewhat naively presumed her efforts would ensure Matthew's interest and he would only have eyes for her. How wrong could she have been?

Regardless, Anna was determined that today, for her own self-esteem and the benefit of anyone who had hoped she would turn up looking like a bedraggled, dowdy mother of three, they would be sorely disappointed. Anna had chosen a pale grey, sleeveless shift dress which finished just above the knee and a matching three-quarter sleeved fitted jacket, trimmed in black. Her patent shoes had quite a heel but they emphasised her good legs and made her feel taller and more confident.

On the advice of her daughter, Anna hadn't put up her chestnut brown hair as she'd planned. While she watched her mother apply her make-up that morning, a solemn, pale-faced Melanie spoke up.

'Dad always liked your hair down, Mum. You should wear it like that.'

Anna wisely decided against voicing the acid-laced comment that popped straight into her head. Her bitter thoughts were always bubbling away, just under the surface but somehow she managed to hold her tongue and instead, simply smiled and agreed.

Some members of the congregation may have thought the sunglasses were a touch over dramatic but Anna didn't care because no amount of make-up could conceal the dark rings around her pale brown eyes. Sitting on the front row also excluded her from prying eyes and no one seated behind them would be remotely aware of her lack of tears, but the second the service was over she would put them straight back on. They were her shield and protector of the truth.

Anna was brought back from her reverie by the sound of crackling, forcing her to cringe and close her eyes, knowing instinctively what it was. Earlier in the day, following the comments made about her attire, Enid predictably took the huff and stomped off into the kitchen where she remained for a while, stomping about and making herself useful (as she put it) while Anna had been distracted by the arrival of other mourners. She was about to make her peace with Enid when she heard Joe call out.

'Mum. The cars are here.' His voice had a ring of thinly veiled panic to it.

Anna's stomach lurched and her whole being froze. This was the part she had been dreading. She steeled herself to go to the front door where the stark reality of Matthew's death was rolling up outside the house. There before her, in the glistening sunshine she saw the unavoidable truth that was her husband's coffin.

Her children were soon beside her and she felt Melanie squeeze her hand tightly, not quite sure if the grasp was giving or receiving strength. Anna held on regardless, at this point, far too stunned to let go. With practised ease and compassionate authority, the funeral director took over, arranging the flowers in the hearse, escorting people to the cars and taking much needed command of the proceedings thus allowing Anna to relax slightly – until Sam passed by. Just before getting into the limo, he spoke to Anna in a hushed tone, checking over his shoulder for Enid.

'Mum, Gran's got a picnic in her bag!'

Anna didn't believe him at first and hoped it was a joke.

'You had better be kidding, Sam, please tell me you are.'

'No, honestly, Mum. I saw her make it in the kitchen. Sandwiches, biscuits, and she's even got a hip flask. I told her you can't eat in church but she said you can as long as you don't get caught. She reckons she might get hungry if it drags on a bit. I wanted to warn you before we left but the cars arrived. Seriously, Mum, you need to have a word with her, she's on one today!'

Sam looked ashen and Anna was furious with her mother for piling undue stress upon them.

Feeling completely drained, and that was before they'd even set off, Anna thought she could cheerfully kill her mother who was getting worse as she got older. Enid was far too outspoken for her own good and at times bordered on being plain rude. She was also prone to bizarre behaviour (including her dress sense), an over fondness for the brandy in her hip flask and now this, a picnic, today of all days.

The funeral director was waiting for Anna and Sam to get into the car, so to avoid another scene with her mother she did as she was told. Consequently, in the middle of her husband's funeral service, Anna was forced to look around where, lo and behold, her mother sat chomping away. She had a sandwich and a packet of biscuits on her lap and a hip flask tucked neatly between her and Philip, who it had to be said, was mortified.

Following the service, everyone followed the coffin to the burial plot in a slow, mournful procession. At the head of it, Anna's nerves jangled, her legs felt like lead and she was managing to hang on to her poise by a thread. The tension and grief in the air was palpable and at times she felt detached, like an actress on the set of a film. Right now she desperately wished someone would shout 'Cut' and they could all rush off, back to reality for a cup of tea and a smoke.

As their immediate family gathered around the grave, Anna knew that this would be the hardest part. She had attended both burials and cremations and was acutely aware that the moment the curtain closes around the coffin or it is lowered into the ground, this is the point at which saying goodbye becomes very real, very final. Matthew's mother was being visibly supported by her husband; this was after all her only child and today, their last farewell. Anna could not imagine how terrible that must feel.

By Anna's side were Melanie and Sam. Philip stood opposite, next to Joe. As the vicar gave his final blessings they each took a handful of earth from a box and as the coffin was lowered they sprinkled it over the descending object. Melanie passed Anna one of the cream roses which she had removed from the arrangement on the top of the coffin, they threw them in together. As they did so, Anna noticed Joe put one hand inside his jacket, pull something out, and then throw it into the grave.

Looking down into the dark space below, mingled with the earth and flowers, lay a tiny teddy, a football mascot dressed in a Portsmouth F.C. strip. Anna recognised it instantly. It was Joe's souvenir from the first football match he attended with Matthew.

It was the bear that broke her, finally allowing the tears to flow from her eyes like a river bursting its banks. Anna clasped her hand over her mouth to trap the sobs and stop them from escaping. As her heart experienced a wrenching, splitting pain she became aware of loving arms wrapping tightly around her. Hearing the calm, comforting words of her family Anna somehow regained control. Once order was restored and she felt able to speak, with all the strength she had remaining Anna took Melanie's hand and then a long, deep sustaining breath. Looking downwards she said simply, 'Goodbye, Matthew,' then turned and walked away.

As they made their way back to the cars Anna realised that some of the mourners had remained by the graveside to say their own personal goodbyes, causing a shiver to run down her spine, her heart missing a beat, skin prickling. Perhaps *she* would be there as well, lurking behind headstones, waiting for everyone to leave so she could weep tears of anguish for her lost lover, or worse, she could be standing there at the graveside, right now, brazenly mourning, defiantly stating her silent right to grieve.

Since leaving the church Anna hadn't had the opportunity to survey the mourners, they had been behind her most of the time but now, as she reached the funeral cars, she allowed the others to be seated, which gave ample time to turn and search amongst the people by the grave.

Dennis was there with Mary, both gazing down in quiet contemplation. With no children of their own they had adopted Anna, Matthew and the children as their family, and they were now heartbroken. Others, employees of the company, friends and neighbours past and present, stood chatting or were beginning to walk away but she could see no one who stood out, looked out of place or even an unknown, lone female. Anna scanned the surrounding headstones for a skulking shape amongst the shadows but to no avail, she just wasn't there. Hearing a soft familiar voice broke Anna from her trance, causing her to jump and turn away. It was Jeannie. Laying her hand gently on Anna's arm, she motioned for her to move.

'Come on, let's get away from here and take you home. You've been really brave but it's time to go now.' Jeannie smiled and waited for her lost-looking friend to respond.

Anna squeezed Jeannie's hand gratefully, thankful for her support and glad of her presence then took one last look towards Matthew's grave, trying hard not to succumb to the dreadful feeling she was abandoning him, then silently, doing as she was told, got into the car.

CHAPTER 3

Back at the house the caterers had done a wonderful job preparing the buffet in the dining room. Laid out on starched white tablecloths there was an assortment of sandwiches, sausage rolls, quiches and cakes, all the usual traditional wake offerings and there was enough to feed an army. Tea and coffee were on offer along with wine or spirits which Anna was now beginning to regret, her mother had been at the brandy already. She didn't want Enid causing further embarrassment and had told everyone to keep a close eye on her, just to be on the safe side. Anna had made a point of inviting everyone to the house and was relieved to see that most of the office team along with some of the garage staff and drivers from the firm had also come back.

Matthew and Dennis prided themselves on the company being a family concern and even though they looked slightly uncomfortable she hoped it was more to do with circumstance than being in their boss's home. Samantha, Matthew's loyal and trustworthy personal assistant was there, chatting quietly in the corner, her early pregnancy not quite showing yet. Anna hadn't had a chance to speak to her but made a mental note to catch her before she left. Maybe she knew something of this other woman, on the other hand, perhaps now wasn't an appropriate time to interrogate her especially as they could be overheard.

Anna was sitting by the fire trying not to encourage conversation, happy just to sit quietly and observe. Next to her was Naomi, her only cousin and dear friend. Naomi was one of nature's children, with very long, naturally curly strawberry blonde hair. She favoured floaty dresses, beads and bangles and always wore perfume that smelled of summer flowers and now held Anna's hand in silent support while listening to Melanie describe her chosen university.

When Mel eventually got up to fetch some food, Naomi turned to Anna and nodded in the direction of Enid.

'I see Mum's fox fur has turned up at last.'

Naomi's wry smile told Anna that her cousin wasn't cross, which was a relief.

'Oh God, I know. I'm so sorry, Naomi, I honestly had no idea she had it. She's got some nerve that one. When she turned up with it today I wanted the ground to open up and knowing you would see it as well, I could've strangled her. She's such a flaming tea leaf. What are we going to do?'

'To be honest, Anna, I don't really care. It's hideous and I've never agreed with furs for fashion as you know. But Mum does keep on about it. She's not been well and gets upset about the smallest of things lately. I think I might liberate it and then arrange for it to be miraculously found. Looks like Aunty Enid's getting a bit merry so she probably won't notice, what do you think?' Naomi smiled impishly and looked to her cousin for encouragement.

'I think she deserves everything she gets; she's been a complete nightmare today. Just give me the nod and I'll distract her if need be. Anyway, from the way she's knocking back the vino over there I reckon she'll be comatose before too long.' Anna shook her head wearily as Naomi changed the subject.

'Will you come over to visit us soon? We don't see enough of you and Mum loves it when you visit her. I was so busy last time and we didn't have chance for a proper catch up. I really miss you, Anna, so don't be a stranger.' Naomi squeezed Anna's hand in a gentle plea.

Anna was touched by her cousin's words and felt a huge lump form in her throat as hot tears pricked her tired eyes. She didn't trust herself to speak so instead nodded a yes, squeezing Naomi's hand in reply. It wasn't only the sincerity of Naomi's words that had prompted this reaction; her cousin had no idea of the part she had unwittingly played in exposing Matthew's affair. Simply remembering the dreadful day turned Anna's blood cold, because that morning, as she innocently left the house without a care in her everyday, normal world she had no idea that by the time she returned later in the evening, it would be shattered beyond repair. The hurt and shock of her discovery would change Anna's life forever.

***

Matthew had been away on a business trip for three days and was due back that evening. Having cleaned every inch of the house, washed and ironed the entire contents of the laundry basket then filled the fridge with all his favourite things, Anna decided that she would drive over to Swanwick and visit her Aunty Elsie who had recently moved into a care home and was now almost housebound. Anna loved her aunt who was the polar opposite of her sister Enid because where Anna's mother was practical, organised, house-proud and strict, Aunty Elsie was liberal, disorganised and, most of all, fun and cuddly. Anna had spent many happy weekends and holidays at her aunt's house in the countryside, running free with Naomi in fields of wild flowers, getting dirt on their knees and eating pasta and tasty food with herbs and spices for tea. It was another world and one in which Anna had always felt welcome and at ease, not that she wasn't loved by Enid, but her affection was harder won.

So, it was with a happy and expectant heart that Anna set off that late May morning, her car loaded with chocolate themed treats, slushy romantic novels and a bottle of cream sherry for Elsie. She never bothered with flowers as Naomi owned the florist shop in the village therefore her aunt was never short of sweet smelling blooms. After spending a lovely morning drinking tea and reminiscing, Anna helped Elsie look for her precious fox fur which had mysteriously gone missing. The prized possession had been given to Elsie by a sweetheart and forever coveted by her jealous sister, Enid.

Anna met Naomi around one o'clock for a late lunch in town where her cousin was rushed off her feet preparing floral tributes for two large weddings, one being held later that day. As Naomi had said, they didn't have much time together as during lunch she received a frantic phone call from the shop. Apparently, one of the large arrangements had been left behind and the wedding planner was screaming blue murder. The delivery van was miles away on another call and they were up to their eyes in it preparing centrepieces for the second wedding. Anna could see the panic on Naomi's face; she hated to let people down, her reputation was everything.

'Where's the wedding venue, Naomi? Maybe I can drop them off for you on my way home.' Anna had nothing planned for the rest of the day and was happy to help out.

'That's really kind of you, Anna, but I couldn't expect you to do it. It'll take you quite a bit off your route.' Naomi was already wishing she hadn't even left the shop and really needed to get back.

'Nonsense, there's no rush for me to get home. Matthew won't be there until late tonight and I'll just be bored for the rest of the day, I'm happy to help out. Just give me the address and I'll set off as soon as we get back.'

Anna saw relief wash over her cousin's face and within the hour she was being waved off by Naomi, who was so grateful she'd filled the car with enough thank you flowers to start her own shop. As she drove east, Anna's heart remained light despite the dark grey storm clouds gathering up ahead of her. There was definitely going to be an almighty downpour, she just hoped the wedding was taking place totally indoors otherwise there may be a very soggy bride.

Three quarters of an hour later having followed the satnav instructions, Anna drove through the imposing gates of Connalston Hall Country Club, Hotel and Spa. The gravel drive opened out into a courtyard car park to reveal a very grand, late Tudor style hotel. The views across the countryside were breathtaking, despite the pitter patter of rain and ever blackening skies. Anna decided she would tell Matthew about this place, maybe they could spend a weekend here and he could play some golf while she relaxed in the spa. He'd been working too hard recently, staying late at the office and travelling, so he could do with some rest, and it'd be nice to have some quality time together.

Anna drove around the back of the hotel as Naomi had instructed and parked at the tradesman's entrance. She had just managed to get inside with the flowers when the heavens opened, hearing a loud rumble of thunder somewhere in the distance as the heavy oak door closed behind her.

After taking directions, Anna followed a plush blue and gold carpet through to the lavishly decorated lobby and at reception asked where she needed to take the flowers, having promised Naomi faithfully to deliver them to the wedding planner in person. Once the display was placed in the grateful hands of a very hyper wedding planner she decided to take the stairs down and admire the oil paintings which were hung at intervals along the winding staircase.

On the first landing Anna stopped by the large, ornate, cut glass window which overlooked the car park. From here she was able to take in the sweeping landscape, however, the dramatic view was partially blurred by the pounding rain, somewhat spoiling the effect. She was about to move away when a huge bolt of lightning flashed overhead and for a second everything turned silver grey, like an old black and white snapshot. In that precise moment something caught her eye. There, directly below her, was Matthew's car.

Anna squinted to see if she could read the number plate but the rain obscured her vision. Surely it wasn't his car, but it had the same 'Dad's Taxi' sticker on the bumper – Sam had put it there for a joke and Matthew had left it on, a double bluff. Anna was just about to go down to the car park to make sure she wasn't seeing things when two figures appeared from the front of the hotel below, hidden behind a large umbrella. Anna leant forward, peering through smeared glass until her eyes rested on what was unmistakably Matthew and a woman. They were running towards his car, she was pulling a small case and his overnight bag was over one shoulder while the other arm was wrapped protectively around his companion, pulling her close and shielding her from the rain. Anna knew it was Matthew. She recognised how he walked and moved and could spot him in a crowd of a hundred people.

Gripped by terror, frozen to the spot, her eyes fixed on the scene unfolding before her as her heart pounded. The only sound she was aware of was the blood rushing through her ears. On reaching the car, Matthew, ever the gentleman, opened the passenger door and then Anna was forced to watch with horror as the woman pulled him closer, her arms locked around his body in a tight embrace. Out there, in the pouring rain her husband was being kissed by his lover. Anna's hands covered her mouth as a mixture of sheer terror and nausea ripped through her body. She was unable to move so remained transfixed, like a rabbit in the headlights, while whoever she was got into the car. Matthew walked quickly around the back and placed their luggage in the boot. Just before climbing inside, Anna got a glimpse of his face, the face she had loved and adored for over twenty years. In stunned silence, she watched helplessly as her beloved husband drove away while there on the stairs, Anna's wounded heart simply snapped in two.

She couldn't remember for how long she stood there. All she heard was the rain pounding on the windows and maybe people passing her on the stairway. It must only have been minutes but it could've been a lifetime. Anna felt like she'd been drugged, it was an effort to move and her brain refused to function until she was disturbed by a large group of businessmen squeezing past. As if in a trance, she walked slowly down the stairs, barely acknowledging the goodbye from the haughty receptionist before retracing her footsteps back to the car. She must have turned on the engine, set the satnav and followed the precise instructions but to this day could remember nothing of the journey home.

It was still light when she pulled into the empty drive and after sitting motionless in the car, finally summoned the energy to venture into the empty house. There, alone with only her pain and thoughts for company, Anna waited in silence for Matthew the stranger to come home.

***

Anna was brought back to reality by one of the mourners leaving. People were beginning to drift away now, saying their goodbyes, promising to keep in touch and offering to be there should Anna need anything. She thanked them warmly for coming, for their support and condolences but in truth couldn't wait for them all to be gone. She was even thankful that Matthew's parents had decided not to come back to the house. Elaine had been too distressed, so Bob thought it best to take her straight back to their hotel for a lie down. Her parents-in-law had retired to Spain and only returned for family functions or shopping trips. Bob promised to visit before they left England to say goodbye, by which time Anna hoped to muster enough strength and patience to comfort Elaine.

One of the earliest to leave had been Samantha. At four months pregnant she was experiencing the tiredness and nausea that accompanies the early stages and had been offered a lift home by one of the other secretaries. As they came to say a brief goodbye, Anna sensed that Samantha felt awkward in her company and if she was honest, felt slightly hurt that she hadn't come over to speak earlier. '*Perhaps it was my imagination*,' Anna told herself, realising that Samantha was probably overemotional and it was sometimes hard to know what to say to the bereaved, a struggle to find the right words, if there were any.

Naomi was next to make a move and held Anna in a long, scent-infused, strength-inspiring hug before they parted. On reaching the door she turned to wave, gave a cheeky smile and then a wink before tapping her bag. The fox fur had been liberated.

Dennis and Mary followed shortly afterwards. Her husband's loyal business partner looked so sad but despite the loss of his best friend, tried to comfort Anna before he left.

'I don't want you to worry about the business, Anna, everything is under control. We'll do a bit of a shuffling and muddle through.

Caitlin has been a great help. She offered to go up to Birmingham this week and manage Matthew's accounts. Sometimes it pays to have a power-crazy egomaniac in the office.' He smiled kindly as he held on to Anna's hand.

Anna laughed in agreement. Since joining the company last October, Caitlin had managed to ruffle quite a few feathers and was not popular at Harrison Haulage. With a reputation for being driven, competitive and heartless, Anna could see why people didn't warm to the Ice Queen. However, Anna recalled there was another side to Caitlin that others may not have witnessed because she had been very kind and extremely concerned the day Matthew died.

***

Anna had turned up at his office in a state. Matthew had been missing all day and he couldn't be contacted by anyone because his phone was switched off. He hadn't arrived for their lunch in town or any of his morning appointments, either. Again, Caitlin had held the fort and despite being rushed off her feet, still took the time to come out of a meeting to speak with Anna, offering her coffee and attempting to calm her down before asking as tactfully as possible if there was any reason why Matthew would be behaving this way. Anna, not wanting to admit to anyone, not even herself that he was probably with his mistress, said nothing.

It was humiliating enough sitting alone in the restaurant for almost an hour, sending messages, listening to his phone go to voicemail and knowing full well that the waiters were whispering about her. Eventually, feeling incredibly stupid, she paid for her drink and then took the walk of shame across the restaurant floor and straight out the door. Matthew knew this lunch was important, she'd told him so that morning just before he left for work, reminding him of the time and the need to talk.

Now, to add insult to injury, Anna had come to the office, desperately hoping he would be there dealing with a crisis which forced him to miss their lunch, but she was wrong. She now realised that Matthew was actually the crisis and whilst Caitlin tried to reassure Anna that there must be a reasonable explanation and not to worry too much, her kind words fell on deaf ears.

***

Dennis's soft voice broke through her reminiscing and dragged her back to the present.

'And what shall we do about Joe? It's such a shame that his trip has been cut short. Would you like him to come into work? Perhaps it will help him take his mind off things and it really won't be a problem.'

Anna thought his hand felt strong and comforting. Dennis was like a father figure to all of them, even Matthew.

'No, Dennis, it's fine. I'm going to speak to him tomorrow. I'm hoping to persuade him to go back and continue his journey. I don't want his adventure to end like this. He'll only get one chance and Matthew wouldn't have wanted to be the reason why Joe's trip was ruined.'

'Very well, Anna, but if you need anything, Mary and me, we're here for you, anytime.' Filling up and holding in his tears Dennis turned to leave, but stopped and whispered.

'Please remember, Anna, Matthew loved you very much. Just hold on to that.'

CHAPTER 4

Once everyone had left, Anna gave into exhaustion and slumped into the nearest armchair, allowing the tension to drain from her body. Closing her eyes, she rested back her head and listened to the sounds of the house. Enid, who had actually managed to behave for the rest of the day, had mysteriously disappeared. The children, after making polite conversation with the mourners, had eventually taken themselves off into the small room at the front of the house which had started life as a playroom but as they grew up, morphed into a TV and computer den. Melanie's best friend, Tania, was there to give her support, so Anna left them to themselves. Taking everything into consideration, the kids had coped well with the funeral and she was really proud of them. She could hear Jeannie and Philip clattering around in the kitchen clearing dishes and the sound of their chatter was comforting, they had both been wonderful today. Who'd have thought that after all the years of friction between them they'd finally manage to get along. Perhaps their truce was just borne out of necessity in order to help Anna, but whatever the reason, she was glad. They had so many shared memories between them and the thought of their growing-up years still made Anna smile and, sometimes, wistfully sad.

***

After her father died it seemed like Anna's whole world changed. Her mother was locked in a long spell of mourning where the curtains always seemed to be closed and their home became gloomy and dark. It felt like a sin to be remotely happy or even smile so Anna avoided watching the television in case something made her laugh. She simply couldn't deal with the guilt she felt afterwards. Then one day, quite out of the blue, Enid was suddenly reborn following a visit from Dr Mason.

Philip had tonsillitis, and in the days when doctors actually made home visits, her mother had called the local surgery. Dr Mason's visit entailed just five minutes with the patient, which included a kind pat on the head and a prescription for antibiotics. The next half hour was spent sitting in Enid's lounge (curtains miraculously having been opened) eating cake and drinking tea as he unburdened himself with tales of domestic woe and, apparently, near starvation. Anna knew all this because she was listening at the door. It seemed that his wife, Myrtle, was almost bedridden and with two teenage sons, a home and the surgery to contend with he was at his wits' end. Enid, never one to miss an opportunity, eagerly offered any assistance he may require. Consequently, by the time he departed, the good Doctor Mason had quite unexpectedly secured himself an enthusiastic housekeeper.

Overnight, Anna's mother was completely transformed. With brisk determination and near regimental organisation she not only managed to fulfil the needs of her son and daughter, but the everyday running of Dr Mason's home and given half a chance, his surgery. To Anna, it was like a gift from heaven, it meant that whilst her mother was out reorganising and controlling someone else's life, she and her best-friend-in-the-world, Jean Brown (changed to Jeannie in their teens in a desperate attempt to sound glamorous) had the run of the house. They could watch whatever they wanted on telly, eat as many packets of crisps as they liked, stay in their pyjamas all day and play records loud enough to annoy the neighbours. It was pure, liberating bliss.

They didn't bother much with Philip or him with them. Being four years older, his sister and her giggly sidekick were of no consequence. He had his own mates and seemed always to be outside playing football, or at the youth club, or somewhere. Then they hit puberty and suddenly, boring Philip and his smelly friends changed overnight from noisy lads, eating jam sarnies in the kitchen to God-like objects of desire.

Anna decided she was in love with Philip's bespectacled friend, Jason. He wasn't good-looking or interesting, or anything really, but all the others seemed too cocky and confident, and quite frankly scared Anna to death so she took the easy option. She didn't want to be left out, having nobody to talk about with Jeannie, who unfortunately was obsessed, to the point of becoming a bit scary, with Philip.

Anna's brother and his friends were naturally oblivious to their mini fan club but undeterred, led by Jeannie, they spent the best part of their time pestering, stalking or just irritating the hell out of the boys. Still, no matter how short Jeannie hitched her skirt or how tight and revealing her top, and regardless of the hours spent titivating in front of the mirror, Philip was just not interested. Eventually, love bred jealousy and hate when Philip started dating Celia from the off-licence. Jeannie was distraught because after all her efforts she'd been spurned and soon, the constant presence of a lovesick teenager began to rankle with Philip.

He was in love for the first time and a mutual barricade of resentment was built between him and Jeannie, with Anna stuck firmly in the middle. From then on, whenever they clapped eyes on each other there was sniping and sarky comments, and a horrible atmosphere. Bespectacled Jason turned out to be gay so Anna was relieved not to have wasted too much effort in that direction and swiftly moved on. Jeannie, however, seemed doomed to be unlucky in love and despite being a blonde, vivacious lad-magnet, she always picked the bad boy, and once unwittingly became involved with a married man.

At the ripe age of thirty-five, Philip eventually married grumpy Gail who was totally unsuitable and extremely hard work. He was a fireman and during a routine safety inspection, met his wife-to-be at the community centre where she worked. To this day Anna couldn't see the attraction. Gail wasn't much fun unless she was talking about one of her hobbies, banging on about nutrition, women's rights or her beloved Nick Clegg. She was into sports and outdoor adventure, she dressed to compliment her interests and was decidedly unfeminine and a complete contrast to all the rather dainty creatures Philip had previously dated.

Anna could only conclude that when he decided to settle down he wanted someone less glamorous and more practical. Maybe Gail was a challenge and after all, there was no accounting for taste. Jeannie said that what Gail lacked in personality and dress sense she must make up for in the bedroom because it was the only logical explanation for his bizarre choice. It hadn't lasted of course and now they were separated. In the middle of their troubles were two young children, Summer aged ten and seven-year-old Ross, so consequently, Philip had been having a hard time dealing with the separation, mainly because of his kids.

Jeannie, on the other hand, flitted from job to job, one unhappy romance to another and was always the butt of Philip's jokes. However, when she was twenty-one, she finally got lucky after applying to become a flight attendant. With her developing charm and eye-catching good looks Jeannie sailed through the whole process, found her niche in life and began a new career. She was now extremely popular and very successful doing a job she loved, flying around the world and in the process, proving her many detractors wrong. Anna was proud of her friend who, apart from still never managing to find Mr Right, had made something of her life. Therefore, it was with great relief that when she needed them the most, Philip and Jeannie had managed to take down the wall of animosity they'd built up over the years.

She hadn't had a minute to spend with either of them all day and desperately wanted a few moments with Jeannie because she'd missed her lately. Anna hadn't confided in her best friend about Matthew's affair; it was the first time in all their years of friendship she'd kept a secret. Fate and timing also played a hand, during her moments of deep despair, when Anna rang Jeannie in desperation and need of advice, her friend had been flying or her phone was switched off. In the meantime, Anna had foolishly kept her heartbreak bottled up. She also suspected there was a man on the scene, which usually accounted for her going off radar for a while. Anna only hoped that whoever he was, he was nothing like Matthew.

Philip came into the lounge carrying a tray and continued tidying up. As he approached, Anna stopped him in his tracks and held out her arms for a hug. Putting down the tray he embraced her without question, spending a few moments in silence, taking comfort in each other's closeness, words not required. When Anna pulled away she looked up into her brother's face. He had the same chestnut hair and pale brown eyes as her and his handsome face was kind and full of concern.

'So, sis. How are you doing?' Philip brushed a stray lock of hair from Anna's face.

'I'm surviving... but I'm more concerned about you. I had a text from Gail saying she was sorry she wouldn't be attending the funeral but under the circumstances, it wasn't a good idea. What did she mean by that, is she being a pain?'

Philip opened his mouth to speak, only to be interrupted by the dulcet tones of Enid reverberating from the landing.

'Has anyone seen my fur? I can't find it anywhere. I'm sure I left it on the coat stand. Anna, Anna, have you seen it?' Enid stopped for no one and always expected her daughter to come running first.

Philip rolled his eyes before escaping into the kitchen. '*Big fat chicken*,' thought Anna as she went to find Enid who was in a total frenzy. She had searched everywhere but her fox fur had simply disappeared. Without being given much of a choice, Sam, Joe, Mel and Tania were enlisted to assist in the hunt, even if it was a bit half-hearted.

Eventually, knowing the truth and wanting to get the kids out of a wild goose chase, Anna placated Enid with the idea that maybe she had left it in one of the cars and would telephone the funeral directors first thing in the morning to ask. Once calmed and with a nice cup of tea in her hand, leaving her mother to be soothed by Mel and desperate to get away, Anna busied herself with collecting the cups and saucers that were scattered around the room. On making her way to the kitchen she was stopped in her tracks by the sounds of Jeannie and Philip in the middle of what she could tell was a very heated discussion.

In hushed, angry voices, the type used by grown-ups not wanting the kids to hear, they had obviously ended their truce and were back to bickering. Despite knowing full well that she should turn around and make herself scarce and that it was wrong to eavesdrop, Anna remained curious so, from the safety of the hallway, listened in.

'I don't care what you say, Jeannie, my mind's made up. She's my sister and she needs me now. I can't be there for her and give my support if I'm lying and keeping secrets. She needs to know the truth. As soon as everyone's gone I'm going to tell her whether you like it or not.'

Anna heard the dishwasher door slam.

'But, Phil, you can't, please, you're not thinking straight. She's got enough to cope with. Trust me, today is not the right time.' Jeannie's voice was beseeching, desperate almost.

'No, Jeannie. I've decided. And if you can't deal with it just go home, but you're going to have to face her eventually so you might as well get it over with today. You can't keep living a lie.'

Anna was frozen to the spot, holding cups and saucers in her trembling hands and momentarily in shock.

One thing was for sure, she wasn't going to wait until later. She needed to know what Phil had to tell her and she needed to know right now. Before she even had time to move Anna heard Mel's voice behind her and the discussion in the kitchen came to an abrupt halt. They'd heard her too.

'Mum, what are you doing? Gran is totally doing my head in and she's getting all weepy. I think she's had too much sherry. Can you go and sit with her and I'll make some coffee?' Melanie looked at her mother and waited for a get out of jail card.

Anna sighed and had no choice but to pass the crockery to Mel and head for the lounge. She didn't want her hearing whatever it was Philip had to say and she was almost positive that it would have something to do with Matthew. Worst of all, it meant that her best friend knew the secret too, and had kept it from her.

Anna sat down next to Enid, telling herself to be patient despite visibly shaking hands and churning stomach. She also knew her face was flushed from nerves and anxiety and prayed that her mother wouldn't notice. Desperate to deflect attention, Anna decided instead to reflect on the day's events.

'It all went very well, Mum, don't you think?' Anna tried to keep her voice calm and even.

'Mmm, the vicar was a bit doom and gloom but apart from that you did a nice job.'

Enid had always been frugal with her compliments so Anna basked in this unexpected praise.

'Did you have something from the buffet? I thought they did an excellent spread.' Anna knew her mother wouldn't have missed out on a free feast but she was grasping at straws, preoccupied.

'If I'm honest, Anna, I thought the food was a bit boring! I fancied something spicy like Mexican nibbles or perhaps some sushi.' Enid loved food but even for her, a taste of Japan was a trip into the unknown.

'Sushi! Mum, you can't have sushi at a funeral. Anyway, do you even know what it is?'

'Of course I know what it is, Anna. It's bits of raw fish and rice all rolled up to look fancy and for your information, I expect Japanese people have sushi at funerals all the time.' Enid tutted loudly and rolled her eyes in annoyance.

'Yes, I'm sure they do, Mum, but this is England, and I bet you haven't even tasted it. I know you won't like it.' Anna was becoming irritable because as usual, her mother's praise had turned into criticism.

'Actually, Miss Know-It-All, I do know what it's like. Me and Gladys went to a sushi bar in town a while back because her doctor told her she needs to eat more fish and we were sick of going to the chippy. I don't think it counts if it's in batter but anyway, it was a very swanky place and the food was nice, just a bit on the small side. I didn't actually eat any of that raw stuff though. I just had the vegetarian rice. If you don't believe me ask Jeannie, she was there with your Matthew.'

At first Anna didn't register what her mother had said, still feeling smug at being partially vindicated in her judgement of Enid.

Then an awful realisation dawned on her. Red flashing lights and shrill alarm bells started to ring in her head as fear gripped her heart. Cold dread swam through her veins as she grasped Enid's hand tightly.

'You saw Jeannie and Matthew in a sushi bar. You never said, Mum, what were they doing?'

'Anna, let go of my hand. You're hurting. If you must know I didn't tell you because they told me not to.' Enid pulled her hand away and looked at her daughter crossly.

'What? Mum, please just try to remember, it's really important. What were they doing and why did they say that?' Anna's voice was quavering now and her mouth had gone dry.

'For goodness sake, Anna, they were eating sushi, what do you think they were doing? I was coming back from the loo and I noticed them in the corner. I can remember telling Matthew not to have any of the green seaweed stuff; they get it off the beach and you know how filthy it can be, full of nappies and bits of plastic. Anyway, Jeannie asked me not to let on that I saw them because they were planning a surprise for your birthday. She had some holiday brochures on the table so it must have been that. Maybe Matthew wanted to take you somewhere nice. Now stop making a fuss, Anna. I'll be in trouble with Jeannie now because you've made me let the cat out of the bag.' Enid stood up in a huff.

Anna was speechless.

'Right, I'm going to see the boys. I've not had five minutes with them today. Honestly, Anna, you do go on sometimes.'

Stomping off, Enid went in search of her grandchildren, no doubt to spread a little more anxiety.

She didn't hear Anna's whispered words.

'Don't worry, Mum, you haven't spoiled anything. Matthew won't be taking me anywhere now, will he?' Left alone on the sofa, Anna had never felt so pathetic, so humiliated in her whole life.

Dazed and almost paralysed by her mother's revelation, she had to get out of the room. The walls were closing in and she was having difficulty breathing while her heart beat so fast she thought it may burst through her chest, spurting fountains of blood over her cream carpet. *'At least this will be over,'* she thought, *'I'll be dead and I'll be glad, because I just can't take any more.'*

Forcing herself up from the chair and willing her legs to move, Anna made her way towards the stairs, hoping to God she had enough strength to make it to her bedroom. Once inside she closed the door behind her and sucked in deep gulps of air, willing herself not to be sick, and somehow made it over to the bed on legs like jelly. She hadn't the strength to sit up. Heavy bones filled with the burden of her new-found knowledge forced Anna to lie down as she allowed the cool cotton of her bedspread to calm her. With the palms of her hands laid flat by her side, eyes firmly shut; she tried desperately to blot out the inevitable truth that she now had to face.

It wouldn't take a genius to put two and two together, join up the dots and fill in the blanks. Philip had somehow discovered her best friend and husband were having an affair. He intended telling her later that day and Jeannie was trying to stop him. Her mother had spotted Matthew and Jeannie sneaking about, obviously making plans to fly away to the sun, so they hastily made up an excuse that they were planning a birthday surprise. He'd actually bought her a silver bracelet. There certainly hadn't been a wallet containing tickets for a romantic holiday. It was all so obvious now.

She thought back to Matthew's late nights and extra workload and it was no coincidence that on these lonely evenings, whenever

Anna had phoned Jeannie to suggest they got together, she was either working or unavailable. She had suspected her friend was seeing a new man but never in her wildest dreams would she expect that man to be Matthew. Recalling Jeannie's tears in the church, Anna realised what a fool she had been. It was almost unbelievable that after all these years, when she needed her the most, the friend she had grown up with, confided in, trusted and loved like a sister had betrayed her in the worst way possible.

Tears burned under her eyelids: hot, angry blobs of salty liquid ran down her cheeks and neck, streaking the remnants of her make-up with white tracks. Anna lay there in silence, trapping in the sobs, waiting for the tears to subside. When they ceased, she soaked up the peace of her bedroom and from somewhere deep within, a welcome calm enveloped her body and a strange, peaceful sensation evolved, building steadily into a wave of ice-cold anger. The anger gave her strength and a surge of super-human power, which she needed to help move her leaden limbs. Feeling somehow detached from reality yet acutely aware of what she was doing, Anna sat up and went over to her dressing table.

After slowly removing all her make-up she looked hard at the blank canvas that stared out from the mirror, then taking a deep breath, Anna started again. Reapplying everything, she created a mask that would hide the tears she'd shed and give her the confidence required to go downstairs and face her foe. She was calmly applying her lipstick when there was a gentle tap at the bedroom door.

'Mum, are you okay? Gran's leaving now. Uncle Phil is going to take her home, are you coming down to say bye?' Melanie's voice was tentative and slightly nervous.

'Yes, love, I'm fine. I was just coming.' Anna looked at her reflection and was satisfied with the result so put away her make-up, checked her image one more time then steeled herself for what was to come.

With her last ounce of determination, Anna opened her bedroom door and went downstairs to meet the enemy.

Enid was already waiting at the door when she reached the bottom of the stairs and carrying a covered plate of boring leftovers to which Anna made no comment. She kissed her mother goodbye, promised to call her later in the evening and then ushered her and Phil out of the door with as little chat and fuss as humanly possible.

It would only take Philip about thirty minutes there and back; maybe longer if he went inside to settle Enid in and as the children were around, she wondered how she would be able to get Jeannie on her own. Her dilemma was soon solved when Anna wandered into the TV room and found the boys with Mel and Tania, watching the music channel.

She walked over to Joe and ruffled his hair, it had grown longer whilst he'd been on his travels and apparently, what they called a surfer style, suited him. In total contrast, Sam, who was texting as usual, had his hair cut military short, but still the same light brown as his brother and their dad's. Joe turned away from the television and grabbed her hand, looking rather sheepish as he asked a question.

'Mum, Sam's going to drop Tania off at home and then the three of us might go to the beach for a bit, just to get some air. You could come too.' Joe waited for his words to sink in, hoping he hadn't said the wrong thing.

Anna knew they would have been discussing whether the question would hurt or offend her; she also knew they wanted to get out of the house and also why they'd chosen the sea. All through their childhood, Hayling Island Beach was their favourite weekend destination, alone with Matthew or as a family.

In the summer holidays they would spend whole days there, playing football on the sand, riding on the little train, picnicking and swimming. As the kids got older they would stay until late and watch the sun go down, faces burnt and tingling from the sun and after-effects of the sea breeze. Matthew would cook sausages on a foil throwaway barbeque and they'd drink hot chocolate from a thermos.

Even when the weather turned cold and winter set in, Matthew would still take all three kids down to the beach on a Sunday morning to get some fresh air and work up an appetite for their lunch. Anna didn't mind being left out; she enjoyed the peace. She had them all to herself during the week and it was Matthew's special time, the four of them together on the beach, having fun.

'Of course it'll be okay, son. It's been a really long day so go out and get some fresh air. I'll be fine here with Jeannie.' Anna's heart lurched involuntarily the second she spoke her so-called friend's name.

They didn't need telling twice. Tania hugged Anna as she passed by to collect her coat and each of her children gave her a near suffocating squeeze and a warm kiss as they left the room. Mel, Sam and Joe raced up to their rooms and threw on jeans and T-shirts, keys were collected, promises of not being too long made, and then the door banged shut. At last, in the silent house, Anna and her best friend were alone.

CHAPTER 5

Having heard the children leave, Jeannie emerged from the kitchen drying her hands on a tea towel. She smiled broadly when she saw Anna.

'Peace at last, shall I get us a drink? I'm sure you could do with one, I certainly could.'

Anna didn't return Jeannie's smile, instead, she gave her a cool look.

'Not for me, thanks, but you obviously need a bit of Dutch courage.'

For a moment Jeannie was lost for words and looked confused. Anna could tell she was gathering her thoughts, perhaps trying to work out what to say next. When Jeannie found her voice it sounded nervous, tense. Eventually, she put down the tea towel and sat on the sofa looking warily at Anna.

'Why would I need Dutch courage? Is something wrong, Anna, have I done something to upset you?'

Anna threw her head back and an involuntary snort of sarcastic laughter burst from her mouth.

'You are something else, Jeannie, you really are. I cannot believe how hard-faced you can be and actually sit there and pretend you don't know what I mean. Did you really think you'd get away with it, that I wouldn't find out, do you think I'm that stupid?' Anna paused for a moment to let her words sink in. 'I heard you talking in the kitchen with Philip. I know about the affair so stop your play-acting and let's get this over with.'

Anna was shaking with rage while Jeannie's blue eyes were wide with shock and misting with tears as her hands flew up to cover her red face.

'I'm sorry, Anna, truly I am. I didn't want you to find out like this. I promise I didn't. It just never seemed the right time. I've wanted to tell you for ages, I swear. Please, Anna, don't be angry... let me explain.'

More tears began to well in Jeannie's eyes but Anna didn't care. Her face burned hot with rage, and emotions she'd kept buried for so long erupted in a torrent of hate and hurt. Anna was bordering on hysteria now and knew she was shouting but it felt good, letting it all out was cathartic.

'Explain! How the hell are you going to explain sleeping with your best friend's husband? Go on then, Jeannie; give it your best shot.' Anna flung herself into the armchair opposite Jeannie and leaned forward, staring straight into Jeannie's startled eyes.

Jeannie gasped. 'What do you mean, sleeping with your husband? Anna, I wasn't having an affair with Matthew, I swear! My God, how can you even think that? I cannot believe that's what you are accusing me of.'

Jeannie shot up from the sofa and knelt in front of Anna, grabbing both hands in hers.

'Look at me, Anna. You've got this all wrong. I think I know why but please, just calm down and I can explain.' Jeannie was crying and trembling.

Anna pulled her hands away sharply, still angry, not quite believing Jeannie.

'So, what were you and Phil arguing about in the kitchen, what did he want to tell me that you were so keen to keep a secret?' Anna was mistrustful and petulant and at the same time praying that she was wrong.

Jeannie sat back down on the sofa; her cheeks flushed red and eyes swimming with tears. She looked up at her friend and spoke softly.

'Anna, you are right, in a way. I have been having an affair but not with your Matthew. I've been having an affair with Philip.' Jeannie held Anna's gaze, watching her face, waiting for her to react.

Anna opened her mouth then shut it again; words wouldn't come out, there were none. Her mind was whirling. Not Matthew, not Matthew, thank God, not Matthew. Pure relief and elation flooded through her body as she stared at Jeannie. With shaky hands, she stood and took the one that was being offered by her friend then flopped down onto the sofa, totally exhausted.

Placing her head in her palms, from deep inside Anna's body, an earthquake of soul wrenching sobs erupted. She didn't know if she was crying in grief for her husband, in anger for the hurt his affair had caused or from the sheer gladness she felt knowing she still had her beloved Jeannie. Her friend wrapped her arms around her and just let her cry. They stayed like that; Jeannie rocking Anna gently, smoothing her hair and telling her it'd be okay until eventually the tears subsided. When finally she looked up, Anna saw her friend's lovely face covered in tears too and she begged for forgiveness, apologising over and over again for making cruel, wild accusations and shouting angry, bitter words.

'Anna, there's nothing to forgive, truly there isn't. You've been through the mill lately and if I were in your shoes I would have thought the same. But there *are* some things I've held from you and I'm sorry. Let me explain and I might be able to make you understand what's been going on and why we kept everything secret.' Jeannie got up, poured them both a glass of wine then passed one to Anna.

Sitting down, she took a large gulp to steady her nerves and turned to face her friend. Then she began.

•••

The spark of something between them began last September, before Joe left to go backpacking. Anna and Matthew threw a huge farewell party where friends and family gathered to give him a good send off and everyone had been having a great time, except that was for Philip and Gail. While their kids had been tearing around having fun, they seemed to be locked in an angry heated debate over in the corner. She was hard work to get along with and not much fun to be around at the best of times and judging by the look on her face, you could tell Gail wanted to be anywhere other than a party, or at least not one with Phil.

Consequently, well before the end of the night, Gail made her sour-faced excuses and left with Summer and Ross. Rather than being annoyed, Philip looked relieved and now, being absolved of car driving duties, threw himself into having a bit of fun and freedom. Jeannie arrived later as she had just flown into Southampton Airport and true to form, was also intent on catching up and having a good time.

At the end of the evening, Anna's brother and friend, both being slightly worse for wear, had to be sobered up with as much coffee as they could stomach. Surprised that for once they were not bitching at each other and in an attempt to get them to go home so she could go to bed, Anna suggested they share a cab. During the ride in the taxi and feeling a little less inebriated, Jeannie noticed that Philip was subdued and looked decidedly fed up. When she enquired as to what was troubling him she was rather surprised when he opened up and told her exactly how miserable and downright naffed off he was with his pain in the arse of a wife.

By the time they reached hers, Jeannie was feeling genuinely sorry for Phil and it was obvious that the last place he wanted to go was home, so she invited him in. Nothing happened that night except for drinking lots of tea, eating toast and listening to Philip pour his heart out. It seemed that things had been wrong for a long time and during the last year his marriage had deteriorated badly. Gail spent the evenings Phil was at home sleeping on the sofa and only went to their bed when he was on a night shift. They barely talked except to discuss the kids and apart from them, had absolutely nothing else in common and were now like strangers. Gail arranged so many activities for her and the kids that the only time Phil saw Summer and Ross was when he was ferrying them about and during occasional, very miserable mealtimes.

Jeannie was shocked and sad for Philip. He was still handsome and if he was so inclined could have his pick of lots of women, it was just a shame that for some reason, he'd chosen Gail. Starting to feel tiredness creeping up on her and having talked till the early hours, Jeannie offered Philip the sofa which he declined. He had to start his early shift so instead, she called for a taxi. They hugged platonically at the door where Jeannie assured Philip that should he need a friendly ear in the future, she would be there for him.

Jeannie never thought for one minute he would take her up on her offer but later that week he called and asked if she'd like to meet up for a drink. The drink turned into dinner where they laughed all night and talked about everything under the sun, from films to music and holidays, teasing each other mercilessly about how much they'd argued as teenagers. They continued to meet as often as they could between their shifts and before long and quite unexpectedly, after all the years of falling out, Philip and Jeannie fell in love.

•••

Anna was dumbstruck while Jeannie felt emotionally drained from her confession and the events prior to it. When she found her voice, Anna asked how long they'd been together.

'It became serious just before Christmas. That's when we both realised how we felt about each other and when Philip left Gail at Easter, he came to live with me, not with one of his station mates like he told you. I was so scared you'd be angry with me, Anna. I thought you would blame me for splitting them up but I swear I'm not completely at fault. And I was terrified you'd catch us at my place, that's why I kept putting you off if you wanted to call round. I feel so bad for neglecting you but our shifts conflict a lot so when we get some time together, it's rare. Anyway, Gail knows about us now. Philip told her at the weekend because he wants to see Summer and Ross more, maybe at my place. That's what she meant in her text, she was referring to me being here so Philip knew he had to tell you before she did.' Jeannie took another sip of her wine and waited for Anna to get her head around everything.

'You know what, Jeannie, I'm not angry at all. The writing has been on the wall with those two for ages. I do feel for the kids though. Summer and Ross are lovely but thinking about it, they probably don't miss him half the time, what with all the sports and clubs she takes them to, otherwise he's at work. You never know, maybe this way he'll get to see them more often. How did Gail take it?'

'Philip got the impression she was more concerned about staying in the house and maintenance payments, that sort of thing. She didn't seem that bothered it was me either, which is a relief but truthfully, I'm more worried about what you think. That's why I was so upset in church. I got myself into a right old state because I deceived you when you really needed me. And now, I realise you were worried about what Matthew was up to as well. I've really, really let you down. It would've been so perfect, the four of us being friends and getting old together, it's all so unfair. I got my man at last but now you've lost yours.' Jeannie burst into tears again.

Anna smiled and held her friend's hand tightly as she spoke.

'Please stop crying, Jeannie. You and Philip are happy and I've not had to disown my best friend, thank God. As for Matthew, there wasn't anything you could do, apart from listen to me rant and rave so stop worrying and give me a hug.' Anna took her turn at being the consoler and wiped away Jeannie's tears.

The jangle of door chimes signalled the return of Philip who looked extremely hassled. Enid had driven him mad all the way to hers and his impending confession only added to his mood. They quickly put him out of his misery and told him the secret was out. Anna pretended to be cross for a few seconds, just to put the wind up him but she couldn't punish her startled brother for too long. Secrets were terrible things and made you miserable and he looked so relieved that at last everything was in the open. Then a thought occurred to Anna, she understood all of what Jeannie had told her except for one thing.

'Jeannie, there's one thing that doesn't make sense, why *were* you and Matthew at that sushi bar when Mum saw you? She told me about it earlier today and said you asked her not to tell me.'

Jeannie sighed, closed her eyes and shook her head. Then, for the second time that day she told Anna a secret.

'I rang Matthew and told him to meet me there because I wanted to ask him something. I thought rather than interrogating him on the phone, if I did it face to face I would be able to tell if he was lying or not. I did actually get him there under false pretences by pretending I wanted to arrange a birthday surprise for you. I chose the sushi place as it was right next door to the travel agents and I needed some holiday brochures for me and Phil.' Jeannie looked over to Phil who was looking confused and probably unprepared for what he was about to hear.

'The week before, I was in the multi-storey car park at the airport when I spotted Matthew through the mesh fencing, he was on the level below. I was on the phone at the time so couldn't call out to him but he was standing by a red Audi, bent down and talking to someone in the driver's seat. Before I knew it, a woman's hand came through the window, wound her hand around Matthew's head and pulled him towards her for a kiss. Well, that's what it looked like to me. It only lasted a few seconds and I got the impression Matthew was conscious of being seen. She held his hand for a moment then Matthew laughed at something she said, waved and walked away. She drove off and that was that. The thing is, at that point I stupidly thought the woman who'd dropped Matthew off at the airport was you, in a new car. I rang you straight away to tease you about your fancy new motor. I was joking that you'd kept it a bit quiet but it was instantly obvious you didn't know what the hell I was talking about and thought I'd gone a bit mad. Don't you remember, I fobbed you off with a case of mistaken identity?'

Anna recalled the conversation which she'd completely forgotten about, until now. 'Now you mention it, I do remember.

You were going on about me being a bit of a poser. But why didn't you say anything then?'

'Because I wanted to get my facts right and the messenger always gets shot, so I wasn't going to risk that. I ran like mad to see where Matthew went but he'd gone into the terminal and I had to get to work. I couldn't rest until I'd spoken to him and it was eating me up so I arranged our meeting. He nearly died of shock when I confronted him. I just came right out and asked him what was going on because there was no point in pussy-footing around.'

Jeannie looked sheepishly from Philip to Anna, who then asked the obvious.

'So what excuse did Matthew come up with? Whatever it was would've been a load of rubbish.'

'He told me I was overreacting and assured me the woman wasn't his lover, just a rep from a courier company. Apparently, they'd been in a meeting and afterwards he needed to get to the airport so she offered him a lift rather than call a cab. I asked him why she didn't just dump him at the drop off zone and he said that they were early for his flight so she parked in the multi-storey and was using the time trying to persuade him to do a deal. He said that he knew she was flirting so got out of the car as quickly as he could. When she attempted to kiss him it was totally unexpected and embarrassing, that's why he shot off. At first it all seemed a bit unlikely but there are some very pushy women out there with no shame and I presumed she was desperate to make her commission, something like that. Matthew was adamant that nothing was going on, begging me not to jump to any conclusions and was terrified I'd tell you.' Jeannie felt like a fool because she should've known he was lying through his teeth.

Phil was in complete shock and pacing around the room, unable to believe what had been going on in his sister's life and worse, Jeannie hadn't told him about her suspicions over Matthew. But knowing how tense the situation was already, he wisely kept quiet and listened to the rest of the story.

Jeannie continued. 'I'll be honest, Anna, he was so upset that he did convince me I'd misread the situation. I've been out with my fair share of Jack the Lads and listened to a lot of bullshit in my time but I actually believed him. By the time he'd finished explaining he looked like he was going to pass out with the stress of it all and I ended up feeling a bit guilty. I didn't let him off that easy though and warned him that if I ever saw him in a car park, or anywhere, with another woman, he'd be sorry and I would tell you without hesitation. I think he knew I would be keeping a close eye on him from then on. He swore he'd not seen her since and had no intention of doing business with her, or her company. When your Mum spotted us we both panicked, so to avoid any questions I made up the birthday surprise and for a change, Enid did as she was told.' Jeannie slumped back on the sofa, worn out with the telling of it all.

'Well the bad news is he did pull the wool over your eyes. But I understand now why you didn't say anything… you did your best and had the right intentions. Unfortunately, it seems none of us knew Matthew that well, after all.' Anna hated the fact her husband was so deceitful, amongst other things.

Philip, having been totally in the dark about everything until now was horrified. He'd looked on Matthew like a brother and could not believe he'd cheated on Anna. In some ways, he was relieved he hadn't had to carry the burden of that secret, or been the one to tell his sister the truth.

Naturally, both Philip and Jeannie wanted to know how Anna found out so with a heavy heart and trying not to cry again, she recounted the events that since May had turned her world upside down.

By the time Anna had told her tale it was getting dark and she was exhausted so she rang Joe and asked him if he could pick up some takeaway food, she couldn't face cooking and longed for the day to be over. Jeannie and Phil stayed to eat with them and once they knew she was okay, as okay as could be expected, they left Anna and her three children alone. Jeannie had vowed that they would track her down, whoever this woman was, and make her sorry. Philip, however, was still trying to take it all in.

For all of them it had been the hardest day and now Anna was glad of some time alone with the kids. She didn't want to make a flowery, emotional speech and risk upsetting them or cause any more tears and knowing her three, it would only make them cringe. But Anna did want to let them know how proud she was, the way they'd held it together and looked after her and each other.

They had loaded the dishwasher and were all sitting in the lounge watching rubbish on the telly (as to whether they were taking it in, she really wasn't sure), they were subdued, but not morose. Sam was busy texting and Anna suspected he had a new girlfriend, Melanie looked like she was nodding off and Joe was flicking through the newspaper when she broke the silence.

'Well, if you lot don't mind, I'm going to turn in. I'm worn out.' Anna stood and went over to each of them one by one and hugged them tightly, whispering into their ear.

'I love you and I'm so proud of you. Dad will be too.'

Each one hugged her back, replying in exactly the same way.

'I'm proud of you too, Mum. Love you.'

Anna hoped her words were enough, they had to be, they were all she had left. Reaching the bottom of the stairs she added. 'If you need to talk or anything, you know where I am. If I'm asleep, just wake me.'

They all looked up and Joe replied.

'We will, Mum, don't worry. Just try to get some kip.'

'And we're here for you too, Mum. We're going to look after you now, okay?' Sam smiled and gave Anna the thumbs up as Melanie spoke next.

'Yes, just knock on my door if you need a cuddle, there's always space for you in my bed just like when I was little. You're never too old for a hug.'

Melanie's sweet, kind thoughts were actually crucifying Anna. Before they could see her cry Anna made her way wearily upstairs, not bothering to turn on the bedroom light because she hadn't the strength for even that one small task. Neither did she take off her make-up because her arms were like lead. Anyway, there was nobody to see her smudged mascara or care that her hair was a mess. Slipping off her shoes she lay down on the bed fully clothed. Pulling up the covers, Anna closed tear-reddened eyes, her body giving in to exhaustion, her mind too tired to think. She could hear the drone of voices on the television below and felt grateful that the kids had each other because she really had run out of steam and words.

Mercifully, sleep came quickly and for a while it took her to a place without hurt, allowing the dull pain in her heart to vanish along with the great big hole in her life, the one where Matthew used to be.

CHAPTER 6

When she woke the following morning, as with every morning since Matthew had died, for a magical second, Anna forgot. And then it hit her with a sickening punch as the unforgiving truth came rushing in, swamping her brain and tightening its grip around her heart. She forced herself to remember what day it was – Wednesday, but even then her head seemed permanently scrambled. Had Anna been alone in the house she would've stayed right there and let misery do its worst, however, with the children to consider she heaved her weary body out of bed and made her way into the shower.

Letting them sleep late, Anna savoured the peace and used the time to formulate her plans. It was the first time she'd had the opportunity to think about the future clearly, so by the time they trudged down the stairs, bleary eyed and hungry, she had a good idea of what she had to say and how to say it. Once her brood were adequately fed, the four of them remained around the kitchen table drinking tea. Anna loved this room. It was the heart of her home where their days had always begun and ended together – the mad panic of breakfast before the school run and then gathering again in the evening. It was something she and Matthew insisted on; eating together around the table.

As the kids got older they would have the small TV on and watch the news as a family, discussing the day's events, catching up on their school gossip and listening to their grumbles and funny stories. Friday was takeaway day and the only time they were allowed to sit in the lounge with their food on their knees and slob out. This kitchen was Anna's place; it was her territory of which she was the queen. She didn't mind spending all day there with her second best friend, Radio

2, to keep her company. Whether it was making packed lunches and breakfast, loading the washing machine, ironing, baking or cooking dinner, it was her place of purpose.

'Right, you three, we need to make some plans, mainly concerning Joe and Sam but we've got to get you organised as well, Melanie. I've had time to think about this so I don't want any arguments. Just hear me out and then you can all have your say.'

Three faces looked at each other with quizzical frowns, then back to their mother.

'Sam, I know the army said you could have as much compassionate leave as you need but I think if you feel up to it, you should go back on Sunday. Your course starts on Monday and if you miss it you'll have to wait for months for the next slot. I don't want you getting left behind or missing out because you have to catch up.' Sam opened his mouth to object but Anna lifted her hand to stop him. Then, she looked at Joe and continued.

'I know you've travelled a long way from New Zealand, Joe, but I want you to go back and continue your adventure as soon as we can arrange a flight. And before you bring it up, I really don't care how much it costs. What I do care about is that losing your dad doesn't spoil anything for any of you... it's the last thing he would have wanted, we all know that. Mel, your A level results will be through in a few weeks, so when the boys are out of our hair we can concentrate on getting you organised for university. We need to make a start on that huge list you've compiled.'

Anna let her words sink in then submitted to a barrage of objections and questions.

Both boys insisted they should stay and look after her and Mel. They said that everyone would think they were heartless and selfish if they left and Dad would want them to stay around. Melanie pointed out that she might not get into university and even if she did get the grades she hoped for, was considering reapplying for a course in Portsmouth so she could live at home and keep Anna company. Having pre-empted all these arguments Anna calmly talked them round to her way of thinking.

'Okay then. So you boys want to stay and look after me do you? How long do you reckon that it's going to take, not just for me, but for all of us to get over this? Weeks, months, years… maybe never. So you ruin your careers, education and memories to mope around here babysitting me and getting on each other's nerves. That's not going to help anyone, is it? Besides, I would feel so guilty knowing everything you've all worked for will be a waste. Dad and I only ever wanted you to be happy and successful, so please don't take that away from us, not now.' Anna had to force her voice to remain emotion-free and firm.

'But, Mum, will you be okay? After September you'll be here all alone. We'll all feel awful, thinking of you without Dad and none of us around.' Joe's eyes brimmed with tears; he'd made a good point.

'I'll be fine, son. I've got the love birds Jeannie and Uncle Phil for company, then there's Dennis and Mary. Naomi wants me to spend more time over there with her and Aunty Elsie and let's not forget Gran. She's enough trouble to keep anyone on their toes. Sam, you are only an hour or so away if I need you and the same goes for Mel. If I get really, really desperate I'll come over and stay. How embarrassing would that be for you both? Your old mum hanging about in the student union bar or worse, chilling down the pub with your mates.' At last she made them smile and could see their resistance weakening. The cogs in their minds were turning like clockwork, working out the pros and cons and examining their consciences.

At last, Sam spoke.

'Okay, Mum, if it's what you really want, then I agree. So long as you swear that if you get upset or need anything you'll ring and I'll drive over straight away. Do you promise?' Anna made her oath and he seemed content.

Next, Joe reached over and grabbed Anna's hands. He folded his fingers around hers, holding on tightly. 'I'll do it for you, Mum, but only because I don't want one more thing to make you sad. If it's really going to make things easier for you and you won't be too lonely, I agree.'

Those damn tears started to warm the corners of her eyes again and Anna was finding it hard to hold down a lump the size of an apple that had formed in her throat. She squeezed his hands tightly, not daring to speak, willing herself to gain control.

Melanie, perhaps sensing her mother's anguish, spoke up.

'So, it looks like it's going to be just us girls for a while. I've got to admit it's a gold star plan! I couldn't have done better myself. Once we've got rid of these two we can take control of the whole house. Just think, a lad-free zone, no smelly socks, no Dave channel *or* flaming football and the best bit is that I get the bathroom all to myself.'

With cries of 'charming' and 'cheeky mare' from the boys, the tension was broken and the atmosphere in the room lifted and ease spread through Anna. Joe offered to make some coffee but before he did, Anna had one more announcement.

'There's one other thing. As this is the only time we will all be together for a while, I want us to try and make these last few days as happy as possible, so if we support and encourage each other, look forward and make plans, I think we can get through this. Don't think for one minute that I don't realise how hard it is for all of you. I don't expect you not to be sad or show your feelings, that'd be false. I'm here if you want to talk about anything and everything, day or night, okay. And finally, I declare Mum's café is officially open for business, so get your favourite meal orders in and then you can keep me occupied slaving over a hot stove.' Anna knew the way to their hearts and Sam was already firing off a list of his favourite things, and that was before she'd even put the kettle back on.

It wasn't going to be easy, Anna knew that. Any crying would be done in the privacy of her bedroom where possible. Her sole reason for living right now was her three children and she would do whatever it took to keep them on track and where possible guide them through their grief.

The week passed in a flash and holding Anna to her word, they ate her out of house and home. Joe booked his flight for the following Monday and Sam, as planned, left on Sunday morning. Anna knew she would cry when he went. It was impossible not to and he held it together just long enough to get in the car and drive away without looking back. Trying to be brave, Anna focused on positives, there was a new girl on the scene so hopefully Beth, and the technical course he was about to start, would keep Sam and his mind occupied. As she closed the door and wiped her eyes, Anna prayed she'd done the right thing and he'd be okay.

Matthew's parents had called to say goodbye and it was clear that Elaine was having trouble controlling her emotions, even in front of the children. She was little comfort and made them all nervous, constantly teetering on the verge of tears and only managing limited conversation. By the time they'd said their farewells everyone was relieved and even though they'd promised much, Anna had a feeling their words were hollow. Not only that, even in their ignorance of his deceit, the fact they were Matthew's parents somehow made her feel alienated and bitter.

Monday arrived too quickly and for the second time, Anna made the trip to Heathrow with Joe but this time Melanie came along so she had company on the return journey. Before they left she'd resigned herself to the fact that as with Sam, this time letting go would be even harder.

When she and Matthew saw him off last time, Anna was a sobbing mess of snot and tissues all the way home from the airport. Nothing Matthew said could console her, even pointing out that Joe had already left home when he went to university, but Anna didn't care because before, she could get to London in a few hours. New Zealand took days. There were millions of spiders and hideous insects, and he wouldn't remember to put sun cream on and end up with third degree burns. Worst of all, he could meet a New Zealander and fall in love and never want to come home again. To Anna, the whole place was filled with hazards when she was thousands of miles away from her first born child and totally unable to protect him.

Eventually she got used to Joe being overseas and keeping his word, he emailed frequently and rang once a month for a catch up. Anna printed off photos chronicling all his adventures and pinned them to a notice board in the kitchen. She probably bored the pants off everyone who made the mistake of asking after Joe, and with another son in the armed forces (whom Anna also never tired of talking about to anyone who'd listen) she was possibly *the* most avoided woman in Portsmouth.

Melanie was chatting away in the back seat, interspersed with texting and ringing her best mate, Tania. They both had summer jobs working in the café at the ferry port and it was blatantly obvious from the topic of conversation that it was a teenage hotbed of romance and gossip.

Anna's stomach lurched as they approached the airport and before she knew it they were at the departure gate. Joe was clutching his ticket and passport, caught like a rabbit in the headlights, Melanie was in floods of tears, clinging on to him, her arms welded around his waist. Anna, realising this was agony for her son took control of the situation, firmly telling Mel it was her turn for a hug. After reluctantly releasing her brother and wiping her eyes, she said her goodbyes and stood back.

Anna wanted to get it over with yet make the moment last forever as she folded her arms around Joe. She breathed in his scent, closed her eyes and held him tight, committing the feel of her son to memory before letting go and ordering him to get through the gate before she changed her mind. In a strangled voice Joe told them he loved them before turning quickly and walking away, leaving Anna and Melanie standing together, holding on to each other for comfort as they watched the back of his head disappear from sight.

Two weeks later, Melanie received her A level results. Buoyed by the same confidence that the sun would rise the following day, Anna knew her daughter would do well. Leading up to her exams, with her usual enthusiasm and attention to detail, along with Tania, they had devised a rigorous revision timetable. It combined studying with very important leisure time, which they diligently adhered to right up to the start of their exams. Now, with the grades she needed, Melanie could start her degree at Reading University in September where she'd chosen a BA in French and German.

Naturally good at languages, Melanie was always the first one on holiday who learned to say hello, goodbye and thank you, enjoying the attention when she ordered her food or managed a short conversation in Spanish, Greek or French. After much squealing and jumping about in the school hall she ran outside to her mother who was waiting in the car. More squealing followed and with another child to brag about, Anna left Melanie to celebrate with her friends and drove home wearing a smile that would make a Cheshire cat proud.

Before she had time to blink it was the day before Melanie left for university. After a frenzy of shopping for cool student clothes, duvet sets, cushions, posters and what seemed like tons of stationery; Melanie was ready for her own adventure.

On the night before she left, Anna had invited Tania, Jeannie and Enid for a farewell meal in town. As they waited for the taxi, Anna noticed her mother had disappeared, fearing she was having a sneaky swig of brandy, she went off in search of her. On reaching the top of the stairs, she heard low voices coming from Melanie's bedroom so stopped on the landing and listened, worried about what her mother may be saying. Both were sitting on the bed, resting against the headboard. Melanie was wrapped in her gran's arms and snuggled against her chest.

'Do you think Dad knows that I did well, Gran? I miss him so much and there's loads I need to tell him, not just about uni and my exams.' Melanie and Enid were very close. The older woman had softened somewhat in her later years but only where her grandchildren were concerned.

'Of course he knows, sweetheart. He'll be watching down from heaven right now, proud as punch. He's probably a bit miffed, mind, that he can't give you a long, boring, Dad lecture about boys and drugs and whatever young people do at university. But he is keeping his eye on you.' Enid stroked her granddaughter's hair as she spoke.

Melanie chuckled, and then asked a serious question. 'But how do you know for sure, Gran… do you really believe in God and heaven and stuff?'

'Yes, of course I do. How do you think I've kept going all these years? It's only the promise of seeing my Jack again that gave me the strength to carry on and look after your mum and Uncle Philip. It's been thirty-four years since I last saw your grandad's face and knowing that one day we'll be reunited stopped me from giving up.' Enid smiled as she pictured her husband.

'But what if, after all this waiting and hoping there's no heaven after all, how will you feel then, Gran? It'll be so disappointing.' Mel desperately needed some kind of confirmation, or hope.

'Well, that's the thing isn't it? You see, there's really no point in worrying about there being no heaven because you won't know until you're dead, but I've watched *The Psychic Detective* and I know there's more to everything than what goes on here on earth. I'm a believer and that's that! So why not just fill up your days being busy and happy until you meet again? Take comfort in the fact that your dad's there, in heaven, smiling down on you. Make him proud and happy. That's what I've done and it's worked up to now.'

'You are clever, Gran. I do feel Dad's watching over me, you know? I talk to him all the time. There's important things I need to say to him and if I get upset, I just look at his photos and it's like he's making me smile. I hope Mum knows she'll see him again. Have you told her not to give up?' Melanie knew that her gran could be strict and sometimes a bit cool with her mum. Other times she was bonkers.

'Your mother doesn't listen to me, Mel, she thinks I'm potty. Anyway, it's time we were getting going, she'll be thinking I'm up to no good if I disappear for too long and I'm blooming hungry, I could eat a horse.' Enid kissed Melanie on the head and began to heave herself off the bed.

Anna moved quickly away from the door and ran downstairs. Yes, she did think her mother was potty but now and again she came up trumps and made her smile. It can't have been easy for her bringing two kids up alone, Anna admitted that. She thought about what her mother had just said and, unbeknown to Enid, would take her advice and wait for the day she saw Matthew again. Quite what she would say to him when they did was another matter entirely.

Anna drove to Reading early the next day and settled Melanie into her halls of residence. By the time they'd carried a multitude of boxes, bags and bin liners up three flights of stairs then made up her bed, Melanie was beyond excited. Anna marvelled at her daughter's ability to take such a momentous day in her stride. She seemed unfazed by all the new faces around her and Anna was obviously experiencing all the nerves lacking in Mel. The halls were a hive of activity and when her daughter struck up a conversation with the girl in the next room, Anna felt this may be her cue to leave, so recognising the now or never moment, interrupted and reluctantly said her goodbyes.

Compared to all the other farewells she had said of late this was by far the easiest, made possible only by her wonderful, capable daughter. Melanie kissed and hugged her mother goodbye at the car, promised to ring her later that evening and with a cheerful wave, ran back inside. Surprisingly, Anna managed to compose herself quite quickly so feeling relieved and positive, set off for her second appointment of the day, with Sam.

It was only thirty or so miles from Reading to Andover where he was based and it had been arranged that she would drive over after leaving Mel. Anna was waiting in the restaurant when Sam arrived and her heart lifted as she saw him walking towards her. He was easily six feet tall now, lean and broad shouldered, a result of many hours in the gym and when Sam spotted his mum, his smile lit up the room, hugging the life out of her the second he reached the table.

They talked all through dinner, Sam, as usual, eating enough for two and finishing her dessert. The time sped by too quickly and before she knew it, it was time to go. At least she was up to date with everything going on in his world: he was enjoying his course and would soon be fully qualified to work on Challenger tanks. He was a bit cagey about Beth so Anna left it there because he seemed happy enough. Eventually, both reassured of the other's state of mind, body and soul, they reluctantly said their goodbyes and as night fell, went their separate ways. On the drive home, Anna thought back to the day Sam joined up, memories flooded back causing her to smile and wipe away misty tears.

***

The writing had been on the wall since Sam was about ten because he and his friend, Danny, were soldier mad, spending hours playing war with their Action Men or haring round the garden with toy guns. At secondary school they joined the cadets where a serious seed was sown and both were adamant they would join the army. When he hit sixteen, Sam wanted to sign up straight away but Anna and Matthew convinced him to wait until he was eighteen. Not in the hope he would change his mind, more so they could be sure it was a mature decision and he would have two extra years of growing up under his belt.

As there was nothing else Sam wanted to do until he could join a tank battalion as a mechanic, Matthew suggested he went to work in the garages of the haulage company and get some hands-on experience. Anna knew that in the back of his mind, Matthew hoped that one day in the future Sam might bring his army skills home and run the maintenance side of the business.

The day Sam left for his fourteen weeks basic training, Anna thought she would drown in her own tears. He didn't want them to take him to the base; he was going on the train with Danny who, true to his word, joined up too. Sam left in a taxi with the largest, heaviest suitcase in the world, an ironing board, his best friend and a normal haircut. Anna still remembered his naive face that was a heartbreaking mixture of excitement and trepidation.

The next time they saw him, on his first home leave, Sam sported the shortest hair you could imagine and looked so thin that Anna was sure he'd snap in half. He didn't stop eating all weekend, having missed his mum's cooking and a cupboard full of treats. But despite getting up at 5am every morning, running for miles and marching for England in the rain and snow, he was undeterred and had no regrets, waving them goodbye on the Sunday evening without a care in the world.

The whole family went to Sam's passing out parade where the happiness in the air was palpable. Anna would never ever forget the sound of the marching band as it approached. Her heart was in her mouth, eyes scanning the faces of the immaculate young soldiers parading before her, desperately looking for her boy.

When she saw him, Anna's breath caught in her chest. Sam looked so proud and serious, the brim of his cap almost shielding his eyes, so smart in his perfectly turned out uniform, gun resting on his shoulder as he marched along in polished, shiny boots. Overwhelmed with pride and love, Anna realised that her little boy, the noisy, boisterous one, was now a man.

***

By the time Anna arrived home it was late and as she pulled onto the drive, wished she'd thought to leave the porch light on because the house looked gloomy and dark. Entering the hallway, silence overwhelmed her so after quickly flicking on the light she stood at the bottom of the stairs, listening. She hadn't been prepared for this, stupid really, what did she expect?

She knew no one would be here and it was exactly what the children had been afraid of but whilst trying to convince them she would be okay, Anna had managed to fool herself in the process. The awful reality crept up on her as realisation swallowed her whole. Despite her brave words she couldn't escape the truth. It was staring her in the face. After living in a house full of life and love and noise, the sound of laughter, tantrums, arguments and children's voices, as she stood there in the silent, empty hall, Anna felt very alone.

CHAPTER 7

Anna didn't bother to get up the next day, or the day after that. She stayed in bed and drank water from the tap in the en suite. Hunger evaded her so there was no need to go downstairs. She had never felt this tired in her entire life, not even after the children were born. On waking, her body felt inert so lying there in a trance-like state the days were spent thinking too much, remembering everything and crying, always crying.

She spoke to Sam and Mel when they rang, forcing herself to make reassuring conversation. Other than that she sent texts. On the third morning, unsure of the length of time she had been there or even what day it was, Anna flicked on the television and stared vacantly at the screen, not really taking in or even caring about what she saw or heard. A persistent headache was starting to throb so reluctantly and with Herculean effort, she got out of bed. Surprised at how weak she felt and aware of her wobbly legs, Anna took her time going down the stairs, ignoring the dust and the stale odour of her home.

In the kitchen she found painkillers and accepting they would make her feel sick on an empty stomach, made a cup of tea. The milk had gone off but she didn't care and drank it black whilst forcing herself to eat some biscuits from the cupboard and handfuls of dry cereal from the box. Dazed and lethargic she sat at the kitchen table, numb and oblivious to the chill in the air. The ringing of the house phone startled her and the noise was far too loud, piercing her ears making her heart thump. When she finally answered, at the other end was Jeannie.

'For God's sake, Anna, answer your bloody phone! Have you turned it off or something? I've been ringing you all afternoon.'

'Sorry, Jeannie, I was asleep so I put it on mute and I'm in the kitchen now. I've left it upstairs.' Anna tried to sound awake and responsive.

'Well, as long as you're okay. I'm at the airport. I've just flown in. Phil's on a late shift so I was going to come over and have some dinner with you if that's okay?' It wasn't okay and company was the last thing Anna wanted right now but knowing her friend would be suspicious if she declined, resolved to get it over with so reluctantly agreed.

'Okay, that'd be great, Jeannie, but there's not much in. Can you bring something, anything will do?'

'No problem, I'll be there within the hour. Get the glasses out and I'll bring a bottle.'

Anna sighed and held her head in her hands. It would only be for a few hours, she could manage that, surely? Then she would be able to go back to bed and oblivion because that was all she desired, the land of sleep. By the time Jeannie arrived, Anna had given the house a liberal spraying of air freshener, taken a shower and changed into clean clothes. She wore pale blue lounge pants and a white T-shirt which, even though they were loose fitting, felt far too big.

Her friend fussed and asked all the right questions about how Anna was sleeping, what she'd been eating (as she looked like she'd lost weight) and generally chit-chatted and jollied the evening along until it was time to leave. Anna was so glad when Jeannie kissed her goodbye after somehow managing to pull the wool over her eyes, hopeful that she would stay away for a couple of days at least. Without even bothering to wash the dishes, Anna went upstairs to bed.

And then, in the midst of her triumph, after faking it so well, everything started to go wrong. Despite drinking two glasses of wine Anna just couldn't sleep. There were strange noises outside her bedroom door, creaky floorboards, as if someone was pacing up and down the landing. Logic told her it was expansion or contraction but her heart still missed a beat every time she heard it. Next, the pipes started to clunk and groan and after remembering childish ghost stories about spirits tapping on things to make contact, she forced the thought from her head, until a sound from outside the window added to her fear. Anna listened in the darkness to the blood-chilling screech of a prowling fox, then suspicious footsteps and mumbling voices on the street. Fending off panic, telling herself she wasn't a child, Anna turned on her bedside lamp and tried to read but no matter how hard she tried, just couldn't concentrate.

The television didn't help, nor the radio. Yes, they drowned out the sounds that were making her agitated but made it impossible to hear an intruder so instead, Anna lay awake for hours, drenched in sweat with eyes like golf balls, paralysed with fear and the light permanently switched on. She told herself to be brave and grow up while desperately pushing thoughts of ghosts, the witching hour, burglars and murderers from her troubled mind. Even the bloody bogey man came back to haunt her.

At some point she fell into a fitful sleep, tormented by confused, erratic dreams. She was running down the corridor of a hotel, flinging open each door, desperately screaming Matthew's name but she just couldn't find him. Imagining she was awake, Anna felt him get into bed, the mattress sinking with the weight of his body only to open her eyes, disorientated, and find he wasn't there. Next, she was looking through a window covered by flowers, black roses, tearing at the petals and straining to see a woman's face, a blurred image that she couldn't quite make out. She thought she felt someone take her hand but its grasp was stone cold. Anna woke with a start, covered in sweat, trembling and frightened out of her wits.

In her bathroom she still couldn't shake the dreams away; they were lodged in her head, refusing to budge. Anna avoided looking in the mirror, too afraid she would see something hideous staring back at her so splashed ice-cold water over her face as she tried to calm down. 'This is pathetic, you're not a child' she told herself, 'pull yourself together.' Anna climbed wearily back into bed where she waited, praying for the morning, which was still hours away, her eyes wide open and ears on alert. When the light eventually appeared through a chink in the curtains she welcomed the relief that dawn provided and, utterly exhausted, Anna fell into a deep untroubled sleep.

Soon, a disturbing and debilitating pattern took hold when, the following evening, the dreams came back and another night of terror ensued. Anna was so emotionally drained by the morning that the rest of the day was spent sleeping peacefully. When she couldn't face the thought of one more night alone in her bed, Anna brought a spare duvet and pillows downstairs and slept on the sofa. She still heard noises but with all the lights on she hoped that any roaming burglars would be deterred. If sleep still evaded her she put the television on low, avoiding late night horror, watching the news, reading the text moving across the bottom of the screen. When morning arrived, Anna would either drag herself upstairs to sleep or remain where she was, mentally and physically drained.

Mobile phones had previously been a great annoyance to Anna because in her opinion, young people spent far too much time on them; they interrupted conversations or rudely bleeped and buzzed in restaurants. Now, she was thankful for this marvellous invention and acknowledged that it was an invaluable tool for anyone living a lie. Her phone enabled deceit. A simple text could throw everyone off the scent and convince them that Anna was busy or sleeping or happy, anything she wanted really. If she didn't reply for a while she could pretend she'd been in the garden, or taking a long indulgent bath. And a quick text informing everyone she was going swimming or to the gym gave her a good two hours of selfish peace.

Anna became devious and reclusive. Naomi thought she was with Enid for a few days, Jeannie believed Anna was at Naomi's and her mother, well, she could be fobbed off with all sorts of nonsense. Anna managed to fool everyone and got away with it for almost two weeks. She knew what she was doing was wrong and they only wanted to help but this way was so much simpler, even though she looked a mess, hardly ate, rarely changed her clothes and lived in the bubble that was solitude.

Anna tried to be sensible and told herself that it wasn't healthy, poring over photos of Matthew night after night and that picking at the past wouldn't help either, while at the same time became absorbed in grief, wallowing in a pit of self-misery that she couldn't and wouldn't climb out of.

Luckily, Jeannie was nobody's fool and after thirty-five years of friendship knew her best friend well enough to sense when something was wrong. So, after a bit of detective work, a few phone calls and acting mainly on intuition, she headed for Anna's, determined to sort things out.

Anna thought she was dreaming again but this time there was an ice cream van, its bell piercing her ears and a loud pounding in her head, punishing her brain. It wouldn't stop, ringing, banging, ringing and then there was a sharp crack, which shook Anna from her deep sleep. Something had hit the window. Muddled thoughts scrambled through her brain, it was light, so unlikely to be a burglar, a gunshot? Also far-fetched. She threw back the duvet, jumped out of bed and ran to the window, grabbing the curtains and flinging them open, the brightness of a new day blinding her eyes, forcing her to squint.

There, down below in her front garden, hands on hips, stood Jeannie. Yawning, Anna undid the catch and opened the window.

'Jeannie, what the hell are you doing? You nearly scared me to death! You could've smashed the glass, what on earth's the matter?' Her heartbeat began to return to normal.

'Never mind the sodding window, Anna, just open the bloody door.' Shocked and slightly nervous, Anna did as she was told and went downstairs where she unbolted the front door only to find Jeannie standing outside the porch, arms crossed and with a face like thunder.

Not waiting to be invited in, Jeannie marched past Anna and turned left into the lounge, stopping in her tracks when she spotted the rumpled bedding on the sofa and the oppressive gloom caused by the drawn curtains. Without speaking, she trailed her fingers across most of the wooden surfaces, leaving embarrassing tracks in the dust before continuing through to the kitchen. Letting out a loud, dramatic sigh when she saw the state of the room with its unwashed dishes, half eaten food and a pile of unopened post on the table, Jeannie pulled open the fridge door knowing instinctively she would find it empty.

Anna stood watching her friend, fearing she was in big trouble and waiting for Jeannie to speak. The silence became deafening as the two friends faced each other, both had eyes swimming with tears.

'Look at the state of this place, Anna. And more to the point, just look at the state of you. I know you've been avoiding me and telling us all a pack of lies, pretending you are anywhere but here. What good do you think that's going to do? You promised everyone that you would ask for help so why didn't you ring me, why are you being like this?' Jeannie gestured sadly to the detritus in the kitchen before her gaze fell on Anna.

Flopping down wearily at the table, Anna felt dejected and ashamed that she'd been found with greasy hair and dirty clothes, her house no better than a pigsty. Jeannie was right, she'd lied to everyone and it had to stop.

'I'm so sorry, really I am, it just sort of happened. It was easier to be on my own, less effort. I was so tired, Jeannie. I swear I didn't mean to upset you but I think I might be going a bit mad.' A sob caught in Anna's throat, the sound sending Jeannie to her bedraggled friend's side.

Kneeling down in front of Anna, Jeannie wiped away her own tears with her hand.

'Just tell me what's been going on in that head of yours, and then we can sort it out. I can't help if I don't understand, okay?'

Anna nodded and between sobs explained the cycle of misery and lies she'd found herself trapped in and just in the telling of it, felt the gloom begin to lift.

Once it was all in the open, Anna allowed herself to be assured and calmed by Jeannie who convinced her that this was only temporary, a result of hurt and shock and somewhat inevitable that things would catch up with her. But it was just a minor setback and everyone would understand. Once the sobbing subsided and content that her new found counselling skills had done the trick, Jeannie morphed into a mini hurricane. After despatching Anna off to the shower she flew around the house, opening windows and curtains, loading the dishwasher, filling the washing machine, examining the contents of Anna's cupboards and emptying the bin. By the time she came downstairs looking and smelling fresh, the house was also completely restored.

'Come on. We're going out. You've had time to wallow so now I'm going to get you back on track. We'll start with something to eat, then we're off to the hairdressers and looking at the way your jeans are hanging off you, I think we might even need a bit of retail therapy as well. And you're going to have to buy some food otherwise you'll starve. Get your finger out, we haven't got all day.'

And with that, before she had chance to object, Anna was whisked away.

After a long lunch they set off towards the salon to be pampered and styled. Anna was so glad to have escaped from the house and be in the company of other humans and in the spirit of moving on, forced herself not to think maudlin thoughts or dwell on past events. To pass the time as she waited for Jeannie, Anna flicked through the magazines in the reception area.

She was engrossed in an article all about a hotel in France where you could learn to paint and cook. It was somewhere in the Loire Valley, an area they had passed through as a family years back. The hotel, *Les Trois Chênes*, which meant the three oaks, was run by an Englishwoman who was restoring it to its former glory. Anna was miles away, imagining relaxing by the river on a warm summer's day, painting masterpieces before dining on French cuisine when she was interrupted by Jeannie, coiffed and ready for stage three of her mission.

By the time they had shopped for new clothes and food they were both shattered and hungry yet on arriving home, Anna was instantly filled with dread at the sight of the empty house. Jeannie's strong and buoyant presence reassured her slightly and as they went around switching on lights and putting the food away, she began to relax.

'Right, madam, you're going to have to lend me some pyjamas so go and dig some out while I open this wine and stick the pizzas in the oven.' Jeannie was looking for the corkscrew as she spoke.

'What do you mean pyjamas? You can't stay here! You need to get back to Phil.' Anna felt a bit silly and certainly didn't need babysitting, or so she thought.

'Not tonight, Josephine! Phil's at football and I'm sure he can cope on his own for one evening, anyway it's all arranged. I'll stay in the spare room and you can get a good night's sleep in your own bed while I guard you from monsters and the bogeyman.' Jeannie pulled a hideous face as she tore open the pizza box.

'Jeannie, that's really thoughtful but you can't stay here forever and I've got to learn to cope on my own.' Anna was resisting mildly and secretly relieved that Jeannie wanted to stay over.

'No shit, Sherlock! But until you get your confidence back I'm staying put. Any arguments and I'm ringing Enid, so take your pick, it's me or Mother Dearest.'

Anna raised both hands, laughing in mock surrender, knowing when she was beat.

'Okay, you win. But just one night mind, I don't want Phil getting jealous that I'm pinching his girlfriend.' As she scurried upstairs to find Jeannie something to wear, Anna realised she had never been so grateful to her friend in her whole life.

Later that evening after pizza, lots of ice cream, and a nice bottle of red, Jeannie told Anna that she had booked a week away in Egypt for her and Phil.

'Why don't you come too? The three of us would have a laugh and I can't leave you here, just in case you flip out again.'

Anna rolled her eyes knowing she would never live down her greasy-haired hermit episode.

'No way! I am not being a big fat gooseberry. I spent enough time doing that when we were teenagers for God's sake.' Anna was not going to be talked into that scenario ever again.

'But I'm going to worry about you. We go next week and I need to be sure you're okay and you could do with a holiday, you're looking pale and malnourished so some sun and five star all-inclusive will sort you out. Just think about it, please?' Jeannie tried the sad face approach but failed.

'Thanks a bunch! If I need a holiday or a spray tan I'll book one. I'm a big girl and I can go away by myself, you know? It'd be an adventure. You and Phil can go and have some fun, I'll be okay now, I promise.' Anna made the sign of the cross on her chest.

Jeannie tutted loudly and looked unconvinced but left it there knowing she'd pushed the Miss Bossy routine far enough for one day.

Lying in bed that night on clean sheets, Anna felt happier than she had for ages, knowing her friend was just down the hall, so she snuggled down under the duvet, warm and relaxed. Her thoughts eventually turned to Jeannie's offer but there was no way she would go with them, it was their first holiday and they really didn't want her tagging along. Then again, it would be nice to get away but she didn't really have the nerve to go by herself, did she? And then there were practicalities, she had to sign papers at the solicitors and visit Enid, but all that could be done in a day if she felt inclined. It was travelling alone that troubled her. There was no way she'd take her mother, they'd kill each other before they even checked in, Anna knew that for certain. And supposing she did pluck up the courage to go solo, maybe she'd feel like a spare part with an empty seat beside her on a coach excursion or a plane, the saddo dining alone in the hotel restaurant. Anna imagined being homesick, in fact it was inevitable, so all in all it was a stupid idea and the type of thing that strong-minded people do, not her.

Yawning loudly as she drifted off to sleep, instead of seeing torturous images Anna's mind wandered to the article in the magazine at the hairdressers, and instead of turning off, her brain began ticking over. The small country hotel looked charming in the photos. She adored France and it was the end of the season so would probably be nice and quiet at this time of year. Anna enjoyed cooking and had always fancied doing a course but never had the time. Perhaps she should go there. A change of scenery was exactly what she needed and the owner was English so there wouldn't be a language problem.

Unhelpful, doubting thoughts soon returned and ran amok in her head. Did she have the confidence? It was ages since she'd driven abroad and she would be nervous, so maybe that option wasn't ideal and what if she had a crash? Yet despite the battle raging through her brain Anna couldn't ignore the bubble of excitement gathering in her chest. A small smile appeared on her lips, accompanied by a tiny spark of long-lost spirit, which had returned just in time to make her decision for her. She had a head full of plans and an expectant heart and, pre-empting that she might just chicken out by the dawn of a new day, Anna promised herself that first thing in the morning she'd book a holiday.

Something had shifted; a glimmer of hope had stepped out from the shadows. The pipes still clunked and the floorboards creaked but Anna ignored them all, closed her eyes, and at last fell into a deep, contented sleep.

CHAPTER 8

Anna gazed down, through the aeroplane window at the meandering coastline of France as it appeared in the distance. She had tried to read her book but was unable to settle. There were too many thoughts running through her head, one of which was nervously anticipating the drive to the hotel, so instead she settled into her seat and allowed herself to daydream and enjoy the view.

***

Once she made up her mind to book a holiday there was no time to catch her breath or, as she feared, chicken out. Before Jeannie woke, Anna was up and about making coffee, typing the name of the hotel into the search engine and making a note of the necessary details. Not giving herself the opportunity to bottle out, she rang the hotel to make a reservation. Anna was immediately relieved to hear a friendly English voice answer the phone, presuming it was the lady owner, who introduced herself as Rosie, she enquired if they had any vacancies.

'Yes, actually, you're in luck. I can offer you a lovely double room with en suite and excellent views. How long would you like to stay? We're fairly quiet so I can let you have it for as long as you need.'

'I was thinking of ten days if that's okay? It's just me by the way, but a double room would still be great. I'm also interested in your cookery course and wondered are there any places available?' Anna's confidence was growing by the second due, in no small part, to the kind and friendly voice at the other end of the phone.

'Ten days is fine but I'm afraid we haven't got a course scheduled for a while. The demand has dropped off as it's the end of the season.' The owner, Rosie, sounded very apologetic.

'Oh well. Never mind. I can still enjoy myself even if I can't cook. I'm sure there's plenty to do.' Anna cast her mind back to the images in the brochure.

Hearing a hint of disappointment in the caller's voice and hating to let anyone down, Rosie replied.

'Tell you what, leave it with me. My husband's the chef but between you and I he's putty in my hands so I reckon I can wangle you a few lessons, just make sure you bring your pinny.'

Rosie was whispering in a jokey way, causing Anna to laugh. Rosie sounded fun and relaxed so with the reservation made, all Anna had to do was book a flight and wake up sleepyhead and tell her the news. Jeannie was slightly incredulous that her raving loony friend from the previous day had actually booked a holiday but once she was sure that Anna was in fact quite sane, insisted on taking over where flights were concerned. As a consequence, Anna ended up in the executive lounge at the airport and in a very nice seat on the plane where she was treated like royalty by Jeannie's colleagues.

The next few days were spent signing papers at the bank and solicitors, visiting her mother, shopping for a few extra clothes and packing. Melanie and Sam were thrilled she was going away, albeit a little concerned their mum was doing it alone. But having been secretly warned via text by Jeannie to be extra supportive and encouraging, they wished her bon voyage whilst insisting on regular updates and photos. Anna emailed Joe who responded almost instantly saying he was very proud of how she was coping and to have a fabulous holiday. He had settled straight back into Kiwi life where he and his two friends were now chugging around the South Island in their campervan.

Philip drove her to the airport, fussing and worrying like she was a child. He'd programmed his satnav for the journey from the airport to the hotel, reminding her that all she had to do was plug it in. She also had to remember to drive on the right, take her time (especially at roundabouts), watch her speed on the motorway and ring him if she had any problems. Anna tried to be patient and grateful but if he'd told her once he'd told her a thousand times. He obviously thought she was a bit dim so she resolved to prove him wrong.

Trundling her case towards the check-in desk, tiny butterflies tickled Anna's insides. Looking smart in her new outfit, chosen especially to boost morale, anyone noticing this forty-something passenger striding through the airport in her short, tan leather jacket, dark blue jeans and suede ankle boots, her dark hair casually tied back with a silk scarf, may have presumed she was a seasoned traveller. Nobody would even suspect that today, for the first time in years, Anna Harrison was going solo.

***

Anna enjoyed the flight immensely. Taking just over an hour it gave her plenty of time to compose and prepare herself for the remaining leg of the voyage and the only turbulence she had experienced was from inside her own body. Managing to retrieve her case and hire car without fuss and with Phil's satnav now successfully plugged in and operational, she was ready for action. After psyching herself up and practising changing gear with her right hand, she told herself that it would all come flooding back once she got into the swing of things. The last time she had driven abroad was when the kids were younger but to hell with worrying, it was now or never, she could do this, she had to.

Following precisely the instructions given, Anna drove carefully out of Aéroport Nantes Atlantique towards Angers and the hotel. Clearing the busy approach roads around the airport severely tested Anna's nerve as the route consisted of a multitude of roundabouts and everything was the wrong way round, not to mention the gear stick and her seat. She was gripping the steering wheel far too tightly and had white knuckles and sweaty palms. Her eyebrows were furrowed in concentration, leaving deep crease marks above her nose and her body was taut and riddled with tension. Relaxing slightly as she pulled onto the autoroute, Anna checked her speed and settled into the inside lane, all the while listening intently to instructions from the very firm, well-spoken lady on the satnav.

A few kilometres on, Anna found she was becoming quite fond of her invisible travelling companion who so far had kept them safe and on the right track, so when she eventually pulled off the motorway onto a quieter road, her tension level dropped down another notch. The pace of the traffic slowed and even though she still had to concentrate, there was ample opportunity to take in her surroundings and soak up the scenery unfolding around her.

Passing through small villages she admired the rows of pretty shops, the *boulangerie, charcuterie*, small cafés and *Bar Tabac* and the imposing churches, Anna relaxed a little, maybe because everywhere seemed so peaceful. Putting down the windows so the breeze could cool her flushed cheeks, she breathed in the country air. The early afternoon was warm and the honey-gold sun glowed softly in a pale blue sky, patched here and there with white clouds. Her heart felt giddy and as light as a feather with the realisation of her achievement. '*Look at me*,' she thought, '*I'm here, in France, all by myself. I did it, I actually did it.*'

Daphne, as Anna had named her satnav buddy, eventually directed her off the main road where she meandered down a country lane, occasionally passing farmhouses and whitewashed cottages with their slate roofs and tidy woodpiles, already stocked up for the creep of autumn.

Fields abundant with crops lined either side of the road and after a long hot summer of ripening, everything was ready for harvest. Tall, raggedy ears of maize and sunflowers, heavy with their burden of seeds forcing their lion heads downwards, swayed in the gentle wind. Perfectly round swirls of hay dotted the fields, drying in the late summer sun.

Anna could hear the chugging of tractors and farm vehicles and prayed she wouldn't meet one coming the opposite way, paying strict attention to the deep verges at the side of the road that separated her from the fruit filled hedgerows and crops.

As the road straightened out, the fields flattened into uniform rows of apple trees stretching as far as the eye could see. Any time soon, here and all across France the land would be filled with seasonal workers, picking the fruits and vines while farmers would toil long into the night to bring in their bounty, reaping the rewards of their labour.

There was a scent of life about this place. You could breathe it in – a heavenly concoction of flowers, cut grass, and earth, contrasted by tractor fumes, farmyard occupants and muck spreading. The colours of nature put on a show, deep golden corn, ripe purple-red berries, cream and yellow elderflowers and every possible shade of green merging seamlessly into the rusty, sun-baked earth. Surrounded by such beauty, Anna recalled a phrase she'd once read in a tour guide and understood now why they called the Loire the garden of France.

Jolted into reality by Daphne, Anna was informed she had to prepare to turn right where she would miraculously have reached her destination. Skin prickling with excitement, she was eager to see if the hotel lived up to the images that had caught her eye in the magazine and rested in her brain. Lo and behold, as Anna turned off the road and onto a dusty driveway she spotted three grand oak trees, spreading their boughs widely in welcome, proudly guarding the entrance to the property which no doubt they had done for hundreds of years. A signpost said '*Bienvenue*' which Anna knew meant welcome, then another, '*Les Trois Chênes*', bearing an arrow which she followed obediently, passing through white iron gates.

Holding her breath she drove slowly along a tree lined track as it arched gradually, opening into a large courtyard covered in pale natural stone. There, waiting for her in all its whitewashed glory, basking in the afternoon sun was her sanctuary and on seeing it, Anna's face broke into a wide smile.

The large farmhouse and the two renovated barns attached graduated down on levels. In front of each window were boxes laden with the last of summer's flowers. The main section of the cottage had a wide open front porch encased in an arch of dark pink roses. The middle, clearly the old stable section had white wooden shutters, open and welcoming in the warmth of the day. Clay flowerpots lined the floor and hanging baskets festooned the pale stone walls. The final section at the end looked out through large patio doors onto a country garden of wild flowers that continued around the border of the house and encompassed the neat front lawn.

Anna was entranced by its beauty and remained in her car, mesmerised, until a flurry of activity snapped her from her trance. A woman appeared on the porch, waving frantically whilst trying to calm a small pack of three yappy, excitable dogs. She couldn't work out who was most eager to welcome her, woman or beast. Gingerly opening the car door, Anna was reassured that all of them were friendly and big babies really so seeing they were suitably calmed, stepped out to be welcomed by her hostess, Rosie.

An extremely attractive, tall thirty-something, her blonde hair was cut just below her ears in a flicky, fashionable style that showed off her sun-kissed, elfin face and piercing blue eyes. Her cut-off shorts emphasised long tanned legs and a vest top exposed toned, golden brown arms. Rosie instantly reminded Anna of a Nordic goddess, wearing flip-flops.

'Anna, it's so good to meet you at last, did you find us alright? I've been keeping an eye out. Come in, come in. Let's get you settled and a nice cool drink, never mind your cases, we'll get them later, no rush, no rush. Sorry about my clothes, by the way, I've been in the garden.'

Rosie didn't come up for air and Anna found herself being efficiently gathered up and quickly swept inside.

The cool interior of the hotel fully complemented the exterior. Straight ahead was a wide oak stairway that Rosie explained led to the first-floor corridor that ran along the whole length of the property. All the bedrooms at the back of the house looked down onto a small terraced garden, a large pool surrounded by steamer chairs and a stunning view of rolling fields and distant villages. The foyer was actually a large sitting room, its main feature on the gable wall being a huge open fireplace, stacked with logs. Arranged around the fire stood a selection of sofas and armchairs, stylishly designed modern classics in soft, rustic colours, cleverly giving the impression they had been there since the house was built and scattered liberally with cushions, an occasional throw laid over for extra comfort.

Anna could picture how cosy this room must be in the winter months. There was an antique radio quietly playing in the corner and the long, low table in the centre of the room offered magazines and books. It was perfect.

They moved along past a central room that held a small bar and seating area while the kitchen lay at the back. This time the chairs were smaller but still comfortable, set in fours around small tables, obviously a place to sit and chat before dinner. They carried on into the end room which was the restaurant. In contrast to the natural warm colour scheme of the previous rooms, the dining area was painted in primrose yellow. Starched white tablecloths laid over antique dining tables were complemented by softly padded chairs. Glimmering crystal glasses stood to attention surrounded by silver cutlery laid on the palest blue and yellow napkins. It was understated and simple but extremely charming. The patio doors, seen from the front garden were shaded by white voile and at the opposite end of the room French doors opened onto the terrace.

'Come along now, Anna, let's get you a drink. Follow me, I'll be back in a tick, will wine be okay?' Once she had seated her guest who was nodding and slightly dazed, Rosie whizzed off to bring refreshments leaving Anna to catch her breath and take in the view.

Sitting on a comfortable oak deckchair she leant back her head and exhaled deeply. The tension from the drive evaporated as green fields stretched out before her. A small hamlet peeped out from the valley, easily pinpointed by its church spire as a tractor worked its way across the skyline, too far away to be heard or break the silence and tranquillity of the moment. As promised, Rosie returned swiftly bearing a laden tray and after setting it down on the table, collapsed into the chair beside Anna.

'A nice sit down at last, I hope you don't mind if I join you. This is my favourite time of the day, you know? We need a little break before the restaurant opens its doors for dinner. Is rosé okay? I can bring tea or coffee, or juice if you prefer.'

Anna surveyed the tray. The frosted carafe of pale pink wine beckoned, along with a colourful assortment of crudités, a creamy aioli dip and a variety of crisps and nuts.

'I think this is just what the doctor ordered, it's lovely, thank you.' Anna smiled reassuringly at her host who had poured two glasses of the cool, pink liquid and raised her glass.

'Here's to making new friends and having a lovely holiday.'

As Anna chinked her glass against Rosie's, a sensation of belonging and happiness swept over her. And crazy as it was, even though she had known this woman for the shortest of time, Anna had the feeling that the stranger sitting by her side would soon become her friend.

Later, as Rosie showed Anna to her room she wasn't disappointed when the door swung open to reveal her home for the next ten nights. Directly ahead was a large window, the sash left slightly open to allow in the afternoon breeze and full-length, heavy cotton curtains decorated with tiny blue flowers were elegantly held in place by corded rope. The large bed to the right lay in the centre of a soft, duck-egg-blue wall, crisp white sheets and plump pillows adorned the mattress topped with a patchwork quilt. On either side of the comfiest bed Anna had ever seen stood small white bedside tables and fringed lamps.

The remaining walls were painted crisp white, the wardrobe and dressing table were obviously antique but had been stripped bare, repainted and distressed in soft-white and grey. Traditional oak floorboards had been carefully sanded and varnished and were partially covered by a large tapestry rug placed at the foot of the bed. Opposite was a small doorway leading to the en suite which contained a small dresser stacked with fluffy towels. Assorted fragrant candles were dotted around the surfaces filling the room with scents of lavender and vanilla.

Anna inhaled, transported by the aromas. 'This is absolute heaven, Rosie. Thank you so much for letting me have this room and I must say, you have wonderful taste. I might never want to leave.'

Rosie looked proud and pleased by her guest's praise.

'Well, I'll leave you to settle in, shall I? Dinner starts at seven. I'll save you a nice quiet table in the corner. Everyone is very relaxed and informal here so don't be nervous, no need to dress up unless you want to. I only have two other sets of guests at the moment and they are all house trained and friendly. Just come down when you're ready. I'll have a little apéritif with you, if you like?' Rosie sensed the woman standing before her was quite shy so did her best to set her at ease.

'That would be lovely, Rosie, thank you, thank you so much.' Anna realised that Rosie must have picked up on her trepidation at the thought of coming down to dinner alone and was grateful for her kindness.

Left alone to shower and unpack, Anna smiled as she reflected on her day. Just that morning she had been a mess. Apprehension and lack of self-confidence had almost succeeded in making her abandon her trip. Thank goodness she hadn't caved in. If it hadn't been for the encouragement of her family and not wanting to disappoint them in return, she would be sitting at home now watching the news and eating from a tray on the sofa.

Anna moved over to the window from where she could just see the sinking sun, a red ball of fire setting itself down on the horizon. Hopefully this meant that tomorrow would be warm. She couldn't wait for the morning, a ripple of anticipation causing her to smile but first, a grumbling stomach nudged Anna into action. Choosing a pale pink, linen shift dress and matching cardigan she added a bracelet of darker pink and coral beads, then slingback sandals with a low heel for comfort. Her hair was pinned up and fastened with a clip and looked quite chic. Instead of her bag she opted to carry the novel she'd bought at the airport, intending to read it at the table if she felt too self conscious.

Summoning all her courage, Anna mentally ticked off the dos and don'ts that she felt necessary to observe in this new land of singledom. Not too dressy, not too casual – you don't want to stand out or attract attention, and don't make eye contact or look nervous and shy, and don't trip up or drink too much. This silent mantra was repeated as she cautiously made her way downstairs.

CHAPTER 9

Passing through the bar area a tall young man paused from polishing a wine glass and called out 'Bonsoir, Madame'. Shyly, Anna replied, 'Bonsoir' and hurried on into the dining area. Rosie, as promised, was waiting, chatting animatedly to a couple sitting by the patio doors and instantly spotting her new guest, made her excuses and wafted over. Slipping an arm through Anna's she guided her to a table in the corner by the open French windows. Transformed from Nordic flip-flop goddess, Rosie now wore a long floaty dress in a patterned riot of blues and oranges, accessorised with long beads strung around her neck which she twiddled and swung as she talked.

The table was set for one with a lighted candle at the centre and Rosie ushered Anna to her seat, again, plonking herself on the chair opposite. Smiling at the young man from the bar, Rosie introduced Pascal who, as if by magic, appeared at their table. In excellent English he suggested an apéritif, both women settling for Kir, white wine mixed with crème de cassis, and as he sauntered off, Rosie leant over and gave Anna the lowdown.

'Pascal's our local hunk and works here during the summer, waiting on and helping in the garden in between working on his dad's farm, they live on the other side of the village. He's at agricultural college and needs the extra cash. He also likes to practice his English and takes every opportunity so be warned, once he's off you won't shut him up, but he's a lovely boy, always eager to help and a hard worker. I don't actually think he realises his potential where the ladies are concerned though. We've had one or two love-struck teenagers go home with broken hearts, I can tell you. Apparently he's waiting for the right girl, lucky thing.'

Pascal returned with their drinks and the menu before shooting off to attend to the couple in the corner.

Glancing down the list of mouth-watering dishes on the á la carte menu, Anna was spoilt for choice so played it safe and went for the *plat du jour*. They chatted amiably about the weather and the forecast for the coming week, Rosie told her how busy it had been through summer and that she was glad the pace was slowing a little. She also asked what plans Anna had for her holiday and gave her some sightseeing ideas. Once she was content her guest was relaxed and just as her entrée arrived, Rosie excused herself and left Anna alone to eat.

Through the French doors the terrace was lit by hundreds of glowing fairy lights, artistically strung through the trees and bushes and Anna imagined it was a lovely place to end an evening. Reading her book in between courses, she soon forgot her earlier jitters and despite the room being almost full with other customers, Anna found she was enjoying herself more than she could have believed possible. Maybe the bottle of Pouilly Fumé recommended by Pascal had something to do with the warmth she felt inside, but nevertheless, she was content.

By the end of the meal Anna was so full that she could barely move and was glad not to be wearing anything with a waistband. Her entrée had been a delicious warm goat's cheese salad, complemented by a lemon and caper dressing drizzled artistically on top. Her plat principal was breast of chicken stuffed with wild mushrooms, accompanied by a mild Dijon mustard sauce and served with fresh garden vegetables. She only just managed the dessert of crème brûlée and declined the liqueur coffees or digestifs that were on offer.

After thanking Pascal, Anna was just saying goodnight to Rosie when another couple entered the dining room. Two men, the first was tanned and wearing casual pants and a loose T-shirt and accompanied by an older man, maybe in his early fifties, well built and handsome with short, salt and pepper hair, stylishly trimmed at the side to a close fashionable beard. Dressed in a white shirt and dark jeans the elder definitely looked the more sophisticated of the pair.

They could have been father and son, however, still prone to having an overactive imagination and not one to be fooled by appearances, Anna suspected they might be gay. The next words from Rosie's mouth and her actions merely confirmed her suspicions.

'Hi, Daniel, Josh, I'll be with you in a second. Pascal will bring your drinks.' Turning back to Anna, Rosie said, 'That's my other set of guests, lovely boys, they're both in a room just down the hall from you. I'll introduce you later in the week.' Giving Anna a cheeky, knowing wink she continued, 'Anyway, breakfast is from seven till nine but I can always bring you a tray if you prefer a lie in.' Rosie was twiddling her beads and watching Pascal as he chatted away.

'No thanks, Rosie. I'll be down around eight. I can't wait to start my holiday and don't want to waste a second. See you in the morning and thank you for a wonderful evening, oh, and compliments to the chef.'

With that, she left the dining room passing Josh and Daniel on the way. Josh was engrossed with his phone but Daniel looked up and smiled before wishing her goodnight which she politely returned. Anna, in the spirit of her new found independence and quest for adventure, decided that it would make a nice change, getting to know different people and looked forward to being introduced properly by Rosie.

Falling into bed that night, Anna was completely exhausted. The warm fuzz from the wine remained and she snuggled between the sheets, pulling the quilt over her for extra warmth. The air had chilled but regardless, she left the curtains open so the moon shone in and lit her room. Leaving the sash raised just a few inches allowed the sounds and the smells of her surroundings to seep inside. She thought she could hear the engine of a tractor somewhere in the fields beyond and a chorus of frogs croaked, passing messages to one another while muffled voices of late night drinkers on the terrace below, drifted upwards.

Here in the moonlight, Anna allowed her mind to wander and inevitably, the pathway led to Matthew. Out of habit she stretched out her hand and reached into the empty space at her side. He would have loved it here. She even knew what he'd have eaten, unafraid like her of making the wrong choice, eager to sample everything. They would've lain here in the dark, holding hands, making plans for tomorrow, going over the events of the day and probably having a giggle about the other diners, discussing how kind Rosie had been and the lovely hotel in which they slept.

A hot tear forced its way from the corner of her eye, rolling slowly down her face. She didn't want to cry tonight, she'd done okay and come a long way, not just in miles. The nagging voice called Truth whispered in her ear, reminding her of what he'd done, but she refused to listen, shutting it out, forbidding entry to anything that would spoil her day. Anna closed her eyes and instead focused on tomorrow. She would take Daphne out exploring and get some sun on her face, perhaps chat to Rosie and maybe even Daniel and his young lover. As she made plans in her head whilst being serenaded by the sounds of the countryside, Anna wore a contented smile, her happier heart less troubled, and cocooned within her patchwork, drifted off into a dreamless and peaceful, deep, deep sleep.

Having set her alarm for seven thirty, Anna was showered and ready for breakfast by eight. She had woken refreshed but for a few seconds remained confused and disorientated by her surroundings. On remembering, she stretched out in the bed and gazed over to the window at a clear blue sky. It was so peaceful. No traffic sounds, only birds chirping and the clink of crockery and subdued voices from early rising guests below on the terrace. Throwing back the sheets, Anna jumped out of bed and couldn't wait for her day to begin.

Going down to breakfast wasn't anywhere near as daunting as the previous night; she knew the natives were friendly so decided against taking her book, not feeling the need for protection. Rosie was in the dining room setting tables, wearing a white T-shirt and vivid lime green linen trousers, a colour that couldn't fail to wake you up.

'Good morning, Anna. Did you sleep well? It's a beautiful day so where would you like to sit, on the terrace or in here?' Rosie smoothed out the tablecloth while she waited for Anna to decide.

'The terrace, please. I may as well make the most of the weather. I hardly ever get to sit outside at home. Join me if you've got time, unless you are really busy.' Anna wanted to offer Rosie the same courtesy she'd shown her the night before.

'I've always got time for a quick coffee, you go and choose a table and I'll bring it out. It's continental brekkie here so I shan't be long.' And with that she was gone.

Anna chose a table benefiting fully from the sun which hovered at the corner of the farmhouse. Anna quickly scanned her phone. She had messaged all of her family the previous day, just before dinner, informing them of her miraculous and safe arrival, assuring them that everything was fine. Later, each had replied with messages varying from being proud and happy, to relieved and mildly incredulous that she'd made it in one piece. Last but never least, she had a very informative text from her mother telling her what she'd missed on *Coronation Street* and the teatime news. Clearly Enid thought her daughter was somewhere devoid of technology, especially television.

Slipping her phone inside her bag as Rosie approached, Anna's eyes feasted on the plate of pastries set down before her. There was pain au chocolat, croissants, fresh bread rolls and a selection of homemade jams and patties of butter. The heady aroma of freshly ground coffee stimulated her taste buds and her stomach rumbled in anticipation.

'I'm going to need elastic in my pants if I eat like this every day. I hope you're going to share, Rosie?' Anna knew there was no way she would eat everything although she could die trying.

'No, just coffee for me, Anna. I ate earlier this morning but trust me, a few extra pounds won't do you any harm so tuck in.' As Anna did as she was told they both sat amiably in the morning sun, drinking coffee and soaking up the atmosphere.

Rosie enquired where Anna was headed, which was Angers, and assured her that she would love it, giving advice on the best places to park. The conversation was cut short by the arrival of Daniel, alone this morning and dressed casually in jeans, T-shirt and wearing a thin blue sweater over the top. He chose the table next to Anna and once Rosie bustled away to fetch his breakfast, he attempted polite conversation.

'Morning… looks like the weather is being kind to us, are you off anywhere nice today?'

'Yes, Angers. I'm hoping to do some sightseeing and shopping. I was just on my way.' Anna began gathering her things as she spoke, not wanting to appear rude but eager to set off, Daniel, however, obviously wanted a chat, so continued.

'It's a fantastic city, you'll love it. I've been there many times. I don't think sleepyhead up there would appreciate it though. You know what young ones are like, he's not much into culture and by the time he gets up the day's half gone, and then he spends the rest of it texting or complaining, usually that he's starving, or bored.'

Anna laughed and rolled her eyes as if to agree. What she really thought was '*that's what you get for going out with someone half your age, cradle snatcher!*' Instead, whilst biting her tongue, she bade him a polite farewell then made her getaway.

As much as it would probably surprise Philip, Anna managed to programme Daphne all by herself and full of enthusiasm, she set off for Angers. Almost an hour later, and after parking her car right opposite the château as instructed by Rosie, she set off inside to explore. It was truly breathtaking. Perched above the banks of the river Maine its seventeen turrets reached high above the city, encasing the gardens and flowerbeds that Anna wandered amongst before heading inside and marvelling at the huge 600 year old Apocalypse tapestry.

Once she'd taken enough photos to thoroughly bore the pants off everyone at home, Anna left the château and followed the signs for the Galerie David d'Angers. Inside the glass roofed, restored abbey were huge sculptures, quite breathtaking figures depicting legendary French citizens. Anna collected various arty postcards for Melanie then moved onto the Musée des Beaux Arts which held contemporary paintings. Feeling cultured and satisfied she had shown enough interest in the historical aspect of the city she continued along the cobbled medieval streets, not failing to notice the quaint houses with striped timbers, twisted and warped by time.

Anna stopped for something to eat on one of the narrow side streets which were teeming with shoppers and tourists. Gratefully resting her aching feet under a striped canopy, she happily ate her lunch, people watching and reading her tour guide. Interestingly, there was a carving she had missed depicting a three-testicled man which adorned one of the oldest buildings in the city. The Maison d'Adam was over 500 years old but not feeling the urge to gawp at the unfortunate man's body parts, she set off for a touch of retail therapy instead. Maybe she'd have a quick peep on the way back.

Temptations were all around so she gave in and bought some pretty gift boxes from a chocolatier containing intricate handmade treats. Steadfastly sticking to window shopping where boutiques were concerned (the prices on the mannequins making her feel quite weak) Anna wandered into a large cobbled square where, at its centre, stood a grand and brightly coloured carousel with dancing horses. At the far end, to her delight, she spotted a huge department store, Galeries Lafayette. Set inside a nineteenth century building with wrought iron balconies on its facade, the interior held floor upon floor of perfumes, clothes and yes, handbags. Anna spent over an hour browsing and being sprayed with various scents by glamorous assistants. Purchasing reasonably priced gifts after avoiding designer price tags, she chose her mother, Mel and Jeannie scarves, gloves and what she hoped was a cool T-shirt, each one in a trendy keepsake bag bearing the shop name.

With her energy levels starting to wane slightly, Anna wisely decided to head back to the hotel before the evening exodus from the city began so with throbbing feet she retraced her route back to Daphne, detouring slightly in order to glance briefly at the statue of the well-endowed gentleman.

By the time she reached the hotel it was 4pm. The journey back had been uneventful and Anna was becoming increasingly confident on the roads and whilst paying close attention to her mate, Daphne, enjoyed listening to Radio France, even though she hadn't a clue what they were talking about. Having stored her purchases away, Anna wandered down to the terrace with her book and relishing the solitude, soaked up the afternoon sunshine. She could hear the occasional clanging of pots and pans in the kitchen combined with laughter and the chatter of voices. A relaxing hour or so passed reading and watching the clouds skim overhead until Rosie appeared on the terrace carrying a pile of linen.

'Anna, you're here. When did you get back? You should have called me, you'll need refreshments. You really are far too shy, you know.' Rosie tutted and shook her head.

'Honestly, Rosie, I've been fine. I didn't want to disturb you and anyway I've been quite happy just reading. But seeing as you have offered, why don't you join me for a drink, now you mention it I am a bit thirsty.' Anna closed her book, hoping Rosie would accept.

'Say no more. I don't need to be asked twice. I'll be back in a jiffy.' And with that Rosie flew off, taking back the pile of linen she came out with.

When she returned carrying a laden tray, there was a very good-looking man following on behind. Noticing the chequered chef's trousers, Anna deduced that this was Rosie's husband, Michel. With a firm handshake and in good English laced with a heavy French accent, he welcomed her warmly to *Les Trois Chênes*. Anna thought they made a very striking couple. In contrast to his wife's blonde, Nordic looks, Michel had the archetypal Gallic olive skin, dark brown eyes, and jet-black wavy hair. He was friendly and had a relaxed, easy-going way about him as they chatted pleasantly about her day out until finally he left them alone, obviously eager to get back to his kitchen.

'Ten out of ten there, Rosie, where did you find him? Good looking *and* he can cook. Is that why you keep him out of sight?' Anna chuckled.

'He has many more hidden talents which are put to very good use, I can assure you of that, but I've got to drag him out of that kitchen first. I swear his first love is food, and then me.'

'So, how did you two meet and how long have you been here? You are so lucky being able to work together, especially in this setting.' Anna gestured to the countryside beyond.

Taking a sip of wine and relaxing back into her chair, Rosie told Anna how, after working in the hotel industry since leaving college and travelling around Europe, she ended up here with a rundown hotel where she inherited a grumpy, frustrated chef. Five years later, the hotel was in a better state than when she found it and, surprise, surprise, the chef had cheered up a bit, too.

'Well, I'm so glad you did find each other. It was obviously fate because grumpy in there sure knows how to cook, and you are a wonderful hostess, so I think it was meant to be.'

Rosie leant over and squeezed Anna's hand in silent thanks, looking very smug. 'Look, I've got to get on and help prepare for dinner but maybe next time we talk, you can tell me your story, Anna. I hardly know anything about you or where you're from.' Rosie's voice was gentle, concerned.

'What makes you think I have a story? I'm just boring old Anna Harrison, nothing much to tell really.' Anna felt self-conscious and slightly uneasy.

'Everyone has a story to tell, Anna, and if I've learned anything over the years, it's that women rarely travel alone out of choice. Circumstance often has a big part to play and besides, you have a beautiful smile but it doesn't hide very sad eyes.'

Considering Rosie's astute words, Anna swallowed down a huge lump that had formed in her throat and unable to respond, she just smiled and looked away.

Rosie continued, 'Well, I'm here if you need me, Anna. I only want to help. Anytime you need a friend or even if you get a bit homesick, you know where I am.' And with that, Rosie stood, placing her hand on Anna's shoulder before walking away.

CHAPTER 10

The next two days followed a similar pattern. Anna rose early, eating breakfast on the terrace or indoors if the day was slow to heat up, the rest of the time she spent exploring the countryside, returning late in the afternoon. She had visited Château Chenonceau situated on the River Cher near Tours, spending a full day in the magnificent castle and grounds where Anna was enthralled by its history and beauty. The gardens took ages to navigate due to their vastness, combining flowers and vegetables to produce a stunning array of patterns and colour.

Resting in the coolness of the little chapel on the estate, she pondered over the stories in her guidebook. During the Second World War the building had been bombed, destroying the beautiful stained-glass windows but undeterred by the attack and threat from the Nazis, the grounds of the château were used by the resistance to enter Free France as part of the river remained an occupied zone. At the time of the French Revolution, the owner, Madame Dupin, disguised the existence of the small chapel by turning it into a wood store to prevent its pillaging or destruction. In the First World War, the château itself had been turned into a field hospital and the lady of the manor, Madame Menier, nursed the injured soldiers herself.

Anna's favourite story was about King Henri. He gave the château to his mistress, Diane de Poitiers who lovingly transformed most of the house and gardens and built the huge bridge across the river. Unfortunately, after all her hard work, Henri died and his wife Queen Catherine kicked Diane out and took over the castle for herself. *'There has certainly been a lot of girl power going on behind these walls,'* thought Anna, as she popped the guide back into her bag and made her way outside.

The troglodyte caves near Saumur were next on the agenda, an amazing place where dwellings were cut from the high rock faces of the landscape and people still lived in tiny cave houses. Anna explored caverns and underground villages and visited a mushroom museum which she noticed on her way home. After a tour of the subterranean caves where various varieties of mushrooms grew, she bought a speciality selection box for Michel, assuming he would appreciate the array of weird looking fungi.

There were many other attractions Anna could have visited but try as she might to ignore it, a tinge of loneliness was beginning to affect her enjoyment of her surroundings. On spotting something interesting it was natural to remark on its beauty, however, when she turned, there was no one to share it with. As she wandered streets and gardens, despite her attempts to avoid the sight of couples walking hand in hand who seemed to be everywhere, taunting her slightly, causing her to feel resentful of their happiness. At first, being in a crowd had allowed anonymity, she was less self-conscious but now admitted to feeling conspicuous and lonely.

Eating alone was also becoming depressing; having nobody to discuss the food or menu with began to taint the experience. It had been the same at dinner the previous evening and although her meal was delicious and Rosie flitted over at regular intervals to chat, Anna was envious of the other groups of diners. Ironically, even though the odd couple appeared to spend much of the meal arguing about too much texting at the table or yawning, even Josh and Daniel had each other.

During her travels along the roads of France, Daphne was extremely reliable but not a great conversationalist so with a sinking heart and worried that her little bubble of independence was about to burst, Anna returned early to the hotel in search of some company and conversation.

Back at Rosie's, as Anna made her way along the corridor to her room she became aware of loud, angry voices. Josh and Daniel were only a few doors down from her – she had seen them going in a few days before. Trying hard not to listen (which was quite a feat as they were really shouting) she scurried past while wrestling the room key from her bag.

'For crying out loud, Daniel, can't you get it into your thick head that I am sick of your prying? I'm not telling you who I'm texting cos it's got sod all to do with you. I am not a kid anymore so keep your nose out.'

Anna could hear Josh ranting and he sounded mad as hell whereas Daniel took a more conciliatory tone.

'Keep your voice down, Josh. There's no need to shout and I'm not prying, you are just so secretive, you know it worries me and why.'

'Do you bloody well wonder? Just leave me alone, Dan, I'm going out, you're suffocating me and I'm sick of it.'

Anna shoved her key into the lock and almost dived inside to avoid being seen, closing it quickly, just in time to hear the loud bang from an angrily slammed door further down the hall.

'*Well, it's all happening here, the older one is obviously jealous and insecure,*' Anna thought as she retrieved her book and sunglasses. Remembering to check her phone she replied to messages from everyone back home, including her mother who had provided a detailed soap update, leaving Anna relieved that Emmerdale Edna's poorly dog would pull through after chemotherapy.

Walking through the French doors onto the terrace she was met by the sight of Josh. Recognising sullen, adolescent body language when she saw it, hand on chin, legs stretched out, foot tapping angrily, Anna surmised he had the worries of his very important world on his mind. She was about to do an about turn when he looked up and spotted her so knowing it would be obvious and rude to walk away, her mothering instinct kicked in, forcing Anna to go over and sit down next to sulking boy.

'Hi, it's Josh, isn't it? I'm Anna.'

He at least had the grace to look up and say hi, back.

'So, how come you're sitting out here on your own? Should I order us both a drink? I could do with some company and you look a bit fed up.' Anna imagined how she'd approach one of her own children and after hearing the row, felt a bit sorry for him.

'Yeah, thanks, a drink would be great, can I have a beer?' Josh managed a weak smile before continuing. 'And I'm here cos that freaking weirdo is always sticking his nose into my business and never gives me any space. He's doing my head in. I can't do anything without him checking up on me and I wish I'd stayed at home… at least I'd get some privacy there.'

Surprised by his honesty, Anna replied. 'Oh dear. You know, all relationships are hard work at the best of times, Josh, and loads of people fall out when they are on holiday together. It's not unusual. Maybe he's just guilty of loving you a bit too much and that can be suffocating sometimes.' Anna waited for her words to sink in.

Not feeling at all pacified, Josh was indignant. 'That doesn't mean he can poke his nose into everything though. There is such a thing as privacy and trust. He acts like he's my flaming dad sometimes. I am *so* never coming on holiday with him ever again, not even if he begs.' Josh was tapping his fingers impatiently on the arm of the chair.

'Well, I don't really know either of you enough to give advice, but there does seem to be a big age gap between the two of you so you are bound to have different interests and friends. I can see why it would cause tension.' Anna was feeling slightly irritated by cradle-snatching Daniel whilst trying hard not to judge.

'Yeah. Dan is loads older than me… in fact he's nearly a fossil. He just doesn't get me at all. It's as simple as that.'

Anna fought down a giggle at the comment but soldiered on with her best advice. 'Perhaps if you just explain that to him without shouting, it'd help. Forgive me for saying, Josh, but yelling and stomping off like a naughty kid will probably encourage him to treat you like a child, especially if you're acting like one.'

Josh looked up with a shocked expression before laughing out loud and agreeing. 'Yeah, I get your point, fuel for his fire I suppose.'

'Exactly. Now, I'll go and get you that drink and you can practice your "I'm sorry" speech. Oh, and make it quick because you've got a visitor.' Anna had spotted Daniel hovering in the doorway so she waved and smiled, beckoning him over. 'I'm just getting some drinks, would you like one, a glass of wine?'

Looking relieved and grateful, Daniel accepted.

As she walked inside towards the bar, Anna turned to see Daniel sitting beside Josh, deep in calm conversation; they seemed to be making peace.

When she returned, the battle appeared to be over so placing the tray of drinks and snacks on the table, Anna sat down next to Josh. Enjoying being in company and seeing that they had both cheered up she gave herself an imaginary pat on the back. They chatted together about this and that, comparing notes on the places they had visited and how lucky they had been with the weather. Tomorrow would be the first of October and the forecast predicted that the mild temperatures would continue for a few more days, until the weekend at least.

Daniel brought more drinks and Anna's cheeks began to warm as the unsettled feeling she'd had earlier eased. Daniel seemed like a genuine, decent man and she felt slightly guilty for her earlier assumptions. They spent a happy hour together during which Josh texted continually whereas Daniel just appeared relieved that they had finally made up and ignored the fact.

The sun was touching the top of the field on the horizon, preparing itself for bed when Anna decided to make a move and get ready for dinner. You weren't expected to dress up but her cropped trousers looked extremely wrinkled, her flat pumps were a bit too dusty and she was feeling sleepy from the wine so needed a nice long shower to wake herself up. Announcing her intentions, Josh had an idea.

'Hey, Anna. Why don't you eat with us tonight? You always sit on your own and we're like your mates now so go on, say yes, it'll be a laugh.'

Josh had actually interrupted texting to state his case so Anna felt slightly honoured, and then Daniel piped up. 'That's a great idea, Josh. I could do with some adult conversation while you text the entire world and I promise I won't say a word. What do you think, Anna?'

Glad she wouldn't have to sit alone again and feeling safe in the knowledge that she wasn't crossing any Victorian mourning boundaries by eating with her gay friends, Anna the merry widow, happily agreed.

Feeling uplifted at the thought of having dinner with company, Anna decided to make an extra special effort and took time styling her hair, leaving it down in long, bouncy waves. Looking through her wardrobe she chose her maxi dress, thinking that the dark red and gold swirls complemented her slightly tanned shoulders and face. Anna carefully applied her make-up; just a touch of eyeliner, mascara and natural lip gloss and a simple brushed gold chain around her wrist finished the look. Pleased with the reflection in the mirror and with a bit of a skip in her step, Anna went to dinner.

They had agreed to meet at eight and when she entered the restaurant, Josh and Daniel were waiting at the table, as was a bottle of champagne and two glasses. Rosie was there to greet her and seemed genuinely pleased she was dining with others and after declining a glass of champagne, left them to ponder the menu.

Daniel explained that the champagne was by way of a celebration in making a new friend, whom he added looked lovely, and also as a thank you for calming the storm earlier in the day. Josh, not having a taste for anything other than beer or vodka raised his bottle then rolled his eyes, no doubt cringing at Daniel's speech.

Enjoying the crisp dryness of the champagne, Anna and Daniel discussed the tempting menu. Josh had already made his choice of soup, steak and chips, and apple pie which apparently he'd eaten every single night since arriving. Anna chuckled, imagining Michel having a cheffy fit on hearing his lovingly made dishes described in such a British way. After much deliberation, Rosie took their order and as she collected their menus, paused to speak to Anna.

'I forgot to mention it's my birthday on Sunday so we're closing the restaurant for the day and having a party. I've already invited Daniel and Josh and was hoping you would come along to help me celebrate?' Rosie looked flushed and excited at her upcoming birthday.

'Oh, Rosie, that would be lovely, as long as you're sure I wouldn't be intruding. I'd be honoured, thank you.' Anna was touched and pleased that she had been included.

'Of course you're not! Right, that's settled then. Two o'clock on the terrace for drinks, weather permitting. Michel's preparing one of his grand feasts, I'm sure you'll love it. I'll go and tell him we've got another guest.' And within a heartbeat she was off, hurrying towards the kitchen.

During the lull as they waited for their entrées, Daniel asked Anna if she liked the champagne.

'It's wonderful. I'm sure I can taste apples or pears but it's probably my imagination, I have no idea about wine.' Anna had another sip, just to check.

'No, it's not your imagination. If you close your eyes you can smell the fruit, it reminds me of apple sauce.'

Sniffing warily, Anna could indeed smell something; it was more like spiced cinnamon. 'Do you know a lot about wine, Daniel?' Anna smirked as she steadfastly ignored the sarcastic snoring noises emanating from Josh.

'Not really. I'm just interested and try to collect some while I'm here. I always end up with a car full of orders for friends back home. The whole process fascinates me especially the interesting facts I find along the way, even though I obviously bore Josh to death with it. Did you know that the first time Dom Perignon tasted champagne he said to his workers "Come quickly, I am tasting stars"?'

Taking another sip from her glass, Anna remarked, 'You know what? I agree with Mr Perignon, that's exactly what champagne is like, tasting stars.'

They ate their starters in companionable silence. Josh loved his onion soup but Anna was feeling adventurous and chose *poivrons villages*: baked peppers marinated in olive oil, garlic, lemon and herbs, then stuffed with soft cheese and chives on a bed of leaves. Daniel chose *poulet lyonaise*: sautéed chicken liver with garlic, chanterelle mushrooms, and spinach served with onion sauce. Sharing some of her starter with Daniel, Anna politely declined tasting his after spotting the scary little mushrooms she'd bought for Michel. As they waited for their main course and feeling emboldened by the champagne, Anna decided to ask a few more intimate questions of her dining companions.

'So, Josh, Daniel, tell me, how long have you two been together?'

Josh's head snapped up and looked at Anna. Seeming confused, he asked quizzically, 'Together! What do you mean, together?'

'You know, how long have you been an item, going out, or however you say it these days?' In the long expanse of silence that followed and with a creeping sense of doom, Anna realised she had said something very wrong. She could tell just from the look on both of their faces and the hush that settled over the table.

Josh held his phone mid-air, fingers poised on the buttons but frozen to the spot. Daniel was just staring at her, his mouth open but seemingly lost for words.

'Oh my God! You think we're gay, don't you? Daniel, she thinks we're gay! This is hysterical. I don't believe it, and that also means that Anna thinks I'm your toy boy.' Consumed by an uncontrollable fit of laughter, Josh placed his head on the table, his body shaking with hilarity.

In the meantime, Anna whipped her hands over her face, hoping to hide the deep crimson flood of embarrassment engulfing her. Unable to take her eyes off poor Daniel and his shocked expression, not knowing what to say, she remained frozen, mortified.

Eventually, the corners of his eyes began to crease and a large grin crept across his face and his shoulders started to shake with laughter. When Daniel finally controlled himself, he managed to speak, 'Anna, what are you thinking? Josh isn't my boyfriend, he's my brother!'

Thankfully Anna had recovered enough to begin her apologies whilst wishing the earth would swallow her up, desperately willing her brain to find adequate words, telling them both she was so sorry and appalled that she'd offended them by jumping to the wrong conclusion, which was becoming an annoying habit.

Daniel reached over and patted Anna's hand, assuring her that no harm was done and no offence taken, instead, he just thought it was really, really funny. Josh said it was the best thing that had happened all week while Daniel quickly poured Anna another glass of champagne in order to calm her down. As she sipped her drink gracefully, all the time fighting an immense urge to knock it back in one, Josh excused himself from the table while Daniel attempted to explain their situation.

'Firstly, I'm divorced and have been for nearly five years now. Despite being single since then and just for the record, I have definitely not been tempted to seek solace at any time with another man and don't intend to do so in the future.' He smiled as he spoke, winking playfully, teasing Anna slightly.

'My daughter, Louise, lives further south in Limousin with her husband and my grandson. I'm an electrical engineer and I sold my company when my marriage ended. I do consultancy work now, which suits me fine as it frees me up to visit the family whenever I like. I found this place by accident about four years ago and have been using it as a stop-off on the way home ever since. My ex-wife and I get on okay but prefer to avoid each other so I only come to France when the coast is clear.' Taking a sip of his drink, Daniel took a breath and continued.

'As for Josh, and to make things even more confusing, he's not actually my brother, he's my nephew. My sister had him when she was seventeen. She was totally out of control, using drugs and disappearing every five minutes and incapable of looking after a baby. She ran away and sadly died after taking an overdose so my mum brought Josh up, that's why we feel like brothers. My dad passed away when Josh was a baby so he never really had a father figure. I was a lot older and left home while he was just a kid. Mum was his world but she died two years ago and since then he's gone off the rails a bit. He dropped out of college, can't keep a job and got in with a bad crowd. He ended up in hospital a couple of months ago after an all night binge and I found out he's been messing about with drugs. From what I can get out of him it was party stuff, so I just hope and pray that he's telling me the truth. It scared me half to death so I took him in, there was no other option really as he'd been kicked out of his flat and had no one else to turn to.' Daniel looked so sad and slightly weary as he told the story.

Sensing he needed a break, Anna interrupted. 'Poor Josh, at least he has you. I dread to think what would happen otherwise.' Anna's heart felt sad for Josh while being impressed that Daniel had stepped up to the mark.

'Well, I'm not sure he sees it like that but I'm not going to give up on him. I brought him to France because I thought a holiday would do him good, and if I'm honest, I didn't trust him to stay at home on his own. It was okay while we were at my daughter's. He was around younger people but now it's the two of us I'm having trouble juggling being his friend and a brother while trying desperately not to sound like a dad.' Daniel looked exhausted from explaining his predicament, along with living it.

Feeling totally foolish, Anna replied, 'I'm sorry I made ridiculous assumptions, Daniel. It's not the first time recently I've been found guilty on that score. I'm such an idiot, putting two and two together. I'm so stupid, but when Rosie referred to you as nice boys and because you were sharing a room and I overheard your argument which I wrongly mistook for a lovers tiff, I presumed you were gay. I live in a fantasy world and watch too much rubbish on television. I hope you can forgive me?'

'There's nothing to forgive, Anna, although I expect I will never hear the last of it from Josh, especially as it's probably all over Facebook by now. At least it cheered my miserable brother up, that's one good thing anyway. Now, I really need another drink. I'll get Pascal to bring us a nice bottle of red if that's okay with you?'

Josh returned at that point, still finding the whole thing really funny just as with perfect timing, Rosie arrived with his steak and chips. To Anna's great relief, it shut him up as she wanted the whole cringeworthy fiasco to be forgotten as soon as possible. The arrival of their main courses also gave Anna and Daniel something else to concentrate on as they tucked into their food, settling back into enjoying each other's company and savouring the lovely, rich Rasteau they were drinking.

But nothing was ever that simple for Anna and as the evening progressed, the irritating voice of her ever present conscience began whispering in her ear. It reminded her that she had just lost her husband, that it was wrong to be sitting here, laughing with a single, available and extremely handsome man. And what would the children think if they knew? Was Matthew looking down from heaven right now, disappointed and hurt?

Entering into silent, one-sided negotiations, Anna replied firmly, '*It served him right! And actually, I'm sitting here by mistake. We have a chaperone and a room full of diners. I didn't instigate any of this, I'm not flirting and neither is he, and what's more, I am totally and utterly the innocent injured party, so butt out!*'

Unfortunately it didn't work. Anna wasn't convinced by her own defence or bravado, she felt disloyal and heartless and gradually her spirits took a nosedive and as much as she tried to hide it, Daniel picked up on the change in mood. Josh wolfed down his apple pie and took up Pascal's offer to watch television in the bar so taking his beer, he shot off to check out French TV. Once they were alone, Daniel plucked up enough courage to ask Anna what was wrong.

'Anna, are you okay? I can tell that something is bothering you. Have I said something to offend you? I hope you're not still worrying about earlier.' His earnest face regarded her patiently, his eyes kind yet revealing a hint of concern.

Nervously twisting her wedding ring around her finger, Anna decided there had been enough misunderstandings for one night so taking a breath, told him the truth.

'Please don't be upset by anything I'm about to say because you have done absolutely nothing at all wrong. The thing is, I feel I'm here under false pretences and despite having had a lovely evening, I wouldn't have accepted your offer if I'd known that you and Josh were, shall we say, not gay. I lost my husband at the beginning of July and came here for a break, to recharge my batteries, that sort of thing and no matter how I try to justify being here with you and Josh, I feel like a really bad person and *I've* done something wrong.' She looked down at her hands, totally lost for anything else to say, hoping he wouldn't be offended by her words.

Daniel sighed and rested back in his chair, shaking his head before replying. 'Anna, it's my turn for apologies now. Firstly, I'm very sorry about your husband. I'd spotted your wedding ring and was eventually going to ask about him which would've made me feel equally as bad when I heard the truth. I'm also sorry if anything about tonight has made you feel uncomfortable, that really wasn't my intention, but just for the record, I think you're extremely brave coming here alone. It took me ages to sort myself out after my divorce and I imagine what you have gone through is so much worse. You have absolutely nothing to feel guilty about, tonight has been totally innocent, simply eating and talking and trying to keep Mr Moody amused. There's no harm in that, is there? And forgive me for saying, but if I was your husband I'd be very proud of you right now. I would be glad that you were having a nice meal and a teeny bit of fun, you deserve to smile, we all do.' Daniel left his comments hanging in the air, watching Anna's face for signs he'd overstepped the mark.

Anna willed herself not to get upset, breathing in deeply she dug her nails into her palm, finally managing to raise her eyes to meet his.

'Do you really think so? I drive myself mad, overthinking every situation and dithering. It's one of my many faults. I've had a lovely evening and if I'm honest I was starting to feel a bit fed up and lonely. I seem to be making progress then losing Matthew hits me like a wall. There are so many mixed emotions inside me and sometimes I don't know whether I'm coming or going. Thank you for listening and understanding, it means lot.' It felt good to actually say Matthew's name out loud, like he was part of the evening, not cast out and forgotten, and now everything was in the open. Almost.

Despite her honesty, Anna couldn't bring herself to mention his affair; it was too personal and ironically seemed disloyal. Maybe part of her wanted to hold on to the good times and for Matthew to remain perfect because for a long time, he had been.

Daniel smiled at her kindly and nodded. 'I do understand, Anna, really I do, so let's try to relax and enjoy our dessert before Josh comes back to annoy us. I promised him a liqueur coffee so he'll turn up eventually.'

With nothing more to be said, they tucked into their *mousse au chocolat* and the subject of Matthew was relegated, but for Anna, not forgotten. It just wasn't that simple.

Still, despite the blip and maybe due to Daniel's kind words or the relief of her confession, Anna was able to continue her evening clearer of conscience and almost light of heart. It had turned too chilly to sit on the terrace so they drank their coffee in the comfy lounge where Anna half wished it were colder so they could light the fire and gaze at the logs. Daniel explained that the following morning he'd be helping a friend move into his holiday home and owing to Josh being neither use nor ornament, he was staying at the hotel and would have to amuse himself. Then Anna had an idea.

'Do you like swimming, Josh?'

'Yeah, I'm actually quite a good swimmer, why d'you ask?' Josh was busy eating the minty chocolates which came with the coffee.

'Well, I was thinking of having a bit of a lie in tomorrow and a lazy morning but if you fancy it, maybe in the afternoon we could find a pool and get some exercise. What do you think?'

'Yeah, that would be fab, Anna, cheers. Just let me know what time and I'll meet you down here.'

'Okay, I'll ask Rosie for some directions and we could leave about two, after lunch.' Anna smiled when Daniel mouthed a silent thank you, suspecting he was relieved at not having to drag Josh along. Now he could relax and she would have some company.

Feeling the full effect of the champagne, wine and liqueurs, Anna decided it was time for bed so after thanking them both for a lovely and very memorable evening, she wished them both a goodnight and made her way upstairs, happier than she had been for a very long time.

CHAPTER 11

In bed later, Anna ran over the events of the evening. She had no regrets except for putting her size fives well and truly in it, but she'd been forgiven and they had laughed about it again later. Her mind wandered to Josh who'd lost both of his mums and had never even known his dad. Anna felt sad for him and hoped one day he would realise how lucky he was to have Daniel who seemed to be decent and kind, someone who would be able to get Josh back on track. She also wondered why Daniel was on his own – a shame really because he was intelligent, funny, interesting and eligible, quite a lot of ticks in the boxes. You never could tell though, for all she knew he might be a wife beating maniac who drank a bottle of vintage wine a day whilst travelling around France, luring lonely widows to a grisly end. Knowing it was highly unlikely and hoping to avoid a return of her nightmares, Anna forced Daniel from her mind.

Yawning loudly, she turned to face the window, dreamily watching the clouds skim across the moon. Her eyelids were heavy and she began to drift off to sleep, thinking of her children and what they might be up to, wishing she could give them a hug and missing the warmth of her husband's body beside her. Just before sleep finally wooed her, unable to prevent it because the habit was too hard to break, her thoughts were, as always, of Matthew.

Anna sat on the terrace reading and despite the blue sky and the sun's attempt to outrun the clouds it felt slightly chillier than the previous days. It was still pleasant enough to take in the scenery and breathe an abundance of fresh air so she soaked up the peace and quiet, taking full advantage of her surroundings. Before long she began to nod off until a familiar voice disturbed her slumber. Rosie was chattering to Pascal in the dining room and seeing Anna, came outside.

'I'm taking a walk into the village, do you fancy coming with me? I need to go to the pharmacy and perhaps we could have coffee in the café afterwards. It's not far. It takes about ten minutes on foot.'

'That would be lovely. I've only driven through and I'd like to have a look around. I'll get my bag, two ticks.' Anna shot off to retrieve her things and within minutes they had set off towards the village.

Their stroll along the quiet country road was disturbed only occasionally by a car or a rumbling tractor loaded up with hay. Anna had Rosie in fits of laughter when she related the tale of the mistaken relationship, trying hard to blame it all on her blonde companion for calling them lovely boys and winking suggestively. In her defence, Rosie insisted the wink was in reference to Daniel's good looks, nothing more and Anna couldn't deny it, he was rather gorgeous.

On nearing the village they passed the sign which welcomed you into St Pierre de Fontaine. The medieval church right at its centre could be seen from the road while the shops and houses were spread protectively around it, in a circular, ordered fashion. The small village consisted of the *Mairie* and the post office, both housed in the same building, with carefully arranged flower beds and lawns while the Tricolour flag blew proudly in the wind. There was a small grocery store, a *boulangerie* selling fresh bread and cakes, a well stocked *pharmacie* and lastly, the village bistro. As they approached the *pharmacie*, Anna continued along the path, hoping to buy some cakes for later; apparently they were made on the premises and sold out really quickly.

Purchases made, they headed for the little café whose interior consisted of archetypal round tables and wooden bistro chairs. A news channel played on the small television, strategically placed above the wooden bar which was propped up by two extremely old men. They were perched precariously on stools, drinking small glasses of wine while chatting to the owner who Rosie introduced as Sebastian.

They found tables by the window which looked out onto the cobbled courtyard of the church. Its dark-green, stained-glass windows reminded Anna of wise eyes, keeping watch on the citizens of St Pierre, missing nothing, remembering everything. As they waited for their coffee, talk turned to England and the things Rosie missed. It was quite a short list really consisting mostly of food such as Cheddar cheese, Heinz beans, salad cream and Mars bars, and even though some English produce could now be bought in France, it was quite expensive. The other thing Rosie missed was the soaps, but even if they had satellite television she admitted that her day was so full she'd never be able to keep up.

Naturally, Rosie wanted to know about Anna, did she have children, where she was from and so on? Until now they'd only had a chance to pass the time of day at the hotel and there'd never been the opportunity to have a heart to heart. Sipping her coffee, Anna realised it would be nice to stay in touch with Rosie after her holiday, maybe return one day and become friends so there was no point in telling half a story, the situation with Matthew would eventually come out in the wash. Secrets were a burden. When Anna began, it was with her three children, knowing that was the easy part.

Rosie had listened to all of it, the hard part in silence, her eyes full of compassion, never interrupting, understanding the storyteller's need to unburden a secret without the distraction of irritating questions. The result was that once the final word was spoken, an invisible yet gloom-filled cloud lifted from above Anna's head and flew swiftly out the door.

'Anna, I am truly sad for you. How you have managed to pick yourself up after the past few months I really can't imagine. One thing I know for sure is that you are an incredibly strong person and if you can get through that, you can deal with anything that life throws your way.'

'I don't know if that's entirely true, Rosie. I think I've been on autopilot for a while, going through the motions and every type of random emotion you can think of. Being here has really helped. It's not been easy, I'll be honest. But like you said, I've proved to myself that I can be independent, and now I have to get on with my life. Coming to France may have been a knee-jerk reaction and frowned upon by some but I had to do something proactive. I needed a confidence boost and an injection of self-esteem because Matthew took most of that away.' As she spoke the words, Anna affirmed them in her head. She did feel strong, a touch more confident and borderline happy.

Rosie, who was impressed by Anna's defiant streak, then asked a burning question. 'So, this other woman, you have no idea who she is, are you going to try and find out or leave it in the past? I don't know what I would do, apart from killing her if I clapped eyes on the cow.' Rosie looked perplexed and angry, defensive of her new friend.

Sighing, Anna shook her head and replied, 'No, I haven't a clue who it is and no idea how to find out either. The children don't know and I'd rather keep it that way for the moment. As far as I'm aware it was their secret, Matthew and this woman, so I can hardly go marching around interrogating everyone who knew him, it's too embarrassing. It will always be in the back of my mind and I will always wonder but I can't let whoever *she* is, spoil the future, can I? Anyway, that's enough of all that maudlin stuff. I'm glad I've shared it with you but I think we need to get these cakes back before they go soggy, or we could eat them on the way, nobody would know!'

The mood had lifted and sensing it was time to move on, both women gathered their things. After bidding farewell to Sebastian and the two ancient customers, the two women walked slowly back to the hotel, getting to know each other more with every footstep. Anna felt so comfortable in Rosie's company; she had a kind heart and an honest, open personality, the type who makes a good friend.

Back at the hotel, Rosie invited Anna up to her apartment which was directly above the lounge area. It was compact but cosy with a small seating area at the front, overlooking the garden and drive, simply furnished with two big comfy sofas set either side of a log burner and a coffee table in between. There was a tiny kitchenette on the back wall and through a small door was their bedroom and en suite. Rosie explained that even though it was small it was enough for the two of them; somewhere private to relax and take time for themselves. Emerging from the bedroom, Rosie had an idea.

'Come on, I'll show you around the garden and grounds. You've been gadding about so much you haven't seen our mini-empire so now I can give you the grand tour.' Rosie ushered Anna towards the door and passing a young woman in the hallway, Rosie stopped to introduce her.

'Anna, this is my cousin, Ruby. She lives here with her two children Oliver and Lily, our absolute angels. Ruby is also my wonderful housekeeper and ruler of the linen cupboard. If it wasn't for her this hotel would collapse around my ears and that's a fact. Ruby, this is Anna, our new guest and friend.'

Laughing and rolling her eyes the pretty, fair-haired woman replied, 'Stop creeping Rosie, you could exaggerate for England. It's nice to meet you, Anna.' Ruby was obviously far too busy to stop and chat so with that she picked up her bucket and carried on.

As they made their way downstairs and out towards the rear of the hotel, Rosie explained that Ruby had come to stay with them just over two years ago. Her husband was a complete psycho and she had a lucky escape. They were just getting the hotel organised at the time so she slotted in nicely with their plans and took over the housekeeping side, leaving Michel and Rosie to concentrate on the restaurant. Ruby's children were at school and nursery and had both fitted into French life with ease.

Passing the pool they turned left and followed a well trodden dirt path, then through a small wooden gate where Anna found herself in the kitchen garden surrounded by neat rows of vegetables, herbs and small fruit trees which grew in abundance. Continuing to the end of the garden and through another gate they followed the path to a clearing and came upon a large barn, in great need of repair but certainly not a lost cause.

'One day this is going to be our family home. We need to wait a few more years before the bank will lend us enough money to restore it but I just love to look at it and know that one day it will perfect. I have it all planned in my head, every last room and how I'm going to decorate it.' Rosie gestured towards the run-down building, obviously seeing something completely different than a ramshackle barn.

Anna glanced at Rosie, now totally lost in her imagining and was happy for her, that she had dreams and plans. She remembered wistfully how it had been the same for her and Matthew, building everything slowly, making their family and their home.

'I think it's going to be wonderful, Rosie, it's very secluded and private but near enough to the hotel for you to keep an eye on things. If what you have done there is anything to go by then this place will be fab. So when do you plan to start a family? You will make a lovely mum.'

Flushing slightly, Rosie explained they had been trying for a while but she was so busy and the hotel refurbishments had taken so long, plus, up to now, nature was being a bit on the stubborn side. Changing the subject she moved to the right and followed the path through a copse of small trees and bushes which opened onto a large field. In the distance was the same wonderful view you could see from the rear of the hotel and the terrace.

'And this is our present project. The four outbuildings have been here as long as the barn and we've converted them into gîtes. Ruby and the children live in the nearest one; the other three are almost ready for painting and decorating. Once we close for the winter we will get cracking so they're ready for the new holiday season. They will be self-catering but obviously guests will have the option of eating at the hotel if they prefer. We're having a small play area and paddling pool fitted in March, then it will be ready to go.' Rosie looked immensely proud.

A lot of thought had gone into every aspect of their little empire, not to mention hard work and Anna suspected that a baby would be the icing on the cake and a reward for all they had achieved. They started to make their way back, past the copse and towards the hotel via a different track, finishing by the pool.

'I'll get Michel to fix us some lunch. And you'd better go and wake sleepy Josh otherwise he'll be in bed all day.'

As Rosie walked towards the kitchen, Anna stopped her.

'Thanks for today, Rosie, you know, listening to my troubles and showing me your home, it means a lot to me. I hope your dreams come true and you get the barn done, you deserve it and I'm sure if you keep practising really, really hard a little one will arrive eventually.'

Rosie chuckled. 'Thanks, Anna and I'm glad we got a chance to get to know each other. Sometimes things are meant to be and this place, well it's magical, good things happen here, you'll see. Now, you go and find Josh while I track down Michel, we all need to eat.'

After lunch Anna and Josh set off for the swimming pool. He was in good spirits and fun to be with, telling Anna quite openly that he'd been a bit of a dickhead recently but was trying to sort himself out. You could tell he was actually really fond of Daniel but tried hard to be cool and cover it up. Being with him reminded her of Joe and Sam and how much she missed their banter and jokes. But she was not allowing herself any maudlin feelings for the rest of her trip so decided instead to focus on positive things, like actually finding the pool.

It was a bit of a trauma once inside because neither of them spoke French so they had to manage with hand signals to find the changing rooms. They were both relieved to finally hit the water where little communication was required, happily swimming lengths, and racing each other. The afternoon passed quickly and they drove back to the hotel in high spirits, feeling like they'd known each other for ages. Josh asked about Anna and her kids; he didn't know about Matthew and was taken aback when the story unfolded, so Daniel had obviously kept the details to himself. In return, Josh opened up about his mum dying, she knew he was referring to his actual grandmother but aware of the situation, let him talk.

Anna listened to his touching stories about how he would take her to bingo and wheel her round the shops. She had to rely on Josh after her legs gave in and he made her laugh by going really fast along the aisles when nobody was looking. What touched Anna the most was that Josh had singlehandedly nursed his mum at the end. Daniel helped too but the main role of carer fell to Josh. He said it was the best thing he had ever done in his life and apart from loving her to bits, it made him feel useful and was his way of repaying his mum for everything. Now, Anna realised that since her death, Josh had been cast adrift and there was a gaping hole in his life and it needed filling, quickly.

Later that evening while they ate dinner together, realising it was almost the end of his holiday, Josh announced that he wanted to have some fun on his last day in France. Apparently he wasn't looking forward to Rosie's birthday on Sunday, expecting it to be full of old people, like Daniel. He really made Anna laugh sometimes so she asked him what his idea of fun was.

'Well, apart from going clubbing which is *so* not happening round this place, or watching Chelsea, I wouldn't mind going to the sea. Is there a sea near here, Daniel, or is it just fields and cow poo?' Josh looked semi-hopeful.

'Actually, you'll be surprised to hear that the nearest seaside resort is about an hour away. So if you can stop moaning for five minutes I might consider taking you and if you're really good, I'll get you a bucket and spade as well.' Daniel smiled, never missing a chance to take the mickey out of his brother.

'Very funny. But can we take Anna too? It's *sooo* sad just the two of us. I'll let her sit in the front as well then you can bore her to death about wine and classical music instead of me. Will you come with us, Anna, please? It'll be a laugh.' Josh swung his head around to Anna and settled his pleading doe-eyes on her rather surprised face.

Put on the spot slightly, her brain switched straight to overthinking-mode where it was assisted nicely by her conscience which persistently gnawed the inside of her head, day and night. As it continued to sprinkle guilt and worry over her thoughts she was gallantly rescued by Daniel. He had sensed her hesitancy and understanding her dilemma, gave Anna a get out clause.

'Josh, leave Anna alone. She might already have plans and besides, it's not really that warm so maybe the beach isn't a great idea so stop pestering us, you're not five anymore. Sorry, Anna, just ignore him, he must have had too many E numbers this afternoon.' Daniel carried on eating, hoping the situation was diffused.

It was actually his act of chivalry that made Anna decide. '*Sod this!*' She thought. '*I'm sick of feeling guilty and beating myself up about everything, this nice man and lovely lad are doing no harm. Neither am I for that matter. Matthew didn't feel guilty about sleeping around so why the hell should I feel bad about a day at the seaside?*' With the problem totally resolved and her mind firmly made up, Anna turned to Josh.

'You know what, Josh? I think that's a great idea! Shall I ask Rosie if Michel can make us a picnic? It's not the same without one. I reckon if we wrap up warm we'll be fine and the sea breeze will do us good and we can eat our lunch on the beach, what do you think?'

Josh's face lit up with a beaming smile. 'See, Daniel. Anna's cool. I knew she'd want to come, she's not a fossilised killjoy like you.' He turned and winked at Anna who laughed and gave him one back.

Basking in his victory, Josh decided to go on Facebook and tell anyone who cared (and probably loads that didn't) all about his plans for the next day.

As he walked away, Anna smiled and glanced quickly at Daniel, noticing that he looked quite pleased too.

CHAPTER 12

Beach day turned out to be dry, mild and sunny. You couldn't help noticing a cooling of the temperature but it was far from cold. They loaded Daniel's 4x4 with their Michelin starred picnic and true to his word, Josh plonked himself in the back, plugged in his headphones immediately saying there was no way he was listening to Daniel's grave music before happily texting and humming his way to the beach.

They headed towards the coast and whilst Josh spent the entire journey in a world of his own, the other passengers used the time to talk about each other. Anna soon realised that Daniel was extremely witty and far from the fossil Josh made him out to be. He had loads of interests and, more importantly, showed an interest in her as she told him all about the children and her life. He was particularly interested in Sam as his own dad had been in the army and even though mentioning Matthew still felt strange, Anna was comfortable enough to talk about their haulage business. By the time they arrived at Saint Marc sur Mer they knew as much as they needed to and not only that, Anna was completely relaxed in his company and looking forward to the rest of their day together.

Anna fell instantly in love with the small seaside resort. Daniel had been many times before and said it was one of his favourite places. He explained that it had been the setting for a famous French film, *Les Vacances de Monsieur Hulot*, or, *Monsieur Hulot's Holiday*, and the hotel on the beach was the central point of the story. As they approached along the narrow road that ran along the coast, they passed affluent holiday homes with palm tree gardens and striped canopies covering their terraces. When she spotted the sea, Anna turned to alert Josh who dragged his attention from his phone to look.

On one side were beach shops and cafés and directly ahead, a large promenade made of polished timber. The floor resembled the deck of a ship, encased by a curved handrail giving the impression you were at the helm of the vessel looking out to sea. There was a life-size statue of a man; hands on hips, looking over the edge and Daniel informed them that this was Jacques Tati, the director of the famous film.

Anna was surprised to see that even off-season, the beach was still quite busy and suspected most were probably retired residents, lucky enough to have the sea on their doorstep or perhaps holidaymakers wanting to avoid marauding children. As they padded down the stairs of the wooden promenade to find a spot on the long sandy beach, to the left, just as Daniel had described, Anna spotted the Hôtel de la Plage.

Anna admired the grand building which looked out onto the Atlantic Ocean, thinking it would be lovely to spend the evening gazing out to sea from one of the balconies, breathing in the air as ships floated by on their journey to who knows where. On the ground floor was a long terrace filled with tables topped with elegant cream parasols and she imagined dining there, relaxing under the stars after a long day at the beach.

To her right, the sand curved in a horseshoe shape to form small coves, protected by the high cliffs that edged the beach. Daniel explained that a path ran right along the top accessible by steep stone stairs that led down to each cove. Finally, they settled on a place against the rocks which gave them some protection from the heavy sea breeze, spreading their towels on the sand as the midday sun valiantly attempted to warm them. Josh slipped off his jeans and went to explore the rock pools along the shoreline as Daniel searched for his book and sunglasses.

Anna wiggled her toes in the sand, feeling the grains cooling her feet. Already the sun was making her warm so she removed her sweater and rolled it up, laying it behind her head before relaxing against the rocks, relishing the heat on her face, amused by Daniel's mutterings and fervent rustling of bags. When he eventually found his book, he too rested against the rocks a few feet from Anna and began to read, every now and then checking on Josh, his parenting instinct still alive and kicking.

They soon immersed themselves in their setting and rested in companionable silence, reading and enjoying the peace. Anna loved the sound of the beach, the waves sloshing against the shingle and sand, hungry cries from seagulls overhead, faraway voices carried on the wind and then some awful, pounding rap music, getting closer and closer. Anna opened her eyes and as suspected, saw Josh making his way towards them.

'I'm starving, can we have our picnic now?' Josh patted his stomach and looked expectantly at the basket of food.

Daniel, however, wasn't amused. 'Josh! Turn that rubbish off! Everyone is staring, just sit down while I get it ready and don't get sand everywhere.'

Josh did as he was told, totally oblivious to the stares of the other beach people as he trampled wet feet marks and sand, everywhere, intent on having the last word. 'Dan, you're such an old woman, try and be a bit more like Anna, she doesn't moan every five minutes. You need to chill out more.'

Daniel whacked him playfully with his book and then got on with the picnic.

As Anna expected, Michel had prepared a feast. They had fresh baguettes, pâté, thick slices of ham, garlic sausage, goat cheese tart, and large, misshaped tomatoes straight from the kitchen garden. A circular box of Camembert ripened in the heat and was accompanied by new season apples. Wrapped in kitchen paper they found a selection of pastries filled with raisins and custard plus a giant bag of crisps, no doubt for Josh. Bottles of sparkling water and white wine had been kept cool in a separate case and Michel had even packed napkins and plastic wine glasses. It truly was a picnic to remember.

Once the box was almost empty, Josh lay flat on his back, arms and legs stretched out like a star, too full to move while Anna and

Daniel drank their wine and gazed out to sea, spotting ships and people watching. As they did, two rather large ladies came into view, waddling along the beach. Wearing tight white swimming caps, causing their heads to look like alien domes while their full, black swimming costumes had huge, pointy bra sections. Placing their towels nonchalantly on the sand, chattering constantly, they made their way confidently into the strong waves that lashed the shore. Josh was fascinated as the water was freezing and he didn't believe they would be brave enough to swim, but they did. Without fear or trepidation they simultaneously launched themselves like killer whales into the cold, grey, rolling sea, front crawling in unison, showing the wimpy Brits on the beach how it was done.

They were out there for about fifteen minutes, thrashing away, back and forth, oblivious to their gob-smacked audience. Emerging from the waves looking nothing at all like Bond girls, they carried on with their chat then reaching for their towels, dried off their weather beaten bodies, picked up their flip-flops and sauntered off.

'Way to go, grandmas, that was awesome!' Josh remarked loudly, giving them the thumbs up as they smiled and waved back, before heading off towards the stairs.

Unable to ignore the cooling temperature, Daniel suggested they pack up and, after dumping their stuff in the car, they took a walk along the coastal path. From here they admired panoramic cliff top views of the coastline all the way down to the port of Saint Nazaire and envying the large sea front houses that perched high above the ocean.

'*One day I'd like to live near the sea,*' thought Anna, '*somewhere I can watch people go by and look out like this, at ships and cruise liners, imagining which far-flung corners of the world they are heading to.*'

After a long trek they made their way back to the car with tired legs and tingly windswept faces. Anna felt a little sad as she said goodbye to St Marc, it had been a lovely day and as they drove away, wondered if she would ever return. It was getting late and as they neared the hotel, Daniel suggested a change of location for dinner that evening.

'Do you know what I fancy? I would kill for some pizza and I know a great restaurant near here. What do you think, Josh? Do you like pizza, Anna?'

Josh, who was getting sick to the back teeth of steak and chips, was definitely up for it and knowing that she had a few more days of her holiday to savour Michel's cooking, Anna also agreed.

Seated in a lovely pizzeria whose walls were painted terracotta red and hung with paintings of Catalan mountain scenery, Anna breathed in the pungent smell of basil and garlic. The dimmed lighting gave it a very cosy feel as they shared a plate of olives and reminisced about their day. Josh ordered the hottest, spiciest pizza on the menu while Anna chose a seafood special in honour of her day out. Daniel plumped for the duck and apple which Anna thought bizarre until she tasted it and quickly changed her mind, it was delicious.

By the time they finally rolled up at the hotel it was after ten. A mixture of sea air, lovely food and red wine were making Anna sleepy so declining coffee and thanking them for a lovely day, she promised to see them both tomorrow. Not failing to notice the look of disappointment on both their faces she stuck to her guns and made her way upstairs, realising as she turned the key in her door that thanks to her lovely new friends, she had also turned a corner because hold the front page – Anna Harrison, widow of the parish, was extremely happy!

A bright, sunny Sunday morning dawned and Anna awoke full of energy and anticipation. She was looking forward to Rosie's birthday party and had to admit she had grown fond of Josh and Daniel so the fact they would be there too, was a bonus. After staying in bed until gone ten (a world record since she'd arrived) and after taking a long shower, Anna relaxed on the bed and decided to ring home.

Starting with Enid and intent on getting the most difficult over with first, she listened patiently to her mother's laborious version of the past seven days' events, the highlight of which was

Gladys (from next door) had started a romance (at her age) with a chap from ballroom dancing. When the subject of *Emmerdale* arose, as she feared it would, Anna crossed her fingers, knocked on the table and told Enid it was room service, mercifully ending the conversation.

Next was Mel, who was having a ball, full of news and enthusiasm especially about her *amazing* new friend Paloma. Parties and socialising were the main topic of conversation when perhaps the emphasis should have been more focused on her studies, however, relieved to hear the happiness in Melanie's voice Anna opted for leniency, making a mental note to be much firmer when she got home.

Sam was obviously in the land of nod when she rang but recovered quickly and between yawns, sounded genuinely pleased at all her news. On the down side, the guard duty list for Christmas had gone up and this year it was his turn which meant that for the holiday week, he would be guarding the base. She could tell he was stressed about it, but what could they do? The last thing he needed was her giving him a guilt trip so they settled on an early celebration, the week before.

Hoping this was sufficient to reassure him Anna sent her love and said bye, knowing he would go straight back to sleep the second his head hit the pillow. Jeannie and Phil were still in Egypt so she sent a happy text then emailed Joe and attached some photos of the beach, and a duck and apple pizza!

Putting away her phone, Anna went over to the window where she could hear a great deal of activity below on the terrace as tables were dragged into position and Michel barked orders; the sound blending with the clink of crockery and muttering voices.

She had offered to help but Rosie was adamant that she was a guest and wanted her to enjoy the experience so Anna decided to stay in her room. The noise outside didn't disturb her one bit, it was actually quite comforting while she killed time before the party, choosing her outfit and ignoring the unexpected urge to look nice for Daniel.

Even though the day was dry and sunny it was cooler than before so she chose charcoal jeans and a sheer red blouse with a black floral print and long floaty sleeves. She found a beaded bracelet and matching necklace, fastened her black sandals, then adding just a touch of perfume, she was ready. Hearing a gentle tap, tap on her door, Anna opened it to find Josh waiting outside.

'Hi, Anna. I thought I'd call for you. Daniel's taking ages with his make-up and I'm bored. He said it was okay and we still need to get your flowers out of the car. I thought you might forget.' Josh was standing with his hands in his pockets looking eager and hopeful.

Anna's heart went out to him. It had occurred to her that he lacked having a mother figure in his life and while Daniel tried to be everything to his brother, nothing would ever make up for their mum or his gran. Anna sensed that Josh was possibly drawn to her because he missed talking to someone with a softer side and resolved that while she had the opportunity and with what time they had remaining, she would take him under her wing.

'As long as he doesn't want to borrow my lipstick, it's not his shade so perhaps we should just leave him to it. You look very smart by the way. Have you got Daniel's keys? You can do the honours with the flowers.'

They had stopped off in a village on the way back from the beach and bought Rosie a bouquet. Praying that the bubble of water the flowers were arranged in had kept them alive, Anna and her escort set off to retrieve them.

Entering the dining room they saw it had been completely transformed and looked wonderful. The groups of tables were now placed together to create just one, running the length of the room. Set for around twenty people, bowls of bread and fresh salad, decorated with tiny borage flowers, had been placed down the centre. Shiny pink and silver stars were sprinkled over the white tablecloth and bottles of ice cold water were dotted along the table. Balloons and streamers were hung from the lamps and '*Joyeux Anniversaire*' banners stuck to the walls.

Following the sound of voices on the terrace, Anna and Josh shyly made their way through the doors. Rosie was laughing with a tall man of around Anna's age while others sat at the garden tables, drinking and talking. Noticing the arrival of her guests, Rosie flew over and welcomed them to the group. Thanking Anna for her beautiful flowers she introduced the tall man as Henri, the older brother of Michel, and then continued around the group, helpfully explaining who everyone was, starting with Michel's parents and his extremely fragile grandparents, Albert and Monique.

Ruby tried to stop to say hello but was busy chasing after her children as Rosie steered them towards another couple, introduced as neighbours and wonderful friends from the house along the lane, Dominique and his wife Zofia. They both spoke perfect English since Dominique had once owned a restaurant in London which was where he had met his Polish wife, Zofia. Introductions over, Rosie served drinks then passing them a bowl of potato chips, left them to chat.

As more people arrived, including Daniel, Rosie flitted around everyone, pouring drinks and making introductions. The final guests were Michel's aunt and uncle who turned out to be the *very* important Monsieur le Maire and his rather snooty wife.

Pascal appeared from the kitchen door carrying clean glasses followed by an extremely pretty dark-haired girl who he proudly introduced to Anna, Daniel and Josh as his little sister, Océane. She worked here during the summer helping in the kitchen and on special occasions like today. Smiling shyly she gave a little wave, blushing slightly as she caught Josh's eye. They both helped themselves to drinks and joined Anna's group, Océane chatting in French to Zofia while occasionally chancing a sneaky glance at a very flustered Josh.

It was almost three o'clock when Michel emerged from the kitchen and placed his arm around his wife's shoulders, asking for quiet. Anna thought Rosie looked particularly radiant today in a floaty, silver-grey dress, platinum-blue beads draped around her neck, all complemented by a simple wrap of electric blue chiffon to ward off the chill. Making sure everyone had a drink, Michel proposed a toast to his beautiful wife and wished her a very happy birthday, thanking everyone for being there. Once the cheers had died down, he added, to everyone's interest, that there was another very special announcement he had to make.

Looking down into Rosie's eyes and unable to hide his joy and excitement a moment longer, he told everyone gathered that his perfect, wonderful, amazing wife, was going to have a baby. The terrace erupted as the guests clapped and cheered then gathered around Rosie and Michel to hug and congratulate them. Waiting until everyone had calmed down or wandered off to refill their glasses, Anna approached Rosie, who was flushed and teary-eyed, gleefully taking her hands.

'Rosie, I am so happy for you both, you will be a fantastic mum, when did you find out?'

'Oh, thank you, Anna. I'm so excited. I only found out on Friday, that's what I went to the chemist for, to buy a test kit. I wasn't sure so didn't mention anything. I've had quite a few disappointments and didn't want to get my hopes up. I managed to get an appointment at the doctors while you were out yesterday. Being the niece-in-law of the Mayor has its advantages sometimes. I'm about two months on so we expect baby Rousseau around Easter and I just can't wait.' Rosie was fizzing with happiness.

'Michel looks over the moon, was he surprised?' Anna looked over to Michel who was surrounded by his family.

'Just a bit. I was dying to confide in you on Friday but wanted to be sure and then as soon as I told Michel he almost rang everyone straight away. I suggested we wait until three months but he was too excited so I agreed on today. Otherwise he would've popped with the sheer strain of keeping it secret.'

Anna laughed and hugged her new friend, glad she had been here to share the start of a new chapter in Rosie's life, making her trip even more special. When Michel announced it was time to eat everyone flowed inside and in that moment Anna had the urge to pinch herself. Surely this couldn't be happening? Never in her wildest imaginings would she have expected this and if she woke up now, at home, alone in her room, she'd throw herself out of the window and willingly impale herself on the rose bushes, she really would!

CHAPTER 13

Anna was seated between Daniel and Josh, who had two vacant seats by his side. Next to Daniel was Zofia, then Dominique and near the top of the table was Michel's parents, Yves and Marie, with Rosie the queen at the head. Along the other side sat the Mayor and his wife with the elderly grandparents and opposite Anna were Ruby and her two children, both very well behaved and tucking into slices of bread. At the end were Henri, and Sebastian from the bar in the village, both already quite raucous.

Pascal and Océane appeared carrying enormous platters, each filled with fresh oysters, langoustines and mussels which they placed at intervals along the table before settling down next to Josh, who looked decidedly flustered. Michel sat at the opposite end to his wife; their eyes never straying from one another for too long despite the distraction provided by Sebastian and Henri who clearly regarded the impending birth as an excellent reason to drink their combined body weights in wine.

The noise level rose around the table as plates were passed around, glasses clinked and everyone savoured the seafood. Anna had never tasted oysters but Daniel persuaded her to have a go, assuring her they were delicious while pouring a little of the dressing over the top and handing it to her. The only thing Anna could think of as the oyster hit her taste buds, was the sea: a kind of zingy, salty combination of vinaigrette, garlic, lemon and the ocean. The mussels were coated with a creamy garlic sauce and the fresh langoustines were plump and delicious, especially when dipped in a homemade mayonnaise. Anna was in heaven but glancing to her right saw that poor Josh had definitely landed in hell, doing his best to enjoy a slice of bread as he picked at his salad; obviously a seafood feast was not his idea of fun.

Pascal was doing his best to entice him but he remained unconvinced causing Océane to intervene. Placing her hand gently over Josh's (sending him a lovely shade of puce) she delicately peeled a langoustine and dipped it in the mayonnaise before passing it to Josh and telling him to taste, it was just like fish, he would like it. Josh silently took the disguised langoustine from Océane and like an obedient puppy, swallowed the lot. Anna swore he went a bit green at first but to her amazement he then allowed his eager assistant to peel more as she chatted away, ten to the dozen in her best, broken English. Josh point blank refused the oysters and bravely had a go at a mussel but didn't seem keen; satisfied he wasn't going to throw up all over the place, Anna turned her attention to Daniel.

Deciding to save some room for whatever culinary delights would follow, Anna declined more seafood and sipped her wine. It was a lovely white Savennières, a regional speciality, full-bodied and smooth and a perfect accompaniment to the food. Daniel had promised to write her a list of recommendations so she could buy a small selection of wine for home. Whilst Daniel chatted, Anna tactfully observed him as he joked with Rosie and the others and couldn't quite believe how comfortable she felt with this man whom she'd known for barely a week. He made her laugh and had kind blue eyes; she didn't feel at all threatened by his singleness, maybe it was because he was well mannered and polite and importantly, he understood how she felt about being here on her own.

Remembering he was leaving in the morning made her heart feel heavy and Anna was surprised to realise that she would miss him, the notion left her slightly confused. Thankfully the arrival of the next course dragged her back into reality. It was pâté de foie gras and a selection of French sausage de Montagne, subtly infused with herbs and garlic which when inhaled, transported you to the Alps.

Anna prayed Pascal wouldn't give Josh the low-down on how or what the pâté was made from but watching Océane lovingly spread some on a piece of bread for him, she suspected that he would eat it anyway, and the mountain sausage!

The two children sitting opposite her were happily tucking in, assisted by the spindly, ancient fingers of Michel's grandmother who was obviously smitten by them, stroking Lily's hair and chatting in French to Oliver. Anna formed the impression, from watching them from across the table, that whatever story had brought Ruby and her children to France it had ended well as all three looked extremely content amongst their new family.

Sebastian and Henri were thoroughly enjoying their meal and the ambience of the gathering. Anna suspected they both had their eyes on Ruby as now and then they would attempt to draw her into conversation. In a mixture of English and French they flattered and joked with her and she returned their banter in a good-humoured way, teasing them back, completely ignoring their flirting.

Pascal and Océane had disappeared into the kitchen with Michel to prepare the next course and Anna, feeling slightly tipsy already and spotting bottles of a deep red Chinon being placed along the tables, knew it would be a good idea to pace herself. Turning to Josh, she asked him if he was enjoying the meal.

'Yeah, Anna, I am actually. The sausage and pâté were really nice; I wish I'd tried it before, I think I need to be a bit more adventurous in the future. I wonder what's next. I hope it's not going to get weird though cos I can only go so far with this food lark. I'm not eating brains or horses or anything disgusting like that, I mean it!'

Anna laughed out loud at his determined, horrified face. She was really going to miss Josh.

Across the way, Michel's grandfather tentatively tried to stand and leave the table, stick thin and looking as though a gust of wind would do for him he shakily tried to lift his spindly, bent frame from the chair. It was clear he couldn't manage alone but his inebriated grandson Henri was oblivious and his equally fragile wife was busy with Ruby's children. Before she had a chance to move, Anna saw Josh whip around the table to the old chap's aid.

Unable to speak French and relying solely on body language, he gently tapped Albert on the shoulder and offered him his arm. Relief and gratitude washed over his weather-beaten face as he pointed to the terrace then at his cigarettes and lighter on the table which Josh quickly retrieved and they began shuffling towards the doors. Anna watched as Albert was settled into a garden chair then brought his drink, an ashtray and assisted ably by his young and very caring helper, with trembling fingers, lit his cigarette. Rather than leave the old man alone, Josh remained by his side and kept him company, happily listening to whatever this very contented French man was telling him, despite not understanding one word.

As the main course was being brought in, Josh helped chatty Albert back into the room and settled him in his place, cheerfully replying in English to whatever he thought he was being told. They laughed and shook hands, ending a conversation needing no translation, just two men from different places and times forming a bond of understanding and friendship. For the rest of the evening, with translation services provided by Pascal and Océane, Josh and Albert got to know each other and between each course they shuffled back and forth together.

After a feast of roasted duck and vegetables all washed down nicely with the red wine, Anna was starting to wish she had worn stretchy pants and was relieved her top was covering a very full and ever-expanding stomach. Michel shouted up the table to Anna, asking if she was enjoying the food.

'This is how I love to eat, French family food, from the earth and the farms around our home. I hope you are liking it, Anna?' Smiling he raised his glass to her.

'It's all wonderful, Michel, thank you. And now, you will have to get used to cooking lots of family food in the future, congratulations.' Anna raised her glass in salute to him as the noise of happy people filled the room, eating and drinking the night away.

The next course was the cheese, ignored by Josh and Océane who were engrossed in his phone, giggling at funny videos on YouTube so Pascal swapped places and sat next to Anna. It was the first time she had the opportunity to talk with him other than in the restaurant so she asked him about his father's farm and his college course. He came alive as he spoke, telling her how things were changing so fast in the farming community that unless someone kept up with the paperwork and all the EEC rules and regulations, his father's farm would go under. His family had farmed in this area for generations and at one time there were seven farms around the village, now his papa's was the last one.

'He cannot afford to employ more workers so I help him, and my mother also works on the farm. We have one hundred and fifty dairy cattle, forty hectares of fields for the animals to live on and fifty hectares of cereal crops. We grow wheat and colza, the small yellow flowers which makes oil. Did you know that France could be self-sufficient but still we import beef from Spain and *ours* is sold to Italy? The price we are paid for our cattle and wheat is reduced each year and when a calf is born we have to prepare pages and pages of forms for the EEC. So I am there to help. I want to learn at college how to make our farm profitable again and help my father.'

'That's very admirable, Pascal, and I can tell you are passionate about farming but you must be exhausted, working here and going to college as well.' Anna felt weary just imagining his workload.

'Yes, it is hard work but it depends on the season. In the winter there is little to do in the fields except make sure there is hay for the cattle to eat and then the calves are born and the paperwork begins. The rest of the time Papa maintains the farm and helps clear the roads with his tractor if it snows. In the autumn he works in the woods, chopping down the old damaged trees for firewood then he sells it to the villagers. We are a strong community and when the harvest starts, all the farms in the area work together to help each other, and our friends and family come too. Sometimes, we work late into the night but it is the best time of the year for me. The problem is that we are ruled by people in city offices who have no idea of our lives and they push the prices down for our produce to make more money for their pockets. It is becoming very hard to exist.'

Pascal's impassioned speech had taken Anna by surprise.

'Well, you make such a strong case for farmers, Pascal, perhaps you should become a politician and fight for them. You are obviously very clever and you should use your intelligence to get them a fair deal.' Anna admired this young man so much and really hoped he would be successful.

'Thank you, Anna, for your compliment. I am very interested in politics but first I am going to concentrate on our farm and try to persuade my father to plant a small area for organic produce in one of the grazing fields. I would love to grow some vines but that is just a dream… along with ruling the world.' Pascal smiled and raised his glass to her.

Once he'd drank some wine he passed Anna the plate of assorted cheeses and as she selected a few small pieces, commented that in England they ate this course last. Pascal thought this extremely odd as the French believed that sweet always follows salty, the palate should be clear and that was how they have always done it. Anna didn't mind either way as she preferred cheese to puddings so tucked in, secretly thinking that the English way was best, especially as here they didn't serve crackers, just bread. In her opinion, there was no better end to an evening than sitting around a table with friends, eating stilton and crackers, and drinking wine.

Eventually, Pascal returned to clearing duties and Anna was left with the neighbours, Dominique and Zofia. They were just as Rosie described, wonderful people, extremely warm and welcoming and eager to hear about where she was from and how she had enjoyed her stay in France. They had a lovely story to tell of how they met. Dominique had lived in London for ten years and owned a French restaurant in Crouch End; he loved his work as his eyes lit up when he spoke of it. Zofia was an accountant when she lived in Poland but decided to throw caution to the wind and go on an adventure, following her nephew to live and work in London. Rather than her usual type of employment, she took work cleaning and in bars, and then Dominique came to the restaurant where she was working and they ended up falling in love.

They were married in London and continued working in the restaurant but after Dominique suffered ill health they decided to relocate to the French countryside, buying a large renovated house just down the lane. They chatted for ages about all sorts: Zofia had a daughter and two grandchildren in Poland who visited each summer, then on to Rosie's good news, the merits of French and English food, London (which Zofia missed a lot) and before she knew it, Anna had been invited for coffee the next day.

More bottles of wine were brought out, this time a very sweet dessert wine, golden and syrupy which left tear stains in the glass. A large *tarte aux fruits*, light pastry with a custard filling topped with berries and apples, was passed around and even though Anna had intended to stop at the cheese, she decided it would be rude not to sample a small slice, and if the worse came to the worst, could always buy bigger pants.

CHAPTER 14

Later, as the pace slowed, Anna asked Daniel what time he would be leaving.

'We'll be on our way before seven thirty so I'm taking it easy with the wine which is a shame because Michel has some good stuff. We have to be at the ferry port at St Malo by nine thirty. I haven't told Josh yet; can you imagine how much he's going to moan? I wish we could have stayed an extra day but I have a meeting on Tuesday.'

Anna noticed her heart sink slightly in her chest. 'Well, I'll make sure I'm up early to see you off. I might be a bit worse for wear but I can have breakfast with you then crawl back into bed.'

Daniel smiled, he didn't try to persuade her to sleep in or miss their departure, instead he had a mini confession to make. 'I'm glad I'll see you in the morning. I was worried that tonight would be the last time I saw you.' He hesitated then gathering courage, continued.

'Anna, I know that under the circumstances I really shouldn't be asking but I will kick myself all the way home if I don't. I was wondering, and I will totally, utterly understand if you say no. Well, I'd really like it if we could stay in touch when you get back, just by email or text, whatever you like?'

Anna's heart skipped a giddy beat and for a second she felt like a sixteen year old again, being asked for her phone number at the end of the school disco, so going with her instinct (whilst being prepared to suffer guilt-ridden thoughts about it later) Anna threw caution to the wind and replied.

'Of course we can stay in touch, Daniel. I'd like that too, and anyway, I want you to be my dedicated wine advisor so if I'm ever out and don't know what to have with my steak, I'll send you a quick text and Bob's your uncle, everyone will think I'm genius.' Anna was making light of it to appear casual but for now, didn't actually care if it was right or wrong.

A look of pure relief washed over Daniel's face, 'Really, Anna? That's great. We can swap numbers in the morning. I was so worried you'd be offended but I feel like we've made a connection and it's a shame to waste the chance to make new friends. I'd like see how you are getting on and maybe, if we are ever in France at the same time we can meet again. I know Josh will be so pleased, he's become very fond of you.' Daniel looked a bit flushed after his speech.

'Just pour me another glass of wine, Daniel, and then shut up.' Anna was laughing at his nervous waffling which was endearing but she was really touched, he'd obviously got himself a bit worked up about asking her.

Sebastian and Henri, fully tanked up and refuelled after the meal were now on their feet and ready to sing 'Happy Birthday' to Rosie, so Michel and Pascal began pouring glasses of sparkling wine. Daniel, just to ensure his job of wine advisor was safely in the bag, informed Anna that it was Crémant de Loire and would add it to her list of what to buy. Glasses filled and ready for action, the two raconteurs began a lovely French rendition of the birthday song aided merrily by the rest of the guests, the English contingent were happy just to listen and cheer at the end. Pleased with their performance and buoyed by claps from the audience, Henri and Sebastian decided that they would continue with their repertoire and entertained everyone with well-rehearsed French classics.

Daniel was dragged away to explore the cellar and Michel's wine collection so Anna sank into the chair next to Josh who was showing Albert an app on his phone that made a photo of your face go really fat. She watched amused as Josh took a photo of a bewildered Monique and then proceeded to make her skinny, craggy face expand to huge proportions, sending Albert into fits of laughter, his little body shaking as tears rolled down his face.

Positively unamused, Monique gave him a slap and gestured that she required a refill. Poor Albert was almost unable to pour through laughing, his shaky hands now out of control and wine slopping everywhere. Being married many years and knowing when he was on thin ice, Albert dutifully controlled himself and gave Monique his full, albeit sniggering, attention. Unperturbed, Josh turned to Anna and showed her the photo which was really quite gruesome.

'I've got one where you take a photo of two people and swap their heads. I reckon that'll really freak Albert out, shall I do you and Daniel?' Josh was clicking away on his phone.

'No you will not, you monster, pick on somebody else. Perhaps I should take one of you and Océane?

I'm sure all your mates will be very jealous when you show them your pretty French friend, she won't mind.' With that, she grabbed the hand of an unsuspecting Océane as she passed to collect dishes and asked for a photo, whipping Josh's phone out of his hand before he could object.

More than happy to oblige, Océane plonked herself on Josh's knee, put her arms around his neck and leaning her head against his, gave Anna a 100 megawatt smile. Praying she didn't mess up, Anna took a few shots just to be on the safe side and before Josh had a chance to recover, Anna thanked Océane, who continued with her chore, and passed Josh his phone. Trying to be cool, he didn't look at the results straight away so Anna changed the subject.

'What were you studying at college, Josh, before you left?'

'Computer science. It was *so* boring. I hated it but I didn't know what else to do, I still don't.'

Anna decided to stick her neck out and make a suggestion. 'I was watching you earlier and you seemed to have a knack where old Albert is concerned. You've been very kind and patient with him tonight. Some younger people don't have time for the older generation but you looked like you we're enjoying his company.'

'Yeah, old people always remind me of my mum. I liked looking after her and taking her out and stuff. I think old biddies are interesting. My mum's bingo friends were all a bit potty but nice with it, if you get what I mean?'

Anna smiled thinking of Enid, her very own mad old biddy. 'Josh, I've been thinking, have you ever considered being a nurse? Not necessarily a hospital nurse but maybe one who specialises in looking after older people in care homes or maybe in the community. I think you would be really good at it. You'd probably have to go back to college but Daniel told me you're a clever lad so I'm sure you could do it.'

Josh raised an eyebrow, obviously not sure if she was serious or not. 'A nurse? Don't you think that sounds a bit gay? What would my mates say? I think being a nurse is more for girls.'

Anna didn't give up that easily. 'No, Josh. It's not just for girls. And I'm sure that sometimes men prefer to be looked after by another man, especially the older ones. Not just that, if you run your life by what your mates reckon is cool then you'll never get anywhere. I bet there's not much call for rappers and drug dealers down the Job Centre. Just have a think about it. I know Daniel will help you find out more about it, or Google it on your phone, do something useful with it for once. Anyway, lecture over; I'm going to get some coffee. Do you want some?' Anna thought she pitched it just right and from experience knew when to shut up.

'No, ta, Anna. I'm going to take some sneaky photos then swap everybody's heads about. And coffee makes me hyper and Dan can't cope with me when I'm normal, never mind full of beans.' Josh winked and the conversation appeared to be over.

Watching as he shot off, Anna sighed, she'd tried her best.

It was obvious that the menfolk were in for the long haul when an assortment of bottles appeared on the table. Pascal joined them, bringing a tray of coffee and chocolates. The older guests were saying their farewells so a long round of kissing and hugging took place where nobody was left out.

The Mayor was driving Albert and Monique but before they left, Josh politely shook the old man's hand, promising via Rosie to send him a postcard from London and a Chelsea football souvenir as soon as he got home. Albert, having none of this formal British nonsense, grabbed the startled young man firmly by the shoulders and kissed both his cheeks before holding Josh's face in his hands and saying his own goodbye.

'À bientôt mon jeune ami'. On impulse, Josh put his arms around the frail old man and tenderly hugged him back, confirming Anna's belief that the younger man definitely had an affinity with the older generation.

Daniel and Anna sat alone drinking their coffee. It was one thirty in the morning and Rosie had already given in to tiredness but insisted she'd be up to wave them off in the morning. Océane and Josh were in the corner exchanging contact details and the four musketeers were merrily becoming merrier. Anna had never seen people drink so much and still be able to stand up.

It also occurred to her that she could easily sit there all night. Anna felt very at home, or was it because she didn't want the night to end with Daniel? During the evening, now and then, she had found herself searching the room for him and acknowledging a flicker of excitement when she spotted his face. Was there really a spark when they caught each other's eye and he smiled just at her, with those laughing blue eyes? On one occasion she had looked up and found he was watching her, not in a creepy way, it was as though he was deep in thought and admiring her. Was she being vain? Anna decided that she didn't care because it made her feel special and boosted her confidence, it felt good.

As the thought pinged into her head it made her feel odd and a bit too hot. Had she imagined the smile and the look? Perhaps she was just a bit tipsy and tired and she always got a bit emotional saying goodbye – there had been too many of those lately. Giving herself an imaginary slap, Anna pulled herself together and pushed any sentimental thoughts away. She had to be sensible otherwise she would spend the rest of the day replaying her actions, especially if she said or did anything stupid.

With this in mind she turned to Daniel and placed her coffee cup on the table, deciding to tell him in a light-hearted, carefree, way that it was time to go to bed. Alone, not with him, to sleep. *'For God's sake, Anna, grow up and get a grip,'* she shouted silently, angry at her own thoughts.

'Well, Daniel, as much as I've had a lovely evening, my eyes really can't take much more and if you want to make it to the ferry in one piece I think you'd better tell Romeo over there that he's got to get up in six hours. He's really going to love you when he hears that!'

'True. And if I was younger I'd try and stay up all night, just to spend a bit more time with you. But I know when I need to give in… and shut up.' Daniel smiled ruefully as he spoke.

His blue eyes looked straight into hers and Anna knew exactly what he was inferring and hoped he wouldn't continue. Quickly, taking the initiative, she stood and called over to Josh, telling him she was going to bed and would see him in the morning. He waved goodnight and carried on, deep in conversation with Océane. Daniel stood up and seemed at a loss as what to do or say next. He looked pensive and shy, his hands were in his pockets and Anna wanted them to stay right there. They were acting like love-struck fools who'd had a holiday romance.

Desperate to keep control of the situation and get away quickly because the tension was becoming unbearable, Anna pulled herself together and decided that levity was the best way to play it. Tapping him jokingly on the chest (which, she noticed, felt very firm beneath her fingers) she took a breath and smiled cheerily. Unfortunately, her previous thought had sent a flush straight up to her cheeks, perhaps giving her away. *'God, Anna, could you be more obvious?'* She asked herself.

'Right you… go and get some sleep otherwise you'll miss your ferry. I'll be waiting here with extra strong coffee in a few hours time so we can save our goodbyes until then. We need to write down our addresses so we can be pen pals so don't be late, or else!' Anna backed away slowly as she spoke.

Daniel was smiling. He gave in gallantly and replied simply. 'Okay, Anna, see you soon. Sleep well.'

With that, Anna turned and legged it.

Reaching her room with hot cheeks and a pounding heart that had nothing to do with running up the stairs like the devil was on her tail, her blood pressure was raised from the thrill of it all as she questioned her giddy state. *'Was she getting ahead of herself? No, definitely not. Did she like him? Definitely, yes!'*

Sitting on the edge of the bed with her mind running rampant, Anna forced herself to think clearly. *'Just be sensible, Anna, don't over think this, and calm down. You've had too much wine, you are over emotional, and you know you'll feel really stupid in the morning.'* Taking her own advice and setting her alarm she slipped off her clothes, threw on her nightie and jumped into bed, curling up under the covers from where she had to stifle a giggle.

'Right, that's it, Anna, enough of this. Grow up and go to sleep,' she told herself firmly.

Within a few minutes of forcing any thoughts of Daniel from her mind, overexcitement, fatigue and red wine thankfully did their job, sending a very confused, slightly giddy widow lady into a deep, contented sleep.

Anna didn't want to open her eyes, the duvet was far too warm and her head was cocooned in a lovely comfy, squashy pillow. Just five more minutes she told herself as her heavy eyelids succumbed to sleep. She allowed herself to drift back off, thinking as she snoozed that the alarm hadn't gone off so she still had plenty of time.

THE ALARM HADN'T GONE OFF!! The shock of realisation forced Anna to snap open her eyes and focus on the clock. Her heart thudded in her chest – ten forty five; it definitely said ten forty five. Bolting upright, Anna grabbed her phone to check the time on that, it was the same, she had missed him. Daniel had gone.

Throwing herself back onto the pillows she felt a huge surge of anger, directed at herself. *'Stupid, stupid, stupid woman,'* she ranted silently as she grasped her throbbing head. '*How hard is it to set an alarm?*' She felt so bad. '*What must he have thought, and Josh too? They would've sat there in the restaurant waiting for her because they wanted to swap numbers and say goodbye. I bet they thought I couldn't be bothered, or that I didn't want to keep in touch. Anna Harrison, you are a cow.*'

By the time she had showered, dressed, sulked and fumed it was lunchtime. She had decided to seek out Rosie and see if she'd spoken to Daniel before they left; maybe he had given her a message. Rosie was in the kitchen with Michel when she found her and was drinking herbal tea which she offered to Anna.

Rosie hadn't seen Daniel and Josh before they left. Michel insisted she had a lie in while he prepared the breakfasts. Feeling too guilty to admit why she was asking, Anna let the subject drop. Michel was chatting to them about the party and it was obvious that he didn't have a message from Daniel to pass on so with a heavy heart, she did her best to sound interested and not let her disappointment show. Rosie announced she was going to the supermarket and suggested that Anna came along for the ride. They could get some lunch in town, an idea to which Anna gratefully agreed, knowing that to remain at the hotel would only allow her to brood.

As they drove along the country lanes, Rosie, sensitive as always, picked up on Anna's mood.

'Are you okay, Anna, you seem a bit down this morning, is something bothering you?'

'No, Rosie, I'm fine, just a bit of a hangover and I always feel like this near the end of a holiday. I've had such a great time so after yesterday it's a bit of an anti-climax.' It was half true, not really a big whopping fib.

'As long as you're okay. I just thought you might be pining for Daniel. You two were looking quite cosy last night, not that I'm matchmaking or anything, but I can see you're blushing so don't deny it.' Rosie giggled as she glanced sideways at a very red-cheeked Anna.

'There's nothing going on, Rosie, honestly. He's a lovely man but it's too soon to even think of anything like that. I did enjoy his company though, and Josh's, of course. But maybe I should just leave things as they are, you know, nice acquaintances and holiday memories.' Anna knew her words were merely bravado, she felt so deflated.

'Yes, you're right. Best do the sensible thing and ignore a really hot, single man who was obviously smitten with you. I'm sure blokes like that come along every day in Portsmouth, but think on, someone like Daniel won't be single for long so maybe you should snap him up. I've known him for years and he's one of the good guys. But as long as you're sure.' Rosie sighed dramatically and sneaked another look at her passenger.

'Stop being sarky, Madame. You know it's complicated and anyway, even if I did like him I think I've blown it now. I promised I would meet them for breakfast and I overslept. He must think I'm a right bitch and I feel terrible. He didn't leave a message with Michel so he can't be that keen. I think that's that and I'll just have to try and forget about him. It's probably for the best or maybe it's just fate. I'm not exactly the luckiest person in love, am I?' As they waited at traffic lights Anna sighed, noticing at the same time that Rosie was grinning as she turned to speak.

'Well, if that's how you really feel I suppose you should just move on and he can go down in history as the one that got away. And you definitely *won't* need this, will you?' Rosie reached into her jacket pocket and pulled out a piece of paper, waving it around just out of Anna's reach.

'What's that? Rosie, tell me what it is right now. Give it here.' Anna was laughing because she knew exactly what it was. A bubble of happiness and relief floated straight towards her heart.

'Oh, this… well, my dear friend, I have here the phone number and email address of the aforementioned single, hot man you have wisely chosen to forget, mainly because you are a big fat chicken. Océane gave it to me when you went upstairs to get your bag. Apparently, she managed to drag herself out of bed to say goodbye to Josh, unlike someone else I could mention and Daniel asked her to give you this. Shall I chuck it out the window then?' Rosie pretended to wind down her window as Anna grabbed the piece of paper and quickly unfolded it.

To her delight, she saw Daniel's contact details and a simple message.

Anna,
Sorry we didn't get to say goodbye.
Please keep in touch and take care of yourself. I will miss you.
Daniel x

CHAPTER 15

The last three days of her holiday had flown by causing Rosie to suggest Anna extended her stay. There would be a last rush of guests during the half-term break but her room was vacant until then. Tempted as Anna had been to accept she decided that she had to face reality and go home. Melanie was due at the weekend and was bringing the 'fantastic Paloma' to stay and she wanted to check out this new wonder-friend in the flesh. And Sam was also coming home to go to the Portsmouth match so she had plenty to do.

Anna smiled, remembering her private cookery lesson with Michel, making millefeuilles: delicate, wafer thin pastries filled with fresh fruit and cream. She had spent a lovely morning with him, talking about food, Rosie's plans for the hotel and the barn and, obviously, the baby. Next, they prepared the ingredients for cassoulet, a rich stew which was packed with duck, red meat, sausages and haricot beans. Later that evening, as she sat with Rosie and Michel in their apartment sharing the fruits of her labour, the line between guest and friend totally crossed, Anna promised faithfully to return in the spring when they opened for the new season. The only condition was that she could have her room back; it wouldn't be the same otherwise.

She had also spent a day in Nantes shopping with Rosie. It was a huge city of many contrasts, ancient and modern combining together where the quaint streets and vast shopping mall provided an exhausting day out. When it came to it, saying goodbye was quite easy since Anna knew she would be going back. The fact that they were going to keep in contact by phone and email convinced her that the friendship wouldn't fade the way most well-intended holiday promises of staying in touch usually do.

***

Anna leaned against the window of the plane, looking down through the white wispy clouds as the earth raced below her. The seatbelt light came on overhead and Anna's thoughts strayed to Daniel. Once she had calmed down she sent him a very apologetic text from the car, he replied almost instantly, forgiving her totally for oversleeping and telling her that Josh had been semi-comatose anyway and only perked up when Océane appeared to wave him off. He'd been asleep in the cabin since they boarded the ferry and Daniel admitted he was on deck, hoping he would get a signal and a message. They simultaneously promised to email as soon as they were both in England and not wanting to sound too eager, Anna ended the conversation by wishing him a safe journey home and sent her love to Josh.

After a grilling by Rosie and once her teasing had subsided, she agreed with Anna that they should take things very slowly. Having only known each other for a few days she advised building a friendship first, yet believed totally in love at first sight, and even if that wasn't quite the case, that some things were meant to be.

Anna confessed she had so many mixed feelings whirling around in her head at the moment that her heart didn't know whether it was coming or going. She thought of Matthew every day and still couldn't take in the fact that he was gone and she would never see him again, knowing if she dwelled on it for too long she'd just break down. Then sometimes she would get really angry and experience such terrible feelings of hate towards him and his mistress for ruining everything, even her grief process. His betrayal was too much to bear so Anna had to banish it from her mind, so strong was the rage inside her.

Then there was Daniel. How could you just click with someone in such a short space of time? Try as she might she couldn't avoid the truth. He made her laugh, she felt relaxed and comfortable with him, he was gorgeous and the fact he wanted to stay in touch made her feel extremely special and happy.

But then there were the children to consider, what would they think? Not wanting to cause upset in any way, she knew their friendship would have to remain a secret for now. Agreeing, Rosie thought it wise of her to keep Daniel to herself and enjoy getting to know him but also to bear in mind she had done nothing wrong. It wasn't a crime to make friends, however handsome, and without sounding harsh whilst stating the obvious, Anna should remember that life goes on.

A smiling, sun-tanned Philip was waiting outside the terminal at Southampton Airport and their drive home was filled with holiday stories. Anna purposely omitted her friendship with Daniel, she would tell Jeannie when she was ready and when they were alone. Philip was best left in ignorance so she was happy listening to his tales of the Sphinx and the pyramids. It was mid-afternoon by the time she was settled at home and as she unpacked the groceries that Jeannie had instructed Philip to buy, Anna chuckled at her henpecked but extremely happy big brother.

Once he left, she loaded the washing machine knowing full well that her dear children would very likely return home laden with plenty of dirty laundry of their own to keep her busy. Listening to the hum of the machine as she wrote a shopping list, looking forward to the prospect of cooking for the kids, she was startled when the phone rang. It was her mother.

Settling down for the long haul, Anna listened patiently to an in-depth exposé of Gladys's fast developing romance with Walter from ballroom dancing and that Chastity had finally been released from prison on *Emmerdale*. This clearly pleased Enid because apparently, poor Chas was completely innocent. As Anna's will to live ebbed away, the conversation turned, and tactful as always, Enid decided to broach head on the subject of her daughter's pre-holiday meltdown.

'So, Anna. Are you going to be alright in the house by yourself? I don't want any more of that nonsense from before you went away.' Enid's voice was firm and her opinion forthright.

'Thanks for asking, Mum, but I'll be fine, honest.' Anna was determined not to rise to Enid's apparent lack of compassion or defend her behaviour in any way. She had just lost her husband for crying out loud; surely she was allowed to have at least one wobble?

'Well, just in case you get the collywobbles again, just you answer me this. Have you ever, in all the years you've lived in that house, seen a ghost?'

'No, Mother.'

'Exactly, and have you ever been burgled, or been disturbed by a prowler or had to call the police?'

'No, Mother.'

'And I take it you set your alarm every night and your security lights work?'

'Yes, Mother.'

'Well, there you go then, you've got absolutely nothing to worry about so stop being a drama queen and pull yourself together. I don't want you going all mardy again but I'll ring tomorrow and check how you get on. If need be I'll come and stay with you until the kids come home, I really don't mind. Now, I've got to go, *Heartbeat's* starting.' Having imparted her wisdom Enid needed to get off.

'Yes, Mother. Thanks for that, can't wait! Love you too, night night.' Anna said her goodbyes and Enid, thankfully, was gone.

Putting ghosts, burglars and bogeymen out of her mind, Anna settled down for a relaxing night in front of the telly, happily eating her egg on toast and texting Melanie and Sam to let them know she was back safe and had settled in. She emailed Joe next and commented on all his recent photos.

He had been to a tourist spot where you dig a pit in the sand (while the tide is out) and the hot springs underneath the beach gradually fill up the hole with steamy water, turning it into a natural sauna. It sounded amazing. She was so glad he had gone back, totally vindicated in her decision.

Signing off to Joe, she hesitated, knowing she should also fulfil her promise to Daniel and let him know she was home. Anna felt a bit shy but she did have an inkling that he would wait for her to make the first move this time, so gathering her courage she typed out a very simple message.

> Hi Daniel, it's Anna. Just to let you know I am back home safe and sound and getting into normal life – the washing machine is on already! Say hello to Josh for me and ask him to drop me a line when he gets the chance. Hope you are both well. I've got Melanie and Sam home this weekend which I'm looking forward to. Anyway, take care, Anna.

She reworded the message about five times, worrying about its content – was it too much or too little, too cold or too brief? Anna realised she was back into over thinking mode so hit send and logged off, adamant that she was not going to sit there all night waiting for a ping telling her she had mail.

The weekend flew past in a blur of young people's voices and the non-stop whir of the washing machine, plus lots of cooking, or not in the case of Mel's best friend, Paloma, who turned out to be a right royal pain in the backside. Anna did try to like her, she really did, but there was something very irritating about this extremely posh, pink- and purple-haired, charity-shop-reject.

Firstly, it was the food thing. After spending the previous day shopping and preparing what Anna regarded as a feast of Mexican food for them both, she was airily informed (in the nicest possible way) that 'I'm a vegetarian'. It was also something Anna had presumed her normally very considerate daughter would've had the decency to inform her of.

After picking through salad and nibbling a dry tortilla, Paloma explained to Anna that she had previously been a vegan *and* a fruitarian but since going to uni was finding it difficult to maintain her high standards, obviously dropping down a few levels of self-righteousness by becoming a lowly vegetarian. Anna asked innocently what exactly a fruitarian ate which elicited exasperated sighs, rolling of eyes and a withering look. As though she was talking to a complete moron, Paloma explained that one only ate fruit or vegetables that fell naturally from a plant or could be harvested without harming or killing it, adding airily that some fruitarians believed that it is improper to eat seeds as they contain future plants. Paloma's lecture left Anna completely lost for words and silently thanking God that Sam hadn't been there – knowing full well that he would have laughed his head off and thought she was a complete mental case. Anna also sent a sarcastic note to self to personally suck the pips out of any food she served Paloma whilst thinking it might be wise to keep veggie-girl and Sam apart for the duration of the weekend.

When Paloma asked Anna what *exactly* one does all day when one doesn't have a job, through gritted teeth and trying not to let her annoyance show, she explained that every day for over twenty-four years she had been a homemaker, a mum and a wife. Her job was looking after her family.

Raising her black, badly-drawn-on eyebrows her young guest looked slightly shocked and very definitely bored by Anna's job description because whilst Paloma didn't say as much, she hadn't been burdened with such a drudge for a mother. Hers sounded infinitely more exciting and was definitely not a stay-at-home mum.

Star (yes, that really was her mother's name) had travelled around Eastern Europe and all of Asia on the hippy trail, leaving university with a first-class degree before lecturing in sculpture, exhibiting her work and socialising with the 'In People' of the art world. Star, now tired of a jet-set life resided in Tenerife, spending her days relaxing and making art.

Fan-bloody-tastic, thought Anna sarcastically. Paloma had only been here two hours and she was sick of her already. Daddy, it seemed, was retired and played golf most days but still had dealings in the city. Paloma was used to not seeing them as she'd been a boarder at a private school in Hampshire and now she was at uni they were happy for her to be a free spirit, to find herself and be independent.

'Well, if you were my daughter I'd want you to be independent too and if you did get lost while you were off trying to find yourself, I certainly wouldn't be in a hurry to organise a search party. That's for damn sure!!' Anna felt not an ounce of guilt at her secret thoughts; instead she checked the clock and looked forward to waving Miss Snotty Pants off.

The arrival of Sam on Saturday morning brought much needed sanity to Anna's life. Luckily, the girls had gone shopping in town, probably buying some more stinky clothes from the charity shop for Paloma. Anna was sure that being a fan of grunge didn't mean you had to pong the house out, because her guest was decidedly lacking in the personal hygiene department and it was starting to tick Anna off. Feeding up her grateful, non-vegetarian son took her mind off Paloma while she listened to all his news and before she knew it he was dashing off to the match with his mates.

Knowing she had a few hours peace, Anna dared to check her emails, hoping for a reply from Joe and maybe Daniel too. Hearing the multiple ping of her inbox resulted in her heart having a stupid little flutter as three messages popped up. They were from Joe, Josh and some spam. Deleting the rubbish straight away she read Joe's whilst ignoring the disappointment that neither were from Daniel. Joe was moving on down the coast and had attached more photos in which he looked tanned and healthy; his cheeky-faced friends waving and pulling faces behind him.

Opening the email from Josh, she smiled, hearing his chilled-out voice in her mind. His big news was that after thinking it over during the long, boring drive home, he'd talked with Daniel about being a nurse and they were going to check it out. He also wished she'd join Facebook as he'd put loads of holiday photos on but attached a few to the email. Josh didn't mention Daniel and signed off by telling her he was looking forward to hearing from her soon.

Anna opened the attachments and cringed when she saw the first photo. It was of her and Daniel sitting at the long table, Josh had swapped their faces which bizarrely morphed into each other, it looked pretty grotesque so she deleted it. The second was more pleasing on the eye. Here, Anna was laughing at something Daniel had said and he was leaning forward, his blue eyes looking straight at her, obviously very amused by his own joke. It was a lovely happy photo, one of those that instantly make you smile. The last one was of Josh holding an oyster and a mussel in each hand and pulling a terrified face. Saving both messages and slightly concerned at not hearing from Daniel, she logged off.

Mel sent a text saying that they would be back around seven as wonder girl wanted to eat out. Anna thought of her well-stocked fridge and seethed inwardly. She had hardly spoken to Melanie since she arrived home and wished that Paloma would just sod off back to La La Land. Sam rang after the match and insisted on bringing home some food so she could relax, suggesting they could watch a film together later. At least he wanted to spend time with her!

By the time Melanie and Paloma rolled in past midnight both Anna and Sam had gone to bed. Anna was actually still awake but far too annoyed to acknowledge their arrival. Melanie hadn't even bothered to ring and let her know where she was, which was out of character and inconsiderate. Listening in the dark as they noisily banged doors and giggled in the hallway there was no way Anna was going out there to complain. It would make her look like an uncool fuddy-duddy and Paloma would just love that. *'I'm sure Star lets people run around her house completely drunk at three o'clock in the morning and doesn't bat an eyelid,'* Anna fumed, resolving to have a few strong words with Melanie in private.

At eight thirty the following morning, with the unmistakable smell of meaty bacon and sausage being liberally and deliberately wafted around the house, Mel was soon tempted downstairs (minus Paloma) where she joined Anna and Sam for breakfast. The three of them spent a happy morning catching up and drinking tea, laughing and teasing each other. Anna was having such a good time she decided to leave speaking to Melanie about her poor choice in friends and selfish behaviour for another day.

Sam left at lunchtime, stocked up with goodies and clean clothes and a little bit curious about his sister's friend who he'd managed not to clap eyes on. By the time an unwashed, greasy haired Paloma surfaced there was just enough time to palm her off with a glass of organic orange juice before they packed up and set off.

Anna was actually relieved that they had gone which instantly made her feel guilty and irritated but the change in Melanie around her new friend was startling, she lacked conversation and seemed apprehensive whenever Anna opened her mouth to speak, suspecting that her daughter might be slightly ashamed of her. The thought really stung but for now she would put it down to Melanie being naive and easy-going and Paloma just being a cow.

CHAPTER 16

The arrival on Monday morning of a bright orange leaflet wrapped around a bin liner gave Anna pause for thought. It was from the local Church committee who were having a Christmas Fair. They needed donations for the jumble sale and would be collecting in the area on Friday. Anna thought instantly of Matthew's clothes hanging in the wardrobes upstairs. She hadn't even looked at them since he died, except to give a suit to the undertaker just before the funeral, the memory making her shudder. Perhaps it was time to have a bit of a clear out and donate some winter clothes that would be useful this time of year, and maybe the rest of his suits. The rest she could save in case the boys wanted anything, that way she wouldn't feel too guilty. It had to be done sometime, no matter how much she dreaded such a heart-wrenching chore.

Anna managed to put it off for most of the day yet realised she was just avoiding the inevitable and it began to torment her, so grabbing the bin liner, she marched purposefully upstairs and flung open the wardrobe doors. Despite the fresh smell of fabric conditioner there was no denying that when she got close, the unmistakable scent of her husband lingered on his clothes. The urge to pull them close and breathe him in was too strong. The chunky sweater he always wore in the garden was rolled up on the top shelf so she pulled it out it and held it to her face. Yes, it was there. Closing her eyes, she imagined Matthew. The suits had a faint tinge of aftershave around the collar and the football jerseys instantly reminded her of Saturday afternoons and his post-match hugs and kisses, especially when his team had won.

This was going to be harder than she thought so swallowing down her emotions and wiping tears from her eyes, Anna avoided the more personal items that she would save for Joe and Sam and began removing the shirts and suits from the rail, checking each of the pockets carefully, not liking the thought of a stranger coming across anything of Matthew's. Anna was on the final jacket when she felt something in the inside pocket, a business card, nothing unusual there, apart from the fact that it was for an estate agent in town. '*Why on earth would Matthew have this,*' thought Anna? She sat on the bed and turned it over, reading a handwritten name and phone number on the back, Simon Stanhope, who the hell was he? Her mind raked through the past, desperately trying to remember her husband mentioning or even needing to see an estate agent.

The card unsettled Anna but keen to finish her task she placed it on the bedside table and folded the suits and shirts, pulling the bin liner around them. Carrying the bag downstairs, she couldn't shake the feeling that the mysterious business card in her hand, meant something. It was in one of his summer suits so Matthew must have worn it sometime just before he died. Anna's heart began to thud loudly, something was wrong, it was an omen, and panic was setting in. She sat by the phone in the lounge, staring at the card, willing it to give her a clue, knowing there was only one way to find out. With a shaking hand she picked up the receiver and before there was time to bottle out, Anna dialled the number on the back. It rang for a while during which Anna hoped it would go to answerphone.

A confident male voice answered. 'Simon Stanhope speaking.'

Desperately trying to match his tone Anna breathed in deeply and replied. 'Hi, Simon. I hope I'm not disturbing you, it's Mrs Harrison here, Matthew's wife, from Harrison Haulage.' It was a bit vague but all she could think of on the spur of the moment.

'Ah yes, the lovely Mrs Harrison. How is Matthew? I was wondering if we would hear from you both again. I'm afraid the apartment you viewed has been sold, if that's why you're calling. I did advise you not to dilly-dally. It was very popular and went the following week but I do have similar properties available if you're still interested.' Simon was obviously not one to waste time if a sale could be had.

Anna, however, was rendered speechless, totally dumbfounded. Blood converged from every part of her body, flooding up to her face and fuelling her pummelling heart. She could feel her cheeks, hot with shock and embarrassment and her hands were really shaking now. Forcing something, anything from her lips, Anna managed a few words, she knew her voice was quaking but stumbled on.

'I'm very sorry we haven't been in touch, Simon, but unfortunately, Matthew passed away in July.'

It was a good line because he obviously accredited her quavering voice to the bad news she'd just imparted; it also bought her some valuable thinking time. Registering Simon's shock down the phone, followed by his sincere apologies and soft words of sympathy, gave Anna the opportunity to regain composure. By the time he'd finished his embarrassed rambling and even though her mouth was dry with nerves, Anna enquired if it was possible to arrange a meeting, hoping to discuss any properties he may feel suitable as she was still interested in relocating.

Desperate to help a grieving and possibly loaded widow, Simon offered Anna an appointment for the very next day, promising to do anything he could to help and no doubt hoping he'd bag a juicy sale in the process.

Once polite goodbyes were exchanged, Anna slowly replaced the receiver. She sat like stone, in shock, unable to move, she stared into space as the day lost its light and the darkness of the evening gathered around her.

Finding out Matthew was having an affair had destroyed her world yet, secretly, Anna had held on to a shred of faint hope that maybe it was just a fling and a huge mistake. Now she knew otherwise and she'd been kidding herself; deluded, a fool. It was obviously much more than that because he had viewed an apartment with his mistress and worse, passed her off as his wife. That meant one of two things – he was either buying a love nest, or worse, he was actually going to leave Anna. Bizarrely, in the midst of the revelation she thought of King Henry giving the chateau in France to his mistress, Diane.

Finally, Anna reached for her mobile, automatically pressing number two on speed dial where, on hearing the voice of her best friend, words failed her and instead, hysterical ramblings mingled with sobs and gulps for air were all she could manage. Within what seemed like minutes, the front door flew open and Jeannie was there, desperately trying but unable to make sense of whatever it was her inconsolable friend was trying to tell her. Anna, racked with anguished tears, made no sense so all Jeannie could do was wait patiently for them to stop.

When they finally subsided and the story was told, both friends sat in subdued silence and Anna waited for Jeannie's verdict. She really needed someone to tell her what to do, what to think and where to go from here. Realising she had to take the lead, Jeannie announced that tomorrow, they would go to the estate agents together and interrogate Mr Simon Stanhope and find out exactly what Matthew and his tart were up to. One way or another, Ms Jeannie Brown was going to get some answers and then, she was going to kick some arse.

Anna had hardly slept a wink but nevertheless was raring to go when Jeannie picked her up and they headed off into town. Anna was bubbling with pent-up anger and driven by steely determination. As they entered the shop her heart pounded in her chest, fast losing her nerve, terrified of what she might hear and even more worried about Simon's reaction to her deception.

Jeannie, on the other hand, had no such qualms and marched confidently up to the receptionist and announced their arrival. After what seemed like hours the snooty receptionist informed them that Simon was ready and directed them to the door at the end of a corridor. Anna was ready to bolt but bolstered by Jeannie they trooped into a small, modern office to be confronted by the top of a very bald, shiny head. Hearing their arrival, Simon looked up from his scribbling and after casting his eyes over both of them seemed somewhat confused.

Taking the lead, Jeannie, who was quite enjoying the drama of the situation, held out her hand and introduced herself and then Anna, the *real* Mrs Harrison. The light quickly dawned on poor Simon Stanhope and they watched as his wide-eyed, open-mouthed face turned a delightful shade of purple. Jeannie again took the initiative and without being asked, plonked herself down on a chair and gestured for Anna to do the same, reasoning that it would be harder to throw them out once they'd got comfy.

'Well, Simon, can I call you Simon? As I'm sure you have worked out by now, the woman who you *thought* was Matthew Harrison's wife was actually, for want of a better phrase, his bit on the side.' Jeannie defiantly stared Simon out as Anna winced.

Sometimes her friend could be a bit too in your face and was very scary when riled. Composing himself and shuffling nervously in his seat while he twiddled his gold pen, Simon coughed and smiled weakly at the two angry women staring at him from across the desk.

'I can assure you both that at the time of the viewing I had absolutely no idea of the true facts and if I have inadvertently caused you distress, Mrs Harrison, please accept my utmost and sincere apologies. Nevertheless, I was led to believe that the young lady in question was indeed Mr Harrison's wife and I conducted the viewing in total ignorance.'

Simon seemed quite genuine in his response causing Jeannie to ease off slightly.

'Okay, Simon, relax. We realise that it wasn't your fault and you can't be blamed for being lied to, so apology accepted. However, we *would* be grateful if you could throw some light on the matter. For a start, when did you meet him and could you describe the woman who was with Matthew?' Jeannie leant forward slightly, looking Simon directly in the eye.

'Well, it was a while ago now, I'm not good with faces and I do feel that you are putting me in a very awkward situation. There is a matter of client confidentiality to respect, after all.' Simon wasn't used to being confronted like this and desperately struggling to know what to say for the best.

'Don't talk rubbish, Simon! It was obvious from the moment we walked in that you realised Anna wasn't the woman you met that day; therefore, you must have some recollection of her. And do I really need to remind you that you haven't actually got a client anymore? Sorry, Anna, but it needed to be said. So stop pussyfooting about and tell us what you know.'

Simon looked like he had been slapped and Anna suspected they were on the verge of being forcibly ejected from the building. Interrupting and using her kindest voice, she leant over to Simon and smiled, hoping to appeal to him as a grieving widow, desperate for answers, unlike the red-eyed psycho sitting beside her.

'Simon, I understand this is very difficult and turning up like this may have embarrassed you but I'd be so grateful of any help you could give me. I've been through a terrible time lately and I'm just seeking closure. So if you could tell me what you know it would maybe set my mind at rest.'

Jeannie gave Anna a conspiratory wink, obviously thinking good cop, bad cop was the best way to go.

'Alright, alright. This really is highly unorthodox, however, under the circumstances I suppose I should help. I met them the last Friday in June, I remember because I was going to my niece's wedding the next day. The young lady, as I recall, was perhaps in her very early thirties and, I suppose, quite petite. She was wearing a baseball cap and sunglasses so I couldn't tell you the colour of her hair or her eyes. I do remember she was extremely excited about the apartment and eager to get things moving.' Simon prayed that would be enough to satisfy them.

'Do you have any details about her on paper?' Anna was grasping at straws.

'No, sorry, nothing like that. I knew your husband from the golf club. I presume that's why he came to see me.'

Anna was despondent, they still had nothing to go on. After all this it was a dead end.

Then Jeannie piped up with another question. 'Out of interest, where was the apartment they viewed, do you still have a photograph?'

Simon sighed before leaving his chair to open his filing cabinet and eventually found a folder from which he extracted a brochure and passed it to Anna. The glossy photos showed a high-spec, modern, luxury apartment overlooking a marina filled with expensive yachts. The price tag caused her to gasp before exchanging a quizzical look with Jeannie.

'*How on earth could Matthew have afforded this?*' The whole thing was too unbelievable for words. Dazed and feeling queasy, the shock of Simon's revelation had unsettled her stomach so she silently passed the brochure to Jeannie who, after reading it, must have also read Anna's mind.

Jeannie came straight to the point. 'Simon, did Matthew mention how he was going to pay for this apartment, presuming he told you they would have it? Did he need a mortgage or indicate whether it was for both of them, or just the woman?'

Anna immediately wished Jeannie hadn't asked and dreaded the reply.

When Simon coloured up and looked extremely uncomfortable, she feared the worst. He was avoiding their eyes and pretending to rearrange the papers on his desk. Sensing his reluctance and before her evil twin stepped in and scared him to death, Anna leaned over and spoke gently to the perspiring and beleaguered man.

'It's okay, Simon, just tell me. I'd rather know the truth, however unsavoury it may be.' Anna knew in that second that whatever she was about to hear, wouldn't be pleasant.

'I'm so sorry, Mrs Harrison, but yes, they did say they would have it and I got the impression it was for both of them. During the negotiations regarding the price of the apartment your husband did seem a little concerned about the hefty amount, however… the young lady reminded him that after the sale of his home they would have ample funds to make the purchase. Naturally, I offered our services, thinking that it would be beneficial if I could arrange both sales.' Simon looked embarrassed and rather distressed, witnessing instantly the impact of his information.

He may as well have punched Anna in the face.

While Jeannie gasped, Anna's hands flew upwards in an involuntary reaction, covering her mouth in utter shock; her whole body trembled as a wave of nausea sent her head spinning. Anna felt Jeannie's hand on her leg, squeezing tightly as she suggested it was enough for one day and they should go. Anna agreed instantly, able only to nod, knowing she couldn't cry there, poor Simon had been punished enough and hysteria would probably finish him off. Relying on Jeannie to end the conversation, Anna could only manage a weak smile to the perplexed, baldy man who shook her friend's hand, still intent on apologising profusely for something that wasn't actually his fault.

Unfortunately, just as they reached the door, Simon called out to them, suddenly remembering something. Turning, Anna and Jeannie waited for him to speak. Anna knew instinctively that whatever it was, wouldn't cheer her up.

'I've just remembered her name, it came to me in a flash, it's a little unusual but maybe it was a nickname, anyway I'm almost sure that during the viewing your husband referred to the young woman as Kitten.'

Then Anna really was sick.

By the time Jeannie got her home, the trauma of the afternoon's revelations and the humiliation of throwing up all over poor Simon's carpet had left Anna exhausted. While Jeannie made tea, Anna lay on the sofa, eyes closed with a cushion over her face, praying her headache would go and this nightmare would end.

She tried to force the image of the sick-splattered office from her mind (she had even managed to get some on his desk) and then the cringe-inducing scene that followed, with Jeannie dabbing away at Anna's face while Simon froze in horror before turning a strange shade of green himself. Remembering the look of pure disgust on the secretary's face as she surveyed the mess and knowing she would be the one cleaning it up, caused Anna to groan out loud, consumed with shame.

On the journey home, neither Jeannie nor Anna had spoken. Anna felt physically and mentally drained and for once in her life Jeannie seemed at a loss for words. Banishing the scene from her thoughts Anna turned her attention to Matthew. Not only had he been having an affair, the scumbag was actually preparing to buy a shag-pad with his tart and if that wasn't bad enough, he was planning to sell the family home to finance it. Anna noticed lately that her language and tendency towards aggression was getting out of hand, she must get a grip and stop swearing; then again – he deserved it!

How could he do it to her and the children? How on earth did he expect them to deal with it? Maybe he'd have mentioned casually over dinner that he was in love with some young bimbo called Kitten, before calmly suggesting that once they'd eaten, they should nip upstairs and fill some bin liners with their stuff because he'd flogged the house and was moving to a swanky new apartment on the proceeds?

Without warning, an uncontrollable fit of rage consumed Anna, like an infection running through her veins, its poison gave her strength, propelling her from the sofa, focusing her mind and driving her on. Bolting into the kitchen and causing Jeannie to jump in the process, Anna yanked open the drawer and grabbed a roll of bin liners. Ignoring her friend's questions and pleas to calm down, Anna raced up the stairs to her bedroom.

Flinging open the doors of Matthew's wardrobe, she angrily pulled armfuls of clothes from the rails then ripped the bin bags apart, stuffing everything inside. Hot tears of hate and humiliation pumped from her eyes, blurring her vision, undeterred, she wiped them away, intent on clearing Matthew's presence and memory from the room. Pulling open drawers she dragged everything out, ramming socks and underwear into the bags as quickly as she could. The room looked like they'd been robbed but Anna didn't care, she had to take it out on something. Jeannie stood silently at the door and let her continue, a tiny bit scared and unsure of what to say or do.

When Anna finally flopped onto the bed, out of breath and drained of tears, she asked Jeannie to help her take the bags downstairs and after a couple of silent trips to and fro, everything was piled in the porch and only then did the shaking inside her body begin to subside.

Later, sitting in the lounge with a cup of very sweet tea, Jeannie ventured to break the silence. 'Feel better now? I must say you really scared the crap out of me running about like that. I thought you'd been possessed or something.'

'To be honest, Jeannie, I don't. But I had to do something. I just want to punish him, both of them for what they've done. How dare he even think of selling this house, it's our home and what would it have done to the kids? I still can't take it all in. And did you see that apartment; was he having a mid-life crisis or something, and how many sugars have you put in this tea?' Anna sat back and closed her eyes, rubbing her hands across her face, exasperated.

'They say sugar is good for shock, and there's only three spoons, just drink it! And as for Matthew, God only knows *what* that man was thinking. I can't get my head round it. And then there's bloody Kitten, what type of weirdo calls themselves that? Surely it can't be her real name, it's pathetic.' Jeannie was full of venom but running on empty where answers were concerned.

Anna agreed. 'I know, I half wish Simon hadn't remembered that bit, it just makes me feel sick, knowing she had a cringey pet name. It doesn't help though does it? Because at the end of this truly crappy day we still haven't got a clue who she is. All I do know is that it wasn't just a fling. It was serious and Matthew was really going to leave me.' Anna's voice broke again as sad, slow tears ran down her cheeks.

Jeannie sighed, desperately wishing she could help. Looking over at her heartbroken friend she felt completely useless and grappled for something, anything that would cheer Anna up; even a scrap of constructive advice would do. But no matter how hard she tried, it just seemed like an impossible task.

CHAPTER 17

Anna lay in bed and was actually enjoying being alone. The house was peaceful and after everything that had occurred, it comforted her as she dissected the day's revelations, trying to be calm, taking time to reflect and think. Perhaps the house was in shock too because it would have overheard everything, now fully aware that its master was going to sell up. There had always been a good feeling about their home, Anna felt connected to it, a bond. Matthew thought she was totally crazy when on the day they moved in she stood in the front room and said loudly, 'Hello house, we're the Harrisons and we've come to look after you.'

And look after the house they did. They lovingly restored it, brought their children home from the hospital into its warm embrace, and filled every square inch with happy memories. Before they went on holiday, Anna always placed her hand on the kitchen wall and whispered, 'Don't worry, we're not leaving you forever, we'll be back soon.'

As they drove away she imagined the house had a sad face and when they returned it would be smiling as they came up the drive, so Anna always said hello as soon as she got inside. Yes, it was a bit mad and the kids took the mickey but she felt these walls and rooms were alive. Now, she imagined them falling silent when she was talking to Jeannie earlier, the lounge passing a message to the kitchen then the bedrooms and bathrooms heard the news. '*He was going to sell us,*' they whispered. '*He was going to leave us, can you believe it? We thought he was happy here.*'

All the rooms were hushed now, watching over Anna, guarding her as she lay in bed and a steady stream of thoughts ran through her head. '*How on earth could it have come to this, where did it all go wrong, how could I have missed the signs, am I really so gullible and naive? Or perhaps it's my own fault and I was arrogant, believing our marriage was perfect and nothing could come between us. It must have been me. Had I let myself go, did I stop trying or become complacent? Perhaps he just went off me, simple as that!* The questions tormented Anna, going round and round in circles. Eventually, after racking her brains, the earliest event she could recall which caused a memorable ripple in their life was when Joe decided he was going away. Yes, maybe it began there.

***

Joe had left university and was due to start at the haulage company in the September. He was going to work his way around all the departments in a junior managerial role until he felt confident and the other members of staff could see he had earned his position. Matthew didn't want any resentment or lack of respect due to the fact he was the boss's son.

Over dinner one evening, Joe dropped the bombshell that he wanted to take two years out and go travelling and whilst their son looked on nervously, Anna thought Matthew was going to have a heart attack. Apparently, Ed, Joe's best friend at university had an uncle in New Zealand who had offered both of them a job on his sheep farm – they could use their earnings to fund their travels. It was a chance of a lifetime and even though Joe knew that the master plan had always been for him to go straight to the firm, he wanted to have an adventure and some fun. Matthew didn't get it at all and threw a blue fit. The row rumbled on all weekend and the atmosphere in the house was unbearable, and Anna was stuck in the middle.

Seeing things from both sides, Matthew's disappointment and her son's thirst for life, Anna really didn't know what to do for the best. Thankfully, Dennis came to the rescue when he and Mary came for Sunday lunch. Joe had made his excuses and wasn't around, so over roast beef, Matthew explained everything as his old friend listened patiently.

Dennis sympathised with Matthew, understanding that he had been looking forward to the day Joe came to work for them properly and because of that, he was naturally disappointed. Then he reminded Matthew how young they both were when they started the business, working all the hours God sent, missing holidays and their wives, but they also missed out on having fun. It had worked out well in the end because now they could provide for their families and the sacrifice had been worth it. Yet on reflection, would it really do any harm to let Joe have some of the fun they had missed out on?

He reminded Matthew that his son had always worked hard at school and university and spent every holiday at Harrison's being the odd-job boy, just so he could earn money for his first car and driving lessons. Dennis suggested that during the two years he was away, Joe would mature and gain some life experience in the process. It wasn't as though he was asking Matthew to pay for his trip either; Joe had worked it out and could stand on his own two feet. The firm would still be there when he got back and by then, Joe should have got the travel bug out of his system and be ready to get stuck in.

Later that evening when he finally sloped in, Matthew was waiting for Joe and told his extremely relieved son that even though he was disappointed at not having him by his side straight away, he wanted him to be happy so it was okay to go off globetrotting, he had Matthew's blessing. He also wanted him to know that he would be waiting with a suit and a new set of biros the second Joe's foot stepped off the plane and then they could take over the world of haulage together. It was never meant to be.

A frenzy of organisation followed, mostly form filling and trying to stuff far too many clothes into the biggest rucksack they could find. At his going away party, Matthew quietly slipped Joe an envelope. Inside was enough money to buy a campervan that Joe and his friends could use for their travels and hopefully, sell it on before they left. Joe was ecstatic. Anna remembered them both laughing when they got their first photos from New Zealand of Joe and his friends, the surfer dude posing on the beach with Molly, the bright orange campervan.

Exactly one week after Joe had left, John, the financial manager from the company had a massive heart attack and it seemed very likely that he wouldn't be returning to work. One of the oldest members of the firm, he would be sadly missed but despite the shock felt by all the staff at Harrison's, a replacement had to be found. On the day of the interviews Matthew returned home in a foul mood. According to Matthew, all the candidates were unsuitable except for one, a Miss Caitlin Winifred Walsh. She came with glowing references and was more than qualified for the job. Dennis thought she was an ideal candidate. Matthew, however, didn't take to her.

Over dinner he was like a bear with a sore head, explaining to Anna and Mel that it was sheer stupidity to employ a woman whose biological clock would be ticking in a year or two and then they would end up paying maternity benefit and God knows what else. He was instantly slapped down by his wife and daughter for being a male chauvinist pig but apart from that, Anna respected her husband's opinion. Years of experience told him that this extremely ambitious and slightly egotistical woman was wrong for his company. Unfortunately he was talked round by Dennis so at the beginning of October, Caitlin Walsh or Winnie the Pooh as Melanie scathingly named her, joined the team at Harrison Haulage.

It was December when Matthew began his really grumpy stage. Apparently, Caitlin was planning a complete financial overhaul of Harrison Haulage beginning with the traditional giving of Christmas gifts to employees. Again, over dinner, he nervously informed an astounded Anna that this year, for the first time, they wouldn't be giving the staff their usual present from the directors of a bottle of wine and a tin of chocolates. Plus, their Christmas bonus would be cut by twenty-five percent.

Anna was livid, knowing only too well that most of their staff relied on and looked forward to that bonus and as for the giving of gifts, how dare Caitlin put a stop to that? It had been an idea conceived by herself and Mary years ago, just a little thank you from them to the people who worked so hard over the year. It was something to take home to their families on the day they finished for Christmas, to show that their bosses appreciated them. Laden with personally hand-wrapped gifts, Anna, Mary and the children would go around each department giving out the presents and wishing everyone a Merry Christmas before they shut up shop for the festivities.

Well, Anna couldn't interfere with the bonus issue, that was out of her hands but the presents were her and Mary's department and she would not stand for it. Seething inside, Anna waited until Matthew was distracted and watching television then went upstairs to ring Mary who, it seemed, was equally annoyed by the situation. Between them they vowed to exert their rights as directors' wives and teach Miss Fancy Pants a lesson she wouldn't forget, along with their wimpy husbands!

On the day the firm closed for the Christmas break, Mary, Anna and Melanie rolled up at Harrison Haulage loaded up with lovely presents. They had halved the cost between them, deciding that Caitlin could stick her petty cash where the sun doesn't shine and just out of spite had added a Christmas cake to the pile, thinking this would send a 'don't mess with us' message to the tight-arsed, misery guts. They started with the office staff, breezing in with arms full of brightly coloured gift bags and were warmly and genuinely welcomed, with the exception of Dennis and Matthew who both looked scared shitless. The Ice Queen (as Mary and Anna had named her) on hearing the commotion outside, eventually emerged from her office and surveyed the scene with a face like thunder.

Anna spotted her instantly and picked up a gift bag then calmly deposited it in Caitlin's hands, and with the smile of an innocent angel, wished her a very merry Christmas from the directors and their wives, giving Matthew a cheeky wink as she walked away. That night at dinner, Matthew had to admit he was really proud of his wife despite the dent in his bank balance. It also transpired that much to the amusement of everyone, the Ice Queen had remained in her office all afternoon in a sulk, stomping home without so much as a 'ho, ho, ho' for anyone.

Then, Anna remembered something else. It was thinking of the Christmas period that brought it back. Traditionally there were two special events around December, firstly there was the Directors and Management dinner where Matthew and Dennis took the senior team for a meal at a swanky hotel to discuss the year's events and plans for the future.

It seemed there had been a bit of an atmosphere at the office due to the fact Samantha, Matthew's personal assistant, had been invited for the first time and Caitlin had objected on the grounds she didn't qualify as a manager. She was overruled by both Dennis and Matthew who insisted that Samantha was their most senior secretary. She knew just as much about the day to day running of the firm as any of them so they thought it would be useful to have her input and wrongly assumed that Caitlin would welcome some female company around the table.

Mary and Anna never went along as they both agreed it would be too boring and they had little to contribute so instead, they booked a quiet table for two at the local Italian and merrily gossiped the night away. On this occasion, Anna's lovely night ended in a huge row when Matthew uncharacteristically rolled in at three in the morning, totally plastered, unable to remember where he had left his car and soaking wet. He also thought it was a good idea to walk home, completely drunk in the pouring rain which resulted in a dreadful case of man-flu and him being in a foul mood for days.

The second event was the works Christmas party where other halves and girlfriends could attend. It was always a great success and held at the same place every year with a traditional dinner and disco afterwards. On the night in question there were two dramas.

Firstly, Samantha, had a ding-dong with her husband, Rob. It was obvious during the meal they were not on speaking terms and at some point afterwards, Melanie found Samantha in the foyer, upset and in a bit of a state. Anna offered to go and check on her but Matthew insisted he would deal with it. After some time passed Anna followed, thinking that maybe a friendly female ear would help and eventually tracked them down to the hotel steps. It was obvious they were in the middle of a row and that Samantha was tearful. Anna's arrival coincided with that of a taxi whereupon Matthew abruptly ended the conversation and his secretary jumped inside the cab, slamming the door and leaving them standing on the steps.

When Anna quizzed her husband about what was going on he was vague, the row was something on the lines of Rob wanting to start a family and Samantha being unwilling to give up her job. Matthew nonchalantly put it all down to free wine, hormones and women's lib. Samantha had taken umbrage with Matthew for taking Rob's side in the argument and thought he was being disloyal, simple as that.

To add to the evening's excitement, an extremely inebriated Caitlin had turned up with her long-term boyfriend, Gavin. As the evening progressed, to Gavin's obvious embarrassment, Caitlin became increasingly more amorous. Her very tight, revealing dress left nothing to the imagination to start with so as she groped and fondled him in full view of anyone brave enough to look, they were left in no doubt of her devotion to her beloved boyfriend or her apparent insatiable sexual appetite.

Dennis and Mary were totally disgusted and Matthew was fuming, reminding Anna that he knew Caitlin was trouble from the start and tonight's performance was no way for senior management to behave. Sam, on the other hand had been mesmerised and filmed Caitlin's hilarious version of dirty dancing then put it straight on Facebook – his mates loved it.

The New Year rumbled slowly on. Regular updates from Joe warded off the winter blues then, at the end of January, Caitlin announced her engagement to Gavin, confirming Matthew's conviction that she would soon start breeding like a rabbit and was totally vindicated where the maternity benefit issue was concerned. Unfortunately, just as they landed two huge contracts, Mary had to have an emergency hysterectomy and was quite poorly afterwards which meant Dennis needed to be at home more than usual. Matthew took on his workload whenever he was out of the office and that's when the very late nights began.

At first Anna didn't mind but they became more and more frequent and Matthew even started working weekends. Even Samantha had to work overtime and take on extra duties. If Anna brought the subject up, suggesting maybe he took a break or delegated more of the work to Caitlin, he was like a bear with a sore head, accusing her of being unreasonable or not knowing what she was talking about. It usually ended in a row followed by Matthew apologising, blaming his harsh words and short temper on stress. Anna was then guilt-ridden and felt selfish so after a while tended not to complain, that is until she decided to book a holiday.

They had always gone away for Matthew's birthday in early April which most years conveniently coincided with the Easter break and school holidays. Dennis had been back in work full-time since the beginning of March but only worked a four-day week; Mary's illness had scared them both to death so he decided to take things a bit easier.

After work one evening, Anna settled down next to Matthew on the sofa with a pile of brochures, she fancied a holiday to Greece and wanted his input. However, rather than his usual enthusiasm he told her it was a no go this year, he had too much on and had appointments he had to keep for a new contract. Anna was shocked and hurt but, after their recent run of arguments, suggested they could go later. It would just be the two of them since Mel would be revising for her mocks so they were flexible with the timescale. It was then that Matthew snapped and hit the roof, accusing her of constantly nagging and pressurising him. Could she not see he was busy and needed to be at work, not gallivanting off when it suited her?

That night his words were excessively cruel and there was no apology later in the evening or the next day for that matter. He point-blank refused to discuss it and a very miserable, sulky atmosphere settled on the Harrison household, lasting for a good few weeks. Matthew eventually attempted to smooth things over and appease Anna by suggested they postponed plans until things eased off but after twenty-three years of marriage, she knew when she was being fobbed off.

Looking back, it was a pity that she didn't also recognise that she was being lied to. Between the rows and the sulks and the late nights, Anna remembered that gradually things had begun to suffer in the bedroom department as well. At first, his extra workload and stress took the blame, interspersed with the odd argument that seemed to drag on longer than usual, then more frequent business trips which always entailed Matthew staying away for the night. Whenever they did spend time alone or make love, Anna began to feel they had to make the effort, Matthew more so. At the time she assumed it was a blip in their married life, something that they could work through. Surely plenty of couples went through this after years of marriage? Instead of smelling the coffee and taking action she'd been blinkered, assuring herself that eventually it would sort itself out. It didn't.

***

God! She had been so naive and trusting, they must have thought she was a prize idiot. Tears of humiliation welled in Anna's eyes as she imagined them both laughing at her expense every time they got away with a sneaky overnighter or as they concocted their next cock-and-bull excuse for an evening of passion. Keeping it all to herself had probably been a mistake, if she had at least confided in Jeannie maybe the woman-of-the-world would have been able to help and no doubt suspected straight away that Matthew was up to no good.

Anna turned on her side as tears streamed down her face and the usual cocktail of hurt and anger enveloped her. As she reached over for a tissue her mobile buzzed. She wasn't in the mood to chat, even by text, but as she focused on the screen her heart did a triple somersault. The message was from Daniel. Wiping away her tears and blowing her nose she swiped across and in an instant, her dark and lonely mood lifted and the ominous cloud that hovered above her bed was blown away. Reading the words, a large grin took control of her face.

> Hi Anna, how are you? I promised myself that I would wait to hear from you first as I didn't want to pester you. My gormless brother was supposed to pass on a message but forgot – as usual. I spilt coffee over my laptop the day we got back from France so it has gone off to, hopefully, be repaired. If you have emailed me I haven't received it, and I was worried that you would be waiting for a reply. When Josh told me you had written to him I was unsure of what to do, so I am breaking my promise and texting you instead. I had to do something. I have been checking my phone every five minutes hoping for a message from you. Please don't be cross, your promise-breaking friend, Daniel x

For once, without thinking it through, Anna acted on impulse and pressed call on her screen then holding her breath, she listened. Apart from the marching band thudding around in her chest you could've heard a pin drop. Daniel picked up on the second ring. He sounded cautious but said simply,

'Hi, Anna, I'm so glad you rang.'

And as soon as she heard his voice, Anna was glad too.

CHAPTER 18

With the winter sun streaming through her window, Anna decided she had had enough of Matthew and his tart making her life a misery. She would start the day as she meant to go on, making a pact with herself to be positive and not let his infidelity drag her down. The fact that she had spent over an hour on the phone the night before, talking and laughing with Daniel about every subject under the sun probably had a lot to do with it. Anna had gone from being trapped in a pit of despair to feeling elated and hopeful. There was something refreshing about being able to have an adult conversation with a member of the opposite sex without feeling threatened or flirted with, knowing in her heart that if Daniel did push things too quickly it would put her off for sure. That he was respecting her feelings made her warm to him even more.

She'd had quite enough of disappointments and if they took things slowly it would give her a chance to adjust to her new life at the same time as getting to know one another. Anna still hadn't told him about Matthew; it was bad enough living with the thoughts in her head without actually going over them again. Anyway, it made a nice change not thinking or talking about it at all.

Next on the agenda was to email Rosie. Sitting at the bureau under the stairs that housed the small home office, Anna decided that in order to be a real friend with Rosie she would have to be honest. So after enquiring after everyone in France and dishing the dirt on dirty Paloma, she related the story of the estate agents in all its glory, ending with the phone call from Daniel.

Once she had signed off and in order to seal the deal of friendship, Anna took herself off to the shops and bought a selection of the

English goodies that Rosie missed and a baby book containing a stage by stage guide to pregnancy. Anna loved reading her own baby book and she would sit for hours looking at the photos, imagining the same thing happening inside her own bump, three times over. Her last stop was the supermarket, if she was going to play the part of a cheated-on widow, then she would damn well do it in style.

Anna happily cruised the aisles choosing meals for one from the gourmet range plus desserts (well, everyone kept mentioning that she was too thin) and being very loyal to her new French friends chose wine from the region and hoped that Daniel would approve of her selection. Having learnt her lesson regarding coming back to a dark, gloomy house, Anna had attached timers to the lights so as she pulled onto the drive, her home looked warm and inviting. That evening as she waited for her meal for one to cook whilst drinking a cool glass of Vouvray, Anna gave herself a little pat on the back, congratulating herself on her positive thinking. Today had been a good day.

The remainder of October was taken up mostly by Enid. Anna took a trip to see Naomi and her beloved Aunty Elsie who was full of concern and sensible advice for her bereaved niece. Elsie was also extremely pleased to inform Anna of the miraculous discovery of her lost fox fur. Bizarrely, it had turned up in one of her old suitcases which she could've sworn she'd emptied. Luckily, her Naomi had found it when she was having a sort out for the jumble sale so all was now well in the world.

'Thank goodness she looked inside,' remarked Elsie, 'otherwise it would've been flogged for twenty pence in the church hall. I was so relieved. And there was me suspecting our Enid of pinching it. I wouldn't put it past her though, she's a sly one but I do feel a bit guilty about accusing her.' Anna sipped her tea and smiled sweetly, if only Aunty Elsie knew the truth.

Returning home late on Sunday evening, when Anna rang Enid to check on her before she went to bed, her mother sounded full of cold so promised to call in the next day. When she arrived at her mother's tiny bungalow it was clear that Enid had worsened overnight, her cold was much worse and it had gone to her chest. By the end of the week, despite Anna visiting each day, bringing every type of remedy she could lay her hands on, Enid didn't improve. Next she developed a fever and was definitely wheezing, so when she complained of a pain in her chest the doctor was called and she was diagnosed with a bad case of bronchitis. Anna, not relishing the thought of sleeping on the sofa persuaded Enid to stay with her and suspected that the ease with which her mum agreed indicated just how ill she actually felt. So, for the next ten days (and with the patience of a saint) Anna cared for Enid, bringing, fetching and carrying whatever her poorly mother needed.

One afternoon during Enid's stay, Anna crept into the spare room and sat quietly by her sleeping mother's bed. Her fever had reached its peak and abated but Enid was still tired from the exertion of coughing and looked terribly frail, even for a woman of her proportions. The peaceful Enid she gazed upon reminded Anna of a child and despite her tiredness was glad that she'd been given this opportunity to look after her cranky old mum. Listening to Enid's raspy breaths and the ticking of the bedside clock lulled Anna and in the peace of the bedroom, memories that were stored away came flooding back from her childhood.

It occurred to Anna as she watched her dozing mum, that Enid really must have worked hard to look after her and Philip as well as she did. Following Mrs Mason's death, Enid became invaluable and was relied upon even more by the doctor and his two sons, but it was never at the expense of her own children who always came first, never shirking her responsibilities at home. They came down to breakfast each morning to find the table set with cereals and toast, then Enid would go off to Doctor Mason's. Anna and Philip always left for school with a clean uniform and a freshly made packed lunch and in the evening they would eat their dinner together around the kitchen table, the three of them, her family.

After her husband died, Enid had to lead the way, pick herself up and carry on, reinventing her role when single parent families were in the minority, not like today where it was the accepted norm at every level of society. Reaching out her hand, Anna slid it inside the liver-spotted, wrinkled palm of Enid, smiling at her mother's red, painted nails, feeling the beginnings of a lump in her throat as she stared at the two rings on her finger, engagement and wedding. Enid had never taken them off. Holding on gently and fighting the desire to squeeze really hard in a symbolic thank you, Anna tried to remember the last time she'd held her mother's hand. It felt nice, and she vowed to make contact more often, relish the feel of Enid's soft skin. Anna remained there, reminiscing and being thankful until Enid began to stir, so she leant forward and stroked her mum's head with her free hand, comforting her until she woke up properly. Eventually Enid opened her bleary eyes and focused on her daughter, smiling and yawning before she spoke.

'Hello, love. Oooh, I do feel much better after that sleep, what time is it, I'd love a cuppa?'

Anna smiled right back and leaning over, she kissed her lovely old mum on the forehead and smiled before answering. 'Coming right up, Mum.'

Later, sitting there drinking her tea as Enid nibbled contentedly on some toast, Anna noticed her mother was indeed looking a bit better. Their chatter soon turned from the weather to the rest of the family.

'Our Philip seems a lot happier these days since he got together with Jeannie. I always knew they'd end up with each other, I just don't know why it took them so long, but it was a happy accident waiting to happen.' Enid reckoned she was psychic and wasn't afraid of telling anyone about her special powers.

'Well, *I* certainly didn't see it coming, Mum. After chasing after him for years I thought that ship sailed a long time ago so I'm obviously not as switched on as you.' Anna was teasing but Enid took it as a compliment.

'Well, I never could understand what he saw in Gail, she was wrong from the start but he was adamant that he'd found the one. Bloody fool! And if you ask me, I reckon she bats for the other team!' Enid raised her eyebrows and gave Anna a knowing nod of the head, making her daughter almost choke on her tea.

'Mother! You can't go saying things like that, believe me, I know all about jumping to conclusions. Anyway, what on earth makes you think that she likes women? She's got two kids for goodness sake and don't go repeating your crazy assumptions in front of them, because if it gets back to Gail she'll go mad and I reckon you'll end up with a black eye. I've always found her a bit scary.' Anna thought it best to nip this unfounded suspicion in the bud straight away.

Dramatically tapping the side of her nose and winking, Enid replied in a knowing voice. 'Just you mark my words, Anna, I have a way of knowing these things and anyway, don't be so naive, it takes all sorts to make the world!' Then without divulging her source, continued to eat her toast.

Chuckling, Anna ignored her, she was not going to encourage this little fantasy and hopefully Mystic Meg would forget all about it, otherwise she'd go blurting it out in company like she always did and then there'd be murders. Although, come to think of it, as far as anyone knew, Gail hadn't replaced Phil and she'd read about women leaving their husbands for another woman so perhaps Enid was on the right track. Her mother's voice soon cut into her silent musings and halted her vivid imagination.

'Anyway, Anna, what about you, how are you coping? Me and Gladys agree that you've done very well up to now, apart from your little blip, but we think it's high time you got out there and started dating, got back in the saddle if you know what I mean. You could join one of those agencies. I'm sure there must be someone who will fancy you.' Enid gave Anna a cheeky wink before looking her daughter up and down, as if to check her suitability.

'Mother, let's get this straight right from the start. I do not want to start dating and I certainly won't be joining any agency or getting into any kind of saddle! Do not even think about doing something stupid like signing me up in secret, either. I know what you and Gladys are like once you get an idea. And for your information, I'm coping very well, thank you, no more blips.'

Enid, however, didn't look convinced. 'Oh alright, spoilsport. But maybe you can get cracking after Christmas, don't drag your feet though, you're no spring chicken!' Enid ignored her daughter's horrified expression and continued.

'Anna, don't look so shocked and just listen to me for once, take some advice from your old mum and don't leave it too late like I did. After your dad died I threw myself into looking after you and your brother because it took my mind off things, then there was Doctor Mason, but keeping busy was really my way of avoiding reality. I remember I was very conscious of the fact that I was a widow. I suppose in those days you had to act in a certain way but nobody told me how long I should be in mourning or the respectable length of time to stay single. I was the odd one out at parents' evenings and sports days; nobody invites a lone woman to parties or for dinner because you make an uneven number, or they likely think you're going to pinch their husband. The years flew by then before I knew it you and Philip had left home and I was on my own. By then it felt like it was too late to meet someone new and I think I'd lost my confidence as well. So when you're ready, just go for it. Don't give what other people think a second thought. I want you to be happy, Anna, so please don't be lonely, that's all I'm asking.' For once Enid's tone was softer, and she sounded a little bit sad.

Anna's eyes were brimming with tears. Her poor mum had felt left out, lonely and unsure, and nobody knew. It also occurred to her how selfish children could be, however unwittingly.

'Mum, I'm so sorry, I never realised. Phil and I just took it for granted you were there and that you were happy. I feel awful now. But I know what you mean about being self-conscious and I do think people will judge me, no matter how long I leave it. They'll think I'm being disrespectful and God knows how the children would take to me meeting another man, they'd hate it. I know they would.'

On hearing this Enid huffed and folded her arms.

'Well, I'm telling you, Anna, just sod what anybody else thinks, you deserve to be happy, we all do. So you get on with your life the way you want to and if anyone dares to comment they'll have me to deal with, you mark my words, and that includes the children. You've been a bloody good mum to all three of them and while they're off living their lives you should be having fun too, with whoever you want.' Two little red spots of anger had appeared on Enid's cheeks as she pointed her finger in defiance.

Anna leaned over and hugged her tightly. 'Thanks for sharing that, Mum, and I promise I'll do as I'm told.'

The topic closed, Enid said she was going to read the paper for a while and see if anyone she knew had died lately so Anna went downstairs to make their dinner. Over the past few days she'd been glad of the company; it was nice to feel useful and she had gained a totally different perspective of Enid and her life. Anna had always loved her mum despite the fact she sometimes gave her a hard time but now, felt she understood her better and appreciated her even more.

Taking her tea up on a tray, Enid's all-time favourite of grilled bacon and tinned tomatoes, Anna sat at the side of the bed while they watched *Coronation Street* together. Enid had no idea but it was Anna's private tribute to the good old days and an unspoken thank you to her wonderful, funny old mum.

CHAPTER 19

During her stint as Florence Nightingale, Anna had kept in touch with Daniel by phone and email. He would often send her a text during the day and always a goodnight missive which she thought was sweet, knowing he was thinking about her. He'd been travelling extensively and kept her entertained with his stories of hideous hotel food and getting lost in the misty Highlands of Scotland. Rosie rang, thanking her for the food parcel and the book. Michel was now nicknamed Doctor Rousseau as there was absolutely nothing he didn't know about babies and was becoming a bit of a know-all after reading it from start to finish.

Jeannie called in to keep Enid company but got her ear chewed off for bringing red, not green grapes, and to add insult to injury they had pips in which played havoc with her dentures! Soldiering on, Jeannie recounted the weekend with Summer and Ross who had stayed over for the first time and had great fun camping on the lounge floor. Jeannie had panicked because she lacked a spare bedroom so Anna suggested they bought blow-up beds, torches and cartoon character sleeping bags. Jeannie left them out a midnight feast so in the end, they were happy as Larry, making patterns on the ceiling with their torches.

Enid casually asked about Gail and wanted to know if the children had mentioned anyone new in their mother's life only to be silenced by Anna. Jeannie would just love hearing Gypsy Rose Lee's prediction.

Sam was busy and enjoying work and Joe faithfully continued his email correspondence. The fridge was almost covered now with photos from his trip, however, apart from the odd text from Melanie, Anna hadn't heard much from her daughter and suspected pongy Paloma had a lot to do with it. With this in mind she thought it was time for a word in Mel's ear and hoping to avoid confrontation decided an email was the way to go. Taking the bull by the horns, Anna sat down to type.

Hi Mel, remember me, your mum? I've been missing our chats but don't want to interrupt you if you are studying or with friends so thought I'd drop you a line instead. Gran's on the mend now but is going to stay for another week just until she gets her strength back. Hopefully next time you get home you can find some time to fit in a visit – she was very disappointed when you were here with Paloma and didn't call in to see her.

This brings me nicely on to the subject of your friend who wasn't quite what I'd expected. As you know I have always made everyone welcome here and I like getting to know the people you and your brothers socialise with, however, I was a little surprised by Paloma. I appreciate you are going to meet all sorts at university and are old enough to form your own opinions, but she doesn't seem like your type at all and to be honest, Mel, I thought she was very rude and bad-mannered when she stayed here. Did you see the state of the spare room when she left it? The curtains were still drawn and she had made no attempt to make her bed or tidy up. It was like a pigsty with empty carrier bags, clothes tags and half-eaten food cartons strewn everywhere.

I know she's a vegetarian but had you thought to let me know in advance I would have happily catered for her but instead, it looked like she'd had some kind of bulimic midnight veggie feast up there. And I am sorry to have to mention it but she is extremely lacking in the personal hygiene department, does it not bother you? I know it's very cool to buy second-hand clothes when you are a student but they do need to be washed now and then.

Finally, she didn't even have the manners to thank me for letting her stay, she may talk posh but Mummy and Daddy definitely wasted their money on that private school. I would be mortified if you behaved like that in someone's home. Anyway, take a hint from me and don't let her bad habits rub off on you. She may think it's hip to look like the great unwashed but it's not exactly endearing and if you are hoping to attract the opposite sex on a night out, no one is going to want to get stuck with your smelly mate. Harsh, but true! Anyway, I hope you're not offended because we have always been able to talk honestly with each other and I'd rather speak up than regret not warning you.

So – what would you like for your birthday? I was hoping that if you hadn't anything planned maybe you could come home the weekend before and I can take you clothes shopping, then in the evening you, me, Jeannie and Gran could go out (birthday girl's choice) and celebrate.

I know it's not exactly rock and roll but you can have a wild student celebration on your actual birthday, even though Wednesday is a rubbish day for partying. Let me know if you can come back, obviously Paloma is welcome if she can manage to be polite but she will have to sleep on the sofa if Gran is still here, I'm not having her contaminate the boys' rooms. Have a think about it and get back to me, oh, and a nice email telling me how you are getting on with your studies (that's what you're there for, remember) would be great. I need some ammunition for when I'm in brag mode at the supermarket.

Love you lots. Mum x.

Anna pressed send, slightly concerned that Melanie might be offended at the criticism of her friend but it needed saying, she wouldn't put up with rude people in her house and neither did she want Melanie being badly influenced. She wasn't kidding either when she said Paloma couldn't sleep in the boys' bedrooms, not only was she a walking health hazard, those rooms were sacred and not to be touched or invaded until her sons came home!

After cooking dinner for Enid, Anna checked her emails and found one from Daniel telling her he had arranged for Josh to do some voluntary work at a home for the elderly. He knew the owner well after installing their electrical system and as a favour she was going to show Josh the ropes. If he enjoyed it there was a good chance that they would take him on and arrange the training he required. Apparently Josh was raring to go; sitting at home all day, watching telly and getting nagged at by Daniel was finally wearing thin.

Anna was pleased that at last Josh had some direction and prayed it would be the career for him, while at the same time trying hard to ignore the twinge of irrational jealousy she felt at the thought of Daniel being friendly with the owner of the care home. Shaking the thought from her head she concentrated on her mail. The next one was from Mel which she opened cautiously, expecting an ear bashing.

> Hi Mum, sorry I've not been in touch but I had quite a few essays to finish. We are focusing on German economic and social history at the moment, it's a bit dull so I won't bore you with it cos believe me – I'd have you snoring in seconds.
>
> I know that Paloma is quite different to all my other friends, which I think is due to her family and upbringing, her parents are very bohemian so she finds it suffocating if she can't do her own thing. I'm really sorry about the mess she left in the bedroom though, she is a bit of a scruff and you would pass out if you saw

her room here in the halls. None of us will go inside and I think she may get fined when we move out – pest control will <u>deffo</u> be called in – it's gross!!!!!! And I'm sure she doesn't mean to be rude but isn't used to boundaries or rules, which I suppose makes her a bit of a rebel.

As for the food thing, I agree, it is a bit tedious. Now she reckons she's got a wheat allergy so there's hardly anything left in the food chain she can actually eat and it does get on my nerves when we want to eat out or get a takeaway.

I will come home next weekend and YES PLEASE to all your ideas. I can spend lots of time with Gran if she's still there, if not I will go round on Sunday and watch a musical or something with her. I don't think Gran and Paloma would have hit it off (do you?) so it was better I didn't visit last time.

Give her a hug from me and tell her I will see her Friday night. I hope you are looking after yourself too and not being Gran's slave. See you soon, Mum. Love you a million zillion xxxxxxxx

PS Forgot to say, Paloma won't be coming as she's visiting her brother Mungo, he's at Cambridge, so you won't have to cover the settee in plastic sheets AND you've got me all to yourself – you lucky thing!

Anna laughed when she read Melanie's email, as usual her daughter let the criticism wash over her like rain and came out the other side oblivious and happy. At least Mel realised that her friend did have some faults even though to her they seemed negligible. And who calls their child Mungo, for pity's sake? She was sure that there was a cartoon dog or a pop group called that in the seventies and as for having bohemian parents, in her book, it was just another way of saying 'we can't be bothered'. Relieved that pongy pants was off to Cambridge to hooray it up with her brother, Anna went upstairs to tell Enid they were expecting a visitor and make some plans for the weekend.

***

November was turning out to be wet and cold and the rain-filled sky seemed to be constantly grey and gloomy. Melanie's birthday weekend, however, was a great success and cheered Anna up no end. Bringing with her some much-needed youthful energy and her own brand of sunshine, she encouraged Enid to venture downstairs for dinner and the three of them sat in the lounge watching the soaps and eating their dinner from trays. Melanie insisted on clearing up and made endless cups of tea for everyone – she even put her own washing in the machine!

After a tiring but fun time shopping with her daughter, teasing each other about their respective fashion sense, catching up properly and gossiping over lunch, everything in Anna's world seemed well. Until, that is, she accidentally overheard a conversation between Melanie and Paloma as she was putting the washing in the airing cupboard; Mel was in her room talking in a semi-hushed tone about Christmas.

'No, Paloma. I haven't mentioned it to her. I just can't leave my mum at Christmas. I told you, both my brothers will be away and if I'm not here there's only my gran and she'll be missing Dad so the last thing I want to do is upset her even more. I should be here looking after her not sunning myself in Tenerife. It's really, really nice of you to ask but the answer will still have to be no.' Melanie was quiet, obviously listening to whatever Paloma was saying, then she continued.

'Yes, I know she would want me to have fun, she's very understanding like that but *I* wouldn't be able to enjoy myself knowing she's here on her own. Maybe I could come with you in the summer or something?'

Anna's eavesdropping was irritatingly interrupted by Enid complaining loudly that the remote for the telly needed new batteries.

'*No flaming wonder,*' thought Anna, '*the bloody thing's never off.*' After sorting out Enid's lack of tele-visual control, Anna sat in the kitchen drinking coffee, pondering over what she had just heard. Picking up the phone she rang Jeannie. She'd an idea how she could solve this little crisis but the plan would need a help from her friend and, unfortunately, even her mother.

In Romano's later that evening, sipping Prosecco, waiting for their food to arrive while heady aromas wafted around them, stage one of Operation Canary-Island-Christmas commenced. On cue, Jeannie brought up the looming spectre of the festive season, commenting on the fact that the shelves in nearly all the stores were packed to the rafters with Christmas paraphernalia and the adverts on television were already grating, and it was only the second week in November. Enid agreed, saying that the Christmas spirit was ruined because it started far too early and it was all about flogging frozen party food and buying rubbish that nobody really needed.

Then Anna chipped in, saying that everyone felt under so much pressure to conform to the perfect traditional Christmas that it wasn't that enjoyable anymore. Instead, it had become a ridiculous spending spree and a bit of a trial, especially for the women who usually did everything, so maybe it was time people went back to basics or tried an alternative Christmas. Melanie listened attentively but said nothing. Ploughing onwards, Anna decided to go to stage two and asked Jeannie what she was doing for Christmas day this year, usually she spent it with them but now she was all loved-up, was she going to dump them?

'Actually, Phil has volunteered to work Christmas Day. He says it's only fair to offer so the lads with families can have a day off. They've done it for him in the past so he's returning the favour. He'll pop round and see the kids in the morning before his shift and I'm going to sit on my bum all day watching telly and scoffing chocolate till I'm sick. Unless I get a better offer, that is.' Jeannie turned to Anna, knowing exactly what she was going to say.

'That sounds just like my idea of an alternative Christmas Day, I'm actually a bit jealous.'

Then, as planned, Enid waded in.

'Well if you must know, I've always fancied going to Bournemouth with Gladys for an all-inclusive Christmas break. They sound marvellous. You get lovely meals for the whole time you're there, morning, noon and night and there's loads of activities during the day like bingo and quizzes then, in the evening, there's a Gala dinner and a knee's up. Gladys asks me to go every year but obviously, I sacrifice my own enjoyment to be there to help Anna and spend time with my family.' Anna raised her eyebrows at Enid who looked like she actually believed the last part. Talk about gilding the lily!

Anna managed to stifle a laugh and restrain herself from throttling her mother at the same time because in truth, Christmas Day for Enid actually meant turning up at eleven o'clock, bagging the armchair by the telly and then completely taking over the remote. The only time she moved her posterior was to park herself at the dining table and complain about the way everything on her plate was cooked, before moving back to the chair from where she'd consume a full box of After Eights and drink copious amounts of sherry. By the time Enid staggered to the car of the poor, unfortunate family member that had been bossed (or bribed) into taking her home, patience, along with the Christmas spirit, had well and truly left the building.

Moving swiftly on and ignoring Saint Enid, Anna turned to Mel and asked her what her alternative Christmas would be. Looking slightly sheepish, Mel took a sip of her wine and replied.

'Well actually, it's funny you should ask but Paloma has invited me to Tenerife for Christmas and New Year. I told her I couldn't go because I didn't want to abandon everyone, especially you, Mum.'

The arrival of their food forced an end to the conversation and the next half an hour was taken up with swapping bits of pizza and pasta and ordering more wine until, feeling that enough time had elapsed since their talk of alternative Christmases, Anna put stage three of her master plan into action.

'If you think about it, there's really no reason why we can't all have our alternative Christmas this year, if we want to. The boys are both away and without dwelling on it, the day will be pretty depressing and weird without our very own three wise men around the table, so I've got an idea.' Three faces stared expectantly at Anna; two of them knowing exactly what she was going to say next.

'What if Mum goes to Bournemouth with Gladys this year? She's had a rotten time with her bronchitis and the sea air might do her good, otherwise, I'm sure the dancing and bingo will sort her out. Mel can go to Tenerife with Paloma and if Jeannie doesn't mind an interloper, I'll stay there on Christmas Eve and then we can spend the next day watching telly and eating chocolates together. And I promise I won't be sick on your sofa. What do you think?' Anna waited for a response.

As rehearsed, Jeannie and Enid were in full agreement and very enthusiastic about Anna's idea, only Melanie was subdued, still mulling the whole thing over. Eventually she spoke.

'Mum, are you sure you wouldn't mind me going away, what will you do for the rest of Christmas, then there's New Year? I don't want you to be lonely or upset. You'll be missing Dad and the boys, maybe you should think it through a bit more and not make spur of the moment decisions.'

Mel was completely earnest in her summing up which made Anna even more determined.

Sighing and trying hard not to let her frustration show, especially as Melanie was unaware that all this had been carefully orchestrated, in her best, reassuring Mum voice, Anna attempted to talk Mel round.

'Listen, Mel. There really is no need to worry because I'll have a great time with Jeannie. We can hit the sales on Boxing Day and buy loads of tat. You have to remember that Christmas is actually just two days, everything goes back to normal until New Year's

Eve and I've never been one for wild celebrating. But if it makes you feel better I will either stay with Jeannie and Phil, Naomi or Gran. Whatever we do this year we will all feel sad at some point and be missing people, so why don't we just do our best to get through it and have some fun? Please go, Mel, it'll make me happy, honestly.' Anna held her breath and hoped she'd got through to her daughter.

Melanie looked around the table at the three expectant faces and gave in, a wide grin spreading across her face. 'Okay then, you win. As long as you all promise to have a good time too. And Jeannie, I'm trusting you to look after her, but you have to swear to ring me if Mum gets upset and I'll come home.' After they both nodded and silently crossed their hearts, Melanie finally appeared to be convinced.

'Can I go outside now and ring Paloma, she'll be so pleased when I tell her?' After they watched a very excited Mel shoot across the restaurant and out the door, eager to phone her friend with the news, Anna turned to her three co-conspirators and raised her glass.

'To a job well done, ladies. Thank you for all your help. I think we got away with that one quite nicely, don't you? Cheers.'

Anna smiled and silently congratulated herself. Covering all her bases she'd contacted the boys and explained her idea, knowing that Mel would want their approval too. Both of them backed Anna up, understanding that she would be happier this way. If she was honest, Anna wished that Melanie was going away with anyone but Paloma, however, was willing to give her one more chance and her daughter a bit of freedom at the same time. She only hoped it was the right decision – for all of them.

CHAPTER 20

December arrived bringing with it gale-force winds and even more rain. Enid was back at home and improving by the day. Her return was warmly and gratefully welcomed by Gladys, who was in need of some TLC herself, following the upsetting if not slightly traumatic end to her romance with Walter from ballroom dancing. It turned out (much to Enid's delight) that Walter was in fact a bit of an octogenarian gigolo. She'd always insisted that he fancied her first but owing to her recently found psychic powers, Enid had him down as a womaniser from the start, hence giving him a wide berth and granting Gladys a look-in.

Gladys was of course devastated and vowed never to return to ballroom dancing again. The shame was all too much, but grateful for Enid's support she offered her Walter's place on the Bournemouth Christmas break, her treat. It transpired that the gigolo was a bit of a freeloader as well as a three-timer. Enid was extremely chuffed because not only had she got Gladys all to herself again, there was no doubt whatsoever about her psychic powers – eat your heart out Mystic Meg.

In the first week of December, Mary called for coffee and over a box of cream cakes they caught up on all their news. Anna spent most of the time reassuring her visitor that she was coping whilst diverting any well-meant reminiscing over Matthew, and was therefore relieved when the subject of directors' Christmas gifts arose. Mary was clearly treading on eggshells and desperate not to distress Anna in any way, enquiring whether this year she would like to give it a miss and avoid going to Harrison's to deliver their presents.

The thought had already crossed Anna's mind but she had mulled it over and eventually put it into perspective. She was now the majority shareholder in the company and therefore had a responsibility to look after their workforce and despite Matthew's failings as a husband, he had always been a good boss so would carry on the tradition in his memory. Kindly brushing Mary's concerns aside, Anna insisted on business as usual and they arranged their annual shopping trip and mammoth wrapping session for the following week.

Anna was also pleased to learn that the Ice Queen had relented and sanctioned the use of company funds this year. She was quite pleased at the change of heart and felt that maybe Caitlin had been slightly misjudged; after all, there was nothing wrong with ambition and at the end of the day it *was* her job to look after the finances of Harrison Haulage.

Sam and Mel came home the weekend before Christmas and even though their number was depleted, they still wanted to swap presents and sit around the table together for a celebratory meal. All the usual suspects were invited for Sunday lunch, plus Gladys, the broken-hearted, man-hungry tart.

There wasn't going to be a tree or decorations this year after Anna made it clear that there was no way she was bringing it all down from the loft for just one person. This year the tree could have an alternative Christmas too, and stay exactly where it was.

Anna pushed the boat out, preparing a feast with two starters: a seafood platter in homage to her French holiday, which naturally included oysters, accompanied by freshly made soup for the fussy members of the family (Enid). This was followed by roast beef and Yorkshire pudding and a trio of desserts. She had risen early and flogged herself to death making mini lemon cheesecake, strawberry Pavlova and mousse au chocolat, but it had all been worth it. To hear the children laughing and see their smiling faces lifted Anna's heart, blessed by having her family and closest friends around her.

After cheese and biscuits, the correct British way, the racy old age pensioners were taken home before they got too cosy and drank the house dry. Dennis and Mary were starting to nod off on the settee so decided to call it a day, soon followed by Phil and Jeannie who drove off into the moonlight. Melanie went upstairs to pack her case after raiding her wardrobe of summer clothes, a surreal experience amidst a wintry Portsmouth.

Left alone in the kitchen with her cup of tea, Anna waited for Sam. He had gone outside with the rubbish and since everyone left he'd been lingering and at times was in a world of his own, a sure sign he had something to tell her and was plucking up the courage to spill the beans. Deciding to put him out of his misery Anna beckoned him to the table as soon as he came inside, pointing to a chair and the waiting cup of tea.

'Okay, Sam, what is it? I can tell you've got something on your mind so let's have it, have you lost your PE kit again or are you in love with someone totally unsuitable who I'm going to absolutely hate?' Anna tried to make light of the situation despite having a sense of foreboding.

Praying that in this instance her intuition was wrong, Anna waited for Sam to speak. When he reached out for both of her hands and folded them inside his own she knew instantly that whatever she was going to hear wouldn't be good news.

'Mum, I've been waiting for the right time all weekend to have a word. I was going to tell you on Saturday morning when I got here, so you could get used to the idea and talk it through. When I realised everyone was coming over today I didn't want to spoil your fun or have family time overshadowed by me, by what I wanted to say.'

Sam was definitely preparing her for bad news. Anna felt sick as her mind raced. They say your life flashes in front of your eyes before you die so perhaps this was a living equivalent, a mother's panic for her child.

Then it dawned on her, the army, causing a lump of lead to hurtle to the pit of her stomach while an ice-cold hand grasped tightly on to her heart, spreading ripples of fear through her body. Anna squeezed his hand so tightly she thought her knuckles would pop.

'Oh my God, Sam! You're going to Afghanistan, aren't you?' And as Anna looked into Sam's eyes, knew she was right.

Holding back a swell of tears she kept calm and took concealed, deep breaths. Reasoning with herself that this was as hard for her son as it was for her, knowing he'd been working up to it all day. She didn't want to make it worse by getting upset; so she listened as Sam explained.

Even though his unit was due to tour Afghanistan the following year, circumstances had changed and owing to the fact that there had been an increase in IED incidents, more armoured vehicles were needed. They had asked for volunteers to go over and since he was now fully qualified, he wanted to serve his country and see some action. Consequently, Sam had put his hand up. He wasn't going to lie to her and say he had been chosen, he wanted to go. This was the reason he'd joined up and what he promised to do the day he was sworn in. He had trained for this, it was his job.

Anna was horrified and in shock. She had somehow convinced herself that by the time Sam was due to be deployed it would all be over and British troops would be brought home. Swallowing down the sob that had lodged in her throat, Anna managed to ask him when he would be going.

'Sometime in February, we haven't been told exactly when yet. There's some extra training to do and other bits and bobs but I promise I will come home every weekend before I go. I'll be back by the summer and get a long leave afterwards so I'll be able to spend loads of time with you. I'm sorry to drop this on you before Christmas, Mum, but I had to tell you sooner or later.'

Anna had pulled herself together by the time Sam finished talking, her tea had gone cold, but she took a sip anyway, and then did her utmost best to reassure her nervous, worried-looking son.

'It is a shock, Sam, and I think you know I'm going to be upset when you go and then worry myself sick for months. I won't lie to you either and tell you that I'm pleased about it, what mother would be? But this is your dream, your life, and something you've wanted since you were little. I'm glad you told me now, it'll give me time to get used to the idea and psyche myself up. And I'm not annoyed with you for volunteering, I would expect it from you, it's who you are. There was never any point in asking you to make promises you'd find hard to keep, so as long as you are sensible and do your best to stay safe AND come home in one piece, that'll do for me.' Anna's voice was on the verge of cracking and she could speak no more.

Sam's eyes were full of tears and as he stood up and leant over the table to hug his mother, Anna felt them fall silently onto her neck.

That night in bed, Anna held back her own stormy tide of tears that were waiting just off shore. '*Don't you dare fall apart now,*' she warned herself, '*you'll have red, puffy eyes in the morning and he'll know you've been crying. Just send him off for Christmas without a fuss. You'll be fine, Anna, you can get through this, you know you can.*'

Melanie and Sam left early the next morning, one had late lectures, the other was on a late shift but before they parted company they had a special call to make, both wanted to visit Matthew's grave and leave some flowers. Anna made an excuse, saying she would pop over at the end of the week when in fact she had no intention of going there at all. She had never visited the cemetery since the funeral, not even when the undertakers rang to say the stone had been laid. She had nothing nice to say to Matthew. He couldn't answer her questions so there was no point asking, and she was still too angry so it was best left alone.

A surge of sadness washed over Anna as she waved them away. Where Mel was concerned, letting her go to Tenerife was all her own doing so she would just have to deal with it, while unfortunately, Sam's situation was beyond her control.

Forcing herself to be busy, Anna tidied the house and stripped the beds then replied to her emails. Joe's was short and sweet, he was looking forward to a party on the beach on Christmas Day and promised to ring her at Jeannie's when the time zones allowed.

Rosie said it was very cold in France but the countryside looked just as lovely in the frost as it did in summer, before explaining their Christmas plans. As Michel loved being the grand host and cooking was second nature, there would be a house full on Monday for Christmas lunch but they were spending Christmas Eve at his parents for the big event, réveillon. Rosie said that things were a lot more relaxed and traditional there with less of the intense media hype she had experienced in England. The focus was more about getting together, eating and being merry, which she admitted the French were experts in.

Signing off, Anna felt slightly envious of Rosie, imagining what the hotel would be like in winter and covered in snow. She'd saved Daniel's email until last. It was sent from Manchester where he was working and although he'd had a productive trip, was looking forward to his trip to France for Christmas with his daughter. Then Anna's heart skipped a beat when she read that he had something important to ask her.

Anna, it seems so long since summer and although I have a few photos to remind me of our time together and keeping in touch like this is great, it would be nice to actually see you again in real life and refresh my hazy memory. Josh and I will be in Portsmouth on the 23rd, we are taking the overnight ferry to St Malo, as usual. We have to check in around 7pm but were wondering if you fancy meeting up with us beforehand? Maybe you can suggest a pub or restaurant near to the ferry port. We both miss you, and Josh is dying to tell you all his news, so will you make an old man and his annoying brother happy this Christmas and agree? If you don't feel comfortable about my idea I totally understand. No pressure, honest. Anyway, have a think about it and let me know, Daniel x

Anna felt slightly giddy, apprehensive, and elated all at once. Her cheeks went hot as they always did when the nerves kicked in. She would love to see Daniel and Josh again and there was absolutely no harm in meeting friends in a pub for a drink and a chat, nothing could be read into that, could it? On the other hand, Daniel might see it as encouragement, the green light to take things further.

'*Stop being big-headed, Anna, how do you know he even fancies you? He might just want to be friends after all. But what would everyone say if they knew?*' Her mind whirred and her heart kept time, beating fast as her eyes read and reread the message, looking for clues. She made a cup of tea and calmed herself down and by the time she sat back down at the computer Anna's mind was nowhere near to sorting itself out.

She didn't need to look for clues as it was plain as the nose on her face that Daniel was attracted to her but why on earth would someone like him waste time wanting friendship? He was a hot-blooded male and could easily attract the opposite sex. At the same time, he'd been a total gentleman and she respected him for that and she was sick to the back teeth of worrying about everything and everyone. She loved her holiday in France and wanted to hold on to the connections she'd made and the happy times with Rosie, Josh and Daniel. It crossed her mind to ask Jeannie what to do but it was about time she started making her own decisions regarding her own life so remembering her mother's recent advice, Anna replied.

> Hi Daniel, that sounds like a great idea, it would be awful to know that you were both here in Portsmouth and not meet up with you. I will think of somewhere suitable and get back to you during the week. Can't wait to see you and catch up. Take care, Anna xx

She hit send without a second thought and felt strangely empowered. Her conscience was clear and if anyone disapproved, she'd set Enid on them. Not waiting for a reply she picked up her bag and with a spring in her step, Anna kept her rendezvous with Mary, then after making a list and checking it twice, they set off to buy Christmas gifts for their workforce.

Santa's helpers arrived at Harrison Haulage on the Friday, just as everyone was finishing for Christmas. Things were winding down in the offices and there was a festive, relaxed atmosphere as Anna and Mary gave out gifts and wished everyone a Merry Christmas. Anna was enjoying herself and felt very at home and welcome, even though her stomach lurched when she saw Matthew's office which was shrouded in darkness. The blinds were semi-closed and the door was locked. She noticed that Samantha had moved her desk from where it had once been, right opposite Matthew's door in a small alcove, and now worked in the main office with the others, a large photocopier occupying her old space.

It was also Samantha's last day; her maternity leave began after Christmas. Anna had always got on extremely well with Matthew's PA and regarded her as a friend so went over to say a special goodbye, causing Samantha to blush crimson. Noticing immediately, Anna put her reaction down to shyness and not comfortable being the centre of attention. They chatted for a while about pregnancy woes and baby names then out of curiosity and concern, Anna asked Samantha why she had decided not to come back to work after the baby was born. Anna had been surprised when Dennis mentioned it, both presumed Samantha loved her job so reminded her she could easily go part-time after the baby arrived, adding they were all very sad to be losing her.

'I'm sorry, Anna, but my mind's made up. I do love it here, it's been a big part of my life but I think it's time for a change and anyway, Rob reckons we can manage for now. We've talked it through and I'd like to be a full-time mum.'

Anna got the feeling that Samantha was repeating a rehearsed speech that lacked conviction, but let it go. 'As long as you've thought it through, Samantha, but if you change your mind please let us know. I'm sure Dennis will pull a few strings and sort it out.' Anna gave Samantha a long hug and wished her well, making her promise she would let her know as soon as the baby arrived.

As she walked away, Anna noticed a box of Samantha's belongings on top of the desk, packed up, ready to take home.

Amongst the goodbye cards and baby gifts, was an old photo of all the office girls along with the bronze nameplate that used to be attached to the front of her desk. It read, 'Samantha Kaye. PA to Matthew Harrison'. The simple words made Anna feel so sad.

Things were always changing, everyone seemed to be leaving and nothing was the same anymore. This time last year she hadn't a care in the world and now look at her life, it had been completely turned upside down. In years gone by, on days just like these, never in her wildest dreams would Anna have imagined this place without Matthew and it tore at her heart, the emptiness he'd left in his wake.

All in all, and despite her sadness, the visit to Harrison's went well. Caitlin made a brief appearance and accepted her gifts gracefully, making polite but boring conversation with Mary and Anna. For want of anything else to talk about they asked how her wedding plans were coming along. Caitlin informed them that she'd booked the registry office and honeymoon in Mauritius, the delay was due to an important business trip in September but after juggling the dates she had somehow fitted it in. As she scurried back inside to answer her phone, Anna and Mary were left unsure whether she meant it was the wedding or the business trip she had managed to fit in, giggling that the others were right and Caitlin really was the Ice Queen.

Mary couldn't fail to notice that Anna's eyes were constantly being drawn in one direction so on the way out, mentioned that Dennis had insisted Matthew's office was locked and left untouched, but if she wanted to go inside they could get the key. When Anna silently shook her head, rejecting the offer, Mary smiled sadly, assuring her that it would remain closed until Joe's return when they planned to give it a lick of paint and put a shiny new nameplate on the door. Mary assured her that soon it'd be bright and cheery and another Harrison would be sitting behind that desk.

Mary meant well but she didn't understand. Sometimes, Anna thought her heart would really break in two, facing up to the fact that she would never pop her head round the office door and see Matthew's face smiling back at her. She remembered how during the school holidays she'd get the bus into town with the kids and then meet Matthew for tea. They'd get there early and while Mel sat in his chair, spinning around and messing with the phone or stapling all his files together, Matthew would take the boys into the yard and drive them around in one of the trucks or on the stacker. In Sam's case, he'd get every single tool out of the mechanics drawers and pretend to fix the engine. Then they would all go for something to eat before driving home with Matthew – a big treat that they all loved. There were so many memories here, so much love.

Walking down the stairs towards the foyer Anna spoke to him in her head, wondering if his spirit rested within the walls and he would finally give her some answers. *'How could you have ruined it all, Matthew, why would you waste all that?'* Nobody replied.

So they could unload their gifts easily, Mary had parked at the front of the building rather than in the car park at the back. Now, as she fastened her seatbelt, Anna looked up at Matthew's office, hoping to see his face at the window, wishing with all her heart that he would smile and wave, that it had been a terrible nightmare. But this was no dream; he wasn't there. Only real life remained, harsh and cruel, along with bittersweet memories, half-closed blinds and cold, grey glass.

CHAPTER 21

Hoping to shake away her black mood, Anna rang Jeannie as soon as she got in and after a few minutes of bringing each other up to speed on the day's events, listening to cabin crew gossip and making final, feast related plans for Christmas, she felt much better. She decided she would have a nice hot bath then raid her wardrobe for something appropriate to wear when she met Daniel the next day. She still hadn't mentioned him to Jeannie yet. Apart from a casual reference after her holiday, she was waiting for the right time to tell her that they'd kept in touch and how she felt about him. First though, she had to work that out for herself. Anna felt slightly deceitful about not telling her best friend everything but didn't want any pressure and at least this time, she was keeping a happy secret from Jeannie.

Her mind then focused on what to wear. It had to be warm but not too boring or sensible, a bit dressy without looking like she'd tried too hard, definitely not revealing but certainly flattering. Most of all she admitted she wanted to look so good that he wouldn't be able to get her out of his mind all over Christmas.

'Anna Harrison,' she said out loud, 'what are you thinking of? Behave yourself!'

When Saturday arrived, she purposely kept herself busy and tried to ignore the butterflies that were causing havoc in her stomach. She couldn't wait to see Daniel and was counting down the hours; in a childish attempt to encourage time to go faster she forced herself not to look at the clock.

After collecting a very excitable Enid and Gladys at 10am she swiftly deposited them at the coach station to join a horde of eager revellers. Anna's Christmas present to her mother was a complete wardrobe of holiday outfits and evening wear, plus a new suitcase to store them all in. Admittedly, the shopping spree was one of the single most trying experiences of her life but with the help of a patient store assistant who expertly steered her mother away from stretchy, sparkly disco dresses, they had managed to make Enid look quite sophisticated.

Next stop was Aunty Elsie's. No matter how many times Anna would make this journey in the future she knew that it would always, always remind her of the day she stumbled on Matthew's affair during her fateful errand to Connalston Hall. Banishing the memory from her mind, Anna spent the rest of the morning with her Aunt, helping her wind wool and tidy her knitting box, just like she did when she was little. Elsie was a brilliant knitter and crafter, and passed her knowledge to Anna and Naomi during the school holidays where they would spend hours crocheting or making macramé knick-knacks.

At lunchtime she nipped over to the florist to see Naomi. As anticipated, they were rushed off their feet so Anna made herself useful and volunteered to be the sandwich girl, heading off into the village with her list. Naomi had recently opened a craft shop so Anna decided to pop in and buy something for Jeannie. While browsing she noticed a handmade patchwork quilt just like the one on her bed at Rosie's and instantly her hankering for the little hotel returned. It also reminded her of the knitted blankets she had made for her babies when each came along. Feeling inspired, Anna decided to make one for Samantha's baby.

Driving back to Portsmouth later that day, Anna's head was swimming with thoughts. She smiled, imagining Enid arriving in Bournemouth and wished the entire hotel staff the best of British where her mother was concerned. Daniel popped into her head which she ignored, reminding herself to ring Mel before her flight, then Daniel's handsome face appeared, so she diverted her thoughts to Joe and wondered what he was up to, then she saw Daniel's blue eyes. He really was getting under her skin and despite her best efforts, couldn't ignore the way he made her feel.

As she motored along listening to Christmas songs on the radio, she couldn't help thinking that the words from the songs were trying to tell her something. According to Mud she'd be lonely without someone to hold and then Wham! reminded her that sometimes, people give their hearts away at Christmas and without warning, her mood began to change for the worse. Jangling nerves soon made their presence felt and before she knew it, self-doubt joined the party and to make matters worse, guilt came along for the ride.

By the time she got home Anna had decided to make up an illness related excuse and cancel her meeting with Daniel. She felt bad but couldn't stand being tormented by her conscience. Her husband hadn't been gone, what, six months? And here she was, fantasising about a date with someone she barely knew. It was 3pm when she let herself into the house which felt chilly and unwelcoming so she grumpily checked the boiler which had been playing up and now failed to come on.

Her mood spiralled further; she was on a real downer because the house felt cold and creepy which she could do without. Grabbing her phone book she rang the service company only to be told that it would be after Christmas before they could get anyone over there – typical! Resigned to wearing thermals for the duration, Anna tried Melanie, hoping to catch her before she left for the airport.

Hyper wasn't an adequate enough description of her daughter which made Anna feel totally vindicated in her decision to let Melanie go, after making promises to take care, keep in touch and apply lots of sun cream they reluctantly said their farewells. But just before she signed off, Melanie remembered something.

'Hey, Mum. I've been meaning to tell you about when we went to the cemetery to see Dad. There were some flowers on the grave already. I thought they were from you because it was a huge bouquet of red roses. Anyway, they were all dried up so I threw them in the bin but I read the card, it was in a plastic wallet and I could still see the writing, it just said, "Love always, K". Who do you think K is? I showed it to Sam and he had no idea so we thought maybe they'd blown there in the wind or got put in the wrong place... Mum, are you listening?'

Anna was listening all right, but was totally shell-shocked as a million venomous thoughts raced through her head. '*How dare that woman go there and taint his grave with her flowers, how dare she take the risk of being seen and flaunt her sordid little affair?* Anna was incensed. God help whoever she was because if she ever found her, the way she felt right now she would kill her with her own bare hands. Then she would dig a very deep hole, right next to Matthew, and chuck the cow in!!!

The pub was in Gunwharf Quays, just a short drive from the ferry terminal. From where Anna was sitting she had a fantastic view of the Spinnaker Tower as lights from the ships and apartments dotted all along the river glowed in the dark. Gazing through the window by her side, Anna imagined it must be lovely to live by the water, to catch the sea breeze and watch the boats going in and out all day. You could people watch from your bird's nest and never feel isolated because there was always something going on down below or out there on the waves.

The traditional pub was one of the oldest in Portsmouth and the festive decorations along with the log fire in the corner added to the cosy atmosphere. It was quite busy with last minute shoppers calling in for food and to rest aching feet. Anna hoped she looked relatively anonymous, pretending to read the paper and trying desperately to give the outwardly calm appearance of a woman who regularly met men in bars on her own.

The thought that had gone into tonight was bordering on ridiculous but had been necessary to provide Anna with enough confidence to go through with it. Melanie's revelation was the catalyst, leaving her feeling like she'd had her nose well and truly rubbed in it by the Kitten, who, having had the audacity to place flowers on her husband's grave, sent Anna into a rage worthy of a Tasmanian devil. Thank goodness her house was detached and the only person that heard her screams of frustration and some shocking swear words was Anna herself, otherwise she risked being sectioned, or arrested.

She'd somehow managed to feign ignorance in answer to her daughter's question, masking her shock and hurt. When Paloma urged Melanie to get off the phone because the taxi was there, Anna was for once glad to hear her grating voice which resulted in a premature end to the call. After that, any feelings of guilt flew right out of the window. She stormed into the en suite and with the aid of the kettle ran a shallow, lukewarm bath then stomped around her bedroom, flinging open her wardrobe doors and pulling out the outfit she'd chosen the night before. '*Sod it!*' She thought. '*I am so bloody tired of beating myself up about everything I say or do. I'm sick to death of overthinking what goes on in my head, not like that tart and my unfaithful, sex-mad, so-called husband.*'

They had arranged to meet at 5pm but Anna got there early on purpose as there was a huge cringe factor involved in the whole scenario. Her options were either to walk into a strange pub alone, looking nervous and stupid as she searched the room for his face or, sit there like Billy-no-mates and wait for Daniel to find her while she attempted to look cool and at ease. She went for option two, needing time to compose herself and had bagged them a nice seat into the bargain.

Placing her black military style jacket and soft scarf over the back of the chair, she checked she wasn't flashing her bra because the pale grey, metallic knitted jumper was v-neck, low and quite clingy, emphasising her body as did the charcoal fitted jeans. Her black suede ankle boots were quite high and another reason she didn't want to risk prancing across the pub and doing a comedy fall at Daniel's feet. Quite pleased with her image as she scrutinised every detail in the bedroom mirror, she'd left her hair down and wavy then given her eyes a slightly smoky, evening look, applying lip gloss and a touch of heady perfume just before she left the house.

Anna prayed she'd got it right and wasn't making a huge mistake; she was lost in thought whilst tracking the course of a ferry leaving the port when she heard a soft voice, whisper in her ear.

'Can this weary traveller buy a lovely lady a glass of red?'

Anna looked up quickly and he was there, his kind blue eyes smiling down at her. Getting up from her chair she flung her arms around his neck, hugging him tightly, surprising them both with her reaction, a natural response which completely broke the ice.

'Yes, please, and make it a large one.'

They both laughed and the nerves were gone, their eyes locking just for a second before he turned and headed towards the bar.

Anna watched him as he ordered the drinks, laughing and chatting with a stranger at the bar. She turned away quickly as he made his way back, her heart was pounding in her chest, and she couldn't wait for him to be beside her. Daniel removed his coat and placed it on the back of the chair opposite. The hammered copper table was small and round and even though he wasn't sitting next to her, he still felt very close. Anna took in everything about him, the soft crinkles around his eyes when he smiled, the faint scent of his aftershave, broad, muscular shoulders underneath his sweater and his strong hands that were just centimetres from hers, wrapped around their wine glasses. She swore she could feel static between them and it definitely wasn't the effects of her drink because she'd only had one sip.

Josh, it seemed, was shopping in some of the many shops housed by Gunwharf Quay, buying last minute presents and would be joining them later. Anna was looking forward to seeing him but admitted to herself she was glad to have some time alone with Daniel before Josh arrived. They chatted about his holiday plans – they were staying with Louise for Christmas and New Year as her mother was in the Canary Islands with her latest man. He would drive up to Rosie's on the 3rd and stay overnight as usual, adding that it wouldn't be the same without Anna there. He wanted to know if she had any plans, especially for going back to France next year.

She explained that once Sam had left for Afghanistan (just saying the word made her heart freeze) the house would be even emptier and Anna nearly added, so will my life, but knew it sounded melodramatic. Instead she told Daniel she intended to visit early in the spring. She thought it would be nice to experience a different season at the same time as bridging the awful gap her son was leaving. Daniel brightened on hearing this as he always went over at Easter so hoped they could meet up.

Anna assured him it was a great idea and had also noticed that their body language had altered and both were leaning a little more forward, perhaps it was so they could hear better because the pub was filling up and had become noisier. Anna hadn't been conscious of it at the time but now, as they spoke, their faces and bodies almost touched. The thought alone warmed her, or was it the log fire? Their drinks were almost empty and she was just about to offer to fetch some more when she realised that Daniel was staring downward, deep in thought, and what felt like a long silence followed.

Anna began to feel slightly uneasy when quite naturally, Daniel slid his arms forward and gently covered her hands with his, stroking gently with his thumb, sending a shot of pure electric through Anna's body. Daniel looked up, had he felt it too? Then he spoke.

'Anna, please don't think I'm poking my nose in but is everything okay with you at home? I know you told me that you'd been nervous at first on your own but you're over that now, well I hope you are. Only, on a couple of occasions when I've rang you late at night I sensed you were upset and trying to hide it and on the verge of telling me something, then changed your mind. If there's anything bothering you I'd like to help. I hope you know I think the world of you and if there's anything I can do, just say the word. Sometimes it helps to share, even with a stranger because they can have a different perspective on things. Or you can tell me to shut up and that I'm a complete idiot if I'm wrong, I won't be offended.'

Daniel didn't take his hand away and she was glad, it felt nice.

Anna looked into his waiting eyes, which were full of concern. She was touched and deep down quite impressed that he had picked up on her distress during a simple telephone conversation. Perhaps this was just the right time to tell him about Matthew's affair, at least then he'd understand her a bit better. He probably thought she was playing games or being a tease. When Anna opened her mouth, ready to spill her guts all over the shiny copper table, a familiar voice brought them both back to reality.

'Hey, there you are, found you at last. I've been looking everywhere. Happy Christmas, Anna!'

Laughing and slightly frustrated at the same time, she stood up and hugged Josh and despite him crashing an intimate moment, Anna couldn't resist his cheeky face, he always made her feel happy. Flopping down on the chair she'd saved for him and shoving his carrier bags under the table, Josh instantly made himself at home, talking away ten to the dozen, firing questions at Anna and telling Daniel to hurry up and get the drinks in.

Daniel sighed and looked resignedly at Anna and knowing the moment was lost, he went off to the bar. Josh, totally oblivious to the charged atmosphere when he arrived ploughed on and brought Anna up to speed with all his news, mainly about his job in the care home. He loved it and already had a few favourites amongst the residents and would be starting college in January. She was so pleased it had all turned out well for him because he was a lovely boy and deserved a fresh start. Daniel returned and as Anna accepted her drink, asked them why they always took the ferry rather than going by plane which was quicker.

Daniel explained that going by car allowed him to take much missed supplies over for Louise; it also meant he was independent when he arrived plus, he liked to collect wine and stocked up during his stay. Apart from that he really enjoyed his mini cruise. They always booked a cabin, which was extremely comfortable with bunk beds, an en suite bathroom and a television – there were even luxury cabins if the fancy took you. They would go for a relaxing meal as they sailed down the Solent, have a quick look round the shops and then get some sleep. There were nice bars on board and live entertainment but as he was getting on a bit, preferred an early night. In the morning, they would have breakfast on board and watch France appear on the horizon before setting off for the drive south.

Anna thought it all sounded lovely. When she had gone over to France in the past with the children they always took the cheapest and quickest ferry across, eager to get on with their holiday but she supposed that when there were two of you, or if you were single, there was no such rush and it was nice just to take your time. In a weird way, those sentiments made Anna consider her situation with Daniel and as she looked over to him, thought the same thing. '*There's no rush, Anna, he's lovely and single and kind, so just take your time.*'

The time flew and when Daniel checked his watch, he reluctantly announced that it was time they made a move. They had to check in and it was the last boat before Christmas, if they missed it there would be murder. Anna didn't want the night to end and two hours had gone so fast. How stupid she had been, wasting so much time worrying about what people thought, she should've used her brain efficiently and met earlier in the day. Now they were going, Anna felt sad and, oddly, as though she was being abandoned until an idea popped into her head.

'When you sail back to England why don't we meet up again? You said your boat gets in around six thirty in the evening so perhaps we could all have something to eat before you set off again for home.' Anna instantly felt silly and too eager, what if he declined?

She needn't have worried as Daniel agreed instantly, smiling broadly as they began to wrap up against the winter night and the harsh wind blowing in from the Solent. As they left the pub, Daniel had to nip to his car to collect something, telling Anna he would follow to where she was parked so Josh accompanied her across the dark car park and while they were waiting for Daniel he pulled a present from one of his bags.

'This is for you. I wanted to say thank you for being my mate on holiday and for all your advice. If it wasn't for you I'd still be acting like an idiot and wasting my life. I got the woman in the shop to wrap it up because I wouldn't have time and anyway, I'm rubbish at it. I hope you like it.' Josh looked very bashful and a bit nervous too.

Anna was truly touched and rather emotional; having boys of her own she knew that was quite a speech for Josh and the fact he'd bought her something made her day. In an effort to stop herself blubbing she grabbed him quickly and gave him a big bear hug.

'Thank you, Josh, you don't know how much your gift means to me and I'm so proud of you for turning things around. Have a lovely Christmas and I'll see you soon.' She kissed him on the cheek as she let go, making him blush.

Noticing Daniel was on his way back carrying a box, Josh made his getaway and said his goodbyes.

'Right, I'm getting in the car, its flipping freezing out here. Have a great Christmas, Anna, oh and by the way, thanks for cheering the old man up.' Giving her a cheeky wink Josh turned and ran into the darkness.

Anna couldn't help laughing; maybe Josh wasn't as daft as he made out after all. Daniel approached with what was obviously a case of wine which he popped into the boot of her car then turned, nerves making him talk quickly, or was it just the fact he had to rush?

'There's a bit of everything in there for you and Jeannie to sample over Christmas. You can decide what you like best then I can bring you some more, oh, and there's a little something in the box just for you, but save it for Christmas Day.' Daniel looked over to Josh who was flashing the headlights and pointing to his watch but he continued anyway, eager to make Anna understand how he felt.

'And would it be okay to ring you and say hi at some point? Just text me when it's convenient. I don't want to intrude but I'm going to miss you all over again now I've spent tonight with you. It seems a long time until January.' Daniel was stalling for time and reluctant to leave.

He was standing so close and Anna had an incredible urge to kiss him and feel his lips on hers, to hold him close and not let him go. Then Josh honked the car horn warning Daniel that they were cutting it fine, making them both jump.

Needless to say, Daniel was the braver of the two and reaching out he pulled Anna towards him before wrapping his arms around her, holding her tightly. Her cheek was against his and she relished the feel of his skin, breathing in his scent, trying to save it to memory as she slid her arms under his open jacket, sensing his firm body under her hands. It felt right being in his arms and Anna didn't want to let go as he whispered in her ear.

'Will you be alright, Anna? Promise you'll call me if you need me. I've been worried about you these past months and I wish you were coming to France because then I could take care of you. I'll be thinking of you every minute, I just want you to know that.' Daniel's voice was soft and sincere.

Anna squeezed him tightly, wordlessly trying to tell him how she felt. 'I'll be fine, Daniel, honestly. And you can ring me anytime… whenever you want to, and I will tell you what's bothering me, I promise. Now's not the time so I hope you've got the patience to wait?' Anna wished they'd had longer together, there was so much to say, she'd left it far too long and seeing him again had confirmed just how strong her feelings were.

'Anna, we've got all the time in the world, of course I'll wait, don't worry. Just keep in touch. I couldn't bear to lose you now.' With that he pulled away and kissed her on the cheek, lingering for a while.

Feeling his lips against her skin Anna fought hard the desire to return his kiss, properly, but Josh might see and she was overcome with shyness.

'Right, I'd better go, otherwise we'll end up swimming across. I'll text you when we've sailed. Just take care going home and let me know when you're in. See you soon.' Daniel held Anna's gaze as if giving her one last chance to say or do something.

Laughing at his bossiness, trying hard not to be hypnotised by the look he was giving her, Anna then remembered her own presents so grabbed a large gift bag from the boot and passed it to him, insisting that it was nothing much, just something to open on Christmas Day.

Grinning, Daniel backed away slowly, saying nothing, then Josh honked the horn again so with a final smile, he turned and ran to his car.

Anna closed her boot and waved them off before getting inside and starting the engine, resting back against the headrest she closed her eyes, remembering how it felt in his arms and the softness of his chaste kiss. It was only brief but it was enough, perfect actually. Putting her car into gear she laughed and shook her head. Who would have thought that boring Anna Harrison, dithering widow of the parish, actually went to meet a man in a public house, on her own, and got kissed in the car park? Ooh la la!

CHAPTER 22

Anna was thoroughly looking forward to her alternative Christmas at Jeannie's, especially after enduring a freezing cold night at home because the central heating was still playing up. The next morning, she packed up her gifts and Daniel's box of wine then set off with a light heart, making a concerted effort to put all thoughts of Christmas Eve's gone by firmly from her mind. It would only bring her down – a fact which had been annoying her immensely. Today had always been her favourite part of the holidays and now she had to blank out precious memories because they hurt too much. Still, no matter how hard she tried they all came flooding back so in the end, she just gave in.

Anna saw and felt it all so clearly, the excitement and anticipation before the big day arrived. Her overtired and giddy kids were finally tucked up in bed, the vegetables had been prepared, including Rudolph's carrot and Santa's mince pie, and as soon as they knew everyone was fast asleep (and not pretending) they would sneak about, putting presents under the tree. Once everything was done they would relax, watching telly, cuddled up together on the sofa and at midnight, open one present each. Now, because of what Matthew had done she couldn't bear to think about it, he had ruined it all. Any precious memories she had which included him were now tarnished forever.

Phil ordered a takeaway and the three of them ate together, happily wandering down memory lane remembering their best and worst Christmas presents. Anna rang Enid who was obviously far too preoccupied with getting glammed up for the Gala party to talk for long so she spoke to Sam instead. He was having a great time in the guard hut watching telly with his mates and eating pizza, courtesy of their corporal. Melanie was off to the golf club for a dinner party with Paloma and her parents. Anna couldn't recall Mel packing anything suitable for such an event and prayed she had enough money to buy something over there or God forbid, she'd have to borrow something, preferably clean, from the grunge monster. Joe, she imagined, was on the beach and would contact her whenever he could.

Philip wimped out of an all-nighter so with him well out of earshot, Anna decided to let Jeannie into her secret about Daniel. It wasn't because Anna thought she'd disapprove that she hadn't mentioned it, in fact it was quite the opposite. Knowing all about Matthew's unfaithfulness Jeannie would've encouraged Anna, but she'd wanted to do things her way and not be pushed into anything, no matter how well intentioned her friend may be. Now was the right time to confide in Jeannie, and besides, it would be nice to share some good news for once. Pouring another glass of wine from one of the bottles Daniel had sent, Anna passed one to Jeannie and giggling slightly, asked if she wanted to hear a secret.

'Go on then, as long as it's nothing to do with those randy old pensioners. I don't want to curdle my chicken korma. Come on dish the dirt, what's going on?' Jeannie perched cross-legged on the sofa in her Mrs Santa onesie, waiting expectantly.

'Well... you remember me telling you about the man I met in France, when I stayed at Rosie's? Well, we've kept in touch since then, mostly by email and text and in between all my dramas I managed not to scare him off. Anyway, he's turned out to be really, really nice and I like him – a lot!'

Jeannie's eyes were wide with surprise; her wine glass remained suspended in mid-air while she listened, rapt and for once silent, until she found her voice.

'Why didn't you say something? I can't believe you didn't tell me! Ooops, sorry, sorry, I'm interrupting. Go on, I'm all ears.' Jeannie put her fingers over her lips and waited.

'Well, you're going to go mad when I tell you the next bit. I didn't mention it before in case I bottled out… but I met him again last night in town, we swapped presents and he kissed me in the car park! What do you think about that?' Anna squealed and then wished she could have taken a photo of Jeannie's gobsmacked face.

Once Jeannie recovered from the shock and then battered Anna with her best Christmassy cushion, they both squealed a bit more, like giddy teenagers. Next, Jeannie insisted on a full confession, demanding a very detailed account of the story so far.

After Jeannie had interrogated Anna then forgiven her for keeping yet another secret, she demanded to see a photo of Daniel which made her start squealing all over again. Once she'd calmed down though, Jeannie looked a bit teary, becoming all serious and grown-up.

'You know what? There have been times over the last few months when I thought I'd never see you smile again. I didn't think you'd ever get over what happened but look at you now. It's so good to see you happy and have something positive to talk about. So promise me that no matter what, you won't let anything or anyone spoil things for you. You are doing nothing wrong and if anyone dares upset you by saying otherwise, they'll have me *and* scary Enid to deal with.' Wiping away a tear, Jeannie took a slug from her wine before giving Anna a huge hug.

Knowing her unusually soppy friend was deadly serious, once composed, Anna wiped away her own tears and agreed. Jeannie then made Anna promise on Donny Osmond's life not to wimp out with Daniel, because he was too gorgeous, then not to keep any more secrets because it was becoming a bad habit and especially not to hold back on any juicy bits. Most important of all, Anna had to go for a proper snog next time, no more shy kisses on the cheek.

It was actually Christmas morning by the time Jeannie calmed down and went to bed, and once the coast was clear, Anna slipped the gift from Daniel out of her handbag and quietly removed the wrapping paper. She knew exactly what the tag said. *With love, have a happy Christmas, Daniel x.* She'd read it about 500 times already.

Bubbles of excitement forced her to stifle a giggle as she opened the long, slim jeweller's box where inside was a brushed, white gold bracelet inlaid with tiny Swarovski crystals. It was very simple in design but so beautiful. Hugging the box to her chest she sent Daniel a text, it was 2.30am but she wanted him to know how much she loved her gift. Buoyed by happiness she was tempted to admit how she felt about him but putting on her sensible hat and, knowing that bold statements were best left unsaid, especially when you were in a highly emotional state and had drunk copious amounts of wine, she decided to snuggle down under her duvet and fell asleep.

Christmas Day morning was spent mainly on the sofa drinking Buck's Fizz and eating bacon sandwiches. Anna and Jeannie swapped presents as they listened to Slade and as tradition dictated, they'd bought each other a pair of bad-taste pyjamas. Jeannie's had huge yellow bananas with the words 'Bite Me' emblazoned everywhere and Anna's were fluffy fluorescent leopard print, and truly hideous. Josh had bought her a silk scarf which, unlike the pyjamas, was very tasteful. Anna then confessed she'd already opened Daniel's and showed it off to Jeannie who was suitably impressed and completely forgiving but warned that as she'd broken the rules, Father Christmas might not be amused.

Anna spoke to her children who thankfully were enjoying themselves in their respective parts of the world. Sam had been well looked after by the officers who brought the soldiers on duty a variety of treats throughout the day, even sharing a glass of whisky with the Company Sergeant Major who had taken the time to call in.

Forcing themselves to get dressed up and sit at the table, they ate their lunch in a very merry state but being proper didn't last long because Jeannie and Anna soon decided to rebel. If they wanted to wear their new pyjamas and eat their pudding on the settee they damn well would!

Daniel rang in the afternoon so Anna scuttled off to the bedroom to stop Jeannie from ear-wigging. He was having a great time but it was perishing there so he appreciated the woolly jumper she'd bought him and Josh loved his hoodie. Daniel was glad Anna liked her gift and she assured him it wasn't too over the top while in return, he said he'd just wanted to spoil her and make her smile.

When Phil finally returned home he was met by two very inebriated women who'd done justice to half a case of wine and were now at the stupid, giggling stage of merriment. By the time he'd finished his warmed up, soggy Christmas dinner they were both comatose so he covered them with the duvet and went to bed. As he switched off the light and heard the chorus of snores from the sofa, Philip laughed, convinced that neither of them would make it to the sales the next day.

Boxing Day turned out to be fun when they finally made it into town. Convincing themselves that there would still be plenty of rubbish left they waited for their heads to stop pounding before they headed for the shops. Anna had intended to go home that night but Jeannie and Phil persuaded her to stay, convincing her she wasn't in the way *or* a big fat gooseberry.

After saying their goodbyes the following morning, all were light of heart after what they considered to be an excellent couple of days, and then Anna arrived home to a freezing cold, empty house. By the time she'd put on some warmer clothes and waited for the engineer to call, then tried to find something to do, she started to feel a bit fed up. She sat morosely drinking tea and watching television but wasn't really concentrating. She was trying to fathom out whether her deflated mood was just post-Christmas blues or whether a combination of factors had resulted in her feeling very lonely. The chilly, quiet house certainly didn't help, and having nobody to talk to or look after was in stark contrast to laughing non-stop during her two days with Jeannie and Phil.

There were four empty bedrooms upstairs and she certainly wasn't looking forward to spending a night alone in the fifth, especially if the heating didn't get fixed. Perhaps this house was just too big now, the memories made her sad, not happy, and the protective walls failed to comfort her. She'd always known that one day the children would fly away but still, Matthew would've been there. Unfortunately and against the odds, her nest had emptied a lot sooner than she'd anticipated. Anna's gloomy thoughts were interrupted by the doorbell and the boiler repair man. '*Thank goodness*,' she thought, '*someone to talk to*.'

By the time he'd fixed the heating, Anna had talked the poor engineer to death and he most likely thought she was either a sex-starved housewife who was after his body or just plain bonkers, and he couldn't wait to get out the door.

Anna was washing the cups and the plate that she'd put the cake and biscuits on after the engineer had politely refused a sandwich, when the phone rang. '*Yippee*,' thought Anna sarcastically, '*it might be someone selling insurance, or windows. That should keep me occupied for at least half an hour*.' In fact it was Rosie.

'Happy Christmas, Anna, how are you? I was just ringing to catch up and see if you had a good time at your brother's.'

Anna was thrilled to hear Rosie's voice so curled up on the armchair and began passing on all her news.

Rosie was shocked to hear about the 'flowers on the grave' incident and was worried that Mel and Sam might be suspicious. Anna reassured Rosie that especially where Melanie was concerned she'd always put Matthew on a pedestal and the thought wouldn't even have crossed her mind, plus Sam wasn't the inquisitive type so they'd both presumed it was a mistake.

Next, Rosie wanted to know if Anna had anything planned for the New Year. They were going over to Dominique's to celebrate as she wanted a rest from entertaining. Anna confessed that if she could get away with it, she intended to stay at home and have an early night. Rosie thought it was a terrible idea and a recipe for disaster.

'Anna, being alone really is the worst thing you can do. No matter how hard you try to ignore the fact that it's New Years Eve it will be virtually impossible, unless you cut all communication with the outside world by turning the television, radio and phone off. And then there's the fireworks, you'd have to wear ear plugs to avoid the merriment. No matter how hard you try I worry that you'll spend the night going over everything in your head and dredging up the past, it's just not healthy.'

Put like that, Anna had to agree. 'I know, you're right, Rosie, but I don't want to impose or bring anyone else down. I could stay with Jeannie again or even Naomi but they both have partners and deserve some time alone, and as much as I love my mother, a night at the community centre with her and Gladys is not my idea of fun, no matter how desperate I get.' Anna was really on a downer now.

'I know, I've had a brilliant idea!' Rosie sounded excited. 'Why don't you come here for New Year, as our guest?'

Anna hesitated. It was too short notice and she didn't want to be in the way or be invited just because they felt sorry for her but Rosie, sensing reluctance, soldiered on.

'Come on, Anna, I would love to see you again and I could do with some help shopping for furniture. I need to get moving on those gîtes if they are ever going to be finished. It's very cold and there's not much to do in the way of sightseeing but you can relax and keep me company. Michel is always busy doing something or other and it would be fun, what do you think? Please say yes.'

It took Anna about five seconds to decide.

When Rosie said it was cold in France, Anna didn't actually think it'd be as nippy as this. After just ten minutes waiting at the pick-up zone she knew her nose was Rudolph red and she had lost all feeling in her feet. Comparing the dark grey sky with the summer blues she had experienced on her last visit, Anna stamped her feet in an attempt to warm them up and avoid cramp, her breath visible in clouds of white as she breathed in the freezing air.

Keeping watery eyes peeled for Rosie's car she amused herself with people watching. Hugs and kisses were in abundance as loved ones were welcomed or bade farewell in an intercontinental exchange of family members, coming or going for the New Year.

***

It had been a bit of a mad rush to get organised and the first person Anna rang after Rosie's invitation was Sam. She didn't want to stay too long and miss out on spending time with him so therefore her plans hinged on his. Melanie was going straight back to university from Tenerife so in the end she had seven full days in France before she needed to be back in England.

Fizzing with excitement Anna booked her flight, shopped for treats to share with Rosie and Michel and thankfully packed plenty of woolly jumpers and sensible clothes. Noticing in the supermarket some knitting magazines, Anna had an idea. Even though it had been years since she'd knitted or crocheted she needed a new hobby and had read that it was becoming fashionable again. There was no time to go up in the loft, searching through boxes for her old equipment so she found a craft shop and bought new needles and hooks and lots of wool in soft baby colours. Remembering her plan to knit a blanket for Samantha, she decided she would knit one for Rosie as well. Her luggage was filled with a selection of English cheese and chutneys, a special bottle of malt whisky for Michel along with an urgent request from Rosie for a large pack of bacon and Cumberland sausages, a tin of Roses chocolates and a pot of Marmite.

Anna had dithered about Daniel but Jeannie was wearing her bossy boots as they set off for the airport, calling her a wimp and insisting she sent him a message so, obeying a direct command, she passed on her news. Jeannie looked exceedingly smug when almost instantly, Daniel replied saying he was thrilled and would travel back early and meet her at Rosie's. It would only be for two nights but hopefully they could spend some time together. Anna felt a ripple of anticipation and nerves as she read his words but had to admit, she couldn't wait to see him.

***

Flashing headlights attracted Anna's attention so she waved back eagerly to let Rosie know she'd spotted her. Obviously in full bloom, Rosie climbed out of the car and folded her arms around Anna, hugging her tightly. Once their hellos were over they quickly loaded Anna's luggage and dived inside, relishing the warmth from the heater.

'Rosie, you look fab, really healthy, being pregnant suits you and thanks for inviting me. To be honest you're a bit of a life saver. I'm so glad to be here even if it is bloody freezing.' Anna was fastening her seatbelt, raring to go.

Rosie laughed, 'Well, if you think this is bad wait till we get into the countryside, it's a few degrees colder there and I'm warning you, the mornings are a killer. I hope you've brought your thermals.'

'I don't care, I can cope with the cold, and I swear, anything is better than that empty house full of memories. I feel so relieved just to be away and here with you and Michel again.' Anna acknowledged a huge bubble of happiness as it swelled inside her chest, and Rosie's next words only added to the fizz.

'And have you told a certain blue-eyed customer of mine you are here? He's coming up this way, you know? I'm sure it will be the icing on his Christmas cake to turn up and find you here next week.' Rosie winked at Anna and grinned.

'Yes, I've told him and he did seem pleased. And before you ask, I am looking forward to seeing him too but a bit nervous at the same time. Things have sort of progressed and I admit it's all a bit scary. I'm not sure where this is all leading but I feel happier than I have in such a long time so I'm just going to go with it.' Anna meant every word and then laughed, seeing Rosie's raised eyebrows at hearing the news.

During the drive to the hotel, Anna related the events at the pub, hoping for some words of wisdom and advice from Rosie. Otherwise, she feared that by the time Daniel arrived she would have overthought and worried about the situation so much she would most likely say or do something really stupid.

True to Rosie's word, it did feel a lot colder at the hotel. As they unloaded the car, a harsh wind blew across the fields and whipped around the house, chilling the air and biting at their cheeks but once inside, Anna felt the warmth from a roaring log fire engulf her. They set off in search of Michel who as usual was in the kitchen where a heavenly aroma of cooking and herbs greeted them. After hugs and hellos, they were informed that beef bourguignon was on the menu but for now, Michel had prepared onion soup and fresh bread. While Anna sat at the counter, eating and laughing with them both, she thought that if you could really glow with happiness, inside her right now there must be a huge orange fireball.

Once lunch was finished and Anna was unpacked and settled in the same room as last time, she grabbed her bag of wool and needles and taking her magazines for inspiration, set off downstairs to make the most of the log fire and Rosie's company. Her heart was light and her mind was clear and trouble free. All she had to do now was relax and enjoy herself and make the most of where she was, who she was with and soon, about to meet again.

CHAPTER 23

They spent the rest of the afternoon warming their feet on the fire, talking and making plans for the week ahead. Rosie needed to go to IKEA at Nantes. The interior of the gîtes were going to be modern and functional compared with the antique French look of the hotel, so the Swedish style suited them well. Another day they could take a look in some of the *brocantes* dotted around the area in the hope of picking up a few bits and pieces to strip down and restore, which Rosie hoped would add a touch of French chic to the rooms. New Years Eve would be spent over at Dominique and Zofia's; Anna had also been invited the second they heard she was coming to stay.

Anna could see the sky outside darkening through the panes of the windows. The wind had picked up and was whistling around the house, the trees swaying frantically in the garden. More logs were put on the fire and Michel joined them for a glass of wine before dinner, relaxing in an armchair, eyes closed, listening to Radio France which was playing quietly in the corner of the room. Rosie drank mint tea whilst browsing through magazines and the only other sound was the clicking of Anna's needles as she embarked on her first baby blanket, destined for the bottom drawer in Rosie's bedroom.

Despite being miles from home and her family, in the middle of the dark, wintry countryside with two people she'd only known for a short time, pure peace and contentment swept through Anna's veins. Her whole body relaxed while her mind was drained of the anxiety and dark memories that had plagued her for months. Knowing she had seven days of tranquillity along with the prospect of seeing Daniel again filled her heart with a kind of happiness she thought was a thing of the past. '*Maybe, Anna Harrison,*' she thought to herself as the rows of knitting took shape, '*just maybe, things are going to be alright.*'

The days leading up to New Years Eve flew by. On her first winter morning in France Anna woke slightly disorientated, taking a few seconds to remember where she was. Noticing the blue-grey morning light outside her window as it broke through the heavy clouds, so different from the warm, bright, sunlit room she remembered from her last visit, there was a distinct chill in the air and even her nose was cold.

Anna snuggled deeper under the duvet and blankets and realised now why Rosie had insisted on leaving extra bedding in the wardrobe, just in case. She didn't care really, a bit of cold never harmed anyone, having said that, it might take a leap of faith to get her from under her duvet and into the shower, and she would definitely be wearing woolly socks in bed tonight.

Outside, the rolling hills once filled with crops were now barren and the dark brown earth was covered in white mist, rolling in from the fields and settling just beyond the swimming pool. The trees in the garden below were bare and frost covered, as was the pale green grass which Anna knew would crunch underfoot. The wind had died down but she would still have to wrap up warm. If it was chilly inside then it'd be freezing out there. Still, despite the weather, she couldn't wait for her day to begin.

Rosie and Anna set off for Nantes with a book of measurements and a list of things to order, hopefully having everything delivered just after New Year. IKEA was situated in a large, modern shopping mall, rather than being plonked in an industrial or retail area like in England but apart from that, everything was much the same. Rosie had planned a simple rustic theme for the gîtes with contemporary functional utensils and fittings. Anna was sure the effect would be very Scandinavian-log-cabin and perfect in the setting of the wood and fields. By the time they'd walked around and around the store following the arrows from one department to another, their feet felt like they'd done the London Marathon and Anna could tell Rosie needed a rest so insisted they stop for a long lunch.

Sitting in a small Italian restaurant drinking cappuccino, Rosie confessed that she took the opportunity to eat alternative food to French cuisine whenever she could, for no other reason than Michel stuck religiously to sourcing only seasonal produce from the land. He insisted it was healthy to go with nature, however, just now and then, Rosie firmly believed that a fast food cheeseburger or a big bowl of creamy pasta was good for the soul and wouldn't do you any harm.

Talk eventually turned to Anna and her meeting with Daniel just before Christmas. Rosie thought it was all very romantic and made a nice change from people diving into bed with each other at the drop of a hat and just like spaghetti carbonara – old-fashioned romance was good for the soul.

'Do you think Daniel might think I'm a bit boring and lose interest? It's all well and good taking things slowly but like you said, these days, people think nothing of jumping into the sack with someone they've just met and eventually he's going to want more, I know he is.' Anna sat back in her chair, worry etched on her face.

'Honestly, Anna, you stress too much. Have you considered that he may think it's a refreshing change to meet someone like you? Maybe he enjoys the thrill of the chase and a challenge? He's a nice bloke and he knows you're getting over Matthew and if he rushes things he could blow it. Anyway, if he doesn't like it tell him to lump it.' Rosie took a sip of her coffee then continued. 'This is your time so do things your way. Don't feel pressured to behave in a manner you're not comfortable with because believe me, there's plenty of fish out there so if it doesn't work out with Daniel, you'll find someone else. And if you get really desperate there's always Henri.'

Rosie smirked and Anna nearly choked on her coffee.

'Henri! Are you kidding me, he's not my type at all and what makes you think he'll fancy me? I hope you haven't been matchmaking, Madame Rousseau.'

Anna was deadly serious which made Rosie laugh as she replied.

'No, I've not, but I saw his eyes light up when I told him you were coming over. He was very interested and wanted to know if you were single and looking for love, honestly, he actually said that. My dear brother-in-law has a bit of a reputation where the ladies are concerned so you'd better watch out, especially on New Year's Eve.'

Rosie looked knowingly at Anna who looked horrified.

'Please tell me you are winding me up. I admit he is very good-looking but a bit too smooth if you know what I mean, so don't encourage him whatever you do… I mean it, Rosie!' Anna was flustered and knew it was amusing Rosie no end.

Henri was in every way the typical French Romeo, very tall, dark and handsome, black curly hair like his brother Michel but cut short and slightly speckled with grey at the sides, and his midnight black eyes had a way of burning holes into you when he looked your way. Henri appeared to be extremely elegant the last time Anna saw him, in his tailored suit and Italian shoes and came across as being quite cultured and clever. Rosie had mentioned he was a high-ranking civil servant and rumour had it that while he was working his way up the ranks, he was also working his way through every available female member of staff. No, he definitely wasn't Anna's type; people like Henri made her nervous so she vowed to be on her guard from now on.

'Come on you. Stop looking so shocked and eat your lunch, you'll need all your energy for when Henri has his wicked way with you, apparently he's an animal.' Rosie laughed out loud seeing Anna's terrified expression, her mirth attracting stares from the other diners.

Rosie couldn't resist teasing Anna, even though part of it was true because Henri definitely was interested and if she knew her brother-in-law, his New Year Resolution, and unwitting target for the evening was sitting right opposite, nervously nibbling on her pizza.

By the time they arrived at the hotel darkness was creeping across the fields while the warm glow from the windows and the white fairy lights strung along the walls made it stand out like a beacon, enticing you in from the cold. The sky was jet black and the stars twinkled like crystal clear diamonds overhead as Rosie and Anna crunched across the gravel drive and into the warmth of the lounge. Voices and laughter could be heard coming from the kitchen so they followed the sound to find Michel, Sebastien and Dominique enjoying an apéritif. Greetings and kisses were exchanged then more glasses were brought so that Anna and Rosie could join the merry group.

Anna did her best to follow the conversation with Rosie interpreting at intervals while her husband, who was obviously enjoying the impromptu gathering, brought plate after plate of food: sausage, pâté, boiled eggs, and cured slices of smoked duck, salad, and baskets of sliced crusty bread. As Michel fried steaks, the phone rang for Dominique who suffered an extensive ear bashing from Zofia after disappearing once again. Apparently it was his favourite trick but she always managed to track him down eventually. Rosie shouted across the kitchen for her to come over and sure enough a few minutes later a rather flustered Zofia appeared. She gave her husband a gentle slap round the head, obviously resigned to his behaviour then accepted a glass of wine before seating herself next to Anna.

Zofia turned away so as not to be overheard and in good English laced with a strong Polish accent, shook her head and rolled her eyes in the direction of Dominique as she whispered, 'This bloody man. I am going to close the chicken shed and fetch the eggs, he is telling me. Pah, what rubbish! For two bloody hours he is missing. I ask you, Anna, how long does it take to look up the arse of a chicken and find the egg? He is making me crazy this little French man, he is like poffshinogga, I am telling you, he is driving me mad.' Zofia grinned and shook her head.

Anna made sympathetic faces but intrigued, asked what exactly a poffshinogga was.

Zofia pursed her lips and said quite loudly, so that her beloved could easily hear. 'It is a Polish word for somebody who runs around like a busybody, poking their noses into everything, like a fat little pig looking for truffles!' Zofia smiled and nodded her head in her husband's direction.

Anna chuckled, a bizarre mental image of poor Dominique firmly planted, but despite the light-hearted mini domestic, the wine continued to flow as did the conversation, so she soaked up the relaxed atmosphere. Sebastien did his best in broken English to ask polite questions, she also got the feeling he was getting a bit more flirty as the evening progressed; making a concerted effort to catch her eye and fill her glass. Rosie was flagging by the time the cheese from England was served. Everyone loved the Stilton and Cheddar, quite shocked that the organic Welsh goat's cheese was actually edible and *nearly* as good as theirs. Anna helped Zofia load the dishwasher before leaving the men to discuss the merits of British food and naturally, drink more wine.

The three women were sitting around the fire enjoying the peace and sharing the tin of chocolates Anna had brought over when Zofia spotted the work-in-progress baby blanket and commented that she couldn't knit but would love to learn. Enough said, Anna whipped out a large set of needles and before Zofia could protest, began to teach her. For the next few hours, Anna's enthusiastic student watched and copied intently, the only interruption was an occasional burst of raucous laughter from the kitchen, which luckily didn't disturb Rosie who was so tired she conked out on the sofa, blissfully snoring the night away.

Anna had been told to make herself at home so not wanting to waste her days, rose early the following morning and after a very quick shower, made her way downstairs where the aroma of fresh coffee signalled that someone had beaten her to it. In the kitchen she found a slightly hung-over Michel, sitting at the counter, dipping a croissant into his coffee. After she'd poured coffee for herself, Anna had a go at croissant dipping, and noticing Michel's bag on the floor, she asked if he was going out.

'Yes, today is Les Restaurants du Cœur. I will leave soon to collect Dominique.' Anna had no idea what he was talking about and looked blankly at Michel, hoping for further details.

'Ah, you do not have this in England. Les Restaurants du Cœur is a charity, it means restaurant of the heart or love. I am a volunteer and we make hot food for the needy and homeless. There are Resto's all over France, ours is in Nantes.' Michel carried on dipping as Anna asked how long he had been helping and what did he do there.

'I have been there for about three years, Dominique introduced me. We prepare the food and serve it, just like a regular restaurant but the customers are different. It's a big charity here. It was started by a comedian called Coluche who had an idea to feed the poor and began in Paris in the eighties. These days we give away around three thousand meals per day and it is the difference between life and death for some, especially in the winter.' Anna could tell by the way Michel spoke that he was proud of his charity so asked him where they got the food and funding.

'It is mostly from donations and each year there is a big concert on television with celebrities encouraging people to send donations. And, Anna, can you believe this? It costs more money to store all the surplus food in France than to share it out, so Coluche, he went to the European Parliament and pleaded with them and guess what? Now, the food is released to four organisations, not piled up. That is a good result, I think.'

Anna agreed and made a mental note to give Michel a donation before she left, her mind ticking over, thinking of all the people not just in France that were cold, hungry and homeless, like those in England who were in the same predicament. Maybe, when she got home she could do something to help.

After Michel left and in complete contrast to what they had been discussing over breakfast, Anna set off with Rosie to experience the delights of the French supermarket – Super U. It was bustling when they arrived; it was Saturday and on Sunday the shops were closed. There were a few exceptions like the bakers or small convenience stores; Sunday was still holy here and refreshingly, remained a family day.

Everyone was stocking up for New Years Eve, trolleys overloaded with what looked like enough baguettes to feed a village, bottles of wine jingled past and seafood seemed to be especially popular. There was an unmistakable scent of the sea lingering in the air and as they neared the rear of the shop, Anna saw why. She had never seen a fishmongers stall like this one. The long counter was overflowing with every type of fish imaginable, mountains of fresh shellfish, prawns, lobsters, crabs, langoustines, mussels and boxes and boxes of oysters.

Anna wanted to take something to Dominique's the following evening so chose one of the wooden crates containing oysters which she would drop off later when she called to see how Zofia's scarf was progressing. Apparently, she'd been to buy some wool and needles and was raring to go.

At the patisserie counter there was a huge choice of brightly decorated gateaux made from sponge, mousse, and fresh fruit. Anna selected the largest they had and placed it gently in the trolley, it was so pretty with its green, pink and gold icing and fancy ribbons. Her final purchase was a bottle of champagne, at least now she wouldn't turn up empty-handed.

Driving back through the deserted villages, Anna admired the little cottages tucked away amongst the fields. White smoke floated up to the sky from their chimneys where below, log burners worked overtime in an attempt to stave off the cold. Rosie said the air smelt of bonfire night almost every day during the winter. The roads were eerily quiet, hardly any other cars passed them en route; farm vehicles chugged slowly along the lanes, moving feed for the cattle but apart from that you could go for miles without seeing a soul. It was so peaceful and Anna was on the verge of closing her heavy eyelids when Rosie chirped up, saying that she'd been pondering 'the Daniel situation' as she'd taken to calling it.

'I think you need to tell him about Matthew's affair when you see him. He needs to understand how you're thinking. You've been let down and hurt once so you should let him know why you are taking your time because it's not just about getting over Matthew's death, but his affair as well. Trust is a big issue here.' Rosie was waiting at a junction and for her passenger to mull over her idea.

Anna sighed, she'd been on the verge of telling him a few times when he'd called her late at night and she was lonely, wanting to talk it through with him but ironically, at the last minute, felt disloyal to Matthew so kept quiet.

'But there are two ways of looking at it, Rosie. He could understand and be happy to wait for me or he could take the view that if my husband was unfaithful then I've got every right to put the widow's weeds away and start having a good time, especially with him.' Anna turned to face Rosie, keen to hear her thoughts.

'Anna, what is stopping you from doing just that? Is it grief or something else, are you worried about what your family will say or feel you have to observe some outdated Victorian period of mourning before you can move on without feeling guilty?' Rosie fell silent, hoping she hadn't gone too far.

'I suppose it's all of those things rolled into one big, annoying ball of self-doubt. Look, I'm going to be really honest with you. I still get sad days and miss Matthew more than I can say, I think I always will. But the anger his affair caused somehow numbed the grief and now resentment has taken over. What eats me up the most, what keeps me awake at night and won't go away is the not knowing.' Anna fell into silence.

Rosie stopped at a roundabout and waited for the traffic to pass. Once she'd set off her attention turned back to Anna.

'But what do you want to know exactly? Who she is, what their plans were, did he really love her? You've got to face the fact that you may never find out and even if you did, it won't change anything, what's done is done.' Rosie could see Anna shaking her head in disagreement.

'It will help me, I'm sure of it. If I knew who she was it would be a start, and then if she's a stunning beauty that no man could resist, I'd sort of understand that he upgraded and traded me in for a newer model. I still have no idea how long it was going on for. I found out in May, Jeannie spotted them just before. That was the point my marriage ended, for me anyway, but maybe it had been over for months. I had no way of knowing and I also didn't have the guts to confront him. Now, with hindsight, the signs tell me that our relationship had been rocky for a while, maybe as early as Christmas. Part of my life has been a sham and I feel the need for answers before I can fully move on and I admit that it's eating me up.' Anna sighed.

'Okay, I get it, really I do. So perhaps when you go home you can get your thinking cap on and do a bit of detective work. I'm sure Jeannie will be glad to help you, but give it a time limit, Anna. Life goes by so quickly and you don't want to let any chances of being happy pass you by while you get bogged down in the past, searching for answers and mystery women.'

Rosie spoke with passion and feeling while Anna nodded, grateful for the advice.

'I promise. I'll have another go at finding her then give it up, and I will tell Daniel the truth. I also need to stop protecting Matthew's memory when in some ways he doesn't deserve it. It's time to look after number one for a change. Thanks for listening, Rosie, I feel a bit clearer now, you are very wise, and almost as bossy as Jeannie. I'm stuck in between a right pair, aren't I?'

Rosie raised her eyebrows, not sure if she would describe herself as wise, bossy yes, but as long as it helped Anna sort through the jumble sale of confusion in her head, that's all that mattered.

CHAPTER 24

Once they'd stored away the groceries, Rosie went for a lie down so Anna took her knitting things and the box of oysters and walked up the lane to visit Zofia. Rosie advised to take them early so that Dominique could prepare them beforehand and it would also prevent Michel from sampling a few. Inside the farmhouse was warm and cosy, photographs of Dominique and Zofia, their restaurant in London and family and friends adorned the walls. The country kitchen had a huge table and plenty of chairs gathered around it, the worktops held jars of herbs and spices and there was a huge pot of beetroot soup bubbling away on the double range – a Polish speciality. To the side of the kitchen was their lounge; comfy sofas were arranged around a large, glass-fronted wood burning fire where the glowing logs crackled away, enticing you in.

Zofia chatted away while she made coffee and brought out cake, enjoying the peace and time to relax before Dominique and the others needed feeding again. He was in the forest cutting wood where he had an agreement with the owner to chop down the old damaged trees, and then he could take them away and sell the logs; a mutually beneficial arrangement.

Anna asked who else lived there; she had presumed it was just the two of them. While they drank, Zofia explained that they looked after vulnerable adults for a department of the French Health Service called *Familie d'Acceuil* which loosely translated meant a welcome family. Basically, they took into their home people with a variety of problems: alcoholism, mental health, or physically disability. They lived as part of the family and hopefully had a better quality of life than if they stayed in hostels or hospitals. Anna said that it sounded like foster care in England but for adults, to which Zofia agreed that it was much the same.

Zofia was a quick learner and her scarf had very few mistakes so Anna taught her the purl stitch, it was quite easy and prevented monotony. Both spent a relaxed afternoon getting to know each other: Anna proudly described her family and Zofia produced her photo album and showed off her relations in Poland.

At 3pm there was a commotion at the door which signalled the return of Dominique with a couple of strangers in tow, followed by the ritual of kisses and handshakes. Anna was getting used to it now, sticking to kissing the ones she had met before and politely shaking hands with new acquaintances, but still not quite sure how many times you did the kiss, kiss thing. It seemed to vary from one person to the next, sometimes two, other times four, all very confusing.

Like a mini whirlwind, Dominique produced wine glasses and snacks, chatting and joking as he went along, obviously in his comfort zone of entertaining. Anna imagined he had been a perfect host in his restaurant in London, he was a natural with people. She tried in vain on a couple of occasions to leave, not wanting to outstay her welcome but was shushed and told to stay, her glass filled up and another plate of appetisers placed in front of her.

Not used to drinking so much in the afternoon, Anna realised she was getting a bit tiddly so tried to soak up the wine with food but two hours later, admitted to losing the battle. After packing up her knitting and thanking everyone for a lovely afternoon she made a wobbly journey back down the lane in the dark, using the full moon and the lights of the hotel to guide her. In her half-pickled state, Anna had no fear of the night and did her best to focus, sticking to the centre of the path.

After eventually making it back in one piece, the cold night air failing to sober her up, Anna carefully opened the front door and sneaked in, glad to find the hotel deserted. Swaying in the hall, she took off her coat and after a couple of attempts, managed to get it onto the hook of the stand. Hoping nobody had heard her come in she crept up the stairs to her room, planning to sleep off the effects of French hospitality.

As she began to doze, happy thoughts swam around her wine-fuzzed brain. *'Anna Harrison,'* she asked herself, *'what are you like? A mother of three, drunk in the afternoon, staggering home down a dark lane, all alone with your knitting bag! What would the children say? You're turning into a bit of a rebel at last...'*

New Years Eve dawned bright and crisp and Anna lay in bed enjoying the warmth of her duvet as she messaged Sam who was now off duty and, along with his mates, was ready to be let loose on the unsuspecting females near his camp. Apparently, he was going to spread some love that night. Anna really didn't want to know what that entailed, but she could imagine. She confessed to her afternoon of overindulgence which he thought was hilarious, advising her to drink lots of water then get a fry up and she'd be fine. No sympathy there then! Sam mentioned he'd been to the stores to get kitted out for his tour of duty and wanted to show her his new desert gear and boots. In reality, Anna knew this was code and meant she'd have rather a lot of ironing to do when she got home.

Anna enquired if he'd heard from Mel but apart from one text saying she'd arrived and then a bit of bragging about how hot it was, nothing, and no photos or updates on Facebook either. Anna was a little concerned because after sending Mel informative, upbeat messages from France the reply was instant but slightly muted and, in all honesty, a bit boring. She was fine, it was hot and had done loads on her coursework. Anna also thought this was odd as Mel was supposed to be on holiday but maybe they had an assignment to do, or something.

Nevertheless, she knew her daughter well enough to know when something was wrong and if she really was having a great time, then it'd be all over Facebook and in her texts. Giving it one last try she sent Mel a quick message, hinting that it'd be lovely if she could send a sunny beach photo or an email. Ending her message with lots of love and a hint not to work too hard because she was on holiday, Anna signed off.

Before lunch, Rosie and Anna went for a gentle walk down to the gîtes and when Rosie opened the door to the first cabin, Anna knew immediately that the IKEA furniture would be perfect. All the walls were painted in a warm cream which complemented the wooden trims and floors and this one had two bedrooms, an open plan lounge and kitchen area. The gîte next door was almost identical but the third, Anna thought was the most impressive; it had three bedrooms, one en suite and a very cute room nestled in the eaves. This was meant for a large family and she could picture it in the summer, filled with children.

Anna couldn't compliment Rosie enough, the views across the fields were perfect and she could imagine sitting here watching the sun go down after a day sunbathing. Each cabin had a small decked area at the front with room for chairs and tables. All the boxes had been ticked to give families everything they would need: pool, play area and somewhere to run free, exactly the type of place they would have chosen when the children were small.

Later as they made their way through the small copse of bare, spindly trees, fallen autumn leaves crunched underfoot as Anna asked Rosie if they had any bookings yet.

'No we haven't, but as soon as we get the first one totally finished, hopefully by the end of this month, we can take some photos and start advertising on the website. I'm not expecting miracles in the first season but I have been spreading the word all summer with the guests who stayed up at the hotel. I'm hoping that word of mouth will help and once we've had a few rentals we may even get some repeat bookings.' Rosie held up both her hands, fingers crossed.

On their return, Michel had prepared a large lunch which surprised Anna until Rosie explained that they weren't due at Zofia's until after eight, then they would have drinks and spend ages waiting for everyone to arrive (the French never rushed anything) so probably wouldn't start eating until at least ten. The meal would likely last until midnight so it was best to stock up now otherwise they'd starve to death so, taking Rosie's advice and not wanting a repeat performance of yesterday's drunken state, Anna tucked into her food.

The bedroom was filled with the heady scent from a magnolia candle which burned on the dresser as Anna prepared for the New Year party. One thing she really loved about being amongst her new friends was how comfortable she felt, there wasn't so much pressure to dress up or put on a show, you could be yourself. People seemed to accept you as you were and didn't judge you by the label in the back of your T-shirt. The country folk had other, more important things on their minds like getting the animals fed or tending to their fields and making a living. Anna admired their less shallow existence, they seemed to appreciate simpler things in life: family, friends, the land and nature, good food and, obviously, wine.

When her phone beeped she let out a small sigh of relief, seeing Melanie's name appear on the screen. Once again, the text was brief and to the point saying that she was fine and they were going to the golf club *again* for the evening. Anna wasn't comforted by the tone or sure of the relevance of 'fine' and 'again', however, after promising a text or call at midnight if she could get through, Mel signed off.

Anna decided to ring Mel in the morning, knowing she would hear in her daughter's voice if anything was wrong, and her instinct told her something definitely wasn't right.

Joe, on the other hand, had sent emails and photos. It was already New Year there which he'd spent on the beach. In one photo there was a lovely looking girl, very tanned and freckled with long fair hair, wearing a bikini and sporting a huge flower in her hair. She was leaning into Joe and he had his arm around her shoulders and if she knew her son, it was his way of giving her a hint. He was very private and the shyest of her children and not given to telling everyone his business. Anna would casually mention the photo in her next email and give him the opportunity to tell her more, if there was anything to say, and she expected there was.

The last two texts were a joint one to Jeannie and Phil, then her mother who was going to the community centre with Gladys for bingo, a disco and dance, and the obligatory buffet. Her brother was taking Jeannie for a romantic meal. Out of politeness, she sent a message to Matthew's parents wishing them all the best and sending her love, but deep down, Anna had been slightly hurt by their lack of interest or support since his death. She had kept in touch and always made the first move which irked, but then softened, thinking that maybe it was best to leave them to grieve in their own way.

Since her arrival she had been exchanging short holiday stories and weather reports with Daniel, apparently it was much milder in the south, so before she left for the evening Anna sent him a quick message, and as usual, her phoned beeped instantly. Daniel was on his way to a restaurant and promised to text at midnight, adding lots of kisses which caused Anna's heart to flutter and a contented smile to appear on her lips.

After blowing out the candle and popping her phone inside her bag, Anna checked herself in the mirror. She wore claret jeans, a black, soft knit top with a slashed neck and her ankle boots, but then fashion sense went out of the window as she grabbed a woolly scarf and her padded jacket. It would be freezing outside; the glass of the window was like ice and as she zipped up her coat, Anna gazed at the final moon of the year. It was full, a huge glowing ball of silvery white that shone brightly onto the frozen fields. The scene really was like a picture postcard so she closed her eyes, remembering it all, sight, sound and senses, then saved it to her bank of happy French memories.

CHAPTER 25

J ust after 8pm they set off up the lane. Rosie linked arms with Anna who precariously carried the gateau, with the bottle of champagne tucked deep inside her bag. Michel had his arms full, carrying a box of clinking wine bottles and was striding ahead, eager to get the party started.

The room was filled with around ten or twelve people and it was clear from the onset that Zofia was in the mood for a party and had every intention of letting Dominique take control and do his thing. While he flapped about bringing drinks, opening bottles and a hundred other things at once, his wife enjoyed the company and circulated. Zofia took Anna into their sitting room where the large dining table had been lovingly decorated with napkins, streamers, and candles, proudly showing off a beautiful crockery set that had been her mother's and carefully transported over from Poland.

The next to arrive was Henri who seemed very popular and after passing over his gifts of wine, effortlessly embraced everyone in the room, gentlemanly insisting his sister-in-law remain seated while he kissed each cheek. Anna watched him scan the room, obviously searching for someone and when his eyes rested on her, realised he had found his quarry. With a dazzling smile Henri strode confidently over to Anna, his eyes locked on hers and like a rabbit in the headlights she waited helplessly then, without warning, she felt his strong hands pulling her forward into a warm embrace, followed by four kisses, his warm lips firmly making contact each time.

Anna couldn't miss his expensive aftershave, it filled her nostrils, and there was a hint of mint from his hair. Pulling away slowly, once again, locking-on with his eyes which had a definite glint about them, Henri gave her a wicked, suggestive grin. Wearing a crisp blue shirt, open at the neck (and fitted just enough to leave you in no doubt that a strong chest and toned arms lurked underneath) teamed with very dark tailored jeans, gave Henri a stylish look. In a husky voice that he surely must practice in the mirror, perfect English rolling smoothly from his tongue with lashings of his French accent adding to the effect, he held the gaze of his prey.

'Anna, it is so good to see you again. Perhaps this time we will have a chance to get to know each other a little better. I was so pleased when Rosie told me you would be staying with her. I have been looking forward to tonight because I want to find out everything about you. Now, allow me to bring you another drink, don't go away.'

Without waiting for a reply he turned and sauntered off, which was just as well because Anna was lost for words, totally.

Flustered, Anna looked over to Rosie for support only to see she was laughing into her orange juice. Thinking there was safety in numbers, she shot over and sat by her giggly friend's side, nervously waiting for her drink and the return of Henri. Sniggering and loving every minute, Rosie leaned over and whispered into Anna's ear.

'I told you, he *wants* you and from the look of him, he's on a mission to get you! It's true what they say Anna, men are just like buses, nothing for ages then two come along at once. Oh actually, cancel that, I should've said three. Here comes Sebastien! You sure have got your hands full tonight, mate, best of British and all that.' Rosie carried on sipping her drink and watched as a spruced up Sebastien made a beeline in their direction.

Ignoring Rosie's smirks, Anna whispered, 'Oh God', just before the kissing and hugging began in earnest. This was interrupted by a slightly peeved Henri who managed to sandwich himself beside Anna on the bench. Due to the tight squeeze, he was required to turn his body sideways, forcing him to lean against Anna and then slide his arm around her shoulders, resting casually on top. Sebastien was fuming and glared at Henri whilst trying to maintain a jovial and interesting conversation, struggling on valiantly as his English wasn't that good, inviting Anna to his restaurant so he could cook for her.

In turn, Henri made the most of his rather close proximity by monopolising Anna and suggested dinner in the finest restaurant his city had to offer, thus well and truly rubbing his friend's nose in it. Anna could feel the heat from Henri's body on her arm as his warm breath brushed her ear whilst he chatted. The death-ray stare from Sebastien only added to the tension and she was sure her blood pressure had gone off the scale, unsure if she was flattered or trapped in some kind of testosterone fuelled nightmare.

Anna also felt a bit sorry for Sebastien. He was handsome in a rugged way, shorter than Henri but well built. He'd played rugby in the past and had suffered a broken nose but it wasn't one of those you see on meatheads in mafia films, squashed flat – his was just a bit wonky. With his fair hair, pale brown eyes and kind smile he should've been a catch so Anna wondered why he was single, surely out here in the countryside he'd be snapped up by a farmer's daughter. Rosie would know, she'd ask her later or whenever she managed to stop sniggering.

Thankfully, after a very long hour of trying to be equally attentive to Henri and Sebastien, Zofia called everyone to the dinner table. She insisted that rather than a girl-boy seating arrangement it was to be ladies on one side, men on the other, winking slyly to Anna before seating her guests. When they eventually sat down, Anna was between Zofia and Rosie, with Michel opposite, and thankfully, Sebastien and Henri on either side, well out of harm's way.

Not only was she conscious of pacing herself to avoid becoming too merry, Anna also needed to be alert and prepared to fend off her two admirers sitting just across the way. Checking her watch, it said 10.30 and she resigned herself to the fact that it was going to be a long night. The selection of fresh seafood, oysters, langoustine, mussels, and snails was followed by a layered fish mousse of salmon and crab. Dominique was adept in his role of host, filling up glasses and joking with his guests, causing Anna's mind to stray, knowing if Daniel were there he'd be telling her all about the wine. She was imagining his face, close to hers, when Zofia's voice broke into her thoughts.

'Are you enjoying the mousse, Anna? It is delicious. And I hope you are pleased with my seating plans. You wouldn't want to be stuck between those two and soon they will all be completely drunk. I think they are better sitting on their own, far away from us.' Zofia nodded her head at Anna's two admirers, giving her a conspiratorial wink before she continued. 'And now the women can talk about interesting things, not like these bloody men who only care about sport, wine and sex.' Looking pleased with herself, the mousse and her analysis, she carried on eating.

'Thanks, Zofia, it was all getting a bit intense. I can't imagine what a whole night sandwiched between them would be like. I'm much happier sitting here with you and yes, the mousse is lovely.'

And so, the evening went on. The flickering candles and plates of food conveniently separated Anna from her admirers but it didn't stop the flattery or flirty looks, or Henri rubbing his foot against her leg whilst Sebastien gave her shy smiles. Even if she couldn't speak French, Anna could tell when two people were sniping at each other because Michel, who was trapped in the middle, was either telling them to shut up or laughing helplessly at their childishness. The arrival of a joint of wild boar seemed to divert their attention and pacify them for a while, along with the full-bodied red wine that accompanied it.

After the plates were cleared and the dishwasher loaded, the largest tray of assorted cheese that Anna had ever seen was brought out and passed slowly around the table. While everyone made their choice, Anna stuck to those she recognised, especially avoiding the one that had been rolled in green mould. The wine was changed again and Anna accepted a small glass, using the lull as an opportunity to ask Rosie about Sebastien. Turning side on, so she could speak without being overheard, Rosie explained.

'It's a bit sad really. He was married while he was in the army. He was a chef and once his enlistment was up they moved back here to the village and took over the bar from his father. He opened the bistro and it did really well but that meant more hours downstairs in the kitchen and his wife got fed up. The bar is open late and he spent more time either cooking or serving drinks than he did with her. She missed her parents and was really bored with country life so she went away for a holiday with his two kids and never came back. That was about ten years ago and he's been on his own since then. He's had a few girlfriends but nothing serious, maybe he's a bit set in his ways but a really nice guy, deep down.'

Anna looked over at Sebastien who was laughing at something Michel was saying, feeling sorry that he'd lost his family like that and her eyes misted, the wine was making her overly sentimental so she turned away and spoke to Rosie.

'What a shame. I would've thought someone would snap him up, being a self-made man and all that. Does he still see his children?' Anna instantly regretted asking such a potentially depressing question.

'His son comes from time to time; he's about seventeen and independent. The younger son rarely visits but maybe in the future, who knows? As for romance, I think that these days, women are a bit wiser and know French men too well. Sebastien may want a wife in theory but getting him away from that bar, his cooking, and his friends would be a struggle. Apart from female company, in some ways he lives a dream life, everything he wants under one roof.' Rosie peeled a clementine as she spoke, ignoring Henri who had been earwigging, probably wanting to know if she was talking about him.

A very jolly Zofia came into the room, clapping and summoning everyone's attention, it was nearly midnight and everyone should take a glass of champagne ready for the New Year. A tray was brought round and Anna waited nervously by Rosie. Henri, she noticed, had sidled around the table and was only two people away while Sebastien was to her right and looked like a panther ready to pounce. Anna felt nervous giggles coming on; despite pacing herself she had drunk quite a lot of different coloured wine and was well on her way to being half-pickled.

'Pucker up, kid,' said Rosie cheekily. 'I hope those lips are ready for a snogathon, look, Henri's almost dribbling and Sebastien is gearing up for a scrum the second those bells go ding-dong.' Rosie thought she was hilarious and openly laughing, not caring if Henri or Sebastien saw her.

'Sod off, Rosie,' said Anna, laughing too. 'If this is what you're like sober I bet you are a real pain in the bum when you've had a drink, you're supposed to be guarding me, remember?' Anna was definitely developing a nervous twitch and didn't know which way to turn, or run, at midnight.

'Don't you fret, mate. I've got your back, but I've also got ten euros on Henri making a pass before the night's out, so don't let me down, a quick snog and I'm a winner.'

Rosie winked and began counting down with Zofia and the other guests as Anna took an emergency gulp of champagne.

'*Sod it,*' she thought, '*it is a New Year after all and I'm here to have fun. I promised myself to stop overthinking everything so I damn well will!*' And at that moment, the bells on the television rang out. Zofia shouted 'Happy New Year' and everyone cheered. Anna hugged Rosie tightly then Michel appeared and kissed his wife passionately so she made herself scarce and walked straight into the arms of Sebastien who wished her Happy New Year and kissed her chastely on the cheek, blushing slightly. After that, there was a fervent exchange of embraces, nobody was omitted, yet surprisingly, there was no sign of Henri.

Anna filled up her glass, pondering whether she was relieved or slightly offended that Romeo had ignored her, maybe it was part of his chat up technique or a silly game. However, just as she headed towards her seat, she felt a hand slip around her waist and was acutely aware of a tall body, pushed close against hers. Anna looked up, trying to hide her embarrassment and hoping that her cheeks weren't as red as they felt and came eye to eye with Henri. Quite unabashed and confident he smiled down at her, pulling her forward (far too close) while her heart pounded rapidly in her chest as he stroked her back with his thumb.

'Ah, Anna, there you are. I was saving the very best until last, Happy New Year.' And without waiting for any hint of an invitation he bent his head and kissed her.

As Henri gently cupped the back of her head with his free hand, his warm lips pushed against hers and instead of experiencing passion or the thrill of a kiss, Anna felt self-conscious, trapped, and very offended. It lasted only a few lingering seconds but long enough for Anna to know she didn't want to be kissed by Henri, now or ever, and felt an incredible urge to push him away which proved unnecessary. She was saved by the bell, or her phone to be precise. Removing herself from his grasp she avoided his eyes, tersely excused herself then grabbed her bag and marched from the room.

The porch was full of people texting and talking on the phone while Anna rummaged inside her bag desperately trying to reach her mobile. The ringing stopped just as she saw the missed call was from Daniel, causing her heart to lurch as frustration overwhelmed her, so when her phone chimed again, she desperately jabbed the answer button before hearing his voice.

'Happy New Year, Anna, are you having a good time? It's taken ages to get through. I couldn't find a signal.'

Anna smiled and wrapped her arms around her body, it was freezing outside but she didn't care.

'Happy New Year, Daniel. Yes, I'm okay, how's your family?' For some reason the word family brought tears to her eyes and as a huge lump formed in her throat, Anna was suddenly engulfed by a sense of being marooned, alone on a frosty driveway in the dark, desperately missing her kids and even her crazy mum.

'They're all fine. It's a bit noisy inside. Louise invited all the neighbours although Josh is fast asleep on the sofa, he's had one too many and missed everything but apart from that, we've had a good night.'

Anna was choked and desperately trying not to cry, unable to speak.

'Anna… are you there, are you okay, is something wrong?'

Hearing Daniel's voice, laced with concern, Anna pulled herself together and forced out some words.

'Sorry, Daniel, I don't know what happened. I just came over a bit emotional, probably too much wine and you reminded me of home and the kids.' And then, just saying the words, meant that she couldn't hold it in.

Daniel knew she was crying. 'Anna, stop, please. Just listen to me. Don't be sad, it's a special night and definitely not for tears. Anyway, did you know that in France it's against the law to cry on New Year's Eve? If you carry on I'll be duty bound to call the gendarmes and have you arrested for crimes against French hospitality. They'll lock you up and force feed you snails, I mean it, those prison guards can be monsters.'

Anna started laughing, remembering once refusing to sample one of his snails at dinner.

Wiping her eyes, she said she promised and then apologised for being overemotional.

'You've nothing to say sorry for, Anna. I had a feeling tonight might be hard for you, are you sure you're okay now?' Daniel still wasn't convinced.

'Yes, honest… thanks for ringing, Daniel, and cheering me up. At least I got it out of my system before the children call. It's not the New Year in England yet so I've got time to pull myself together, what would I do without you?'

Daniel laughed and said he was glad he'd made her smile; then Anna heard a woman's voice in the background, calling out to him.

'Dad, Dad, can you come inside? Josh has been sick all over the place and Tomas is trying to get him upstairs, it's gone everywhere. I swear I'm going to kill him in the morning.'

Daniel sighed. 'Look, Anna, I'm going to have to go. Josh is in the doghouse again, I'll try to call you back later when I've sorted him out.'

Anna laughed, poor Josh, he'd be in for it now. 'Okay, Daniel, don't worry if you can't get through, tomorrow is fine. I'll go inside and drink lots of coffee and wait for the kids to ring me. And it's freezing out here, I can't feel my toes.' Anna was shivering so started back towards the house.

'Okay will do. Oh, and, Anna… I want you to know that I've not stopped thinking about you all night. I wish you were here, or I was there and I really can't wait to see you again.'

Anna stopped dead in her tracks. 'Are you getting all sentimental on me, Daniel?' Anna heard him laughing as she paused, gathered her courage and continued.

'But just so you know, I've been thinking about you too and I wish you were here as well.' But she was wasting her breath, her words fell on deaf ears, she'd lost the signal.

CHAPTER 26

Heading towards the bathroom to check that she didn't have panda eyes, Anna walked straight into Rosie who, on seeing her friend's face knew instantly that something was wrong so doubled back and once the door was locked, asked what was wrong.

'Don't worry, Rosie. I just got a bit emotional outside. Daniel rang and I suddenly missed the kids. I'm okay now, honest.'

Not convinced and suspecting her randy brother-in-law to be partly responsible, Rosie folded her arms and wanted answers. 'Are you sure it's nothing to do with Henri? He asked me where you were just now and he's been looking rather smug. And I saw him and Sebastien having words earlier. Has he upset you? Don't protect him because I know what he's like.'

Rosie was on the right track so Anna gave in and told her about the kiss.

'I don't know what it was that actually offended me, whether it was because it was so public or that he just thought it was okay. I felt that he was putting on a show or trying to prove something to Sebastien which is mean, and he just really annoyed me. Do you think I'm overreacting, I'm being a prude aren't I?'

Rosie shook her head. 'Henri thinks he's God's gift and has no thought for anyone but himself, that's why he's still single and as for him and Sebastien, they've been like this since they were kids, always arguing over something or other, usually girls. Michel told me they've competed for as long as he can remember, they even had fights at school over football and they were on the same team, for God's sake! Sebastien is a big boy and can look after himself, and as for Henri, he hasn't taken into consideration anything I've told him where you're concerned. In his arrogant head you will be gagging for sex and naturally, thinks he's on a promise.' Rosie looked vexed and ready to throttle him.

'Well, I can assure you he's not! I'll just be cool and give him a wide berth from now on.' Anna brushed her hair which had become tangled in the wind, wiped away the smeared eyeliner with tissue and applied some fresh lipstick before stepping outside, calmer and in control.

As they made their way back to the others, Rosie suggested that they have some dessert and then make their way home, she was getting tired and Michel would want to stay, adding that the party was just beginning and could go on for hours. Anna agreed. She didn't fancy being left there without Rosie or be walked home by two randy Frenchmen.

They entered the lounge just as Zofia was dishing out assorted gateaux. Dominique poured her a glass of dessert wine and looking across the table, Anna made eye contact first with Henri, who did look like the cat who'd got the cream and gave her a wicked smile, which she ignored. Glancing over to Sebastien she noticed that he looked slightly crestfallen so, deciding it would do Henri good to have a taste of his own medicine, Anna turned on a dazzling smile and leant forward, clinking her glass against Sebastien's.

'It's been a lovely evening and I'm sorry we didn't get chance to talk more, so if I have time before I leave, I accept your invitation and will come and visit you at the restaurant to sample some of your wonderful cooking.'

Sebastien's eyes lit up and he told her she was welcome, anytime.

Turning back to face Henri and seeing his thunderous look, Anna simply raised her glass, smiled sweetly and said, 'Cheers.'

Saying goodbye took quite some time, as did convincing Michel, Sebastien and Henri that they were more than capable of walking down the lane by themselves but eventually they escaped and linking arms, strolled along the frozen path, wrapped up against the strong wind that was blowing across the fields.

The frost-covered ground crunched and crackled beneath their feet and even though it was cold and they wanted to get inside, they took their time, guided only by the bright moon overhead. Anna, overly cautious and conscious of Rosie's pregnant state held on tight, just in case they hit a frozen patch, prepared to hold her up or break her fall if she slipped.

As they made their way up the safer gravel drive, Anna's phone buzzed into life and not having heard from anyone in England, received three messages all at once.

Jeannie's said:

> Tried to ring, can't get through, miss you, love you loads. Happy New Year x

Enid's read:

> At the kebab shop with Gladys.

'*The mind boggles*,' thought Anna.

Then finally there was one from Mel saying simply:

> Happy New Year, Mum. I miss you and love you so much. Hope you are having a good time. I will ring you tomorrow. xxxxxxxx

Inside, the fire was almost out so Rosie popped on some more logs and stoked the embers and, after making hot chocolate, both stifled yawns and decided it was time to call it a night. Climbing the stairs, Rosie asked Anna if she had enjoyed her first French New Year party and despite the Henri incident, Anna said it had been lovely, a totally different experience and was so grateful for her invite. At the top of the landing they hugged and said goodnight before making their weary way to bed.

Anna dressed hurriedly into her pyjamas then jumped into bed and was just about to reply to her texts when her phone rang. It was Sam who was taking a break from partying and spreading love, well and truly drunk, fog-horn loud and in very high spirits.

'Hi, Mum, Happy New Year, are you having fun? It's been mental here! Lads, lads, come and say hello to my mum, she's in France.'

Anna was laughing as she heard rowdy voices, then a chorus of 'Happy New Year, Sam's mum'.

'Happy New Year to you, too, take care and behave yourselves.'

This was followed by loud cheers, obviously behaving themselves was the last thing on their minds, and then Sam came back on the phone.

'Sorry it's taken ages to get through but I had some serious snogging to do, you know how it is. Anyway, I've got to get off, the taxi's here. Love you, Mum, see you soon.'

Anna chuckled and said she loved him too.

Now her mind turned to Melanie, the brief text earlier bothered her. Was it possible to get psychic vibes down the phone? God, now she was starting to sound like her mother. The simple fact that she hadn't had one, single chatty message from her daughter in almost two weeks rang alarm bells, her reticence speaking volumes.

Even after all that wine and milky hot chocolate, Anna couldn't sleep; her mind going over the night's events. First, there was Henri thinking his luck was in. He was extremely handsome and whether or not he could teach her a thing or two between the sheets was irrelevant, he wasn't her type at all. Then, Anna felt sad for Sebastien and told herself not to give him any encouragement, he was nice and all that but there was no point in egging him on. She certainly didn't want to end up running a restaurant in France, spending all night sitting on a stool at the end of the bar waiting for her husband to call it a night. She was still annoyed with herself for getting upset, but once again, Daniel had made things okay, noticing that whenever she thought of him she always smiled.

What the hell was her mother doing at a kebab shop? She was supposed to be getting a taxi home, Philip had booked one especially. Anna then had a scary vision of Enid and Gladys, sitting at the bus stop on the high street eating their doner and chips, waiting for the night service with kebab meat and spicy sauce stuck to their chins.

Her eyes slowly began to droop and Anna started to doze; thoughts of kebab meat merged with remembering to ring Melanie, then a blurry image of Joe on a beach somewhere and Sam was crammed into a taxi with all his mates… and the door knob was rattling.

Anna's eyes popped open and almost rigid with fear, she turned to her left and no, she wasn't imagining it, the door knob really was turning and then someone on the other side shook the door. Anna had been just about to scream when she heard a soft, male voice, half whispering.

'Anna, my darling, it is me, Henri. I bring champagne and would like to share it with you. Open the door and we can talk. I have waited to be alone with you all night and I am very lonely out here in the hall.'

Anna was mortified. What the hell should she do, pretend she was asleep and hope he'd go away or just tell him to piss off? The rattling got louder and there was no way anyone could sleep through that so he'd know she was awake by now, especially when his voice went up a notch and he started tapping on the door.

'Anna, Anna, wake up. It is me, your Henri, let me in. Are you in there?'

'*Oh God*,' thought Anna, '*this is so embarrassing. Please let it be a horrible dream.*' One thing she did know was that if she opened that door it would be fatal and she'd never get rid of him, it was time to take action.

'Go to bed, Henri. I'm very tired, I will see you in the morning and please be quiet or you will wake Rosie.' Anna pulled the duvet up around her chin, hoping her firm tone would do the trick.

Undeterred, Henri pleaded through the door. 'Anna, I am tired too, so let me in and we can sleep together, it will be perfect, I give you this as my promise. You will never forget tonight.'

Anna held her head in her hands. One thing was for sure, he was right on that score because the evening would definitely be going down in history as a bloody nightmare. The situation was becoming ridiculous and she was starting to get desperate when to her relief, she heard the furious voice of Saint Rosie coming to her rescue.

'Henri' she bellowed, 'what the hell do you think you are playing at?'

'*Merde*!' Anna heard Henri exclaim loudly. '*Sacré bleu*, Rosie, you scare me to my death, what are you doing creeping up on me like that? I am only talking to Anna. Go back to your bed and rest, it is late and you must think of the baby.' Henri was trying to brazen it out but knew he was in deep trouble.

'NO! I will not go back to bed, now sod off and go back to the party otherwise I'll ring Michel and tell him to come home and he will NOT be pleased about that, so go on, downstairs. *À toute vitesse*!'

Anna presumed that meant quickly then heard Henri grumbling about only having a little bit of fun and that Rosie was worse than his mother. A few more irate words were said in French and then thankfully he was gone. Gently tapping on the door, Rosie asked Anna if she was okay.

Opening it cautiously and peering down the corridor to check Romeo was really on his way, Anna then looked at Rosie before both of them burst into fits of laughter. Trying to control themselves they sat down on the edge of the bed, sides aching and wiping away tears when they were startled by the sound of stones hitting the window and their giggles ceased instantly. Creeping across the room before warily peeping around the curtains they saw Sebastien, down below, gazing up at Anna's room. The bedside light had given her location away and the sight of him set Rosie and Anna off again. Sebastien threw a couple more stones, both missing the target. No doubt he had double vision and was definitely swaying and seemed to be having trouble keeping his balance.

'Anna, Anna, are you there? It is me Sebastien, open the window, I wish to speak with you.'

When Rosie pulled up the sash and stuck her head out, giving him the shock of his life, Sebastien's mouth formed in a big round O. Rosie was definitely not who he expected. He was even more shocked when Henri appeared in the garden, staggering about while carrying his champagne and glasses becoming instantly outraged to find Sebastien attempting to woo Anna. An intense Gallic exchange ensued and not wanting to miss the fireworks, Anna popped her head out just in time to see Henri carefully put down his bottle and dramatically remove his jacket before casting it theatrically to one side and rolling up his sleeves. Sebastien soon followed suit and once prepared for battle, both men held up their fists, glaring angrily at one another.

Exasperated, Rosie decided enough was enough and in fluent French told Sebastien exactly where to get off and that if he and his creepy friend didn't clear off she would get Michel's gun and shoot them both in the arse. Undeterred by Rosie's threats, a drunken bout of what Anna could only describe as comedy fighting commenced. There were arms swinging everywhere, not one single punch connected and after a couple of minutes of circling each other, lots of swearing, hilarious kung-fu kicks and disorientated staggering about, both were definitely getting out of puff. Sebastien had lost one of his shoes which Henri childishly threw in the direction of the pool so in retaliation, his very expensive jacket found itself on the roof of Michel's kitchen.

Rosie had disappeared and despite being enthralled by the performance below, Anna was worried she'd gone to get the gun. She soon returned carrying two plastic buckets from Ruby's cleaning cupboard, signalling for Anna to follow her to the bathroom. Chuckling, they filled both buckets with ice-cold water and taking one each, went back to the window. Outside, the two sparring partners had stopped to catch their breath. Both had their hands on their knees, panting away, but sure enough, after a breather, the battle resumed. Henri lunged forward and grabbed Sebastien around the neck and began dragging him around and around in a circle, demanding he surrender.

'Just wait until they get really close, we don't want to miss them.' Rosie peeped out as they balanced the buckets on the edge of the windowsill, both waiting patiently for the right moment.

Locked together, Sebastien finally managed to wrestle Henri to the ground and they rolled about on the terrace, thrashing wildly, ending up just within reach, right below the window. Knowing the moment had arrived, Rosie and Anna looked at each other, smiled wickedly, and chucked the water onto their unsuspecting victims.

Leaning out to get a good look, Anna and Rosie howled laughing as Henri and Sebastien spluttered and shrieked as they tried to recover from the blast of ice-cold water, looking up to the window above in complete shock.

'Now go home, or I really will get the gun, I mean it!' Rosie pushed down the sash window sharply and then pulled the curtains firmly shut.

The room was now freezing and their feet felt like blocks of ice on the cold wooden floor. Anna and Rosie peeped from between the drapes as the enemies staggered to their feet, one helping the other up, their clothes wringing wet as the heat from their bodies created plumes of steam. Henri picked up his champagne and glasses and as if nothing had happened, the two friends swayed off into the distance in a misty haze. Both had an arm around the other's shoulder, laughing and slapping each other on the back as they went, their feud completely forgotten. As they disappeared out of sight, they even began singing.

'Bloody typical!' said Rosie.

It was 3.30am and Anna could feel her feet again. She put extra blankets on the bed and after being sure Henri and Sebastien had taken the hint, reopened the curtains so she could watch the stars twinkle in the jet-black sky and the moon shine in through the window; a silver glow lighting up her room. Taking her phone from the charger on the bedside table she typed a joint message to her children.

Hi, it's your mum. I'm lying here in my bed in France watching the stars and thinking of you. I wanted you all to know that I couldn't have got through these past few months without my wonderful children. You are my greatest achievement and my life. I know that as time goes by and you spread your wings it means we will spend more time away from each other. So wherever you are in the world, however far apart we are, no matter how many miles separate us, just remember that we are always under the same sky. Whatever time of day or night it is, if we are missing each other, we just have to look up. The heat from the sun, the light from the moon and the twinkle of the stars is reminding you that I am here for you. Never forget that you are always in my thoughts. I love you with all my heart and I am the proudest mum in the whole world. Catch this hug and I will see you soon X

CHAPTER 27

The beeping from her phone woke an exhausted Anna from a dream free, semi-comatose sleep. Barely able to lift her head from the pillow, trying desperately to force open her eyes and fumbling around she eventually located her mobile and squinted her eyes. The room was too bright and it was a struggle to focus on the screen. Finally, she made out the words, it was from Melanie.

Mum, check your inbox, sent email – URGENT!

Sitting bolt upright Anna checked the time, 8.30am. She'd had five hours sleep once last night's shenanigans ended and planned a record breaking lie in. Forcing herself into action, she needed the loo so heaved herself out of bed, flicking on the kettle as she passed to go to the bathroom. Rubbing her eyes and yawning, she desperately needed to wake up in order to read properly so splashed water on her face. The little tray with assorted packets of tea, coffee and hot chocolate were a godsend so as she waited for the email to open, the Internet speed was always snail's pace, quickly poured boiling water into a cup and stirred in the sachet of espresso, hoping it would do the trick.

Sitting down on the bed, Anna felt excited at last to hear from her daughter and wondered what was so urgent, praying that it wouldn't be a three-line wonder and half expecting Mel to say she'd run out of money and needed a top-up. It was much worse than that.

Hi Mum, I am going to start by saying sorry for my lack of communication since I got here. I got a right telling off from Sam yesterday and promised I'd ring you today. It would take too long on the phone and cost a fortune to explain why I've not been in touch so I hope when you read this you will understand.

Everything was okay until I realised that Paloma and her whole family are a bunch of FREAKS. Her mum and dad are not at all how she described them – first off, her dad is a huge snob and talks like Prince Charles. He more or less ignores us and I don't actually think he knows who I am. If he isn't at his golf club he spends the rest of the time locked in his study making money and avoiding his vile wife.

As for Star, I don't think she's an artist at all. I reckon it's just a cover story so she can slob around all day in her studio getting pissed – sorry for swearing. She sits in a smelly old armchair drinking gin surrounded by half-finished scenery paintings that are crap. Honestly, Summer can do better with her felt tips. And the sculptures she makes are just lumps of dried up old clay – a bit like her actually. Star never gets up until lunchtime, floats around in her old hippy dresses and then gets stuck into the booze. Paloma says it's her artistic nature but I just think she's a mad, old alky.

The first day was alright. We spent most of the time by the pool and just relaxed but Paloma hates the sun and didn't want to get brown – she's perfecting the pale, unhealthy look, so sits under a parasol most of the time, then in the afternoon we went inside to watch television which was fine because I didn't want to burn. We skipped breakfast and I was waiting and waiting for something to eat but wouldn't ask because I thought it was a bit rude.

They have a lovely maid called Mariella who I've got to know quite well but she doesn't do cooking, just cleaning up after this scruffy tribe of mingers. Anyway, I was starving and in the end had to ask Paloma, who, as you know, can survive on nuts and seeds so we went into the kitchen but there was absolutely nothing there apart from alcohol, off-milk and crisps. The fridge was empty except for champagne and tonic water so in the end we walked into town and got pizza, well I did, Paloma was being a food-weirdo as usual. Apparently her dad eats at the golf club and if her mum's sober, she rings for takeaway in the evening, not that she's ever bought us one.

Then there's Paloma's new boyfriend, Pete the Protester. She met him at a party before Christmas and spends the whole time texting and messaging him on Facebook, she's besotted. Prince Charles will have a fit when he gets his phone bill cos she's been ringing Pete every day and yakking on for hours about politics and the oppressed.

After that, the days just seemed to drag on in the same boring way. Paloma doesn't get up much before her mum, she refuses to go to the beach because the smell of the sea makes her heave, sand gets everywhere and it's too hot and boring – like her. She prefers to stay by the pool or slob out in front of the telly talking to Pete. I've not had one meal in the house – except for Christmas day which I'll tell you about in a bit and I've had to use all of my money buying food from town, otherwise I'd starve.

On Christmas Eve we went to the golf club which was awful, full of posh ex-pats trying to outdo each other. The only good thing was the buffet but apart from that it was boring. In the end, we snuck off and went into town but Paloma got wasted on vodka and was sick everywhere so we came back here and went to bed. I was hoping that Christmas Day would be better. They had the caterers in because Prince Charles invited some of his cronies and their wives round for dinner.

I know you are going to be fed up when I tell you this but Christmas morning was a non-event, nobody got up, no presents or fun, it was awful.

Paloma was ill and dragged herself out of bed at 11am and we swapped gifts. She gave me a friendship bracelet that she reckons she made herself but I think it was one of her old cast-offs. I left her parents' presents on the kitchen table, they didn't get me anything. Paloma got money in an envelope which they will probably want back for the phone bill.

Christmas Dinner was a complete trial. The food was nice but the guests were totally hideous. Star got trashed on wine, knocking it down like it was going out of fashion, Paloma sat there like a zombie and messaged Pete and, as usual, ate virtually nothing while her mum and dad made sarky comments about each other, sniping and embarrassing everyone so the guests left early.

After that I did my own thing. Paloma was pretending to be ill and festered in her stinky bed so for the next couple of days I just went down to the beach and spent time reading. There were lots of families around so before you stress out I was quite safe. Then, when Paloma recovered we had a bit of a row because I told her I was bored doing the same old thing and wanted to explore the island. She said I was ungrateful and should be glad she'd invited me and what more did I want – I was getting a free holiday after all. I said it was more like prison and I was being punished for a crime I didn't know I'd committed.

We didn't speak for a whole day. Mariella the cleaner was the only person to talk to and I've been practising Spanish with her. She's lovely and one day she made me a packed lunch and brought it with her. I went to her house for tea as well. She told me they are all mad people in that villa and have no manners and live like pigs, she also warned me to stay away from Mungo as he's a bad boy. She even gave me her phone number and said I could ring her anytime if there was any trouble.

I didn't really understand why until the horrible brother turned up on Saturday. Mungo has been skiing with his chums from uni and he arrived with three other Hooray Henrys and then basically took over the villa. Paloma's dad hasn't been seen since – I don't think they get on. And Star thinks Mungo's the bee's knees and he can do no wrong. The house is trashed on a daily basis, they never pick anything up, it's a pigsty, bottles and takeaway boxes everywhere, and poor Mariella gets treated like a slave.

They spend all day drinking and – don't freak – they take drugs. I had my suspicions but last night when Star and Prince Charles went to the golf club for another old-fogey night, we stayed at the villa and had a party round the pool. To be honest I'd rather have gone with her parents as I felt uncomfortable with Mungo and his creepy friends, and at least there would have been some decent food but Paloma had apologised for snapping so I had to let it go.

You are going to hate this next bit but when Mungo joined us outside he emptied a bag of white stuff onto the table and began snorting it. I knew it was cocaine, I've seen it on telly enough times, and then he asked me if I wanted some. DON'T PANIC. I SAID NO. I'M NOT STUPID! What really upset me was that Paloma took it too, and then called me a sissy and a baby for refusing. I said she was pathetic and told her to fuck off and went to bed – I am so not apologising for saying that to you or anyone.

Since then they've been banging on my door and window for most of the night, shouting awful things and calling me names, one of them said he'd do really disgusting things to me if he got in my room. I locked myself in and put the cupboard in front of the door. The party carried on until 6am so I stayed awake in case they managed to open the window. When I got your text I missed you and home so much and knew I had to tell you the truth, and then you'd sort it out for me.

I hate it here and I hate Paloma. She is selfish and rude and smelly. She's not a proper friend and her family is awful. I didn't tell you all this stuff as it was happening because at first I thought it would get better, then I knew it would upset you and spoil your Christmas and that's the last thing I wanted. My plan was to get through it and ditch Paloma the second we got back to uni.

It's my own fault for not listening to your advice and for being selfish and leaving you at Christmas and wanting to do my own thing. I miss you so much, Mum, and just want to go home. I don't know what to do. Please, please, please don't let this ruin your holiday, that will make it a hundred million times worse, but can you think of a way of getting me out of this house. I'd rather sleep at the beach than stay here one more day. I love you, Mum, and I am sorry if you are upset or annoyed or both when you read this. Ring me. Melanie x

Anna was sobbing and angry and horrified. How could people be so vile? She had to pull herself together before she rang Mel. She had to get her home. A million thoughts zapped around her brain and adrenaline pumped through her veins, she must get organised, make some calls, reassure Melanie that it was all in hand, she would sort it out. The first thing Anna did was forward the email to Jeannie. The subject said URGENT – READ THIS THEN RING ME. Then she rang Mel.

'Mum,' Mel picked up on the second ring and instantly started to cry.

'Melanie, don't get upset, sweetheart. It's okay, I understand. I'll sort it out. I'm going to get Jeannie to book you a flight home or try and change the one you've got, but you need to calm down and listen to me.' Anna paused as Mel gulped for air, the sobs slowly subsiding.

'I'm not being a baby, Mum, but I hate it here and the atmosphere will be awful when they all wake up and those boys scare me. I can't even repeat what they said, it was disgusting. What shall I do?'

'Melanie, you are not a baby, you've stuck it out and despite living with a bunch of morons you tried to make the best of it and protect my feelings at the same time. It's a bloody good job I can't get my hands on them though, I am livid.' Anna was raging while Melanie had stopped crying, at last.

'So what's the plan, have you spoken to Jeannie yet?'

Hearing the desperation in her daughter's voice, Anna realised she needed to get things moving.

'No, but I forwarded your email, it was the quickest way of her getting the gist of things. I hope you don't mind but she'd find out eventually. Right, this is what we need to do. I want you to text Jeannie your flight details, if it can't be changed I'll get her to book you on a different one. If there are none today we'll find you a hotel for the night so don't worry about staying there. I'd do it myself but the Internet is so slow here it will take ages. When you've done that, pack your case and stay in your room and wait for me to ring you back. Jeannie can arrange for a taxi to the airport or wherever. I'll book a flight home when I know you are sorted.' Anna heard Melanie let out a loud wail.

'No! Mum, please don't come home early. That will make everything even worse and I swear, if this spoils your holiday I will go outside right now and punch Paloma and Mungo in the face. I mean it, Mum, stay there!'

Anna wasn't convinced, insisting she should be there when Mel got back.

'Mum, it's not necessary. As long as I am away from here I'll be okay. I'm sure I can stay with Uncle Phil and Jeannie or I'll go to Gran's and chill with her, it'll be fun. Then we can have next weekend together when Sam comes home, *please*, Mum.' Melanie sounded like she was on the verge of tears again, her voice beseeching.

Anna said she would decide once she'd spoken to Jeannie, urging Melanie to send her details and pack her case while she made the call.

By lunchtime everything was arranged. Anna was trying to keep calm and not obsess over ways of punishing Paloma and her family, while Rosie had been a soothing influence throughout the morning as Anna liaised between Tenerife and England. They had left Michel in the kitchen clattering around, preparing a late lunch for his family at the same time as insisting he didn't have a hangover, which, judging by the state of his bloodshot eyes and strange green-grey complexion, was a bit of a fib.

Jeannie rose to the challenge and booked Melanie another flight as her economy ticket couldn't be altered. The new one was a red-eye, but Anna was assured that Mel would be fine, the airport was a busy place with lots of holidaymakers around – she'd come to no harm in the departure lounge. Philip would pick Melanie up and she was going to stay with them after Jeannie made Anna promise to remain in France, reminding her that Mel would feel bad enough without having a guilty conscience to deal with as well.

Philip Googled a taxi firm in the town near to Paloma's house which picked Melanie up and took her to the airport. The family from hell was still drugged up or paralytic when she snuck out of the house. Anna told her not to even leave them a note and see how long it took them to notice she was gone, but Rosie's common sense prevailed, suggesting she left a short message explaining she was leaving early. They certainly didn't deserve a thank-you but felt it best to maintain the moral high ground, although in the case of that family, it really wasn't too hard!

Anna was wrung out, sleep deprived and mad as hell, but now things were organised and Melanie was on her way home, she started to relax. Their thoughts turned to the previous evening and the wrestling match outside Anna's window, going over the whole scene, giggling and wishing they'd videoed it. Michel was furious that Rosie had been disturbed and embarrassed that Anna had been pestered by his brother and the mood he was in at the moment, when Henri turned up for lunch he might get a bit more than he bargained for. Anna secretly hoped he'd cry off as she was dreading facing him but accepted the shenanigans were mostly due to high spirits and, as usual, too much wine.

By the time the guests arrived, Anna had helped Rosie set the table and sliced the bread for Michel. He had perked up immensely and was scurrying about putting the final touches to his meal. The main course was lamb shanks *en papillote* with leeks, carrots, rosemary, and orange. Anna had watched him earlier placing all the ingredients inside a paper case to steam inside the oven and the aroma wafting around the kitchen made Anna's stomach rumble.

The gathering was small, just Michel's parents, grandparents, and Henri. Anna made herself useful and served drinks and passed around the hors d'oeuvre, keeping an eye on the door and waiting for Romeo to arrive. When he finally flounced in looking his usual elegant self, Anna took the initiative and greeted him with a drink and a warm hug, wished him a Happy New Year and hoped he hadn't caught a cold after his surprise shower. Henri smiled back, looked genuinely amused and assured her he was fine then clinking his glass against hers, gave a little salute before moving off to embrace his family.

Unable to communicate with anyone except Rosie and Henri, Anna decided to help Michel, so for the rest of the evening, in between courses she tidied the dishes and served the guests. The meal was heavenly: *coquilles de St. Jacques* for starter – scallops in a creamy wine sauce served inside large seashells – then the lamb shanks followed by cheese and a dark chocolate mousse. Anna didn't feel uncomfortable or out of place as Michel's family were friendly and accepting; thanking her each time she served them or removed their plate, attempting to bring her into the conversation using the others to translate.

Anna marvelled at the contrast, comparing those before her to Paloma's family, confirming her belief that no matter how much money you have, it's what is in your heart that matters and how you treat others. Being loaded couldn't buy you genuine love or kindness and it didn't make you better than the next person, in some cases it made people worse. It was a shame that Melanie had learnt the hard way not to be dazzled by wealth or believe everything you're told, it was just part of growing up and thankfully, it had turned out well and she was safe.

Upstairs later, Anna read her messages as she lay in bed, utterly exhausted. Sam had texted, explaining exactly what he would do to Mungo if ever he saw him. He was mad as hell.

Daniel was all packed and would see her around 2pm the following day. Jeannie was looking forward to having Mel stay, insisting that Anna wasn't to worry about a thing before adding mysteriously that one way or another she would 'sort out that lot in Tenerife'. Anna was actually far too tired and a little bit scared to ask what she meant.

Snuggling down under the blankets, Anna dozed with her phone on the pillow, waiting for Melanie to ring before she boarded the plane. Only then could she relax. Reflecting on the last day or so where there had never been a dull moment, images floated in her head of randy wrestling Frenchmen, a kebab-eating, disco-dancing mother, her daughter trapped in paradise, then of herself, crying like a fool in the garden on New Year's Eve. Anna hoped that Sam hadn't expanded the Harrison gene pool on his night out and then she pictured the photo of Joe on the beach with bikini girl. Her mind was weary just thinking about the past twenty-four hours but they were all okay, her little family and her friends.

At 10.15pm when her phone finally rang, it nearly gave Anna a heart attack, jolting her awake. Melanie was at the gate about to board and she could hear the happiness in her daughter's voice.

'Night night, Mum, I love you and thank you for today, you're the best. See you Friday.'

'Night, Melanie, love you too sweetheart. Have a safe flight and I'll see you soon.'

Then, pushing scenes from *Taken* firmly out of her weary mind, Anna slept.

CHAPTER 28

Pascal and Océane called in after lunch to say Happy New Year and stayed until Daniel and Josh arrived. The three of them, Pascal, Océane and Josh, had arranged to go into Angers and do some shopping. Océane looked lovely although a little bit on the nervous side and judging by the way she kept pacing the room and peeping through the window, had a huge crush on Josh. In truth, Anna knew exactly how Océane felt and had a few butterflies of her own jiggling about inside her stomach, whilst trying to appear patient and unflustered.

Just after 2pm, they heard a car pull up on the gravel outside and while Rosie went to the porch to welcome her guests, Anna watched Océane check her hair in the mirror and smooth down her skirt. '*Oh dear,*' she thought, '*she's got it bad.*' All at once they were in the room where Pascal, being his usual effervescent self, was shaking hands and welcoming them in whereas Josh was struck dumb when he saw his love interest. In an attempt to jolly things along, Anna jumped up from the couch and gave him a hug, asking if the cat had got his tongue before turning to Daniel who rolled his eyes at his brother then enveloped her in an embrace of his own. The second his arms wrapped around her, Anna had the urge to hold on and not let go. His body felt familiar, yet strange and exciting all at once.

'Right. You young things had better get a wriggle on if you want to do some shopping otherwise everywhere will be closed.' Rosie was ushering them out the door. 'And drive carefully, Pascal. The roads are a little icy.'

When they were finally gone, Daniel shook his head laughing. 'You know, he's not shut up about seeing Océane since we left and then when he claps eyes on her he goes shtum, he's all talk.' Daniel hung his coat up and went over to the fire, warming his hands on the flames.

Rosie tactfully shot off to make coffee and Anna sat on the sofa, taking in Daniel, just glad he was here. They chatted with ease about the journey up and the weather which had changed and now harsh sub-zero temperatures were expected over the next few days. Both asked about their respective holidays, Anna skilfully omitting the Henri and Sebastien incident. When Rosie returned with Michel in tow they all sat together drinking coffee and warming themselves by the fire until the kitchen finally beckoned Michel. He was preparing a special dinner for the four of them so Rosie announced she was going for a lie down and would see them later. Not seeming at all phased by being left alone, as Anna had to admit she was, Daniel suggested they go for a walk before it got too dark. He'd been stuck in the car all day and could do with some fresh air.

A cold north wind was getting up and an icy blast took Anna's breath away as she stepped outside. Looking up at the sky, Daniel stopped and turned to her.

'Are you sure you want to be out here? It's a bit nippy, I didn't realise.' Daniel shivered and pulled up his collar.

'No, I'm fine, honest. We should warm up once we set off and I need to work up an appetite for whatever Michel has planned.' Anna closed the door and pulled on her gloves, however, just before they set off, Daniel held out his hand.

Looking into her eyes, watching her intently, he waited. Her stomach flipped over and then she smiled. Placing her hand in his, Anna wished instantly that she hadn't worn her gloves because then she could've felt the touch of his skin. Closing his hand firmly around hers Daniel didn't speak but his eyes twinkled as he smiled back. They walked down the drive hand in hand as her chest constricted with happiness. It was so easy and natural and everything felt right, apart from fighting the urge to turn around and check Rosie's bedroom window. Anna fully expected to see her

Patricia Dixon

friend's face, squashed up against the glass, smiling and keeping an amused, beady eye on them.

They walked silently for a while, heading down the lane and towards the village. Every now and then she felt Daniel's thumb stroke hers, sending a thrill through her body and eventually he broke the silence.

'I wonder how Josh is getting on with Océane. He's off drink at the moment after he threw up at Louise's. He's only just recovered so at least I know he won't make a show of himself. Fingers crossed.'

'Poor Josh, he does get himself in trouble but having said that, wait till you hear about Melanie. We had a right performance yesterday. It turns out she's been staying with the family from hell.'

Daniel stopped in his tracks for a second and looked concerned so after assuring him it was all sorted out; Anna began the 'Tale of Tenerife'.

By the time she'd finished they had reached the village and Daniel suggested they go into the bar and warm up to which Anna replied hastily, saying it wasn't a great idea, leaving him slightly puzzled. Grinning, she told him she would explain later, it was just another crazy New Year story that could wait. Instead, they walked into the small garden next to the Mayor's office, well out of sight of Sebastien's restaurant and found a wooden bench in front of a large shrine. The Virgin Mary stood inside a large white stone cave, the Nativity scene laid out at her feet with fairy lights strung around the perimeter, lighting up the grotto. It was very pretty and soothing as Daniel positioned himself close to Anna and folded his arm through hers, saying that they'd soon lose the light and would need to set off before it became pitch black. The country roads had no street lights and when it got dark it was hard to see your hand in front of you.

Anna knew she had to get something off her chest, not Henri and Sebastien, and maybe this was the only time she would get the opportunity. Taking off her gloves she fidgeted about in her pocket, checked her phone for the time then turned it to silent, not wanting any interruptions.

'Daniel, remember in Portsmouth, that night at the pub, you asked me if there was something bothering me or if I wanted to talk to you about anything?' Anna heard the nervousness in her own voice before Daniel replied.

'Yes, then Josh turned up. I got the impression you were conveniently saved by the bell.' He smiled, waiting for her to continue.

'The thing is I've not been entirely honest with you. I haven't told you everything about Matthew and I need to get it off my chest so that you might understand me a bit better. And that, I assure you, will be quite a challenge because half the time I don't understand myself, really.' Anna felt Daniel tense slightly. She was rambling and needed to get on with it.

He probably thought she was going to tell him she'd topped her husband and buried him under the patio or he wasn't really dead at all and she was just a philanderer. Staring straight ahead, focusing on Mary's forlorn face while the lights twinkled around baby Jesus in his crib, Anna took a deep breath and got on with it.

'What I wanted to explain, what I need to say is that in May last year, two months before he died, I found out that Matthew was having an affair.' There, she'd said it and even that short sentence had lifted such a weight, now all she had to do was tell her tale, all of it.

Daniel patiently listened to everything. He didn't interrupt to ask questions, not a word. He simply held on to her hand, glancing up now and then. Anna suspected he was checking for tears but there were none. She purposely kept things matter-of-fact and straight to the point, giving him a chronological breakdown of events, right up until the time they had met at Rosie's and since. Anna didn't want sympathy. Her only desire was that he understood her better, to lift the burden of a secret that she knew was holding her down. Once she had finished, Anna took a deep breath and looked straight at Daniel.

'There, that's it. I'm glad I've told you, for all sorts of reasons. I hope you're not angry with me though, for not saying all this sooner.' Anna was worried and unsure.

Daniel sighed, and then he stood, holding out his hand to her once more. She couldn't read the expression on his face but if she had to choose just one description, she'd have said he looked annoyed.

'Come on you, let's walk back before it gets too dark and no, Anna, I'm not angry with you. I'm not angry at all.'

Letting out a sigh of relief, Anna took his hand. This time she could feel his skin against hers and it sent a powerful bolt of something highly charged through her body so strong that had it been electricity, she'd be dead. Squeezing his fingers tightly she hoped it sent a message, saying thank you. As they began to walk, Daniel placed their hands in his coat pocket to keep them warm, also taking the position nearest the road, protecting her from oncoming cars. Anna kept her eyes downward on the grass verge as she walked, waiting for him to speak.

'There are so many things I could say about Matthew but I won't, mainly because I never knew him and have no right to criticise or judge. And even if I did and despite what he's done, deep down inside you will want to defend him because you're a loyal person. Yes, I think he must have been mad to risk losing you and I can't imagine why he would jeopardise his marriage and his family but he did, and now you are left with the mess and if I'm honest, that makes me angry. You don't deserve that.' Daniel held Anna's hand more tightly from inside his pocket.

'I think that my loyalty to him has been the main reason I didn't say anything before, plus the fact that sometimes I feel ashamed that I wasn't good enough to keep him, so he looked elsewhere. I can't tell you what a blow that is to your confidence and self-esteem. I was in shock and denial at first, and then I just went into autopilot, stupidly hoping that it'd all just go away and we'd get back to normal. I realise now that I wasn't thinking straight and should've confided in Jeannie and taken some advice, or even confronted him sooner, not left it until the day he died. In a way I'd been a widow for a long time. Our marriage was dead even though he wasn't. And on top of that, being left ignorant of so many things made me feel foolish.' Anna realised the gloom from that period in her life was beginning to settle again, like a dark cloud overhead because revisiting that time only brought back the pain.

'Anna, don't ever feel ashamed or foolish, you were deceived. This is not your burden to carry and that's all I will say on that subject. But how did you carry on, day after day, knowing he was being unfaithful, it must have driven you crazy? I know for a fact I wouldn't be able to keep a lid on something like that.' There was disbelief in Daniel's voice mixed with sincere concern.

'I honestly don't know. It seems like so long ago. Melanie was still at home and Sam would pop back now and then so I suppose on one hand, I was terrified that they would find out and wanted to protect them. On the other, I think I was also protecting myself by not facing up to it. I kept looking for clues, listening to phone calls, checking his mobile, observing his every move or conversation, scrutinising what he said or how he said it. God knows why, perhaps I just wanted to be sure so that when I finally worked up the courage to confront him I had all the evidence. I also realised that once it was in the open that was it. I was terrified that if I gave him the opportunity to confess and get it off his chest he might actually be relieved and walk out, and even then I didn't want to lose him.' She hoped saying that hadn't hurt Daniel in any way and was desperate to make things right.

Anna needed him to know that even though she didn't want to lose Matthew at the time, it didn't alter how she felt about what was happening now. The gloom that hovered above her was becoming oppressive and she could feel it seeping into her bones, bringing her down.

'I hate that the past affects me so much. I want to move on but need to take things slowly, not make mistakes and have regrets. I couldn't bear to feel like that ever again, to lose someone or be hurt by them for whatever reason.' Anna looked at Daniel for reassurance.

'You know what, Anna? You could go over and over this a hundred times and nothing will ever change what happened. Please don't think I'm being harsh with you because that's not how I mean it. The events leading up to Matthew's death will always be the same and no matter how much you beat yourself up for not doing this or saying that. It won't change anything and it wasn't your fault. You were stuck in a situation not of your making which you dealt with in the best way you could at the time.' Daniel looked at Anna now, hoping for some hint of understanding or the very least a smile.

She was deep in thought and silent so Daniel ploughed on, trying to make her see sense.

'As I see it, you have got confidence, you just don't realise it. I bet you never dreamed you'd come to a place like this and meet new people, did you? Your strength and support will be keeping your kids going and give them a great example to follow. I'm sure all your family are proud of the way you've got on with your life so you just need to keep up the momentum and not get too bogged down in the past, even though every now and then it will come back to haunt you. But given time you will learn to deal with it, I know you will.' Daniel nudged her arm and smiled encouragingly.

'See, you've made me feel better already.' Anna smiled at last and the cloud of misery began dispersing, floating off into the night sky. 'I hate talking about it all. It just brings everything back but I'm glad I told you. It's a weight off my mind and sort of feels like a fresh start.'

They turned left into the lane that led up to the hotel and Anna suddenly felt sad that their time alone was almost over, even though she was perished and her toes were numb. Noticing their pace had slowed Anna hoped it meant a few more minutes could be added on and as they crunched their way back up the drive, both were lost in thought. To the side of the porch was a round iron table and chairs and without warning, Daniel stopped and leaned against it. Taking Anna's other hand he gently pulled her close and folded his arms around her back and as her body rested against his, she placed her hands on his shoulders, waiting for him to speak as he smiled and looked deep into her eyes.

'So, that brings us to the very tricky situation of you and me.' He was teasing and had a glint in his eye. 'Now I know all your secrets, Madame, I feel I should tell you some of mine.'

Anna laughed and gripped his collar, playfully pulling him just a little bit closer.

'Oh yes, Monsieur, and what secrets may these be?' The way Anna felt right at that moment she really didn't care if he was an international jewel thief or a secret agent.

'Well, I think it's only fair and right that you know I have been totally besotted since the first moment I clapped eyes on you that night in the restaurant.'

Anna stifled a giggle, totally flattered as Daniel continued.

'I think about you twenty-four-seven. You torment my dreams and keep me awake most nights. I've bored my friends to death telling them how wonderful you are and the subject of Anna is now banned from the pub. And absolutely nothing you could confess would ever change the way I feel about you… are you getting the message here?' Daniel gave her a quizzical look. When Anna nodded it assured him he was getting through so he continued, 'Seriously though. Now I know the score I completely understand that you need to take things slowly so rest assured. I am the most patient man in England, or even Europe. And I'll be here for you no matter how long it takes to sort out whatever goes on in that head of yours. There's no pressure, I promise.'

Large, happy tears fell from the corner of Anna's eyes which Daniel wiped away gently. 'There is one thing you might be able to help me with, although it might keep me awake tonight but at the same time cure me of a terrible obsession.'

Anna frowned, curiosity getting the better of her. 'Should I be worried about this obsession in any way? You'd better tell me what it is before I agree to anything.'

Daniel shook his head and lifting his hand, stroked Anna's face and then said quietly, 'I would just like to know if actually kissing you in real life, right here and now, would be as good as it is in my imagination?'

Anna's heart skipped a beat then pounded away in her chest, playing the drums for all it was worth. 'Well, there's really only one way to find out and I'd be more than happy to help.' Anna only had to wait a heartbeat for him to react.

There are so many types of kisses, like a quick peck on the cheek that you forget seconds after it happens. At New Year or the end of a crazy night out, a result of too many vodkas and being egged on by your mates. Or perhaps the one behind the bike sheds with a spotty lad you can't even remember the name of anymore. Truth or dare can be fateful and the work's Christmas party is always a real hazard. But the worst one of all is when you feel the urge to scrub your mouth with Dettol and you cringe at the thought of it for weeks, too embarrassed to tell your friends.

But some kisses are the special ones and you know when it happens. It doesn't matter where you are, either. It can be at the bus stop in the pouring rain, outside the chippy with the taste of salt and vinegar on your lips, on the back, middle, or front row of the cinema, at your mum's front door or on the settee watching *Dr Who*. The setting is irrelevant, it's who you are with that counts. You know the minute your lips meet theirs and feel the heat of their body against yours. Nothing else exists except for that moment because the deal is sealed; it is etched into your memory and carved into your soul forever.

Even if your heart eventually gets broken and the owner of the lips disappears forever from your world, the moment remains and is held as a gold standard for kissers of the future to live up to. Right there and then, in the middle of France in a wintry garden with frozen toes and a red, runny nose, Anna knew that this was one of those kisses. As Daniel pulled her nearer, blue eyes willing her to trust him, his face so close she could hear him breathing, she closed her eyes as his lips met hers. Strong arms held on tight, her body pressed against his and Anna gave in, not caring who saw, what they thought or where she was. This was their moment and it was perfect.

'Well, has that answered your question?' Anna teased, feeling giddy and flushed.

Daniel scrunched his face and shook his head. 'I think I need to double check, just to be on the safe side, in the interests of accuracy and all that.'

So he pulled her close and kissed her again. 'Yes, got to admit it, that's definitely better than I imagined. But now I'll never sleep again and I hope you feel really guilty about that.'

Anna hugged him, laying her head on his shoulder, savouring the heat of his body, the feeling of his arms around her and the scent of his skin, even his clothes smelt good.

'Are you okay?' Daniel whispered in Anna's ear as he kissed the side of her head then held her close.

'I'm fine, Daniel, stop worrying. And thank you for being you. For coming here and having dinner in the restaurant that night but most of all, for being my friend. I'm so glad I met you. You make me feel happy and safe. I want you to know that.'

'Well, I do now.' Daniel's smile showed huge relief until bright headlights broke the moment as Pascal's car pulled into the drive. 'Here comes trouble, perfect timing as usual.'

Josh, Océane and Pascal piled out of the car and announced they weren't stopping long but a change of clothes was needed as they were going to eat out. Daniel passed Josh his car keys so they could get the cases from the boot, lingering with Anna until the commotion died down and they'd gone inside.

'Come on, we can't stay out here kissing like teenagers all night, you're frozen. Let's go in before Rosie sends out a search party.'

After giving her one last kiss, and then another, they both floated inside.

CHAPTER 29

Anna found Rosie making tea in the apartment kitchenette. Daniel had gone to change for dinner and check on Josh, more than likely he wanted to warn him to behave himself while he was out.

'Well, you look like the cat that got the cream, are those rosy red cheeks due to the cold or are you a bit hot under the collar?' Rosie enjoyed teasing Anna whenever the opportunity arose.

'A bit of both actually, anyway sit down and stop faffing. I need to tell you my news and as long as you promise to be serious for once, you can give me some advice.' Anna patted the sofa and gave Rosie a stern look.

Rosie brought two mugs over and sat down, doing as she was told before asking the obvious. 'Come on then, dish the dirt, what's happened?'

Anna related the walk to the village and how she had told Daniel everything, ending with kissing on the porch. Rosie hooted with laughter and clapped enthusiastically, saying it was about bloody time.

'The thing is, Rosie, what about tonight? He said he understands that I want to take things slowly but what if he's half hoping that if he plays his cards right, we might sleep together. I don't want a repeat performance of Henri tapping on my door. I know we're adults but I'm not ready for that.' Anna watched as Rosie sipped her drink, clearly considering her response.

'From what I know about Daniel he's an honourable bloke and I think he's proved that over the past few months. The way I look at it is he's only human and I'm quite sure given any encouragement whatsoever he'd be more than happy to wander along the corridor tonight. That said, I don't think he's going to risk offending you. He will be taking his signals from you, he's not daft, Anna, and he's certainly nothing like Henri, thank God.' Rosie placed her mug onto the table, and then continued.

'And if it makes you feel better, I can't see him sneaking out once Josh is asleep, can you? He'd never hear the last of it if he got caught creeping back in after a night of passion. No, I reckon you're perfectly safe so just relax and enjoy the evening.' Rosie patted Anna's knee, genuinely concerned that her friend's sensitive soul always managed to take the shine off happy times.

'You're right as usual. I wish I was as sensible as you. I've just got to stop worrying and overthinking things, it's my New Year's resolution.' Anna leaned back into the sofa, relaxing slightly, vowing to go with the flow and enjoy her time with Daniel, with all of them.

Later, as she changed for dinner, in celebration of her new positive mindset Anna messaged her kids, letting them know she was having a great time and would be spending the evening with Rosie and Michel, plus one of the guests she'd met in October, called Daniel. There, she'd done it. Mentioning his name felt good. Just a hint would do for now, she didn't want to have secrets from her children so would introduce his existence gradually. Jeannie, however, got a more detailed version as promised, not leaving out any juicy details.

A harsh wind began to howl outside, rattling the window frame with each icy blast. As she dressed, spatters of rain began to tap against the glass, increasing in size until they became ferocious hailstones. Glad she would be safe and warm indoors, Anna got on with the task in hand and chose a peach sweater that was decorated with shimmering sequins and her favourite jeans. She wanted to feel comfortable and not overdressed; she was with friends so there was no need to make an impression.

Daniel was waiting in the bar with Michel when she went downstairs; they were watching the news and drinking pastis. Anna hoped that the dancing butterflies in her stomach would stay forever and not fly away, aware of how thrilling a new relationship could be. She so wanted this feeling to last and maybe, with a bit of luck, this time it would.

That evening, during a wonderful meal, the four of them talked late into the night about every subject under the sun. Josh returned in high spirits, thankfully sober but very tired so went off to bed leaving them to sit around the fire in the lounge. Anna and Daniel were side by side on the sofa, the feel of his body was comforting and she succumbed to the urge to hold his hand, still slightly self-conscious, especially under the watchful and amused eye of Rosie. It was past midnight when their chaperone finally gave in to tiredness and Rosie announced she was off to bed. Refusing any offers of help and tactfully insisting Anna and Daniel remain by the fire, Rosie and Michel retreated to the kitchen. Once they were gone, Daniel pulled her into his arms and whispered in her ear.

'I've been dying to do this all night. You cannot imagine how much self-control it's taken. I hope you're impressed.'

Anna let her body fold into his, relishing the feel of him, his chest was extremely firm and his muscular arms convinced her he must work out. Underneath her hand she could feel his heart beating through his shirt.

'Well, that makes us equal because I feel the same. I just hope my eyes stay open, too much wine makes me sleepy.' Anna rested her head on his chest as she listened out for their hosts.

'Well, before you nod off, I need you to remind me of how good those kisses are.' Daniel managed to make everything sound relaxed.

So feeling quite bold Anna did her very best to refresh his memory, leaving him in no doubt of the quality and definitely wanting more.

Voices approaching along the hall forced an end to their embrace which Anna felt was well-timed as with each kiss, his passion increased and she was doing nothing to discourage him. Michel appeared, alongside Rosie, with a tray and a dusty bottle of brandy, a pack of cards and a bowl of snacks, signalling his intention to make a night of it.

'Hey, Daniel, remember you promised me a rematch last time you were here, shall we play poker? What about you, Anna, do you like cards?'

Anna admitted she was rubbish at poker; she didn't have the attention span for most card games and was easily bored and always, always lost. Seeing this as her cue to go to bed and escape from what could only be described as increasing lust, she hugged Rosie and Michel then turned to see Daniel's slightly crestfallen expression. Rather than playing it safe she surprised herself and him with a firm kiss on the cheek.

'Night night, don't let him beat you. I'll see you in the morning.' There, she'd done it.

By kissing him in full view of Rosie and Michel she hoped it would tell him she wasn't embarrassed and that she wanted people to know about them. Giving him a smile, she stood and followed Rosie up the stairs.

Once they were out of earshot, Rosie turned and high-fived Anna. 'Way to go, mate, nicely done. He nearly died of shock when you kissed him and you also let him know that hanky-panky wasn't on the cards. Mission accomplished I'd say.'

Laughing, Anna shook her head. 'Honestly, this romance lark is hard work. I don't think I can stand the stress. I'm off to bed and thanks for everything, Rosie, I'll see you tomorrow.'

Anna turned and made her way to her room and just when she thought she'd got away with it, Rosie piped up.

'Well, just in case he really can't take a hint and fancies his chances you'd best dig out your best pyjamas and prepare yourself for a night of passion. Just scream if you bottle it and I'll be straight down with my gun and a bucket of water. Night, night, Anna, sleep well.' Then she was gone, tittering as she closed her door.

Firmly resisting the urge to take Rosie's advice, fearing it would tempt fate and trusting that Daniel was a true gentleman, Anna lay alone in bed, admittedly wearing a clean pair of pyjamas.

Also, the fact she'd scrubbed her teeth twice and dabbed on some perfume meant absolutely nothing, nothing at all.

Lying there, pensively listening to the rain lashing against the window and the howl of the wind as it whipped around the hotel, Anna refused to have a conversation with herself about what she would do if she heard a tap-tapping on her door and also refused to admit that she may just be tempted to open it and let him in. Nor would she even consider how good it would be to lie here after making mad, passionate love, safe in his strong arms, her head lying on his naked chest, protected from the storm outside. *'For God's sake, Anna, go to sleep,'* she told herself, *'you made the rules so stick to them.'*

After a long and tormented couple of hours spent trying to get comfy and watching the door handle, waiting for footsteps and checking the bedside clock every five minutes, exhaustion thankfully claimed her. The widow of the parish was freed from an overactive imagination, a touch of disappointment and extremely lustful thoughts.

Josh was spending the day at the farm with Pascal and Océane. Tractor driving and helping in the dairy was on the agenda, leaving Daniel both impressed and surprised at his brother's new-found interest in all things agricultural and he presumed he was trying to impress a certain young lady. So, making the most of his last day in France and taking advantage of the fact that Josh was occupied, Daniel had invited Anna to spend the day with him visiting Saumur.

As they drove thought the countryside on their way to Bourgueil, Anna found it hard to resist sneaking glances at Daniel, fighting the urge to ask him to pull over because she couldn't get his kisses out of her mind. Instead, she settled for holding his hand as he drove, contenting herself with just being near to him. He was taking her to buy some wine from a special cave he had visited before, explaining that while there were plenty of *Cave à Vins* to choose from, the place they were headed really was a cave and something quite extraordinary.

Driving along the banks of the Loire they passed the stunning château at Saumur; perched high on a cliff face, overlooking the river and the town below, grandly guarding the citizens living under its gaze. The day was bright with clear skies but it was still bitterly cold outside. The rain and wind had ceased and everything looked even better in the sun. Heading further inland they passed field upon field of neat vineyards, the rows of vines were empty now yet Anna remembered them full of fruit just before the harvest. How could she have known that just a few months later she would be back, driving through France and holding hands with the lovely man beside her?

When Daniel announced that they had arrived, Anna was slightly confused because all she could see were fields and lanes and a few farms dotted on the horizon. There was definitely no sign of a shop. Daniel parked the car in a small clearing at the side of the road just as a battered old jeep pulled up behind them. Getting out of the car, they were greeted by a tall man dressed in smart outdoor clothes who was introduced as Gerard. Once the hellos were dispensed with he chatted to Daniel until they reached a large padlocked gate which he unlocked. Leading downwards was a steep track, just about wide enough to fit a car and as they walked on, Anna saw what appeared to be a large archway that had been cut into the earth, right underneath the fields above. The track curved to the left slightly so that the entrance couldn't be seen from the road. The arch was supported by rough stonework and a thick iron gate covered a wooden door, reminding Anna of the entrance to a castle.

Gerard unlocked the gate and then the door, and as they stepped inside Anna was glad she wasn't claustrophobic when she realised they were going to be right underneath the fields. Nothing, however, could have prepared her for what she saw once the door swung open and the lights were switched on, even the fact that there was electricity down there left her amazed. Once her eyes accustomed themselves to the dim lights, Anna saw that they were standing in a large underground cave.

On either side, stretching into the distance were stone arches cut into the earth – entrances to smaller caves, all protected by locked iron grilles. Huge barrels of wine were stored along the middle of the tunnel and everywhere she looked was rack upon rack of wine. Gerard lit candles as he walked on. They flickered and swayed, giving the place an eerie feel yet Anna was too in awe to be spooked because it was fascinating.

Daniel explained that the cave had been in Gerard's family for generations and some of the wine stored there was from before they were born. Peering into each cave through the grilles Anna noted that the wine was marked with a year and sure enough, some of it was over fifty years old. Most of the bottles appeared to be sealed with wax; there were no labels, just a number written on the back to denote its age. Not only did Gerard sell cases of Bourgueil from more recent years, you could also buy a bottle of the older vintages as a keepsake. Daniel had previously bought one for his daughter, grandson and Josh, bottled in the year they were born. Taking the initiative, Anna wrote down the birth years of the children and also Summer and Ross, thinking she could keep the wine hidden until they were twenty-one and give it to them as a special gift.

Once the correct bottles were found, covered in dust, Gerard got down to the serious business of wine tasting. They sat at, what Anna could only describe as, a huge round stone table, surrounded by a curved bench also carved from stone, reminding her of something medieval or from King Arthur's castle. From the large cool bag, Gerard produced wine glasses, Camembert and a fresh baguette which he deftly sliced then handed round.

Anna accepted a glass of red wine and left the men to talk business, quite content to sit and take in her surroundings. As she ate, the candles burned on their stands, casting shadows across the walls and the voices of Daniel and Gerard echoed along the tunnels as they examined cases of wine and discussed prices. Once they had sampled three or four different bottles a deal was struck, money changed hands and they emerged from the underground labyrinth with their purchases trundling along behind them on a small cart. Blinking in the glare of daylight, the wine was soon loaded into the back of Daniel's car and after thanking Gerard for his hospitality and promises were made to return, they set off in search of somewhere to eat.

Daniel had arranged to take Michel and Rosie for dinner that evening to give the chef a break from cooking and Rosie a welcome night out, so they bought filled baguettes and take away coffee from the bistro in the *Intermarché* and drove to a car park by the edge of the river. Sitting on a bench by the tree-lined banks of the Loire, watching the odd barge cruise along in the winter sun, Anna was a picture of contentment.

'I love it here,' said Anna. 'I always feel so much calmer and relaxed when I'm in France, don't you?'

Daniel nodded while drinking his coffee. 'I know exactly what you mean. Even though it's a long haul to Louise's, as soon as my car drives down the ramp and off the boat I start to relax, even the roads are more peaceful. I think it's because the pace of life is slower here and they know how to enjoy the simpler things in life, eventually it rubs off on you.' Daniel scrunched up the wrapping paper from his lunch.

Anna agreed and then asked, 'Would you ever move here permanently to be nearer your family? It must be tempting, especially because of Jules.' Anna imagined he must miss his grandson a lot.

'I have thought about it. Maybe when I retire but at the moment I like things how they are. I look forward to coming here for holidays and a break from everyday life and don't want the magic to wear off. Plus, I've got Josh to keep an eye on, I'd want to know he's settled and happy first but you never know what the future brings. Look at you and me. I hadn't a clue when I walked into the restaurant that night I'd meet you. When I looked over and saw you, everything changed from that moment.'

Daniel made Anna blush slightly at the compliment before she recovered and replied.

'It's true. This time last year I was a housewife with three kids and a husband to look after, now look what's happened. Nobody could've predicted I'd be a home-alone widow who'd meet her knight in shining armour on a holiday for one.'

Anna kissed Daniel on the cheek and looking pleased with her reaction, he took her hand in his, both content to bask in a special moment.

They rested there for a while in the winter sun, talking and laughing, getting to know each other more with every passing minute as passers-by smiled and nodded at the happy couple holding hands, sharing a bar of chocolate, completely lost in each other.

Driving back later, Daniel asked Anna if she had any preferences for where they ate that evening, if not he thought they could go into the village to Sebastien's restaurant, saying he liked to put business the way of the locals.

'No, we can't go there! It's really not a good idea. I don't think Sebastien would be too pleased to see us together, he might think I'm rubbing his nose in it and spit in my food.' Anna cringed the second she spoke, knowing she'd slipped up and would have to tell him all about Henri and New Year's Eve.

'Oh really, why's that? I get the impression something's been going on while I've been away, what've you been up too? If another confession is on the cards I hope it's not going to make me jealous.'

Daniel had a wicked look and Anna prayed he was teasing.

While Anna went through the events at New Year, Daniel howled with laughter most amused at the part where she was sitting in bed, mortified with embarrassment and bug-eyed as Henri tried to woo her through the door. He also said he felt sorry for both of them, being drenched with freezing cold water.

'What do you mean, sorry for them? They were both doing my head in, squabbling all night like children. I was a nervous wreck by the time I got to sleep that night so you should be outraged and defending my honour and, come to think of it, jealous as a green-eyed monster, not laughing like it was a huge joke.' Anna folded her arms across her chest and pretended to be offended yet secretly, was glad he'd taken it all so well.

'Nope. I'm laying the blame firmly at your door, tempting these poor, lonely, country folk. They don't get a lot of action round these parts and then you show up at parties, flaunting yourself, they're just red-blooded men after all, so what can you expect?'

Daniel tutted for added effect so Anna slapped him really hard on his chest, laughing.

'Well, it wasn't funny at the time, I can tell you, and for the record, I wasn't flaunting anything and certainly did not flirt! I was just being me.'

At that, Daniel sighed and shook his head. 'I rest my case, Your Honour. See, that's what you don't get, do you? It's about time you realised that just being you is enough to drive any man crazy, look what you've done to me. I was quite normal before we met and now I feel like a teenager again. You've even had me kissing on the doorstep. No, sorry, I have nothing but sympathy for Sebastien and Henri but I might need to keep an eye on you *and* them in the future.'

Daniel pretended to be worried as Anna huffed loudly, hiding a smirk.

'Okay, stop creeping and watch the road, but I still think we should eat somewhere else this evening, especially after that reaction. I don't think I could cope with you and Rosie chunnering away all night at my expense. We'll ask Michel, he can decide.' She was also a bit worried that Sebastien might poison her food. It was a rule of hers to never, ever complain in a restaurant, at least until she'd paid the bill.

'Have you had a good time tonight? That meal was so good. Michel seemed to relax for once and Rosie loved it.' Daniel asked Anna who despite being sleepy agreed, glad that her friends had taken an evening off.

They were on the sofa in front of the fire. Rosie and Michel had tactfully gone straight upstairs when they got in and Anna had the feeling he'd been told to leave them in peace. Josh was already in bed after having a great time on the farm but needed some kip, not amused at having to be up at stupid o'clock to catch the ferry.

Anna leant against Daniel's chest: cosy and warm after he'd covered them with a throw, stroking her hair gently as they talked. Her eyes were heavy but she willed them to stay open. This was their last night and she didn't want it to end yet. Daniel broke the silence with a question.

'So, will I get to see you when we go home or are you going to break my heart and restrict me to secret liaisons in France?'

Anna smiled to herself, glad he had asked the question because she'd been too shy so to put him out of his misery, replied, 'Of course I want to see you in England. I was just waiting for you to mention it. You know I'm a big chicken and slow on the uptake but I'm not presumptuous.'

Daniel chuckled. 'That's a very big word for someone who's had quite a lot of wine, well done. I wouldn't have risked it myself.'

Anna tapped him on the arm. 'Just stop teasing for once and make some plans. You need to be the decisive one in this relationship. I'm too much of a ditherer, take control, man, for goodness sake!' On saying the words, Anna felt his body stiffen for a second, a sure sign she'd put her foot in it.

'Is that what we've got, Anna, a relationship; is that how you see us?' Daniel's voice was quizzical.

Anna's heart thudded, now she really was embarrassed. What if she'd got it wrong and had foolishly jumped onto the next step, going too fast after misjudging everything. But it was said now, no going back. Pulling herself upright so she could see his face, Anna spoke.

'Well, that's what it feels like to me but if you think I'm jumping the gun I'd rather you say. For all I know you might have lots of women that you spend time with and for that reason you don't consider this to be a relationship, perhaps people are more casual these days. I'm very out of practice so have no idea. But I do need to know where we stand. I don't want to be made a fool of, not twice.' Anna's insides were shaking, dreading what Daniel might say, already rehearsing her exit speech if he turned her down, telling herself not to feel stupid. Just to get away as quickly as she could.

'Anna, sometimes you drive me mad! Come here and take that look of doom from your face. You've not said the wrong thing, I promise.' Daniel pulled her to him and kissed the top of her head before continuing. 'Right, cards on the table. I want nothing more than for this to be a relationship and there are no other women who I spend time with, or want to for that matter. I know we live a distance away and there's personal stuff you need to sort out but we can make this work. And before you start panicking I will keep to my promise to take things slowly and at your pace but just so you know, say the word and I'll have you up those stairs and into bed in a flash before you change your mind.'

Anna laughed, she didn't mind his joking. To be honest it made her feel less stupid.

'So, have we got a deal, are you okay with all that?' Daniel waited for a reply, twisting his fingers around hers.

'It all sounds perfect to me and you're right, we can make this work, I know we can.' Anna kissed his hand before making herself comfy.

Sighing with relief Daniel reached over and pulled the throw up over Anna's shoulder. 'Good, that's sorted then, and in future will you try to trust your instincts a bit, throw caution to the wind and all that. Otherwise, one day your head will explode with the sheer pressure of worrying about everything. I saw a documentary about it once, boom, and it blows. Makes a right mess of the furniture and the carpet, I can tell you. Stop laughing, seriously, it was gross.'

Anna snuggled closer and once she'd stopped laughing, promised to chill out more. Relaxed and reassured, they lay contentedly together in the quiet of the sleeping hotel. The fire crackled in the grate where hypnotic red and gold flames danced, warming them as they made plans and promises. Outside, the

Atlantic wind blew against the panes, the fields freezing over as the countryside slept, silently watched over by the silver moon, bathing everything in white.

In the months that followed, when Anna fell once again into despair and her troubled heart felt like it could take no more, she would think of this night with Daniel, remembering how being happy felt and just knowing that it was possible, it would give her the strength to carry on.

CHAPTER 30

The taxi bringing Anna home from the airport chugged along the motorway, her body travelled along the M27 but her mind remained on the sofa in France. It was pouring down with rain in Portsmouth and the windows of the cab were misted over. Anna was glad not to be able to see outside because she preferred to exist in her own private bubble, alone with her thoughts. Slightly depressed, the only thing that cheered her was the thought of Mel, who was waiting for her at home and Sam, who would arrive later that evening and of course, Daniel. Anna smiled, remembering how they had fallen asleep where they lay, lulled by flames and the gentle rhythm of their hearts, spending the whole night together in front of the fire.

***

The alarm on Daniel's phone woke them and, bleary-eyed, they realised that it was morning and soon Josh would realise his brother was missing and his bed not slept in. Giggling like idiots they folded the throw and crept up the stairs, bolting into their rooms and straight into the shower. When they met in the lounge half an hour later, Josh was still none the wiser after being out for the count when Daniel sneaked in. However, in complete contrast, when Rosie appeared carrying a tray loaded with steaming coffee and gave Anna a cheeky wink, both knew they'd been caught out. Their hostess had risen early, suffering from indigestion, and got quite a shock when she came downstairs.

In the end, the morning rush took away the chance to be maudlin over Daniel's departure with just enough time for a hug and a very hurried kiss before he had to jump in the car and set off. Anna's final day in France had been spent finishing her baby blankets, visiting the *brocante* with Rosie in the search of useful antiques, followed by a quiet meal around the kitchen counter with her hosts and their neighbours. The journey to the airport was spent making plans for the next few months. Anna had booked for Easter and promised faithfully to visit when the baby was born.

As she waved goodbye to Rosie then trundled her case through to the check-in desk, Anna felt the usual post-holiday mixture of emotions swirling around inside. A tinge of sadness, laced with memories that made her smile and, of course, looking forward to seeing her family. If it hadn't been for them, Anna realised there would be no point even getting on the plane.

***

The taxi pulled into the drive and immediately Melanie was at the door, jiggling about and waving in excitement, eager to see her mum who darted into the porch to avoid the driving rain then hugged her daughter for dear life, relieved she was home and safe.

'Come on, Mum. I've got you a cup of tea waiting, the heating's on and I bought us some sandwiches.' Mel dragged the case inside and firmly closed the door on the rain.

Anna would never admit to Melanie how lonely she was in the house or that her being there to welcome her home had banished the gloomy experience of opening the front door to nothing but silence. They spent the afternoon filling each other in on their respective holidays, one like hell, the other like heaven. Melanie was evidently over the whole Paloma experience, managing to laugh it off and see the funny side of her alternative Christmas with the Adams Family. Later, on the way back from the supermarket, Melanie asked Anna about Daniel.

'So, who's this Daniel, you mentioned him in a text and said you'd met him before, was he there for the whole time?'

Melanie had turned to face Anna who prayed she wasn't blushing and sounded casual in her response.

'I met him in the autumn. He was with his younger brother both times. He always stays at Rosie's on the way back from visiting his daughter in the south. Apparently it's a convenient break in the journey and then they get the ferry home. He took me to the cave for your wine and then out for dinner with Rosie and Michel.' Anna hoped her explanation sounded totally innocent.

'Where's he from? Why was he with his brother, isn't he married?'

Melanie was either showing polite interest or she was suspicious so Anna explained he was from Hemel Hempstead, divorced and had taken his brother under his wing.

'Well, I'm glad you're meeting new people and getting out and about. Is he good-looking? I bet he fancies you, that's why he took you to the wine place and out for dinner. Have you got a bit of a crush on him? Come on, you can tell me.'

Melanie tickled Anna's ribs, making her squeal and then insist that she behaved.

'Mum, stop blushing, I'm only teasing and anyway I don't care if someone fancies you or you like them. You deserve to have fun. Flipping heck, chill out!' Mel was now looking at her phone and checking her messages, news from Tania ending the interrogation.

Anna had been on the verge of internal combustion and was glad she didn't have to make eye contact with Melanie, not wanting to lie or say too much, not just yet. Grateful they were home, the further distraction of unloading the shopping diverted Mel from returning to the subject of Daniel as they darted back and forth from the car, the persistent heavy rain soaking them to the skin. While they waited for Sam to arrive, and with the aroma of homemade shepherd's pie wafting through the kitchen, Anna suggested Melanie rang Mariella in Tenerife to thank her for her kindness and explain why she had just disappeared. Even though the poor woman worked for a dreadful family Anna thought Melanie should show her that not all English people were rude and ignorant.

Jotting down a few useful Spanish words just in case the conversation became lost in translation, Melanie dialled the number she had saved and rang Mariella. Anna listened from the kitchen, happily setting the table, relishing having two of her children home for the weekend, making her feel useful again. When Melanie entered the kitchen her cheeks were flushed from the concentration required to be understood in English and Spanish, but also wearing an amused expression.

'Mariella was really pleased that I phoned her and I'm okay, but you'll never guess what. She said it was a good job I left because there's been "a big lot of trouble" as she put it, up at the villa.' Melanie mimicked Mariella's accent perfectly.

'You're not going to believe this but in the early hours of the morning, more or less while I was flying home, the villa was raided by armed police with sniffer dogs. Someone complained about being constantly disturbed by wild parties and tipped them off that Paloma's family are a gang of drug dealers. All the neighbours were out watching the goings on and the gossip has spread like wildfire, it's the talk of the town. I reckon they'd stuck most of the cocaine up their noses by the time the police arrived so no one was actually arrested, apart from Star who apparently went mental. Mariella says she takes too many pills and they don't mix with gin, anyway, she whacked one of the police officers when they tried to search precious Mungo's room and she ended up spending a night in the cells. It was only because Prince Charles pulled a few strings that they let her out. She's got to go to court and everything. Paloma is in disgrace after they found her in bed starkers with two of Mungo's creepy mates and they've all been banished for bringing shame on the house. Can you believe it? I'm so glad I wasn't there.' Melanie was pouring a drink as she waited for her mum to reply.

Anna was at the kitchen table listening in stunned silence to Melanie. She didn't feel even slightly sorry for them and was glad that the whole dysfunctional family had been given a wake-up call so maybe now they'd sort themselves and their kids out. It then occurred to Anna that it was all either immense good luck that Melanie was winging her way home when the raid took place, or a bit of a happy coincidence.

Jeannie's words came back to her – now what did she say? Something like, she'd sort them out one way or another. Then the light dawned as to who may be responsible for the tip-off and decided that Ms Jeannie Brown was due a telephone call before the night was out. They were interrupted by the sound of the front door opening and the arrival of Sam, bumping into the doorframe and loaded up with two huge bags containing his desert kit and as usual, a sack of washing.

After their dinner, Sam insisted on unpacking all his kit, loving the fact that he had new sunglasses with *three* interchangeable lenses, a brand-new helmet, rucksack, Magnum boots, and a mass of combat gear all ready for the ironing board. As Anna watched him teasing Mel who was wearing his camouflaged helmet, she swallowed down the panic that billowed up from her knotted stomach, bringing tears to her eyes. '*Remember, he's doing what he loves, it's what he's always wanted, don't ruin it for him,*' she repeated over and over to herself like a mantra until the feeling ebbed and she was able to join in the conversation.

Jeannie and Phil called in and the rest of the evening sped past, sitting around the table drinking tea and poring over their respective New Years. Occupying herself with loading the washing machine and trying to keep the ever-growing pile of clothing in some kind of order, Anna soaked up the sound of laughter that filled the silent corners of the house, making it a home again.

Thankfully, Melanie didn't mention Daniel but when the subject of the drugs raid came up, Anna scrutinised her friend's face for any hint of a clue but as usual, Jeannie was cool as a cucumber and gave nothing away. If anything, she just seemed incredibly interested in the whole story. Waiting patiently until they were alone, Anna decided on the direct approach because sometimes it was the only way forward with Jeannie.

'I wonder who tipped off the police in Tenerife, it seems a bit strange, don't you think? Maybe it was someone seeking revenge. I don't suppose you can shed some light as to who the culprit might be?'

Anna rested against the cooker, her eyebrows raised at Jeannie who appeared totally nonplussed as she sauntered over to the sink with some plates.

'Well, I hope you're not accusing me, Miss Marple. As if I'd do a wicked thing like that. Who, in their right mind, would be bothered to Google the number of the nearest police station and then inform them that a gang of evil drug dealers were hosting a wild party, heaving with prostitutes who were dishing out cocaine like sweets? Honestly, Anna. I've told you about that imagination of yours before. It's going to get you into trouble one of these days.' Jeannie huffed and flounced off, giving Anna a flick on the bottom with the tea towel as she went.

'So, guilty as charged, then.' Anna said, chuckling to herself as she closed the dishwasher and turned off the kitchen light.

After she'd waved off Phil and Jeannie then locked up for the night, Anna smiled as she climbed the stairs, thinking that the house would be happy tonight. It had people under its roof again, guarding them while they slept. But her light mood soon evaporated when a niggling voice, deep inside her head whispered that soon, she'd be on her own again. She chose to ignore it.

Sam had Melanie in fits of laughter when Anna came downstairs the next morning. They were in the kitchen making toast and had obviously suffered a few mishaps as you could smell burning bread from the landing. Entering the kitchen, Anna was instantly aware of the cause of Melanie's hysterics, spotting Sam who was prancing round the room giving a rather camp fashion show, dressed in nothing more than his helmet, sunglasses, army boots and a pair of very tight boxer shorts with the words 'CHOKING HAZARD' emblazoned across the front.

Posing for photos and eating toast, he was a sight for very sore eyes. Anna simply tutted and warned him not to dribble butter down his chest, quite used to Sam's penchant for dressing up in random clothes and acting the fool. She remembered one of his favourite get-ups: a bright red hooded dressing gown, fluffy gorilla slippers, and a huge fake cigar. He would sit opposite Matthew, pretending to puff away and watch TV, swinging his gorilla-clad foot to get attention, patiently waiting for his dad to take the bait. The first time, Matthew told him he looked like a bloody idiot and to get some proper clothes on but the second time Anna saw him laughing silently behind his newspaper and after that, he just ignored him, hoping Sam would get bored. Anna was pouring herself a cup of coffee, lost in thought when the doorbell rang.

'I'll get it,' said Sam, wandering into the lounge, unfazed by the prospect of opening the door looking like a half-dressed action man.

Anna prayed it wasn't the postman.

'Alright, Gran, how are you doing? Give us a hug. Mum's in the kitchen.' Sam followed Enid who bustled in laden with carrier bags and only when she'd plonked down her shopping did she seem to notice Sam's attire.

'Is that your desert gear, love? Ooh, it's very smart. Just remember, you're going to need to rub plenty of sun cream in. It's bloody hot over there so make sure you cover all your bits when you go sunbathing, we don't want you burning.' Looking very serious and oblivious to the fact that Sam wasn't actually going on holiday but to a war zone, Enid pulled out a chair and sat down at the table.

'I won't forget, Gran, promise. Fancy a brew?' Grinning, Sam flicked the kettle on.

Melanie was tittering away as he sat on the edge of the table, still wearing his sunglasses, legs crossed, nonchalantly eating toast while listening to Enid twitter on about the buses and the rain as she doled out the treats she'd brought for her grandchildren. It was something she had always done since they were little, never turning up empty-handed, her bag containing unsuitable sweets packed with E-numbers or giant bars of chocolate. Today it was cakes and biscuits to take back to the base and uni.

Having seen quite enough of her son's lily-white body and hairy legs for one day, Anna suggested they both take their haul upstairs and that Sam put some proper clothes on. Gathering up their goodies they kissed Enid on each cheek, Enid halting Sam as he passed by pulling him closer to read what it said on his boxers.

'What does that say on your undies, love? Choking hazard.' Enid shook her head and tutted loudly. 'Now isn't that just bloody ridiculous. See what I mean, Anna, this government is taking all that health and safety nonsense too far. Why on earth do they need to write that and what type of idiot would choke on a pair of undies, I ask you?'

Once again, Enid left Anna speechless, her mind scrabbling for a suitable reply as she listened to guffaws from Mel and Sam as they ran up the stairs.

Rather than put up with Enid banging on about David Cameron for the next ten minutes and to prevent her from repeating the whole thing down at the community centre, Anna candidly explained to her mother what the slogan really meant. Doing her best not to blush, she told Enid that what was contained inside the boxer shorts could, in some intimate situations, cause one to choke and therefore – be a hazard.

Enjoying having the last word for once, Anna left her mother to ponder her newfound knowledge and loaded the tumble drier. After a moment, Enid worked it out and had a chuckle, then undeterred rabbited on about a number of other political and telly-based issues close to her heart, drank more tea and put the world to rights before announcing that it was time to leave.

Refusing offers of a lift because she wanted to get her money's worth out of her bus pass, Enid marched to the bottom of the stairs and shouted to her grandchildren that she was off home.

'Ta-ra, Sam, ta-ra, Mel. Oh and Sam, those underpants are very rude, you cheeky boy!' And with that she was gone.

The tail lights of their cars faded into the distance as Anna watched Sam and Mel disappear down the road, Mel making use of Joe's car, waving until her arms hurt and they were out of sight. Closing the gates to the drive she rested against them, looking back at the house. Upstairs was in total darkness, the only light coming from the porch and the lounge so folding her arms across her chest and with a heavy heart, Anna walked slowly up the path, not looking forward one bit to her night alone. After a weekend full of life and laughter the rooms would be quiet now, and try as she might she couldn't summon up any enthusiasm for the week ahead. It was as empty as her home.

Lying in bed Anna listened to the sound of the house closing down for the night, the radiators clunked, and the floorboards contracted and outside, suburbia slept. The odd car passed by but apart from that her neighbourhood was lifeless, deserted. There was a time when Anna loved the peace of her quiet, middle-class road where they were rarely woken by sirens or late-night revellers. On sunny Sunday mornings, the worst you'd hear was the hum of a lawnmower and later, the whiff of charcoal and voices being carried over fences as neighbours cooked on a barbecue.

Most people would give their right arm to live there and she sounded ungrateful, Anna knew this, but it still didn't alter a thing. Her mind was on a treadmill, remembering the best years, willing her heart to rejoice in such good fortune, desperate to convince her already defeated brain that she could be happy here once more. Frustrated and unsettled, Anna threw back the covers and got out of bed, then stood by the window and looked out.

The eerily silent road was wet from earlier downpours and the lights in every house were out, they all looked abandoned and still. She thought of her room at Rosie's where even in the middle of the quiet, peaceful countryside there was noise of some description, a cow mooing, a tractor in the field or people below on the terrace. How ironic that here in the middle of a city, loneliness somehow seeped in, it was everywhere. Anna had the sudden impulse to throw open the window and let out a blood-curdling scream, just to see if anyone woke up or a light flicked on, desperate for some sign of life.

At that precise moment, Anna realised that she couldn't stand being there any longer, it was time to let go, move on and leave the past behind. She would always have precious memories but this wasn't a home anymore, just a place to eat and sleep and it was bringing her down. Had it given her comfort then she would have remained here until she was an old lady, rattling around on her own, holding on to her husband's spirit and memory that were immersed in bricks and mortar.

Visions of lovingly tending their garden, keeping alive his roses and dusting ornaments and faded photos, enjoying the shadows of the night and her solitude while waiting patiently for the day Matthew would hold out his hand to her and take her to the next place, faded into oblivion. That is how Anna had always envisioned the end but knowing about his affair had tarnished much of what she remembered. This fact alone played heavily on her mind, in some ways enforcing her decision.

Relying on the children to come home and fill the rooms and make her feel useful wasn't the answer. They would always leave at the end of the day, move on with their lives and need her less. It was time to start again, find a place that was hers, put down roots of her own and make fresh memories. Somewhere she'd be happy to spend time alone and not dread opening the door.

Energised and full of ideas, Anna knew she wouldn't be able to sleep and needed reassurance that she was doing the right thing. Jumping back onto the bed with excitement fizzing through her veins, she rang Daniel. If anyone would give her an unbiased opinion, he would. As she waited for him to answer, Anna looked around her quiet shadowy room and couldn't wait to get away.

CHAPTER 31

Anna waited impatiently to be put through. She'd been up since 7am, drinking coffee and writing lists and couldn't understand why everyone else wasn't raring to go on a Monday morning. Eventually she heard a click and then a rather hesitant voice at the other end.

'Good morning, Simon Stanhope speaking. How can I help you, Mrs Harrison?'

Anna suspected that the poor man was expecting another ear bashing.

'Good morning and Happy New Year, Mr Stanhope.' After attempting to put him at ease, Anna moved swiftly on. 'I was hoping that you could help me with something. I want to get cracking straight away so if you are too busy I'd rather you say so then I can search elsewhere.' It was a bit abrupt but now she'd made her mind up, wanted to get the ball rolling.

Sounding rather flustered and still hesitant, Simon asked her to fire away.

'I'm thinking of selling my house and by way of an apology for our behaviour the last time we visited your office, I'd like to offer you the contract, would that be agreeable?'

Anna really wanted Simon to accept so she was pleased when, after swiftly regaining his composure, said he'd be pleased to act on her behalf. After Anna pinned him down to a valuation later that day, Simon, slightly flabbergasted and somewhat relieved not to have been interrogated or verbally abused, said he was looking forward to it.

Smiling, Anna put a big red tick next to number one on her 'TO DO' list. Number two was telling the children what she had planned, so, praying that they would understand, she composed a joint text to Melanie and Sam then sent an identical email to Joe.

> Hi, it's me. I wanted to run something by you before I commit totally to my idea. I respect your opinions and hope to avoid upsetting you in any way so please get back to me as soon as possible if you have any concerns. I would have rung you all but didn't want to interrupt your day and this way you have time to mull it over. I am thinking of selling the house and finding somewhere smaller and more suitable to live. I have been struggling with being here on my own and I'm becoming increasingly lonely rattling around. Please don't be upset by this admission. I'm fine but weary of it all. I know this is your home too and there are lots of memories here, especially of Dad. That said I can't rely on the three of you to always keep me company – you have your own lives to live, therefore I feel the need to move on. I will find somewhere that has space for all of us. I'm not planning on a studio flat with a pull-down bed so don't worry. I hope I've not shocked you and I'm sorry to hit you with this on a Monday morning. Please be honest and tell me how you feel then we can talk things through. Take care, love you, Mum. x

The rest of the morning Anna spent tidying the house from top to bottom and used enough cleaning products to pop another hole through the ozone layer. Everywhere smelt of beeswax, bleach and lavender air freshener. Killing time until Simon arrived and, in an attempt to quell nervous energy, Anna rang Jeannie and filled her in on her plans, then emailed Rosie. Jeannie thought it was the right thing to do but warned Anna she may upset the kids, so to be prepared. Daniel had said much the same thing the night before but hearing Anna so energised and positive he thought it worth running by them.

At 2pm prompt, Simon arrived, briefcase in hand, bald head nicely polished and looking a little more comfortable than the last time she saw him. Getting straight down to business Anna gave him the grand tour. It felt strange showing someone around her home and slightly disloyal, especially in the children's rooms. By the time they came in from the garden her confidence and enthusiasm was waning and Anna was on the verge of telling Simon that it was all a huge mistake.

Sitting at the kitchen table, unaware of his prospective client's wobble, Simon shuffled papers and scribbled notes while Anna nervously tried to pluck up the courage to ask him to leave. Fastening the lid onto his fountain pen, perhaps recognising the face of a client coming to terms with selling their home, he smiled reassuringly at Anna.

'Mrs Harrison, I'm sure this is very hard for you and the decision to sell must have involved a great deal of soul-searching on your part. But if I may say, without knowing too much about your situation, I think that you are doing the right thing. I've seen it happen so many times before, people hanging on to a home for many admirable reasons, however wrong it may be for them personally.' Giving Anna a kind smile, he waited for her to tell him to mind his own business and show him the door.

It had happened on a few occasions, most embarrassing but a hazard of the job, however, despite their previous encounter and due to being privy to the sad and rather disturbing events that led to their meeting, Simon felt quite sorry for his prospective client and genuinely wanted to help.

Anna was taken aback by his kind words and appreciated his advice. 'I don't think wandering around the empty rooms and down memory lane just now has helped. I've got to focus on how I felt when I made my decision and the reasons why I want to sell. Thank you for being so understanding, Simon, your professionalism has made this slightly easier.' Anna smiled weakly, trying hard to be positive.

Feeling quite pleased with his foray into the world of counselling, Simon had a quick sip of his coffee then suggested they talk figures.

'I don't think you will have any trouble at all selling your property, Mrs Harrison. Southsea is very popular and your lovely home is in an affluent, sought-after area. Being detached with five bedrooms and its own driveway is a huge bonus and there's scope to extend into the spacious garden, perhaps with a conservatory. I'm most confident that we will be able to move you along quite quickly. I'm frequently approached by professionals seeking family homes outside the city and this is perfect.' Once Simon had pronounced his verdict he left Anna to consider his words and began tapping on his calculator, thoroughly engrossed in his sums.

Positivity returned to Anna as excitement began flooding through her veins. She almost fainted when he told her how much he thought it was worth and she definitely wouldn't have to make do with a studio flat. After signing the papers and being assured by Simon he would get things moving straight away, she saw him out and closed the door. As she cleared away the coffee cups her phone beeped, it was a message from Sam.

Hi Mum, I'm totally cool with you selling the house – it's your decision, okay. To be honest I do get worried about you being there on your own and now I'm going away you'll have one less visitor. Just do what makes you happy. Home is where YOU are to cook my tea and do my washing :) I don't care where it is as long as you are there. Let me know how you get on and ring if you need me. Love you, Sam xxxxxx

Anna smiled from ear to ear as she read his message, one down, two to go; she crossed her fingers hoping they would all be happy about it. Melanie rang after lectures, apologising for not being in touch sooner but she wanted to speak to Anna rather than send a text. With a sinking heart, Anna feared a damning verdict from her daughter, fully expecting her to take it the worst as she was the youngest and only recently left home.

'I wasn't really surprised when I got your text, but how come you didn't mention it while we were there this weekend? We could have talked it through together.'

Melanie seemed curious rather than accusing so, somewhat relieved, Anna explained her thought process and how the previous night had been a turning point.

'Mum, honestly, you don't have to explain, I totally get it because when I came back from Tenerife I had to nip home for some warmer clothes and stupidly, I expected it to be like it was when we all lived there. But while I was up in my room I noticed it was different. It never bothered me before, you know, being home alone cos eventually someone would turn up. This time though, it gave me the creeps. It was so quiet and knowing I was totally on my own and nobody would be coming home, well it totally freaked me out. It was really surreal and unnerving. No way would I want to stay there overnight on my own and I couldn't wait to get my stuff and get out. On the way back to Jeannie's I felt sad that our lovely family home had turned out to be somewhere I felt uncomfortable, but worst of all, you must feel like that every day. It played on my mind all night. That's why I made sure I was there when you got back from the airport. I still didn't like it though, opening the door to silence, knowing the rooms upstairs were empty, even making food in the kitchen by myself was unnerving. It was a massive wake-up call and imagining you in the house pottering around made me realise what you've had to go through and how brave you've been.'

Melanie sounded emotional, her voice cracked slightly so after breathing a sigh of relief, Anna tried to reassure her daughter.

'It's not too bad, Mel, honest. Just now and then it gets to me but I realise it's never going to change. Circumstances have altered so much in the last year. If Dad was here and Joe was working at the firm, then the house would still be viable, but for me and the occasional weekend visitor it's just too big. I just don't get comfort from being here anymore, I'm glad you understand though.'

'Course I do, Mum, so you can relax now and make some plans. I'll come back and help you whenever you want, you know with packing and stuff. Have you thought of where you'd like to move to yet?'

Melanie now sounded as excited as Anna had felt the previous night.

'Well as it happens, I have got something in mind. I know exactly what I want and where I'd like it to be. I just have to find it.'

***

Since being a child Anna had always wanted to live by the sea. Romantic notions of walks along the beach with a dog that loved to chase sticks, and the sound of waves lapping at your door had been replaced by a degree of common sense and the ability to consider the ever-increasing problems of global warming and the rising flood plain.

Anna's tick list for her new home – a sea view essential and in her case it would be the Solent as she wanted to stay in Portsmouth. There definitely had to be some life in the area: like people passing by, ships, yachts, boats, holidaymakers, she didn't care as long as she wasn't the only person awake at night. An apartment seemed a good idea; modern and low maintenance. Anna was determined to live somewhere that was impossible to turn into a museum the older she got. Her mother's home was full of mismatched, 1970's cabinets and assorted knick-knacks, therefore minimalism was the key. It had to have three bedrooms. One for Joe when he got back from New Zealand, she presumed he would want to live at home, at least until he earned a regular wage. And she'd need another room for Melanie and Sam and the icing on the cake would be a balcony or some outside space. Simple.

Buoyed by her chat with Melanie, Anna decided to surf the net for her perfect home so typed her criteria into the search engine and waited for a result. On the first site nothing took her fancy. They were mostly high-rise and right in the centre of town, more for the young professional than a pernickety widow because judging by the photos, a sea view often meant a glimpse of the ferry terminal through the toilet window. Some were around marinas but that only reminded her of Matthew's intended love nest and there were plenty of lovely family homes on the seafront, but she wanted something different.

Anna was in the fortunate position of being able to be choosy and once the house was sold she would be able to take her pick of the nicest properties. The life insurance had already paid off the mortgage and still left a hefty sum, so, added to the proceeds from the sale she was well and truly in the black. As she searched the property sites, Anna noticed a new email pop up, it was from Joe.

Hi Mum, only just got Wi-Fi so sorry for the delay. You asked me to tell you if I had any concerns about your idea so I will be honest in my reply. Truthfully, I cannot believe that you are even thinking of selling our home. I was in shock when I read what you planned to do. It's too soon and so inappropriate because Dad has only been gone for seven months. What's the rush? I know it must be a bit lonely on your own but I don't think you have given it enough thought or had a chance to get used to things yet. Sam and Mel come and see you and there's Gran and Phil, surely Jeannie is around to keep you company so maybe you need to get out more or should get a job, perhaps that would keep you occupied and give you an interest. I don't know what the others think but I'm sure they will agree with me. You can't just pack up all our memories and sell a huge part of our life. Dad was really proud of the house and he would've wanted you to stay there and keep it for us. I've been looking forward to coming home and now it will be gone when I get back. Please, Mum, I want you to reconsider and think things through. You might regret it and there's no going back once it's gone. You will be on your own wherever you go so why not just

stay there and make the most of it. I'm sorry if I've upset you in any way but you did ask. I'll be here for an hour or so if you want to email me back. Love, Joe x
PS I've been meaning to ask – who is Daniel?

Totally stunned by the condescending tone of Joe's message, Anna drank her wine and thought hard about her reply before she typed it.

Dear Joe, thank you for your frank and honest response and I'm very sorry if I have caused you any distress. I want to assure you that I have spent many a long, lonely, sleepless night in this house listening to nothing but the ticking clock and my own breathing whilst turning the whole situation over in my head. You should know me better than to make rash or hasty decisions. I take my family and their feelings very seriously and into consideration, always. Bearing that in mind, please remember I have willingly dedicated my life to looking after all of you and considered <u>that</u> to be my job, but now all three of you are getting on with your own lives, maybe it's my turn.

If I make a mistake then I will have to deal with it and yes, I may be lonely wherever I end up but it's a chance I'm willing to take. May I also remind you that you've spent the past four and a half years away from home at university and in New Zealand, doing exactly what you want? If you are so concerned about this house and miss it so much, use your return ticket and come back. Oh, and perhaps then <u>you </u>can get a proper job and live in the real world like the rest of us have been doing while you've been away.

As for the comment about your father being proud of this house and him wanting me to keep it, please remember that you can never know for sure what goes on in someone's head and he wasn't perfect, Joe, none of us are.

In answer to your last question, Daniel is a very nice man who I met in France last year. He was travelling with his brother and they always stay at Rosie's after visiting his daughter. He took me to buy some special wine and then for dinner with Michel and Rosie.

Let me know when you are coming back, I will get your room ready. Love, Mum x

Anna hit send and poured another glass of wine, still in shock that Joe didn't approve. Maybe being away from home made him over-sentimental or he thought he was speaking on Mel and Sam's behalf. She shouldn't be too annoyed, after all, he was only being honest. As she mulled things over, another email pinged onto her screen.

Mum, I think that is a bit harsh and really unfair to mention uni because I earned my degree and worked hard. I may have been overseas for a while and I appreciate that you've had to cope with a lot on your own but YOU insisted I came back here. Dad was the best and I can't believe that now, of all times, you would criticise him. We were a really happy family, he was loyal and honest and he did everything for us, so actually, I do think he was perfect. As for this bloke Daniel, it's very nice that you went out for dinner but I just hope that's all there is to it. You need to remember that once people find out you've got a few quid they could latch on to a lonely rich widow, there are some unscrupulous people out there so beware. If you've made your mind up about the house there's nothing I can do about it but I feel like things are moving too quickly. It's out of character for you and I didn't expect it. Joe x

Anna was livid: lonely widow, best dad in the world, loyal, honest, happy family. Typing furiously, she replied.

> Joe, in future, I will remind you at every available opportunity that if potential girlfriends find out your mum is worth a few quid and you are the boss's son *and* heir to the throne, they might latch on! You should also realise that you have been allowed to spread your wings, take your degree and travel the world because that's what love is, letting people go and being pleased they are happy, not holding them back for your own selfish needs. Also, under normal circumstances it may seem rather previous that I am going on holiday, meeting people and selling the house but these are not normal circumstances and that is why I am doing what I'm doing. Your father was not the god you think he was, Joe, so don't put him on a pedestal, he had plenty of faults and let me down badly which is precisely why I'm moving on! x

Anna pressed send in sheer temper, then realised what she had done. A message came back almost immediately.

> Mum, what exactly did you mean by that? Why wasn't Dad what I think he was? Why did he let you down? Tell me the truth. What's going on? Joe x

Anna dropped her head into her hands, she'd done it now and Joe wouldn't be fobbed off. Even if she made up some stupid story, nothing would explain her hasty words unless it was the truth. Resigned to what she had to do, Anna began to type.

> Joe, please believe me with all my heart when I say that I never ever intended for you to find out. I want you to promise that you will not repeat what I am about

to tell you to Mel and Sam. It's bad enough that you will know. X

The reply was instant.

Mum, I promise, just tell me. x

There was nothing for it so as she wiped away tears, Anna told her son about his father.

Joe, I'm so sorry but in May last year, totally by accident, I found out your dad was having an affair. I saw them with my own eyes so there's no mistake. I kept it to myself and he didn't know I knew. I have no idea who she is or how long it was going on for. Discovering that and then losing him shortly after has been so hard to cope with. I didn't even get the chance to sort things out or know the truth. Can you see that I am trying my best to come to terms with everything and need to do things my way? I also found out he was planning to buy a new place with this woman and intended to sell the house to fund it. I know you will be upset and angry and may not believe it of your dad, but I have never lied to you and never will. Maybe now you will understand. I love you with all my heart and I'm sorry if you are hurt. Mum x

Anna waited for what seemed like forever for a reply, maybe he'd gone offline. Then it came through.

Mum, please ring me, Joe x

CHAPTER 32

Sam came home at the beginning of February, one week before
he flew out to Afghanistan. He was his usual buoyant self
and you would have thought he was going to Ibiza with his
friends, not a war zone. There wasn't a flicker of nerves or anxiety
and that helped put Anna more at ease, reassuring her they had
been trained for any eventuality, would be well-protected at all
times and he'd keep in regular contact with her. He gave her an
official-looking pack with phone numbers and a helpline. If she
was worried about anything she could contact them and get a
message to him. Sam made himself useful by sorting out his room
and packed up anything he wanted Anna to take to the new place
– when she eventually found it.

On the Thursday evening before he left everyone came round
to say bon voyage. Emotions raged through Anna so she didn't
drink any wine, knowing she had to be in total control. She
was forced to keep herself in check more than once after losing
concentration and letting her imagination run riot. Knowing how
it felt to lose someone so close, the terror and threat of a repeat was
magnified and almost tangible. Her son was so precious and the
thought of anything happening to him was unbearable. Her heart
felt strange, as though a cold hand had gripped it and wouldn't
let go. When her fear increased, the grip tightened. Noticing her
friend's mood, Jeannie leant over and whispered in her ear.

'Come on, Anna, smile. The lad's excited and he's going to
notice you are sinking into one of your glooms. If I've spotted
it, so will he. Buck up and enjoy yourself, he's going to be fine
you know.' Jeannie gave Anna a reassuring smile before turning

to listen to a bizarre conversation taking place between Sam and Enid who was asking her grandson a favour.

Apparently, Sam was to get Prince Harry's autograph if he bumped into him while he was out there, failing that, Ross Kemp would do. Hiding his amusement, Sam assured his gran he would even try to get her a nice photo, signed if possible.

Later, after insisting on doing dishwasher duty, Anna used the time alone to write Sam a note. It was something she'd been putting off for days, trying to find the words to tell him what she needed to. The smell of Chinese food lingered in the air and the clock in the hall ticked rhythmically as she sat by the desk and began to write.

When he was five, Sam went through middle child syndrome, vying for attention between his older brother who achieved and experienced everything first, and Mel, the baby of the house who was adorable and never put a foot wrong. Anna had found him in tears at the bottom of the garden where, between sobs, he told her that he was fed up with being in the middle. Joe had got a new bike for his birthday, Melanie had a new pram for hers and for his, he'd asked Matthew for the red bicycle out of the Argos catalogue. Without thinking it through, Matthew said he didn't need a new bike because he could have Joe's old one.

After cheering Sam up by promising faithfully that if he was a good boy, he could have the shiny red bike, Anna sat him on her knee and gave him a cuddle then told him how much she loved him and why being in the middle was so special. Drawing the shape of a heart in the sand pit, she put the initial J on one of the bumps and M on the other and right in the middle, she drew a large S.

'You see, Sam, look where you are, right in the centre. A special spot, just for you.' Anna pointed to her chest and then brushed a lock of hair from his face, his eyes were locked on hers, hanging off her every word. 'And the middle is the very best place to be because you are right over my heart and every time it goes bump,

bump, bump, I think of you.' Anna kissed him on his head and squeezed him tightly.

Resting his head against her chest, Sam listened for a while, confirming his mother's story and once he cheered up, Anna told him she knew a funny rhyme. It was a bit naughty but it could be their secret. Loving it already, Sam wiped his snotty nose on his sleeve and with wide eyes, asked what it was.

'It goes like this,' Anna said. 'First's the worst, second's *the best*, third's the one with the hairy chest!'

Sam chinked with giggles, repeating it over and over until he got it right. From then on it was their secret, although now and then she noticed him staring at Melanie, hoping to catch a sneaky look at her hairy chest.

Holding back tears, Anna took her favourite photo of the two of them from the drawer; it was taken at the beach when Sam was six. His gangly legs and arms were wrapped around her body and his face was covered in ice cream, both of them smiled happily into the camera. Anna had cut out a heart from red card and now, stuck the photo right in the middle. Sam didn't need telling how much she loved him or how proud he made her, he knew that already. She just needed to remind him where his special place was in her heart. So underneath the photograph, Anna wrote these words:

Each time my heart beats, I will be thinking of you.
See you soon, take care. I love you. Mum x

Slipping the card into an envelope Anna wiped away a tear, turned off the light and went to bed.

***

Two weeks after Sam left, Anna had an offer on the house. A doctor and his family were moving from London and relocating to the Queen Alexandra Hospital in Portsmouth. They even offered to buy the furniture, pleasing Anna no end as she was sticking to the clean sweep plan. Apart from whatever the kids wanted to keep, everything was going to the charity shop.

All Joe's stuff was packed up and ready to go, a task made easier once Anna had made her peace with him during a long and upsetting phone call to New Zealand. After he got over the shock, Joe was angry then desperately sorry for his comments and between the two of them, everything was fine. How Joe dealt with his feelings towards Matthew was up to him. The next big issue was finding somewhere to live because nothing Anna had viewed or seen on the Internet was suitable and now that her house was virtually sold, time was of the essence.

Daniel, as always, had been at the end of the phone, cheering her up or calming her down. It seemed like ages since they were in France, not a month and he'd been gently hinting that he wanted to see her, suggesting that she stayed with him. Anna used the excuse of Sam's departure and the house sale as a stalling tactic while Jeannie told her to stop dithering and sod all this 'taking it slowly malarkey'. Her sage advice was to slip Josh twenty quid and get rid of him for the evening then whip Daniel straight upstairs and into bed.

Anna was daydreaming, thinking that Jeannie always made everything sound so simple and uncomplicated, when her phone rang. It was Simon Stanhope who sounded rather excited, she was more familiar with his no-nonsense telephone manner but today he seemed uncharacteristically effervescent.

'Mrs Harrison.' Despite frequent assurances that Anna would do, he still insisted on being formal and today was no exception. 'I'm ringing with some rather interesting news. I was having lunch with an old acquaintance and I think I may, quite by chance, have found you the perfect place.' Simon knew exactly what she wanted and also everything she had rejected so this sounded promising.

'Go ahead, Simon. I'm intrigued, what have you got for me?' Anna's heart beat slightly faster, listening with crossed fingers and toes as Simon explained.

The following day, Anna recounted Simon's tale to Jeannie as they made their way to view the apartment. During his lunch with a fellow estate agent, it transpired that his acquaintance (Gordon) was close friends with a developer who was in the final stages of restoring and refurbishing a prestige apartment block on the outskirts of Southsea. Due to a technical hitch, work had halted for a while but they were expecting to complete the project in the next couple of months. Gordon was selling the apartments and had given Simon the heads-up.

One of the two penthouse suites had already been sold to a friend of the developer so Anna needed to view it quickly as Simon was confident it ticked all her boxes. Jeannie was beyond giddy and they'd both dressed up to give a good first impression. Apparently the developer was quite fussy about who he sold to. Looking very smart in their best clothes, Anna wore a bold, red, two-piece dress suit and ridiculously high black shoes. Jeannie had gone for a very sexy all-in-one, catwoman creation, showing off her assets nicely and assuring Anna that the agent would be putty in their hands.

Thanks to Jeannie's rubbish directions, they finally pulled up outside the block with minutes to spare. Anna's very first glance of the apartments caused the hairs on the back of her neck to tingle. The exterior of the large, three storey, 1930s art deco building was painted brilliant white, setting off the brushed steel balconies and large glass windows. Anna thought instantly of Hercule Poirot, imagining it was the type of place he would have lived in. The canopied entrance in the centre of the building grandly framed an ornate arched double door, embellished with leaded glass in the iconic sun pattern, and on the inside, a polished black and white marbled foyer with a lift. The building faced the Solent, the main road separated the apartments from the grassed promenade and path that led along the seafront.

Gordon was waiting for them and after polite introductions he took them up to the penthouse suite, chatting animatedly about the development at the same time as admiring catwoman's perky cleavage. The lift doors swished open and they exited onto another marbled floor that ran along the rear of the building, the windows to the left looked onto a private car park. There were only two pale oak doors on the corridor and Gordon ceremoniously took out a key to open the one nearest. Anna's heart pounded in her chest and had to tussle with Jeannie to get inside first once Gordon swung open the door and with a wave of his hand, invited the ladies in.

Immediately to the left was a small stairway that curved gently up out of sight. Ignoring this, Gordon guided them further into the apartment. On the right, a corridor led to two adjacent bedrooms, adequately proportioned with large windows that looked over the front of the property and out to sea while opposite was a rather swish bathroom. Passing the stairway once again, Gordon pointed out a small utility room neatly concealed below before they walked into the main and very spacious open-plan lounge area.

Situated on the left was the kitchen that immediately took Anna's breath away. Gleaming in all its black, high gloss glory, the shiny units running around the walls were separated only by a steel range and electrical appliances. A marble counter-top split the kitchen from the rest of the bright and airy room, due entirely to the light from huge windows and the patio doors which opened onto a large decked balcony.

Anna paced quickly over to the window, eager to take in the view. Asking if she could go outside, Gordon unlocked the doors and slid them back. The cold February wind blew in from the sea while the rain-filled clouds overhead were dark grey, fading into white as they touched the horizon. Not the cheeriest of days but it could have poured down with rain and hail because right there and then Anna knew this was it – exactly what she had waited for. Grasping the steel balcony, she looked out on to the tidy gardens and dormant flowerbeds of the promenade that was bordered by Victorian iron rails, edging the pathway and protecting walkers from the rocks and strip of beach below.

Anna watched as a jogger and a couple of dog walkers passed by before her gaze drifted out to sea. The forts at the mouth of the Solent were shrouded in mist, while the choppy waves were dotted with small boats going about their daily business. In the distance, approaching from the channel, a large ferry made its way cautiously towards the harbour, just out of sight to her right. On the opposite coastline Anna could just make out a variety of buildings and apartments that she knew lit up the harbour at night. Further along the road was a row of shops and perhaps a couple of pubs and restaurants. Bursting with glee, Jeannie came to stand next to Anna. She'd been occupied with opening and shutting cupboard doors and examining the fridge-freezer and range but now needed to gauge her friend's reaction.

'Oh my God, Anna, this place is fantastic! Have you seen that kitchen, it's bloody amazing? Come and have a look, you'll love it. Please tell me you like it because if you don't I'm going to have a tantrum right here and now then throw you over the edge.' Jeannie came up for air and spotted Anna's expression, giving her the answer she was hoping for.

Big, blobby tears were escaping slowly from Anna's eyes, and they had nothing to do with the wind.

Before anyone could speak Gordon coughed politely to interrupt, he wanted to show the ladies the *pièce de résistance*. Following obediently they climbed the small set of winding stairs; Jeannie tweaked Anna's bottom and had her hand slapped as they jostled and giggled nervously.

'And this, ladies, is what one would call the wow factor.'

Gordon proudly stepped back allowing Anna into the master bedroom, listening to gasps of delight while Jeannie, just to prove Gordon right, kept saying wow, over and over.

The room had a glass panoramic roof, and French windows that looked straight out to sea. The doors led onto a small patio where pale wooden floors reflected the light from the sun which was peeping through the clouds. Anna could imagine lying in bed at night, watching the stars and the moon, then being bathed in sunlight in the morning. Even rain pounding on the glass wouldn't bother her because she'd be inside, cosy and warm. It would be perfect. Through an oak door she found a perfectly equipped and luxurious en suite, meaning that she would have peace and privacy from the rest of the apartment.

Gordon tactfully took himself off downstairs to speak to the foreman of the site but couldn't have failed to hear the squeals of delight. Anna and Jeannie frantically ran around the apartment, stroking marble and opening doors, running back up the stairs just to have another look before testing how comfy the toilet seats were.

When Gordon returned to discuss business, Jeannie's breasts seemed to take on a life of their own and her twenty years of experience flying in first class came in handy. By the time she'd finished flattering and flirting with Gordon she had wangled a cheeky price reduction and he agreed to have the apartment carpeted throughout, at no extra charge.

Anna signed on the dotted line and taking a last look at the apartment before Gordon locked the door, she tried to commit it all to memory, still not quite believing that soon this beautiful place by the sea would be her new home.

CHAPTER 33

Anna heard the news that Samantha had had her baby, a little boy, via Mary. He had been born two weeks earlier, which Anna thought allowed ample time for a message or a phone call. Mary had presumed that Anna already knew; perhaps Samantha had the baby blues. Both scenarios settled Anna's mind as she wrapped the hand-knitted blanket along with a selection of tiny blue outfits. She was driving over to stay with Naomi for the night and intended to drop the parcel off on her way. Knowing what it was like with a newborn, especially the first time round, Anna had decided to give Samantha the benefit of the doubt and ignore the snub.

When she pulled up outside, Anna presumed Samantha was home as her red Astra was on the drive but to her surprise, nobody answered the door when she rang the bell. Fearful of waking the baby by making too much noise Anna opened the porch door and placed the parcel inside, unable to shake the feeling of being ignored. She walked back down the path, sensing all the time that she was being watched. When she reached the car, Anna took a close look at the house before admonishing herself, suggesting she added paranoia to her long list of faults. Shaking off her doubts she started the engine and drove away.

The contracts on her house were to be exchanged just before Easter and the apartment would be ready approximately two weeks after. The plan was to store her remaining belongings in the warehouse at Harrison's then visit Rosie for a week. Melanie had surprised and delighted Anna by asking if she could accompany her to France so after a bit of rearranging, Rosie offered Anna the twin room Daniel usually had.

There was, however, one issue still to be dealt with. It was over five weeks since Anna had seen Daniel and despite having plenty to keep her occupied, she looked forward to his funny texts and daily phone calls. He had been busy with work so the blame didn't rest entirely with her and was merely a case of bad timing and busy schedules, with a bit of Anna's dithering sprinkled on top. Their first kiss and their last night together was never far from her mind. She found herself smiling like an idiot, remembering waking up on the sofa the next morning and if she was honest, slightly regretting that they didn't make the most of being together. And then there was bossy boots Jeannie who kept reminding Anna that they were adults and she had nobody but herself to answer to – so she needed to get off her backside and have some fun with Daniel.

Anna's needles clicked away furiously, her mind locked in silent contemplation as she pictured Daniel's face and admitted to being tired of having just an image in her head, fearing it would eventually become blurred if this carried on. He was so good-looking and fate had placed a gorgeous single man right there on a plate. And to hell with it, yes, she had imagined what it would be like to make love with him; it kept her awake some nights. She was only human for God's sake! Reminding herself what she stood to lose and that he might get bored or meet someone else on his travels, Anna finally lost patience with self-enforced celibacy. Picking up her phone she tapped on Daniel's name, eager for the call to connect.

On hearing the click her heart fluttered, nervous at what she was about to say when to her surprise, a woman's voice answered and said hello. Speechless for a second or two, Anna recovered and asked if Daniel was there. The woman sounded foreign but politely replied that he was in the shower and told her to hold on, she would see if he had finished. Listening intently to background noise, Anna could tell she was walking on a wooden floor, phone still in hand, before calling out.

'Daniel, Daniel, darling, there's somebody on the phone for you, it says here she is called Anna.'

Before she even heard his reply, Anna hung up.

Hot tears pricked at her eyes. Squeezing her eyelids tightly shut, she willed herself not to cry but the liquid won and pierced its way through, bursting onto her cheeks. *How could you have been so gullible? Did you really think he'd wait for you? He's just a selfish, pathetic man. He's not special like you thought, you stupid, stupid, cow!* Looking down through blurred eyes, Anna saw a whole row of stitches had fallen off her needle so in a rage she flung the knitting to the floor, furious at herself, that woman, and Daniel.

When her phone started to ring and seeing the name on the screen she immediately switched it off. He could go to hell! Anna felt so humiliated and small and whatever he said she wouldn't believe. And neither did she want to hear his excuses or even his voice, for that matter, because he probably had a whole repertoire of bullshit suitable for any situation.

He would think she was immature for hanging up, along with being naive and old-fashioned, the realisation causing her to laugh out loud. Pacing the room, her thoughts were bitter and sarcastic. *'You are so pathetic, Anna! It's your own fault, what did you really expect? They say if it's too good to be true, it probably is. What a mug!'* Wiping away her tears Anna grabbed her coat and keys, leaving her phone on the table, no intention of speaking or listening to Daniel. There was only one person of any use in a situation like this, and that was Jeannie.

It was impossible to interrupt her very upset and confused friend so instead, Jeannie stirred her tea and listened patiently while Anna vilified Daniel as a low-down, two-timing scumbag who had conned her into thinking he was kind and understanding.

Just because he hadn't got into her knickers straight away he had done what all men do and found themselves a trollop! Not wanting to set eyes on him again, she vowed never ever to step foot on French soil if he was there, skulking about, looking for lonely women to woo and talk bollocks too.

Anna didn't take a breath as she paced, ranting and raving, looking manic with flushed cheeks and puffy eyes while silently, Jeannie observed. After getting a word in and suggesting that she calmed down and thought things through, it only succeeded in bringing out Anna's alter ego, the demented sister of Satan, so Jeannie sat back and waited patiently for her friend to start foaming at the mouth.

Eventually, like a naughty child, Anna exhausted herself and hoping she'd got it out of her system, Jeannie plucked up the courage to speak.

'You know what you're doing, don't you?' Jeannie asked as Anna finally sat down to drink her cold tea. 'You're hurt and suspicious and, dare I say it, overreacting because you think he's made a fool of you and this has got more to do with Matthew than Daniel. The second you heard a female voice on the phone you had a knee-jerk reaction and presumed she was his lover, he had cheated on you, it was happening again. You think Daniel is being unfaithful, just like Matthew.' Jeannie waited for a reaction, pleased with her psychoanalysis.

'Yes, I bloody well do! She said "darling" in this sexy foreign voice. And I bet she's a prostitute. He couldn't keep it in his pants so he got a hooker to come round! And before you try and make excuses it wasn't Betty his cleaning lady, and anyway, calling your boss darling is pushing the boundaries of familiarity, even for good guy, two-faced Daniel. Come on then, smarty pants, talk your way out of that one.' Anna folded her arms and looked smug, continuing with her suspicions before Jeannie could reply.

'Plus, he was in the shower and she was close by. You know as well as I do they'd probably been at it like rabbits just before I rang. And I bet she was doing that cringey thing they do in films, where they put on the man's shirt and walk round the room, semi-naked. Everyone thinks I'm a dork but I'm not backwards. I'll have you know that I've watched the whole *Sex and the City* box set and I'm telling you, I've got him sussed.'

Anna was deadly serious, whereas Jeannie had to push her hands against her cheeks to stifle the giggles, trying to regain her composure.

'Anna, listen to me! Just because you won a gold medal in over-imagination and spend most of your time concocting all sorts of rubbish rather doing the sensible thing, you have backed yourself into a corner, again! So stop being a drama queen and call him, otherwise I'm going to ring him myself. What's the worst that can happen? He can hold his hands up and admit it, in which case you can verbally abuse him or you can listen to what he has to say. Even then you might not believe him so if you don't think you can trust him then end it, but please, just give him a chance.' Jeannie knew she had to nip this in the bud otherwise her friend would go into meltdown once again.

Sometimes, it really annoyed Anna when Jeannie was right and as usual she'd made it all sound so simple and solvable. Letting out a huge, drama queen sigh, Anna picked up her keys and after giving Jeannie a long hug, went home. There were fifteen voicemails from Daniel on her mobile when she turned it back on, plus texts written in capitals, pleading for her to call him. Anna felt a bit childish now; throwing a tantrum like that was almost naughty step behaviour. Resigned to getting it over with, one way or another, she rang Daniel.

'Bloody hell, Anna, where have you been? I'm going out of my mind here. Right, I know what's upset you and why, so just let me explain, no interrupting. The woman who answered the phone was Irina, my late uncle's sixty-year-old Ukrainian wife who unexpectedly blows in on the wind now and then, taking over the whole house, outstaying her welcome and offending Betty by finding fault. She is incredibly nosey and overbearing but most importantly, out of habit, calls everybody, including the postman, darling! I was in the shower and left my phone on charge while she was on dust patrol and heard it ringing. I know for a fact that as soon as she saw your name she wouldn't have been able to resist answering. I suspect if you hadn't hung up she would've interrogated you but at least you would have realised who she was, but instead you panicked, didn't you?' Daniel sounded out of breath and desperate. He probably thought Anna was going to take the huff again.

Sinking into the armchair, knowing she'd made a real fool of herself, Anna wished she would learn to stop and think before she flew off the handle or jumped to conclusions.

'Yes, I did panic and I thought the worst of you, which is terrible because you don't deserve to be lumped into the same category as Matthew. That's what I've done and I'm so sorry.' Anna didn't know what else she could say.

'Anna, there's nothing to apologise for, apart from sending my blood pressure off the scale. It was just so frustrating not being able to get through, let's just forget about it. Are you okay now?' Daniel was starting to relax, relieved more than anything.

'I'm fine, honest. Perhaps I can make amends by telling you what I rang for in the first place, before my ridiculous meltdown.' Anna's nerves jangled and noticing her throat and face had gone a bit hot decided to get on with it before he had time to reply. 'I realised that if we don't get together before Easter it will be ages before we see each other again, what with moving house and stuff like that. So I was wondering if maybe we could get away somewhere soon for a long weekend, just you and me?' There was a deathly hush at the other end causing Anna to giggle, just before Daniel replied.

'That would be great, what did you have in mind, just let me know and I'll organise it. Have you anywhere in particular you'd like to go?'

He was trying to sound composed but Anna could tell he was flustered and she quite liked it – him being nervous for once. Having Daniel on the back foot for a change made her feel bold, so she decided that shock and awe would be her next move.

'Well, I was thinking of a country house hotel, spa facilities and a double room, none of this twin bed nonsense. You told me to give you the nod so there it is. You'd better get on the Internet pronto and find us a secret love nest.'

The silence was deafening and when Daniel finally spoke Anna could tell he was amused.

'Okay, leave it with me. You certainly know how to surprise someone. I didn't see that coming but your wish is my command. I'll get onto it straight away and let you know. Apart from almost killing me earlier you've really made me smile tonight. There's never a dull moment with you, is there?'

Anna laughed. 'I will remind you of that when you've spent three days with me, bored out of your head and are begging to go home.'

After assuring her that was never going to happen, Daniel said he needed to get off the phone and find a hotel. First though, he needed something for his blood pressure which was all over the place! Half an hour later Anna received a text and a link to a hotel in Berkshire and after looking at the photos assured Daniel that it was exactly what she had imagined. Melanie was going to be in Manchester that weekend, staying with her new friend Amy, then going to a 'gig' as she called it, advising Anna that nobody says concert anymore. Anna was glad that her daughter had finally met a normal friend after Paloma and the Tenerife incident.

Anna didn't want to tell Melanie where she was going and neither did she want to lie, so instead she said nothing, hoping that it wasn't breaking any mother-daughter covenant. It was like a teenage love tryst but in reverse because Anna was the one sneaking off, absolutely terrified that she'd get caught out by a nineteen-year-old.

Once again, Anna's mind raced, full throttle, realising that sleeping with someone new for the first time in almost twenty-five years would take some preparation both mentally and physically – but she was up for a challenge. Still, this was virgin territory (sort of) and Anna was completely out of her depth and floundering. There was only one thing for it. In a situation like this you needed specialist advice and she knew just the woman for the job. Picking up her phone, Anna rang Jeannie.

CHAPTER 34

Melanie and Anna were on their way to Rosie's and full of beans, due entirely to the dreadful coffee they served on the plane. It was the first time they had travelled abroad, just the two of them, and Anna was looking forward to relaxing and spending time with her daughter. Melanie had resolved to speak only French for the duration of her holiday and get some practice in, but only to the natives, otherwise conversation with her mum would be rather limited. True to her word, Melanie had done Anna proud at the car hire desk when she took over proceedings. They even got a free upgrade. As they joined the autoroute, Melanie asked Anna who would be around and if by any chance Daniel would be passing through. Relieved that her passenger was preoccupied, fiddling about with the radio stations and didn't notice her blushing, Anna replied.

'No, he won't be there. His ex-wife is over here so he's keeping out of the way. But there's Océane who's about sixteen and her brother Pascal, he's the same age as Sam and they're both lovely. I'm sure you'll meet them.' Anna thought she deflected that one quite well but still felt deceitful.

'Mum, please don't do your cringey matchmaking thing with this Pascal guy. You're worse than Cilla Black and I'd never go on a blind date organised by you, the fact you've even mentioned him makes me suspicious, I know what you're like and you have terrible taste. Remember that lad at the supermarket, the one on the meat counter you kept trying to fix me up with so you'd get a discount on your sausages, he was a horror! That's why I wanted to check out Daniel, just in case you fancy him. He might be a real minger for all I know. And anyway, how do you know he's not coming, do you keep in touch… you do don't you?' Melanie was, if nothing else, direct and now right on Anna's case.

Anna laughed, remembering the spotty boy in his stripy pinny, but was more concerned about deflecting the Daniel comment. At the same time she was surprised that Melanie was being so casual about him.

'I'm not matchmaking and anyway, I don't think Pascal is your type. He's really into agriculture and a bit political as well, you know, farmers' rights and all that. He's at college, studying something to do with renewable energy I think.'

Anna glanced at Mel who was snoring and pretending to nod off.

'Flipping heck, Mum, he sounds like a right geek, you can't half pick 'em. Does he polish his tractor at the weekend for thrills?'

Anna smirked, a bit of reverse psychology never did any harm, and she couldn't wait to see what Melanie thought of the dark-eyed, six-foot-two geek with his rather large biceps and six-pack when they actually met in the flesh.

'And you haven't answered my question, Cilla… are you and Daniel text pals? Being a pen pal is a bit old-fashioned even for you!'

Melanie was opening a bag of mints so didn't spot Anna's glowing cheeks.

'Yes, he texts me now and then. Just friendly messages, is that okay? Now stop pestering me. I'm trying to concentrate, and pass me a mint.' Hoping she'd nipped Melanie's interrogation in the bud, Anna nervously sucked her sweet.

They drove on into the countryside. Melanie finally found a radio station that she liked enough to stop her from fidgeting and with the subject of texting laid to rest, Anna's secret thoughts turned to her weekend with Daniel.

***

It had been everything she had hoped it would be and they didn't stop laughing the whole time, amongst other things. They relaxed in the spa, swam in the pool and he treated her to a pampering package in the salon as a surprise. There was a golf course at the hotel but it wasn't Daniel's thing, he preferred to watch football in the bar while she was beautified.

Thanks to Jeannie's romantic weekend preparation routine, along with the aid of the grapefruit diet and Corporal Brown's exercise plan, Anna felt toned and less self-conscious, almost ready to get her kit off and jump in the sack, as Jeannie quaintly put it. There was the compulsory shopping expedition to the lingerie department of a stupidly expensive store but it all boosted Anna's much needed confidence and for that, she was eternally grateful to her friend.

In the final, more pleasant stage of what seemed like a military manoeuvre overseen by a power-crazed dictator, Jeannie took her to their local salon to be waxed, plucked and have her nails polished. By the end of it though, Anna really did feel like a new woman who despised grapefruit, totally exhausted and a few quid down, but one hundred percent ready for action.

Sticking to Corporal Brown's meticulous plan, Anna had to arrive before Daniel and pulled up outside the hotel just as dusk fell. The hotel was once a stately home and as she headed for the reception desk, Anna was a little overwhelmed by the grandeur of her surroundings, not to mention the looming night of passion which she imagined everyone from the receptionist to the porter knew about. Nerves really kicked in as she signed the register. Thankfully, the booking was just in Daniel's name, not Mr and Mrs Wright, saving her blushes and not causing any offence to her ever-present conscience. The room was opulent and very plush but on Jeannie's orders Anna avoided wasting time checking out the mini-bar and pinching the complementary soaps, and got on with preparing herself for Daniel's arrival.

Anna had confessed to her self-styled, love guru that she was dreading the first evening. The thought of dressing up and going down to dinner to eat a meal that she'd be far too nervous to enjoy, knowing full well that while they were making polite conversation and studying the menu, the subject on both their minds would be the events after they'd enjoyed coffee and mints.

It was all too toe-curling to contemplate and Anna was overthinking it as usual so Jeannie wisely pointed out that the last thing anyone needs when you're rolling about stark naked, is a gourmet meal and a bucket full of Dutch courage swishing around in your stomach. To set Anna's mind at rest Jeannie assured her there was a solution, instantly quelling Anna's concerns by suggesting they cut to the chase and got it all over with, as soon as Daniel arrived.

'Just give him a flash of your sexy underwear, drag him into bed, sort him out, and then get straight downstairs to dinner. Job done! Hopefully you'll have worked up a healthy appetite by then, plus you might need a bit of a breather and some nourishment to see you through round two, or even three if you're really lucky.' Jeannie winked and gave Anna the thumbs up, laughter diffusing the tension.

By the time Daniel texted to say he'd arrived and was just parking his car, Anna was calm and in the zone; a panther ready to pounce. As Jeannie had promised, taking control of the situation had given her power and confidence so when Daniel cheerily opened the door, innocently carrying his overnight bag and a bottle of champagne, he was met by flickering candlelight, soft music and a semi-clad, silken robed goddess. The poor man didn't know what hit him.

***

Melanie loved the hotel and hit it off straight away with Rosie who was expanding quite nicely and in full bloom. Once they'd unpacked, Anna gave Mel a quick tour of the hotel where at every turn she was reminded of Daniel. It was becoming increasingly difficult to get him out of her head. Being there, in the place where they met was like an invisible bond, a subliminal connection that led directly to him.

Rosie had invited them up to the apartment, eager to show them the things she'd bought for the baby. In January, Anna had left two cheques at the hotel as a thank you for their hospitality. One for Michel which she stuck on the fridge, to donate to *Les Restaurants du Cœur* and another, slipped inside the reservations book for them to buy something for the bump. As Anna and Rosie oohed and aahed over tiny outfits, Melanie watched television, soaking up the news and French television shows.

Rosie suggested that they take a walk down to the gîtes to say hi to Michel who was doing some last minute jobs before their first bookings arrived and as Melanie was eager to explore, the trio set off towards the fields.

It was clear that Rosie and Michel had worked hard to finish the small complex in time for the season, there was now a small pool enclosed by a fence and a sandy children's play area with swings and a slide. They found Michel working inside the gîte which was once occupied by Ruby and her children, now repainted and ready for use. He was busy sweeping the wooden floors and shouting orders to Pascal who was upstairs, dragging furniture about. Sticking to her resolution to only speak French, Melanie chatted happily with Michel who called for Pascal to stop making a noise and come down and say hello. Doing as he was told, they heard his footsteps moving across the room above them and making their way downstairs. Pascal's feet appeared first, clomping down the stairs in his work boots, then the bottom half of blue, paint splashed overalls, the sleeves tied around his waist, then his body, squeezed into a dusty white vest which showed off his muscular form to a rather stunned Melanie.

Managing to keep her composure whilst shaking hands and valiantly continuing a conversation, Melanie was watched like hawks by Anna and Rosie who passed each other knowing glances and amused smiles, directed also at an unusually bashful and tongue-tied Pascal.

'Okay, everybody, I am finished here. We will go back to the hotel for aperitifs. Come on, you too, Pascal. I think you have worked hard today and deserve to relax in the company of these beautiful women, don't you think?' Michel began packing up his tools, clattering about and totally oblivious to the wonderful shade of pink Pascal had turned.

Anna resisted the urge to tease Mel, knowing full well she'd ignore Pascal just to prove a point so instead, concentrated on the scenery and the lovely guest houses, praising Rosie's work and knack for homemaking. They wandered back up to the hotel, passing the covered pool then through the kitchen garden where the vegetable patch was coming back to life with sprouts of green popping through the soil.

Melanie was sitting on a stool at the counter chatting with her mother and Rosie when the men tramped in and began removing their work boots and washing their hands in the large sink, deep in conversation about last minute jobs they needed to complete the following day. Pascal seemed to have recovered nicely from his bout of shyness and took a stool opposite Melanie while they waited for Michel to bring the wine. Taking a handful of crisps, he leant forward and began asking Melanie all about herself and casually, how long she was staying, thankfully sticking to English so at least Anna could eavesdrop.

Melanie ruined this by responding animatedly in French, pausing now and then when she was mentally translating a certain word, both laughing when she got it wrong as Pascal politely corrected her. The conversation then began in reverse, Melanie quizzed him on every aspect of his life, helping if he stumbled with difficult words and both seemed to be thoroughly enjoying their bi-lingual exchange to the exclusion of everyone around.

As usual, the aperitifs continued into an impromptu dinner cooked by Michel, who then called his neighbours to come over and join them for drinks so before long, the happy faces of Dominique and Zofia appeared at the door. Anna watched with pride as Melanie was hugged and greeted by her friends, realising as she surveyed the scene how welcome and at home she always felt here with these kind, open-hearted people.

Listening to the chatter, Anna silently thanked the God of Hairdressers for leaving that magazine at the salon, knowing if she hadn't read the article about the hotel, then none of this would have happened. Remembering that sunny afternoon in autumn when Rosie gathered her in like a hovering, guardian angel, just waiting to become her friend, made Anna feel special and wanted. Getting on the plane had been a huge leap of faith but once she arrived, her confidence grew a little each day. She had experienced so many emotions here, good and bad, a little bit of loneliness, finding the courage to be the single lady at dinner, ignoring the inquisitive stares, then battling her own demons and defeating her nagging conscience.

Taking a sip of wine, Anna reflected on how life could change so quickly and the mere flick of a magazine page had brought her all this – the friends gathered around this table, laughter, a new start in a place where she felt at home and happy. Anna agreed with Rosie, the hotel was magical. It had allowed her to move on but the icing on the cake was that here, she had met Daniel and for that alone, she was eternally grateful.

Anna and Rosie were in the garden behind the kitchen which was just large enough for a washing line and a small table and chairs. It was also private and away from the guests.

Melanie had spent every day since they arrived with Pascal, juggling her time between him and Anna, enjoying sightseeing while he worked then jumping into his car and zooming off the second Michel said he could go. If he worked in the restaurant Melanie would linger in the bar, chatting away, but as far as Anna could tell, their friendship was purely platonic after explaining in her 'talking to a moron voice' that it was just a cultural exchange, helping each other to perfect their language. Melanie also found Pascal's knowledge of the French political system fascinating, admiring his passion for farmers' rights and his dedication to improving and expanding his father's farm.

In return, Anna admired Melanie's ability not to blush while she tried to pull the wool over her mother's all-knowing eyes, and also impressed that her daughter appreciated the person beneath Pascal's rippling muscles and Gallic good-looks. What her daughter lacked in political tendencies and agricultural awareness she made up for in abundance with her purity of spirit and intelligence, not to mention blonde hair, pretty face, trim figure and bubbly personality. Anna hoped that in return, Pascal also held Melanie in high esteem.

Snapped from her imaginary matchmaking by one of the lovebirds appearing at the kitchen door, carrying a tray of tea and biscuits, Anna could only smile as she watched her daughter step into the sunshine.

'Hi, Mum, hi, Rosie. Phew, it's a bit warm out here. Maybe I should've brought fruit juice instead. Shall I get a jug of water?' Melanie laid the tray on the table and wiped her forehead.

'No, that's fine, thanks, love. Unless Rosie wants some, anyway, where have you two been all afternoon?' Rosie declined water so Anna began pouring tea, trying not to sound too nosey.

'We've been to the farming museum. It was really interesting. Pascal wanted to show me the history of the communities around here and how life has changed over the years. I brought some leaflets back in case I ever need them at uni, maybe they'll come in useful one day.'

Rosie tried to hide a smirk which Anna picked up on.

'So, what excitement has he got planned for you tomorrow, perhaps it really is tractor polishing? I'm sure you'll love that, too.' Anna remembered Mel expected Pascal to be a geek, but that was before she met him.

Then Rosie piped up. 'No, Anna. In France we only polish our tractors on Sunday, it's the law!'

Rosie winked at Anna and drank her tea as Mel defended her honour.

'Ha ha, very funny. I know you two think it's hilarious, me taking an interest in the farm and all that but Pascal knows loads of fascinating things and I really admire his commitment and views. Sometimes, there's no pleasing you, Mum! You'd have something to say if I was driving around France with a drug dealer.'

Mel had two pink spots on her cheeks so Anna did her best to look apologetic and be serious before her daughter really took offence.

'Sorry, love, only teasing. Anyway, what are your plans for tomorrow? We fancy a drive into Nantes to look round the shops if you fancy it.'

'Count me in but I need to be back by late afternoon. Pascal is going to show me how they milk the cows and after that he's taking me for a ride across their land on his tractor. I might even have a go at driving.'

There was a very short period of silence before Rosie and Anna looked at each other and burst into hysterical laughter at which Melanie just rolled her eyes and let out an exasperated sigh.

'You two should grow up. I'm going for a shower while you giggle like school kids, see you at dinner.'

This only sent them into further hysterics with Rosie rushing in the direction of the loo.

CHAPTER 35

Melanie had forgiven Anna's teasing and even managed to see the funny side of it by the time they had eaten dinner and they were friends again when she happily trotted off to perch at the bar and keep Pascal company. The hotel was busy and Melanie had offered to lend a hand but Rosie wouldn't hear of it, saying she was on holiday. A little bird had told Anna that once the boss was out of sight Melanie had got stuck in, assisting Pascal in the restaurant and Michel in the kitchen.

Anna spent the rest of the evening in their room reading, trying hard not to nod off and concentrate on her book. It was past midnight when she was stirred from sleep by Melanie moving quietly around the room so turned on her side as she watched her daughter slip under the sheets then lie silently, staring at the ceiling.

'Are you okay, Mel, you're a bit quiet?'

Anna watched her daughter in the twilight, sensing a problem and hoping it wasn't anything to do with Pascal so, when Melanie finally did speak up, it wasn't quite what she expected.

'There is something bothering me actually. I was just wondering when you were going to tell me about you and Daniel?'

Anna held in a gasp after which the silence in the room was truly deafening. Turning onto her back she too stared at the ceiling and felt like a teenager caught out by her parents, giving herself time to think of a good excuse or at least work out how much of the truth she would have to tell. It was obvious that Pascal had said something but the problem was, Anna had no idea exactly what. There was only one thing for it – she had to tell Mel everything because if she lied now or watered things down it would only come back to haunt her and trust was sacred, she couldn't risk losing that.

'I suppose the honest answer to that is I don't know. I was scared to death of upsetting you or your brothers. I didn't want you thinking badly of me and until very recently there hasn't been that much to tell. I'm presuming Pascal has been gossiping and I'm truly sorry that you've had to find out from someone else. I'll tell you everything because the last thing I want is for us to have secrets.'

Anna was hurt and unnerved by Mel's sarcastic laugh but waited patiently in the moonlit room for her daughter to speak, dreading what she was going to say.

'For your information, Pascal is not a gossip. He genuinely thought I knew and mentioned Daniel in conversation, saying he was surprised that he wasn't here with you. That's how it all came out but you'll be pleased to know I didn't give my ignorance away. It's bad enough that you keep things from me without everyone else knowing that this whole family is incapable of telling the truth.'

'I'm sorry, Mel, I really am.' Anna could hear the anger and hurt in Melanie's voice and for that alone, felt dreadful.

'You know what annoys me the most? It's that when we were growing up you kept banging on about us being honest, that you never wanted to hear things second-hand or from rumours and now look at you, making up different rules for yourself. All this time you've been sneaking about behind our backs and never said a word. I'm sick to death of being treated like the baby of the family and being shielded from anything distasteful. Well, for your information, Mum, I'm an adult. I go to university. I see and read stuff that would probably freak you out. I'm not an innocent child so please, from now on, show me some respect and stop holding things back otherwise that's how I'll behave towards you.'

Anna winced. That was quite a speech and she could hear the barely controlled anger in her child's voice, but she was guilty as charged and felt terrible so all she could do now was apologise and try to make her understand.

'Okay, Melanie, I get it and I am very sorry. Everything you have said is true. I do protect you and I have kept secrets but please try and see things from my perspective. I have to examine my conscience on an almost daily basis and have tried to do the right thing for everyone since your dad died. It's been like a juggling act sometimes, always worrying what people will think. And after the way Joe reacted when I told him about the house I certainly wasn't going to risk mentioning Daniel and anyway, when would have been the right time to tell you all? I'm only just getting used to the idea myself.' Anna lay there quietly. She'd said her piece so gave Melanie time to think.

Finally, after what seemed like eternity, she spoke. 'I understand all that, Mum, and I think you've been really brave since Dad died. We're all proud of how you've got on with your life but I was just really hurt. Apparently Josh told Océane that his brother was mad about you. I felt foolish and hurt and it was obvious that Pascal presumed everyone knew.'

Anna was angry at herself. She should've known there was a chance that someone would mention Daniel. She had been naive and careless. It was a schoolgirl error made by a supposedly mature woman. Feeling foolish she listened as Melanie continued.

'Even though I'm upset, I am glad you've found someone you like and from what Pascal said, Daniel sounds really nice but I'd rather have heard about him from you. The funny thing is I sort of guessed the other day, when you said you'd kept in touch but I didn't want to pry or embarrass you. I was hoping that if there was something in it you'd confide in me. I'm not going to be annoyed, Mum, so just tell me the truth.'

Melanie turned on her side to face her mother so Anna followed suit, sensing a thaw in relations.

'If you're sure you won't disown me or think less of me then I'd be glad to tell you. It'll be a weight off my mind and I'd like to be able to talk about him with you. I hate secrets, Mel. It makes me uneasy but sometimes us grown-ups do stupid things, we mess up too, you know.'

Melanie snuggled down further into her bed and smiled at Anna. 'Come on, Mum, stop stalling and dish the dirt. This is exciting. Not many daughters get to hear about their mother's love life and I assure you I'm totally un-shockable.'

Anna laughed, telling Melanie not to get her hopes up as it was all quite tame, nevertheless, she started her confession from the very first moment she saw Daniel in the restaurant. As the tale unfolded the tension gradually drained away, Anna was relieved and so very tired of secrets; they talked late into the night. Melanie took it all in her stride and once she understood the sequence of events and appreciated that her mum had taken her time, not rushing foolishly into anything, curiosity took over. She insisted on seeing a photograph of Daniel so Anna sat on the end of the bed and waited nervously for Mel to pass judgement, feeling stupidly pleased when he got the thumbs up. Buoyed by her daughter's enthusiasm and giving in to Melanie's inquisitive streak, Anna agreed they could all meet and give her the chance to check him out. One favour she did ask was that Melanie kept the secret a while longer as Anna wanted to tell Joe and Sam herself – she'd learned her lesson on that score.

'Right, Miss Nosey Parker… go to sleep. I'm worn out with all your questions and if I don't call time now you'll be giving me the third degree all night, but there's something I've just remembered. You know earlier you said this family was incapable of telling the truth, what did you mean?' Anna thought it was only fair that Mel took a turn in the hot seat and the comment had made her uneasy.

Melanie didn't speak straight away because she was part way through a long, dramatic yawn, sounding bored and sleepy when she finally answered.

'You know, all that business with Uncle Phil and Jeannie. They were having a secret affair for ages and nobody knew, and Sam never tells us anything about his love life, he thinks he's James flippin' Bond. That's all I meant, why?' Mel yawned even louder.

Anna breathed a huge sigh of relief because earlier, for one awful moment, she feared that Mel was referring to Matthew which meant she'd found out about his affair. But she was barking up the wrong tree as per usual.

'Nothing, I was just being paranoid, it's my new hobby. As long as you don't know some dark family secret, especially about your crazy gran or the boys.'

Anna's eyes were burning and she needed sleep, but Mel had one more question.

'Mum, can I ask you something… were you and Dad happy before he died? We just sort of took it for granted that you were but the atmosphere was awful, you know, just before. And I'd noticed that you looked unhappy, things just felt different. I don't want to upset you but I've never felt it was the right time to talk about stuff like this before, it probably never will be. But if he hadn't had the accident do you think you'd have been together forever, do you still love him, even though he's not here?'

On hearing the words Anna's heart sank like a stone. It was possibly the hardest question she had ever been asked in her life. Tears welled in her eyes and soon seeped out, trickling down her cheeks and soaking her neck.

'Me and your dad had been together for a long time and in the same way you took our love for granted, maybe in some ways, we did too. I know he'd changed a bit before he died. He had a lot of pressure at work and was irritable and moody because he was working too hard but I'd like to think that between us, given the chance, we could have worked things out. Most marriages go through sticky patches and ours was no different. Do I think we'd have been together forever? I really can't answer that one. I always imagined us getting old and grey with grandkids running about all over the place. I never even contemplated him not being around. But one thing I do know without hesitation is that I loved your Dad with all my heart and part of me always will, no matter what happens. He gave me you three and we had so many happy times together as a family, nothing can change that. Does that make you feel better?' Anna wiped away her tears and dried her neck with her pyjama top.

'Yes it does and I'm fine, Mum, honest. Don't worry about me. Night night, love you loads. Let's get some beauty sleep because some of us need it more than others.' Feeling a pillow whack against her bed, Melanie chuckled as she turned on her side and settled down in the darkness.

Anna closed her eyes and tried to relax but sleep evaded her. The grating sound of cogs in her brain were keeping her awake, turning over and over, churning up every word of their conversation. Mel had unsettled her, reminding Anna of the past and the events leading up to the crash. She was also disappointed and saddened that Mel had picked up the problems between her and Matthew. She thought they'd hidden it so well.

Melanie was right, the atmosphere in the house had deteriorated badly, Anna admitted that, and Mel spent most nights in her room keeping out of the way. Meal times, when Matthew actually turned up on time, were dismal affairs. Polite conversation was all that was on offer – the days of happy kitchen-table banter were long gone. The more she thought about it, the night before the crash Melanie was in a foul mood, refusing dinner and didn't come down at all. Perhaps she blamed them both for the tension in the house and was sick of their bickering. Anna had tapped on her door before she went to bed and asked if everything was okay, only to be met by stony silence.

The next morning, Mel had left for work at the ferry port before anyone got up meaning she never saw her dad again. That evening, when the police came to the house to give them the dreadful news, Melanie was hysterical, going on and on about wanting to speak to him one more time, saying she needed to tell him she loved him. It broke Anna's heart.

Fatigue and guilt settled on Anna like a fog, how could she not have noticed that Mel was suffering too? Probably due to the fact she was too wrapped in her own misery and clue hunting, that's why. She had let her daughter down and as for Matthew, he was the biggest let down of all. This was his fault and she was so angry with him. Anna's mind then wandered to Joe and Sam. Had she neglected them since Matthew died? Should she ask them about their feelings and give them a chance to open up, to talk about their dad more and, as with Mel, were they being tactful just to protect her?

'Surely they would ring me if they were upset or needed to get things off their chest, wouldn't they? I remind them often enough that I'm always there for them.' Anna asked herself a multitude of questions and tormented herself with feelings of self-doubt and failure. There was only one solution but there was nothing she could do about it tonight. First thing in the morning she vowed to email them both and ask them outright if they were okay. And she would ask Melanie the same question, but face to face.

When Anna was growing up, when she was worried or upset about exams or silly schoolgirl arguments, Enid used to insist that things always seem better in the morning and most of the time, her mum was right. No matter what worries kept you awake at night or left you sobbing into your pillow till the early hours, sleep, the cold light of day and a clear head seemed to put a fresh perspective on your woes. It didn't take them away completely but somehow, from somewhere, you found the strength to face them head on. The following morning turned out to be no exception to the rule.

As Anna stirred from her sleep to the sound of Mel murdering a song in the shower, a peek of bright blue sky and the promise of another sunny day lifted Anna's spirits no end.

Over breakfast, Anna broached the subject of Matthew, there was no way she would go back on her resolution, what was the point of hours of contemplation and soul-searching if you didn't act on it? As Melanie buttered her croissant, Anna plucked up the courage to speak.

'After our chat last night, I couldn't sleep worrying about you and your brothers and I can't help feeling as though we've not talked about your dad enough, or perhaps I've not made the effort to ask how you feel. If that's the case then I'm really sorry and want you all to know that you can talk to me about him anytime. And I won't get upset so don't think you're protecting me.' Anna drank some coffee while watching her daughter closely.

Melanie, who was about to take a bite out of her croissant stopped and looked wide-eyed at Anna.

'Mother, what is wrong with you? Have you been rehearsing that speech? We know all that and if I was upset I'd ring you, promise, but we're grown-ups now, remember. I reminded you about treating us like babies last night.' Melanie carried on eating, the conversation closed as far as she was concerned.

'But you are all away from home so much it's difficult to know what goes on in your heads. I don't want to psychoanalyse you, so have no idea if you are crying yourselves to sleep or dread coming home because it reminds you of Dad, or that he's not there. Do you understand what I'm saying? Just because I don't ask it doesn't mean that I don't care.'

Anna placed her hand over Melanie's who then gave her an exasperated look.

'Mum, listen. You are seriously doing my head in now. We are all fine. Do you think Sam wants you ringing him up asking in depth questions about his inner feelings when he'd rather be in the gym? No, he wouldn't. And neither would Joe appreciate you interrupting him mid-sheep-shearing or whatever he does over there so you can ask if he's had a good cry lately. And where I'm concerned, I would rather hear all about Gran's latest adventure or if I'm a bit desperate, your secret love life, than have a deep and meaningful conversation about death and closure. So please, stop obsessing or you'll need a shrink, now eat your breakfast like a good girl.'

Mel pointed, giving Anna a death ray stare causing her to laugh and give in, knowing when she was beaten.

The view of Nantes from the panoramic bar was breathtaking, with 360° views of the city, taking in the meandering river and the Château des Ducs. Melanie had specially requested they visit Le

Nid, which translated meant The Nest. The huge 472-foot high tower in the centre of the city incorporated a water reservoir and was designed by a feted and world renowned French graphic artist, Jean Julien. One of Melanie's lecturers suggested she take a look while she was in France.

The bar was the home of an enormous white bird – half stork, half heron – sculpture who watched sleepily over the city and its inhabitants, the body doubling as a bar while gigantic eggshells provided seats and tables. The artist's work adorned the walls – bright, colourful posters depicting scenes and landmarks of the city. Rosie was relaxing in an eggshell chair, content to take in the view and rest her feet and Melanie was off taking photos and writing notes, leaving Anna to herself on the open deck, enjoying the city air, breathing it all in.

They had spent a lovely morning in the Old Town district of Bouffay, passing the half-timbered houses and gourmet food shops, then wandering around Galeries Lafayette and the magnificent glass roofed shopping area of Passage Pommeraye. They ate a light lunch in a street front bistro, people watching, but Rosie was tired now and once she had rested, Anna decided they should head back to the hotel.

Her thoughts as always led to Daniel. He'd been in touch every day since they arrived and never failed to tell her how much he missed her or couldn't wait to be with her again, which only reminded her more of how perfect their weekend together had been.

***

Smiling, she remembered the moment he opened the door and saw her standing there in the candlelight, the look of surprise on his face when she folded her arms around his neck. Recalling the urgency of their kisses and the feel of his hands as he eagerly explored her body through silk and lace still sent shivers up her spine.

Afterwards, as they lay on the bed, wrapped around each other in a tangle of sheets and hastily removed clothing, Anna listened to the sound of Daniel's breathing, soaking up the warmth from his body, taking pleasure from the touch of his skin on hers and the feel of strong arms holding her tight. She couldn't believe that she had worried so much and was glad that a huge hurdle had been crossed. Twisting her fingers around his, she looked up to see if he had dozed off but he was awake, smiling before kissing her forehead and turning on his side to face her.

'Are you okay? You certainly took me by surprise when I arrived!' He stroked her face, his eyes gently teasing.

'Well, I like to keep you on your toes but if I'm honest, I've been so wound up about all this.' Anna motioned towards the bed. 'And the tension of polite dinner conversation would've killed me so I decided to have my wicked way with you as soon as you got here.'

Daniel laughed out loud then slid gently on top of her. 'I quite like the assertive Anna, so feel free to do with me as you wish whenever the mood takes you. I'm all yours.' He kissed her softly.

Anna traced the line of his jaw with her finger, drinking him in. 'Well in that case, the mood takes me right now. I think we need to make up for lost time, don't you?'

And so, the once bashful, dithering, self-conscious Anna spent the rest of the evening and all of the weekend making very sure that the most was made of a huge four poster bed, the mini bar, gourmet food and in particular, a very happy but slightly knackered, Daniel.

CHAPTER 36

Their time at Rosie's had flown by and it was evident by the increasing amount of time Melanie was spending with Pascal, either at his farm or in the hotel, that she would be one unhappy bunny when it came to saying goodbye. Anna and Rosie were on their way to the gîtes to drop off some extra towels, discussing return visits and when would be the best time for Anna to come back.

'I'll definitely nip over once the baby arrives, even if it's just a flying visit. I'd like to see him or her and help out but I don't want to be in the way. Will your mother-in-law do her bit?'

Rosie rolled her eyes and let out a sigh. 'I can't imagine anything or anyone being able to stop her. This is her first grandchild and she can't wait but André should be back from his travels so he can stand in for me at the hotel. You still haven't met him but I know you'll love him as much as I do.' Rosie was referring to her old friend and mentor who was currently making his way across Europe and by all accounts, a bit of a character.

'And I'll have Ruby here for moral support but if I'm honest, I'm more stressed about the restaurant and whether Pascal will be able to cope on his own. Hopefully, once I get organised I can do the odd evening while the baby sleeps but for a while, it's going to be a juggling act. I think we may have to take someone on.' Rosie was the consummate professional so the thought of her precious hotel falling into chaos weighed heavily on her mind.

Anna was deep in thought as they walked, knowing only too well that no matter how organised you planned to be, when the baby actually arrives it's madness and with a hotel to run as well, Rosie might struggle. Then she had an idea.

'Rosie, are you fussy about who you'd want to take on for the summer, I mean, do they have to be qualified or anything?'

Rosie shook her head. 'No, not at all. As long as they are willing and friendly and work hard, why, are you offering?'

The thought had actually crossed Anna's mind but it wouldn't work, she was Rosie's friend and that's how she wanted it to stay.

'Actually, I was thinking of Mel. She had a summer job in the café at the ferry port last year and really enjoyed it so maybe she could come and work for you. It would be good language practice, plus she needs a job during the holidays and absolutely loves it here. She could fill in for you in the restaurant and help Ruby during the day.' Anna hoped she hadn't spoken out of turn but when Rosie clapped her hands in excitement she knew it was okay.

'Do you think she would want to? It's a great idea, Anna. I'd rather have someone I already know and Michel told me that she's been secretly helping out. She could have the attic room that we save for emergencies. Come on, let's go and ask her.' Rosie was thrilled and headed straight off in search of Melanie.

Needless to say, Mel accepted instantly then wanted to see the attic and tell Pascal her news all at once. As usual she fussed and worried about Anna who then surprised everyone with an idea of her own. Rosie had mentioned that the large gîte was still available in August so, while they sat in the garden waiting for Michel to bring out their lunch she had another question for her friend.

'Rosie, do you think you could put up with me for a whole month in the summer? I was thinking of renting the large gîte for August, maybe Jeannie and Phil could come over and I might even persuade my mother to stay for a few days. I don't know what Sam has planned yet but there'd be enough room for everyone in there.'

Rosie looked a bit taken aback by Anna's offer. 'Of course you can have it, Anna, it would be fantastic to have you here, and your family too. Are you sure though? It's quite expensive because it's so big, especially for four weeks but I'll do you special mates rates.'

'No you will not. I know exactly how much that gîte costs because I've looked on your website, so that's what I will pay – no arguments.' Anna stubbornly folded her arms across her chest.

'You are getting very bossy lately, Madame, but it's a deal and I'm very grateful.' Rosie leant over and squeezed Anna's hand. 'And you could even do a bit of babysitting while you're here. You know what? I really like this plan, it gets better by the second.' Rosie was thrilled.

Michel appeared carrying wine, juice and glasses, shaking his head, saying he had left the lovebirds in the kitchen to finish making lunch, the screeching and the excitement was too much for him. It seemed that Pascal had been getting on his nerves all morning, moping around the vegetable patch, barely speaking and in a world of his own. Apparently, he soon perked up when Melanie bounced through the door with her news so hopefully they'd get some work out of him now he was a happy rabbit.

When Rosie and Anna laughed at his comment he naturally assumed he was being amusing and ignored them. 'I will make us a special dinner this evening, let's invite the neighbours and have some fun. The other guests can join in too. Soon we will be too busy with holidaymakers and a baby so we should make the most of the time with our friends.' After he poured the wine, Michel raised his glass and the three of them made a toast to good friends, young love and the summer.

Anna had so much to do when she got home she barely had time to have any last minute regrets or be haunted by ghosts of the past. The packing was done and she had cleaned every inch of the house for the very last time. Keeping busy was the key so in between shopping trips to buy new furniture for the apartment and taping up boxes, she had managed to fend off any of the negative feelings she'd been expecting in the lead up to moving day. Now it had arrived and as she looked around the sparkling, clean house that was devoid of photographs and personal belongings, it didn't seem like her home at all.

Placing her hand on the wall of the lounge she tried to imagine how the house would feel. Was it sad to be saying goodbye to the family it had cared for all these years, a little bit excited perhaps? It was gleaming and maybe proud, full of anticipation and eager to greet the new owners, she hoped so. Anna could feel the tears coming and no amount of talking herself through it could dissolve the swell of sadness deep in her heart.

'I'm going now. Thank you for looking after us, you made us so happy. I'm sorry I couldn't stay forever like I planned but I'm sure the new people will love you as much as I did. I will never, ever forget you. I promise.'

Glad that the kids weren't here to witness a mad woman talking to a house again, Anna picked up her keys and grabbed the handle of her suitcase. With a deep breath, Anna gripped the keys, stepped outside, and locked the door. Swallowing down a sob she turned and walked along the path, refusing to look back, taking just her suitcase and memories with her.

The day Anna got the keys to her apartment felt like the start of a new life, and Jeannie's too if her excitement was anything to go by. They arrived at 9am, the car loaded with food after an early morning shopping bonanza and waited patiently in the foyer for Gordon to bring the keys. Jeannie was marching up and down checking her watch while Anna occupied herself by peering through the glass doors when she had to move out of the way to allow a sweaty jogger inside. Stepping aside to let him pass, to Anna's surprise she heard Jeannie exclaim rather loudly.

'Anthony Rogers, is that you?'

Jogging man stopped in his tracks and turned to face her.

'Well, well, well, if it isn't Jean Brown, fancy bumping into you after all these years, you haven't changed one bit!'

After setting him straight where her name was concerned, smug Jeannie introduced Anna who didn't know jogging man from Adam.

After much trawling down memory lane, it transpired that Anthony Rogers (now preferring Anton) used to live next door but one from Jeannie in the flats on the estate. They went to the same comprehensive school and remained good friends but eventually drifted apart. Interestingly, Anton had done extremely well for himself and now owned a string of nightclubs and pubs around the area and coincidently, the penthouse next door to Anna. Their reminiscing was interrupted by the arrival of Gordon and once he'd passed Anna the brown envelope containing her keys, she and Jeannie swiftly bade him farewell and headed upstairs.

When Anna tentatively pushed open the door of her new home they were met by the unmistakable smell of fresh paint. Walking around the apartment in a daze, she tried to take it all in. At the moment it was a blank canvas of white walls. Anna had decided, rather than choose the wrong thing she ought to get a feel for the place before making firm decisions. Unlocking the patio door and sliding it back, Anna let in the fresh air and the sea breeze, and was joined on the balcony by Jeannie.

'Well, here we are, kiddo, the start of a new life. You did the right thing you know, you'll be happy here, I can tell.'

Jeannie placed her arm around her best friend's shoulder as they looked out to sea, both lost in their thoughts until the buzzer on the intercom sounded, signalling that the furniture had arrived. The rest of the day was a blur – visits from Enid and Dennis, the arrival of Phil and his toolbox, the delivery of packing boxes and pizza.

***

The late May sun poured through the open windows as Anna sat on the balcony, knitting and watching the world go by. The afternoon heat gently warmed her as ferries chugged back and forth along the Solent and the coast guard zipped here and there, keeping watch. Pedestrians meandered along the seafront and the squawk of hungry seagulls pierced the air. So far the apartment had completely lived up to Anna's expectations. She never felt lonely and if she woke in the middle of the night she would lie in her bed with the French doors slightly open and once the traffic had died down, she could hear the waves crashing against the promenade wall at high tide, or the sounding of a ship's horn somewhere in the distance.

Even weekend revellers didn't bother her. They were the sound of life and people having fun as they passed by her home. She loved to look out across the Solent at the lights of the ships and the houses on the opposite shore, twinkling away, signalling that whatever hour, she wasn't alone. Sometimes Anna would set her alarm for 6am so she could sit on the balcony and drink coffee, watching the world wake up. The mist would slowly lift from the sea as fishing boats crept into the harbour, followed in their wake by screeching gulls and the early morning ferries, and then the brightly clad joggers, some of them even gave her a quick wave.

Then there was Anton next door to keep her occupied. He was a bit of a night owl and man about town, very popular with the ladies, all stunningly pretty and never over the age of twenty-five. They had gradually got to know each other over morning coffee or in the evening for a quick glass of wine before he went on the prowl. Anna suspected that he didn't have to look far for entertainment as he had the pick of his lap dancers and clientele.

Daniel had met Anton and they got on like a house on fire, once it was clear that Anna was way too old to even register on her neighbour's radar, even if she was actually two years younger than him. This fact was confirmed by the slightly ditsy, over made-up, under-dressed leggy blonde who had superglued herself to Anton's arm on the night he called in for a quick drink.

Daniel's visit was the second time they had seen each other since the 'weekend of love' as Jeannie mockingly described it. Due to immense pressure from Melanie once they returned from France, Anna arranged a flying weekend visit so she could meet Daniel. He lived in Hemel Hempstead which was about an hour from Reading so after picking Melanie up from university they drove over to his, Anna quaking with nerves and convinced it would all go horribly wrong. Josh was going to be there too and she hoped this would help break the ice and ease any tension while Melanie, as per usual, was totally unfazed and couldn't wait to get there.

They had planned to stay for dinner and then drive back later to Melanie's halls where they would top and tail in her rather small bed. Anna really didn't care if she got cramp or slept on the floor as long as they all got on. As it turned out, the evening went surprisingly well.

Daniel was his calm, laid-back self when they arrived; making a fuss of Melanie and by some strange coincidence had made her favourite Italian meal, cannelloni. Nosey as ever, Mel wanted a guided tour around his home which was a very elegant whitewashed Georgian townhouse, tastefully decorated with antique furniture and full of original features. They ate in the cosy kitchen surrounded by the smell of herbs and garlic where the conversation flowed easily as they swapped tales of France and uni. Josh proudly told Melanie about the people he cared for and how Anna had helped him choose his career.

After dinner they half watched a film, half chatted and in between, Josh had them in hysterics recalling the tale of how Anna thought he and Daniel were gay and her well-meant heart to heart in the garden when she thought she'd smoothed over a lover's tiff. He relished the part when Anna realised her mistake, saying he thought her glowing red face was going to explode.

Daniel then insisted that Anna retold the tale of Henri and Sebastien fighting a duel and how Rosie solved the problem. Melanie was enthralled and totally impressed that her old mum had so many men after her. Time flew and it was getting late and even though they were having a great time, Anna suggested they head off as they didn't want to outstay their welcome. Groans of protest came from Josh and Mel because they hadn't eaten the chocolate fudge cake and insisted it was way too early to leave, prompting Josh's flash of inspiration.

'I know, why don't you just stay here tonight? It's stupid driving all that way. Mel can have the spare room and Anna can crash with Daniel, you old fogey's need an early night and us youngsters can stay up and watch a film. What a plan.'

As Josh high-fived Mel, the phrase can someone take the elephant out of the room, sprang into Anna's mind.

Nobody spoke. It was awful. Then Mel saved the day.

'Go on, Mum, can we? You've got your overnight bag in the car and it'll be fun staying over. Like Josh said, it's daft driving all that way when there's room for us here.'

Anna was still too embarrassed to even look in Daniel's direction when he spoke.

'Well, it's okay by me. I think I've got spare toothbrushes in the bathroom and Mel can borrow some of Louise's things, she always leaves spare pyjamas here and she's about your size. Help yourself.' If Daniel felt at all uncomfortable he didn't show it one bit.

'Right, that's settled then, come on Josh let's get some cake.' Melanie jumped up and headed out the door then popped her head back in to speak to Anna, her face wearing a wicked grin.

'You can breathe out now, Mum. Honestly, you are so old-fashioned sometimes. It's all cool so stop looking so embarrassed.'

Then she shot off to the kitchen as Daniel went over to the sofa, putting his arms round Anna and kissing her on the cheek.

'She's right, you know. I thought you were going to die of shock right there and then on my sofa. As long as Mel's okay with us sleeping together you shouldn't worry, and what would we do without Josh? Sometimes I think he borders on being naive or slightly insane.'

Daniel chuckled and Anna relaxed, but only slightly.

Anna was still a little uncomfortable knowing her daughter would be downstairs or next door while she slept with Daniel, but she'd have that exact situation to deal with when Joe and Sam came home, so they may as well just get on with it. Daniel took a bottle of wine from the kitchen, calling out to Mel and Josh that they were going to watch TV in his room and they'd see them in the morning. As they started to climb the stairs, they heard Josh say sarcastically to Mel.

'Yeah, right, course you are!' After which they both dissolved into fits of laughter.

'*Not quite so naive after all*,' thought Anna as they sheepishly climbed the stairs, but it made her smile and despite her reservations and endless worrying, knew it was going to be okay.

***

Anna had been daydreaming, staring out to sea in a world of her own and thinking of Daniel. Her thoughts then turned to Sam. He would be home in a couple of weeks but her heart still constricted with fear each time she imagined where he was and the cold grip of worry had remained ever since he left. Anna had become obsessed with the 24-hour news channels, almost never turning off the television, monitoring the feeds which ran along the bottom of the screen. For some strange reason, as his return became more imminent the fear had increased. Thoughts of getting this far and something happening just as he was about to come home tormented her nights and hovered on the edge of her consciousness during the day. Sam rang her regularly as promised from secure lines as mobiles were forbidden. There wasn't much to say at his end (for obvious reasons) but for Anna, just hearing his voice was enough.

On strict orders from Melanie, Anna had emailed Joe and written to Sam and told them all about Daniel. After a serious talk on the way home from Hemel Hempstead, Mel had convinced Anna it was the best thing to do because the longer she left it, the more secrets she would be keeping. It would also give them time to get their heads round the idea. Mel promised to stick up for Anna and give Daniel a glowing reference if either of them kicked up a fuss but luckily, there was no need.

Sam said it was cool and just wanted his mum to be happy, then enquired what football team Daniel supported. Joe, having learnt his lesson previously, was gracious if a little less enthusiastic but assured Anna that he was pleased and would take his sister's word that Daniel was a good bloke.

It had been over a year since Anna stumbled on Matthew's affair and the date was imprinted in her mind, pecking at her brain and bringing back ugly memories, forcing her to go over and over things in her head. Her promise to Rosie that she would have one more go at tracking down 'the other woman' had been downgraded in her list of priorities and most of the time Anna managed to forget all about her. But over the past week it had resurfaced, niggling away like a scratchy-clawed rat, unsettling her and making her fret. Jeannie had told her to stop obsessing, look at the positives in her life and not let some evil slapper spoil what she'd achieved. It was sound advice, but a lot easier said than done.

Anna shook the thoughts away and concentrated on something else. Melanie was coming home for the weekend with her friend Amy, so that would keep her occupied. The ringing of the phone made Anna jump, bringing her back to earth. Lifting the receiver she heard Sam's faraway voice, and in an instant, her heart soared, her face beamed and the sun came out.

CHAPTER 37

S abine Rousseau was born on the 3rd June in the very early hours of the morning following a mad dash to the local hospital. Michel telephoned Anna at around 6.30am to announce her arrival, totally forgetting they were an hour behind in England, disturbing her slumbers with his happy news.

Sam arrived home three days later and Melanie and Anna were at the base to meet him along with the other families. If it had been a contest in Crying Tears of Happiness and Relief, Anna thought she won hands down. She couldn't wait to get him back to Portsmouth and spoil him, having to restrain herself from hugging him every five minutes. Sam thought the apartment was cool while Melanie was overjoyed to spend time with her brother, laughing at God knows what (Anna most likely) talking rubbish and catching up late into the night.

They had a welcome home meal for Sam that weekend where Jeannie, after bottling up her fears so as not to worry Anna, became very tearful now her godson was home. Enid was disappointed that she didn't get a Prince Harry photo but instead Sam managed to get one of David Cameron during a flying visit – she wasn't impressed. They were joined by Dennis and Mary and Mel's friend, Amy, who was lovely, polite, normal, and fragrant, plus Anton from next door popped in. Daniel was stuck in Edinburgh working so couldn't make it back.

The apartment was coming together now, three comfy sofas were positioned in front of the patio doors, one facing right out to sea, the other two opposite each other creating a cosy seating area so wherever you sat, you could take in the view. Anna had added splashes of colour with cushions and ornaments, making it feel very homely. A large coffee table sat in the centre of the sofas and a matching bureau stood against the wall that separated the dining area and bedrooms, adorned with family photos and memories, the centre piece being one of them all, including Matthew. In front of the large windows was a dining table from where Sam was chatting to Anton about the club while Mary heard all about Enid's photo, leaving Dennis to escape and make his way over to Anna.

'This is all lovely, Anna, you've done a great job and the apartment is perfect for you all, I hope you'll be very happy here, we've been meaning to come over more often but work has been busy. Anyway, how are you doing?' Dennis looked ill at ease as Anna chatted.

She suspected it was a reaction to change and that Matthew was missing from her new life so she changed the subject.

'I was a bit hurt that Samantha didn't let me know about the baby. I can't put my finger on it but I feel as though she's avoiding me. I got a very short text thanking me for my gift and apologising for not hearing me when I called, she was asleep apparently. Do you think I've done something wrong?'

As she spoke, Anna thought she saw a flicker of something cross Dennis's face, a twitch of nerves maybe, as though was he slightly uncomfortable, but the moment passed.

'No idea, Anna, but don't dwell on it. Perhaps she thought we would pass the message on and I believe new mothers do need their sleep. Don't fret about it. You couldn't possibly have done anything wrong. You always worry too much about other people. Right, I'm going to get a drink then rescue Mary from your mother.'

And without giving Anna the opportunity to reply, he was gone.

It was still there though, that niggling doubt. Anna had known Dennis for years and she had an awful feeling he wasn't being honest with her, evasive.

Sam stayed for another week and soon became Anton's sidekick. How many other twenty-two-year-olds have the owner of a lap dancing club as a neighbour and a free pass to all of his establishments? Then there was the added advantage of a bevy of gorgeous girls who flocked to their boss's side, none of which were impervious to the charms of a handsome, sun tanned, muscle bound soldier either. Having the same ethos about health and fitness, Sam and Anton jogged and trained together during the day and spent most evenings at one of his clubs.

When Anna received a text message from Rosie saying, PLEASE COME SOON OR I WILL COMMIT MURDER. MOTHER IN-LAW DRIVING ME MAD, she obeyed immediately, booking a flight and packing her bag. Sam wasn't due back in work for a while so she tore herself away and after listing a string of dos and don'ts along with a very detailed list of cleaning related expectations, she left him to his own devices and flew to France.

Sabine was a beautiful baby, with her father's dark hair and her mother's blue eyes. She was absolutely no trouble and did nothing but eat, sleep and need her nappy changing. The problem lay with Michel's mother, Marie, who had almost moved in and taken over, driving Rosie to distraction. Ruby was run off her feet with the hotel and her own two children so unable to help much, giving Marie the perfect opportunity to muscle in. Michel was scared to death of *Maman* and even though he was in the same frame of mind as Rosie, didn't have the bottle to tell her to sod off. Anna suspected that Rosie was on the verge of a total meltdown and doting Marie was on the brink of copping for it, big time.

Michel, Anna and Marie were on the terrace while Sabine slept peacefully in her pram, guarded fiercely by her *mamie*. Rosie was pretending to take an afternoon nap but secretly sticking pins in an effigy of Marie. With Michel to translate and using all of her diplomatic skills, Anna attempted to liberate Sabine and her parents from the well-intentioned clutches of Marie.

'You look a little tired, Marie, I expect you have been overdoing things, taking care of everyone here then going home to your husband. I really don't know how you do it, I'd be exhausted.'

Marie agreed, looking slightly martyred while insisting that she didn't mind helping out. Michel quickly backed up Anna's observations, adding he was very concerned about his *maman*, and that perhaps papa would be feeling neglected at home; all the while nodded his head, urging Anna to continue.

'You really ought to get some rest, Marie, what would everyone do if you got sick? The whole family needs you to be healthy so perhaps you should have a break and recharge your batteries. I'm sure Rosie and Michel will understand.'

Marie let out a weary sigh and nodded in agreement, happy that someone had, at last, recognised her sacrifice. Enjoying immensely her saintly role she then asked who would help out here if she took a break, everyone was so busy with the hotel and restaurant.

Anna looked thoughtful then came up with a great idea. She should've been on the stage. 'Well, I'm here for a week so maybe I could step in? If I need advice or can't manage I will phone you and you can come straight over. I really don't mind, as long as you get some rest, that's the main thing.' Anna's acting was now verging on melodramatic.

After mulling it over whilst Michel held his breath, Marie admitted that it was becoming a struggle, keeping her demanding husband fed and watered as well as being here, so if they really didn't mind, would take Anna up on her offer, just until she went back to England.

Michel was off his chair in an instant, saying he thought it was a fabulous idea and before Marie could change her mind, suggested that they should get a move on and he would run her home, right now. Poor Marie barely had time to kiss Sabine and thank Anna before she was ushered out the door, strapped into the car and zoomed off down the lane.

Anna waved them both off before gently pulling back the blanket to gaze at the sleeping baby who was completely oblivious to the trouble her arrival had caused. 'There you go, princess. I think that went rather well. Poor grandma, it's not her fault that she loves you so much but mummy wants you all to herself for a while and I really don't blame her.' After tucking the blanket around Sabine, Anna triumphantly pushed the pram inside and went upstairs to tell Rosie that at last, the coast was clear.

Anna only stayed for another night, leaving Michel and Rosie alone with their daughter. The plan was to tell Marie that she was still there and fend her off for as long as possible. Before she left, Anna also told Michel that he needed to grow some parts of his nether regions, pronto, and start standing up to his mother, or else!

***

It was a lovely sunny Monday afternoon; Anna sat day dreaming about France and smiling to herself as she waited in the traffic for the lights to change. She was on the way back from visiting Naomi and intended to make a quick stop at the supermarket. Mel was paying a flying visit between exams, dropping off stuff from her room before the end of term. Anna's mind then wandered to Joe, he'd want his car back when he came home meaning Mel would need a runabout of her own.

Anna was distracted from her ruminating by the red car that pulled alongside her at the lights, turning to her right she recognised the driver instantly, it was Samantha. Her baby was in its carrier on the front seat and she was fussing over it, oblivious to anyone around. Instinctively, Anna honked her horn, forcing Samantha to look up and wave as she wound down her window. Samantha did the same.

'Hi, how are you, how's the little one?' Anna couldn't see him properly from where she sat.

'Hi, Anna, we're fine, how's everyone?'

Samantha glanced at the lights and before Anna could answer they changed, forcing both women to move off and end their conversation mid-way.

Anna should have been pleased to see Samantha but she wasn't. There was something nervy about the look on her face and she got the distinct impression that she was glad to drive away. Anna was irritated and couldn't put her finger on it but something was niggling, hidden away in the back of her mind and if only she could work out what it was. An early morning phone call from her mother the very next day would bring her the answer she was looking for and finally solve her greatest mystery, the one which had caused her so much misery and rocked her world.

Enid turned out to be the catalyst which led to Anna discovering the identity of Matthew's mistress. Woken by the buzzing of her phone from a gloriously deep and peaceful sleep, Anna conducted the first part of the conversation with her eyes closed and on the verge of drifting back into the happy land of nod. Enid was relentless when she was on a mission so, summoning all her powers of concentration, Anna listened to her mother who was in full, breezy morning-mode.

'Anna, it's me. I need one of those telly thingys, the ones you can record your favourite shows. That man advertises them, what's he called now? Him with the white hair and beard.'

Enid was vague at the best of times so, bored already, Anna attempted to conjure up an image in her head.

'Father Christmas, is that who you mean?' Anna had no idea who Enid was going on about.

Enid tutted loudly, clearly irritated by her daughter. 'Don't be stupid, Anna, no, not him. I mean the one who has trains and planes and talks posh.'

Thankfully, the light dawned. 'You mean Richard Branson, Mum. Why do you want one of those? You won't be able to work it you know, it's a bit confusing and you'll need to get the Internet connected at yours.' Anna rubbed her eyes wearily.

'Yes I will be able to work it and don't be so judgemental, I'm not a dimwit. I had a go of Gladys's and I wouldn't mind getting the Internet, I quite fancy surfing on the web and all that.

Anyway, I'm fed up with missing the end of *Inspector Morse* or *Midsummer Murders* because I've nodded off or I'm out. I never get to know who did it, that's why I want one of those machines. It's not bloody rocket science and if Gladys can do it, so can I!' Enid huffed loudly.

'Right, Mum, I understand, no problem. I'll get onto it today and arrange it but can I ring you back later, I'm still in my pyjamas?' Anna was wide awake now so she might as well get up.

'Thanks, love, I knew I could rely on you and what are you doing in bed at this time? I've been up for hours. Anyway, got to go. Me and Gladys are going bowling later and Mel's coming for tea so let me know how you go on. Ta-ra.'

Anna turned onto her back and sighed. It was 8am and her mother had been up for hours. What on earth did she do at that time?

Half an hour later Anna was sitting on the balcony drinking coffee and watching the world go by, thinking about Enid and her set-top box. She didn't know why her mother watched detective programmes because apparently, they annoyed her, saying that the one whodunnit was always the person you least suspected. While everyone was chasing after the suspicious obvious character, in the background, Mr Nice Guy was getting away with murder. Anna chuckled to herself. Miss Marple had better watch out because Chief Inspector Enid had it all sussed.

As she watched the traffic on the road below, a shiny red car sped past. For some reason it made the hairs stand up on her neck and her heart beat just a little faster, her brain racing, trying to jog her memory. *'Red car, red car, what is it about the red car?'* Whispers inside her head taunted her, *'It's always the one you least suspect, Anna, the quiet one, lurking in the background, someone everyone trusts.'*

And then it hit her like a thunderbolt. *'The airport! Jeannie saw Matthew get out of a red car; he kissed the woman in the red car!'* The whispers were there again, *'Who do you know that has a red car?*

Come on, Anna, work it out, don't ignore it, you know the answer.'
Anna put her hand over her mouth and spoke out loud.

'Oh my God. It's Samantha!'

Bile rose in Anna's throat and her hands shook uncontrollably.
She needed to get a grip, Melanie would be out in a minute, but
her head throbbed as a million thoughts pulsed through her brain,
forcing the blood in her veins to pump faster and faster, adrenaline
helping her think, putting it all together. The pieces of the jigsaw
were falling into shape just as Mel breezed onto the balcony and
instantly spotted the look on Anna's face.

'Mum, are you okay, you've gone white as a sheet, what's
wrong?' Melanie came over, placing a hand on Anna's shoulder.

'I'm fine, love, don't worry. I've got a pounding headache and I
feel a bit sick, that's all. I think it was that curry we had last night,
it mustn't have agreed with me.' Anna didn't look her daughter
in the eye; she hated lying but couldn't even begin to tell her the
truth.

'Look, you go back to bed for a bit but it might be better if
you are sick, get it out of your system. You should have had the
same as me. I told you prawns are dodgy in a curry but you never
listen. I'm going into town now to get some packing boxes then
I'm meeting Tania before I go to Gran's. Will you be alright on
your own? I don't mind staying to hold the sick bowl.'

After Anna assured her she'd be fine, Mel gave her a peck on
the cheek before setting off.

'Okay, as long as you're sure. Get some sleep and I'll ring you
later.' Anna smiled weakly, willing Melanie to go before she had
a meltdown.

Taking her phone the second the door slammed shut, Anna
rang Jeannie but it went to voicemail so she sent a text, telling her
to ring as soon as she got the message, it was urgent – really bloody
urgent. Then she sat there like a zombie, putting it all together in
her head while she waited for Jeannie. Yet another half an hour of
torment passed by until her phone finally buzzed.

'Where are you, I've been going mad here? I need you to come round right now. Or I'll come over to yours, are you at home? I need to tell you what I've found out.' Anna could hear the hysteria mounting in her own voice.

'Anna, I can't, I'm in Barcelona. I told you I was working today, well, I think I did. We're waiting to board right now, what's wrong, are you okay? Tell me quickly, I don't have long.' Jeannie was panicking and just from Anna's high-pitched pleading, knew something was up.

'I've worked out who it is, Matthew's mistress. Remember when you saw him at the airport last year, you said it was a red car, an Audi, are you sure that's the right make?' Anna spoke quickly.

'Yes, I think so. It was ages ago but if that's what I said, then yes. Why do you want to know?'

'Bloody hell, Jeannie, you have to be sure, think! Could it have been an Astra?'

Jeannie was on the spot and frantically racked her brain. 'Anna, I don't know, it could've been, you know I'm not interested in cars and get confused with the makes and models. I just remember it was that type of shape and size, why is it so important?'

Jeannie was under pressure on both sides while Anna let out a frustrated sigh.

'Oh God, it all makes sense now! I've worked it all out. It's so obvious, the person I least suspected, someone everybody likes and trusts and she's been there all the time, right under my nose, laughing at me.'

Anna sounded slightly deranged, her voice getting higher with each word which is when Jeannie lost her temper.

'For fuck's sake, Anna! Just tell me who it is.'

Jeannie cringed as her colleagues and a few passengers turned and stared, while at the other end Anna paused, shocked for a second then rallying, she began to explain everything.

Samantha had a red car, the mistake had been an easy one as Jeannie had been in a rush to get to work and was also distracted by what she saw, both cars were of a similar size and to be fair, she had been concentrating mostly on Matthew.

Then, there was the day Anna spotted him at the hotel. She'd rang Harrison's earlier that morning because his phone was switched off, so, presuming he was in a meeting, decided to leave a message with Samantha at the office. When one of the other girls answered and told her that Samantha had rung in sick, Anna thought nothing of it but evidently, she was at the hotel with Matthew.

Skipping forward to the day he died, Matthew had been missing all day and was supposed to meet her for lunch. When she went to the office in a state, Anna hoped and expected to find him there but he wasn't, and neither was his wonderful personal assistant. Caitlin said that Samantha had a doctor's appointment which was why, when Anna rang her, desperately hoping she'd shed some light on her boss's whereabouts, her phone went to voicemail. Whilst oblivious to the deceit at the time, Anna now knew that Samantha's medical issues were clearly a load of bollocks because she was elsewhere, assisting Matthew with the zip on his pants.

Rewind to December, wasn't it odd that after all these years, Samantha was invited to the managerial Christmas dinner? Matthew reckoned it was so that Caitlin didn't feel like the odd one out, being the only woman, how thoughtful of him but total crap. He had the hots for his PA and now Anna understood why it took him so long to get home that night.

Then, there was the incident at the works Christmas party when Mel found Samantha crying. Anna offered to go and see if she was okay, but no, Sir Galahad insisted he went and was gone for ages. When she eventually found them arguing on the steps they stopped abruptly when Anna appeared and Samantha jumped into a taxi like the devil was on her tail. Anna was such a fool, believing Matthew's cock and bull story about Samantha's husband putting pressure on her to have a baby when in fact, it was a lover's tiff.

At the funeral, Samantha could barely look Anna in the eye and she was definitely avoiding her, and the same thing happened at Christmas when they went to give out presents at Harrison's. She barely managed to make conversation, and then there was the nameplate.

Anna didn't make the connection at first but remembered Melanie saying she had found some roses on the grave. The card said from 'K'. While she chatted to Samantha at Christmas, Anna noticed a box containing her belongings amongst which was the brass plate saying Samantha Kaye PA, and that's what the card meant. It was a code. 'K' was an abbreviation of her surname, or Kitten.

'Anna, I totally get where you are coming from but you need to think all this through. It could be a coincidence and you know what you're like for jumping to conclusions and letting your imagination run riot. Listen, try and calm down. I'll be back in a couple of hours and I'll come straight round so we can talk it through properly then.'

Jeannie was desperately trying to soothe her friend whilst alarm bells were ringing in her ears, soon accompanied by Anna's irate voice shouting down the phone.

'I am not stupid, Jeannie. I know I'm right and get this, that's not the worst of it. Haven't you realised there's someone else involved? The bloody icing on the cake, the cherry on top of my pathetic life.' Anna felt the tears coming and was shaking uncontrollably.

'Who else is involved, Anna, what do you mean? Hurry up. I'm going to have to go any second.' Jeannie's stress levels were in the red and she'd be helping herself to a double vodka the second she got into the galley on the plane.

'The baby, Jeannie. Samantha's had a baby and I think it's Matthew's! It all makes sense now. He was born almost nine months since I spotted them at the hotel. Then there's her not letting me know he'd arrived, hiding from me at the house. I knew she was there, watching me, I could feel it. That baby is Matthew's,

I know he is.' There was total, utter silence at the other end of the phone and for a second, Anna actually thought Jeannie had hung up.

'I can't believe it, Anna. I honestly don't know what to say but we can talk it through as soon as I get back, just don't do or say anything to Samantha, you have to wait for me. Promise you will. Look, I've got to go now, they're calling me. I'll ring the second we touchdown, just hang in there, okay?' Jeannie sounded shocked and slightly upset.

Anna was hyperventilating at the other end of the phone, just saying the words made it even truer, more real. Managing to retain enough composure to reassure her friend, Anna said she would try to keep calm and then the line went dead.

Fifteen long minutes passed. Sitting around, waiting and thinking was just making matters worse. Anna felt sick to her core; she couldn't get the baby out of her mind. She had to see him for herself and would know the second she clapped eyes on him if he was Matthew's because all her children looked exactly the same when they were born. Surely he would look like them. That nagging voice returned, reinforcing the urge to do something, anything rather than sit there, crying like the fool that she was. The cajoling, hissing sound of the truth continued to stir things up, '*This has gone on for too long. You need to go over there right now and confront her. There's no need to go over things again with Jeannie. The facts speak for themselves. Come on, Anna, you're a big girl now, stop being a mug, fight back.*'

A surge of energy flowed through her body as Anna ran into the shower, flinging off her clothes and jumping under the water which hadn't had a chance to warm up, but she didn't care, the cold blast revitalised her. Shivering, she dried herself quickly and grabbed clothes from the wardrobe, pulling on jeans and a white T-shirt as quickly as her damp body would allow. Sitting in front of the mirror she hastily applied make-up, there was no way she would face this woman with dark rings under her eyes and blotchy skin. Dragging the brush through her hair she tied it in a ponytail and stepped into the first pair of shoes she could find, grabbing her car keys and bag.

One way or another Anna was determined to get to some answers and as she drove towards Samantha's house, regulating her breathing as she talked out loud, giving herself advice, warning her reflection in the rear-view mirror not to lose control. If she went in there all guns blazing she would never hear the truth, so no, this time Anna would be calm and sensible. It was the only way and once she saw the baby she would know if he was Matthew's, she was sure of it.

CHAPTER 38

Anna wasn't going to be fobbed off or give Samantha the chance to hide behind the curtains while she rang the bell like a fool this time, so she parked further down the street and watched the house carefully, giving herself time to go over things and compose herself. The postman had called and the red car was parked in the drive, but as yet there was no sign of life inside. Anna texted Mel mid-spying, saying she felt much better but was sleeping it off, thus avoiding being pestered. She had about ninety minutes before Jeannie landed by which time Anna would be vindicated and have the whole sordid story to tell her friend. Looking up from her phone she saw movement, Samantha was collecting the post from the porch so Anna got out of the car and locked the door.

Anna stood close to the porch so that it would be difficult to be seen from the windows, resolving to stand there all day with her finger on the bell if need be. There actually was no need for the subterfuge as eventually she saw a figure approaching through the frosted glass and within seconds Anna came face to face with a rather astounded Samantha, who did her best to appear pleasantly surprised.

'Hi, Anna, what a nice surprise. Is everything okay, I wasn't expecting you?'

Anna smiled sweetly at her adversary – she needed to get into the house. 'Yes, I'm fine. I was just passing and decided to pop in for five minutes and say hi and meet the little one. I hope you don't mind me turning up like this but seeing you in the car yesterday jogged my memory, so I thought I'd strike while the irons hot, if you know what I mean.'

Anna could see the hesitation in Samantha's eyes and suspected she was desperately trying to think of a get out clause when the sound of a baby's cry distracted her and she gave in.

'No, that's fine, Anna, come in. I'll just pop upstairs and get him. You go through to the kitchen. I won't be a minute so sit down and make yourself at home.' Samantha stepped back and allowed Anna inside.

The kitchen was clean and tidy but littered here and there with baby paraphernalia. Anna's heart sank as she took in the scene. Matthew's son lived here. These things were the result of his affair, scattered all around her, a testament to his betrayal. Tears stung at the back of her eyes, which she angrily forced away hearing footsteps returning down the stairs and Samantha's voice, soothing the baby. Anna's heart thudded in her chest and subconsciously, she gripped her bag for support, white knuckles betraying just how scared she really was.

'Come on, Archie, look who's come to see you, this is Anna, say hello.'

Anna turned slowly and almost stopped breathing as she gazed at the little boy in Samantha's arms, unable to speak for what seemed like and age but in reality, was perhaps only a few seconds.

There was no need to scrutinise him and look for minute likenesses to Matthew or the blonde hair and blue eyes of each of her babies, it was quite obvious from one quick look at him who he belonged to. The beautiful dark-eyed baby with jet-black hair was the image of his father, Samantha's husband, Rob. Anna's voice trembled slightly as she managed to say something coherent, aware of tears welling in her eyes as the pounding of her heart slowly subsided.

'Hello, little one, my word you are handsome, and the image of your daddy. Can I have a little cuddle?'

Anna held out her arms as Samantha passed her the baby who sucked on his dummy contentedly, watching his mummy switch on the kettle and begin to warm his bottle.

Anna fussed and cooed over the baby while the shaking inside subsided, reassured to some extent about the parentage of

Archie, but there was still unfinished business left to settle. They made small talk for a while about sleeping patterns and feeds, Samantha asked Anna about the family, nothing too personal or too deep, as though they were both skirting around an issue that was too painful or near the knuckle to bring up. The subject they both carefully avoided was Matthew. Samantha fed Archie while Anna sipped her coffee and waited for the right moment, trying to time it just right so that whatever she said didn't sound like an attack.

'I was wondering, have you had a chance to visit Matthew's grave since the funeral?' Placing her mug on the table Anna waited.

Samantha didn't flinch when she answered. 'No, I've not been up there. I wouldn't feel it was my place to go and I hate cemeteries, but why do you ask?'

This was it, no going back now. Anna took a breath then went in for the kill. 'Because the last time Melanie went up there she found a dried-up bunch of roses, the card said they were from "K". It was a bit of a mystery and the only person I could possibly think of was you, as your surname is Kaye.'

Anna kept her voice steady and this time, Samantha had the grace to blush, shifting in her seat, clearly becoming unsettled.

'Well, it definitely wasn't me, Anna. I sent my flowers at the funeral, why would I send any more?'

When Anna didn't reply, instead staring her out, Samantha was forced to speak. 'Look, is something wrong because I can sense that there is? I'd rather you say than beat around the bush and I get the feeling you're annoyed with me about something.'

Anna saw that Samantha's demeanour had changed and now seemed to be putting up barriers, preparing to defend herself.

'If you must know, Samantha, there is something wrong. There's a little mystery regarding Matthew I need to solve.' Anna looked her straight in the eye and continued bravely. 'He was having an affair before he died and I've been trying to work out who she was and seeing as you were privy to most things, wondered if you could shed some light on the matter.'

There, she'd said it. Now all Samantha had to do was confess, and it certainly got a reaction because on hearing Anna's words, she leant her elbows on the table, hiding her face in her hands, letting out a long sigh which was followed by a tense silence. Then she spoke.

'How long have you known?' Samantha removed her hands wearily and looked at Anna.

'Since May, last year.' Anna's pulse raced and she was having trouble controlling her emotions.

Samantha's eyes were brimming with tears and her neck was red and blotchy as she sat back in her chair, looking resigned and beaten, then taking a deep breath, she confessed. 'I wanted to tell you, Anna, I swear I did. The guilt drove me mad. So many times I almost picked up the phone but I always bottled out. I couldn't look you in the eye at the funeral, or any time I've met you since. I'm sorry, I really am.'

Anna couldn't bring herself to speak, after all this she was completely lost for words. Her mouth was dry and her head pounded as a year's worth of tension pulsed inside her brain while Samantha carried on, words tumbling from her mouth.

'I threatened Matthew a couple of times that if he didn't end it with her, I'd tell you myself, but he called my bluff and I didn't really have the guts if I'm honest.' Samantha wiped away her tear with trembling hands.

Registering the enormity of the last sentence, time stood still and Anna froze. Every sinew in her body went rigid with shock, she actually felt her face lock up, suspended in animation while her brain still functioned.

'*Why did Samantha say "end it with her", end it with who, what was she talking about?*' Then the light dawned and the real truth hit her. '*Oh my God, you stupid, stupid woman, you've got it wrong again, it's not Samantha, it's someone else!*' Anna felt so ashamed and spiteful but gathering her wits, forced out some quiet, calm, intelligible words.

'Just tell me who it is, Samantha. I need to know.'

As she waited in the airless kitchen, Anna sat, stock-still, staring at Samantha, waiting for a reply.

Samantha whispered. 'It was Caitlin. I'm so sorry, Anna. Matthew was having an affair with Caitlin from the office.'

***

According to Samantha, it started around the Christmas before he died. Caitlin had gradually alienated almost all of the secretarial staff with her aloofness and managed to make enemies of every other department to boot. Her cost-cutting and restructuring didn't go down well with anybody, regardless of the fact that it was in the interests of the company. Much of this was down to the fact that she was completely heartless and had a ruthless streak, not to mention being power-driven and determined to get her own way at any cost. The person she disliked most of all was Samantha. She saw Matthew's PA as a barrier and a challenge, resenting their close working relationship, respectful friendship and genuine admiration for each other.

Things soon started to disappear, such as important notes Samantha had taken or typed. Her files went astray. Matthew's meetings were cancelled or rescheduled causing him to turn up on the wrong day or at the wrong time. Caitlin would insist she had no knowledge of important conversations between her and Samantha. Despite pleading her innocence and reminding Matthew of her previously untarnished record, Samantha's perceived incompetence tested his loyalty on more than one occasion.

From her desk, positioned directly opposite Matthew's office, Samantha had a bird's eye view of what went on inside. Alarm bells began to ring when Caitlin insisted on closing the door firmly behind her when she entered, the buttons on her blouse undone to reveal more cleavage than appropriate, heavy perfume polluting the air as she passed by. Then there was the flirting and invading his personal space during meetings. Samantha found it hard to ignore the lingering hand on his shoulder, the flash of thigh and the giveaway: her irritating, girlish laugh.

Sensing that Matthew was becoming increasingly uncomfortable in Caitlin's presence, Samantha wasn't surprised by the invitation to the managerial Christmas dinner. Not only did he want company for the vamp, she suspected he wanted her there as some kind of safety blanket. Caitlin was livid and did her best to undermine, belittle and humiliate Samantha from that moment on. In the end, Samantha went home as soon as she could escape, leaving Matthew to fend for himself. He was a big boy, plus she was sick to death of Caitlin's barbed comments and it was bad enough at work so she wasn't putting up with it in her free time.

By the time Samantha left, Caitlin was seriously drunk and flirting with Matthew like her life depended on it and Dennis was livid. Something must have happened between them that night because from then on Caitlin was unstoppable, lingering at the end of the day, making last minute excuses to have a one to one, conveniently just as everyone was leaving the office. It made Samantha's skin crawl.

On the day of the staff Christmas party, Caitlin had called Samantha in to advise her of further restructuring. She was going to be moved from her position in two ways – firstly from outside Matthew's room into the main office. The new printer had to be accommodated plus, she would now be required to take on extra secretarial and reception duties due to the fact they were letting someone go. Samantha was hurt and incensed but cleverly, Caitlin had chosen a day when Matthew was out at meetings and therefore couldn't be relied on for backup. Instead, Samantha decided to speak to Matthew when she saw him later that evening at the party.

Caitlin turned up smashed, dressed like a tart and the slobbering show of affection towards Gavin was probably more for Matthew's sake, trying to make him jealous and show him what he was missing, therefore assuring his allegiance where Samantha was concerned. Later, when Melanie found her crying in the toilets it was because she had had a huge row with Rob. She'd told him everything on the way to the party and his response was simple, start a family and tell Caitlin to stick her job up her arse. Rob refused to respect the fact that this was her career and she loved working at Harrison's and when the conversation rumbled on through the meal, he stormed off home saying he was sick to death of hearing about the ice maiden.

Matthew found her just as she was leaving; she was in no fit state to party so they went outside and waited for a taxi. That's when Samantha let him have it, no holds barred, warning him what Caitlin was up to and asking him to stand up for her. He tried to cajole her, made excuses and in the end took Caitlin's side. At that moment, Samantha realised the contents of his pants were ruling his head and it was game over. Her parting shot was to remind Matthew what he was risking: his reputation, his self-respect and his wife, just as Anna appeared on the steps and the taxi pulled up outside.

From then on nothing was the same at Harrison's. Samantha was relegated and Caitlin continued to manipulate and monopolise Matthew. As his PA and fully aware of his day to day movements, it became increasingly clear what was going on and that the affair was gathering momentum. Just by monitoring Caitlin's activities and observing her smug demeanour, Samantha knew that Matthew was in deep and more importantly, that she no longer enjoyed coming into work. The upshot of this was maybe a little bit sooner than they had planned, Samantha and Rob decided to try for a baby.

Caitlin's engagement announcement was a master stroke, designed purely to make Matthew jealous while at the same time diffuse or divert any suspicions by giving the appearance of being madly in love with her fiancé. The working relationship had almost completely broken down between Matthew and Samantha by the time she announced she was pregnant, while Caitlin was of course delighted at the prospect of his PA being well and truly out of the picture – hopefully for good.

Samantha granted her that wish, simply because she couldn't be bothered fighting anymore so told Matthew that she wouldn't be returning to work once the baby was born. Stupidly, he played right into Samantha's hands when he asked why not, so she took great pleasure in telling him, in no uncertain terms, exactly why she hated working at Harrison's and precisely what she thought of him. He didn't take kindly to being told a few home truths and they had their first and last row. Samantha stormed out of the office in a rage and never saw Matthew again. She'd booked leave the next day for her first antenatal appointment and to her eternal regret, it was the day that Matthew died which is why she wasn't around when Anna came looking for him.

When she arrived at the office the following morning, everyone was in tears and being sent home and on hearing the news, Samantha was so distraught that Rob had to be called to collect her. She still remembered passing Caitlin's office on the way out and seeing the ice maiden on the phone, holding the fort as she commendably put it, not a tear in her eye and seemingly untouched by the tragedy.

Samantha dreaded the funeral. She was grief-stricken and riddled with angst over her final words to Matthew. She couldn't look Anna in the eye; knowing a secret about the man that the eulogy portrayed as a saint, yet in her eyes he was a sinner and had betrayed everyone who held him dear. Since then Samantha hoped to avoid Anna whenever possible and believed that once she left Harrison's, the guilt she carried at lying to such a lovely person would subside. That's why she didn't encourage any conversation or contact, or even tell her when Archie was born. Naively, Samantha hoped it would all just go away but it didn't and now the reason for her guilt was sitting before her, broken-hearted and in tears.

***

Getting up, Samantha grabbed a handful of kitchen roll, silently passing it to Anna before flicking on the kettle and sitting back down, waiting for the sobs to subside. Eventually Anna's tears slowed and her breathing returned to normal. Looking up with red eyes and streaked mascara she spoke, her voice choked and hoarse from crying.

'I don't blame you for keeping that secret, Samantha, truly I don't. I've done exactly the same thing so I know how it torments you. I'm just grateful you were able to tell me otherwise I would have gone on forever with a mystery hanging over my head. Please don't beat yourself up about it anymore.' Anna dabbed her eyes and tried to pull herself together.

Samantha took Anna's hands in hers as she spoke. 'Thanks, Anna, that means a lot. I've agonised over it for so long and I even blamed myself for his death, thinking that if I'd had the guts to ring you and expose them, then maybe you could have sorted things out. You may have forgiven him or something. God, I hate her so much! Caitlin has ruined both our lives and your kids' too. I loved my job at Harrison's and I didn't want to leave. I'd been there for twelve years and she took it all away from me, but compared to what she took from you, it's nothing.' Samantha was so angry her voice trembled.

Anna shook her head in disbelief. 'Matthew is just as much to blame as she is, and you're not alone in beating yourself up. I've spent many a sleepless night wishing I'd changed the course of events by confronting him sooner. I was a coward and left it too late and now he's gone. Neither of us can change the past. We both did what we thought was right at the time while the two people doing wrong didn't consider us at all. I refuse to carry that burden anymore and you should do the same.'

The kettle clicked and Samantha got up to make some tea. Baby Archie was fast asleep in his rocker, blissfully unaware of the drama unfolding in his kitchen.

'It was probably Caitlin that sent the flowers. At least she had the decency to stay away from the funeral after she made out that someone had to keep the business ticking over while we all fell apart. To be honest I don't think I could've coped if she'd have been there.'

Anna nodded at Samantha's words but one thing still puzzled her. 'Where do you think Matthew was the day he went missing?

When I went to the office to look for him I was convinced he was with his mistress but Caitlin was there, she spoke to me and was full of concern when in reality she just wanted to know for herself.'

Samantha shook her head. 'I've often wondered where he got to. I suppose we'll never know.'

'What I can't understand is why she calls herself kitten. That must be what the "K" stood for on the card that I thought was from you.' Anna cringed every time she mentioned the stupid name.

Samantha huffed as she brought back the tea things. 'Oh, I know the answer to that one. When she was plastered and drooling all over Matthew at the dinner she was telling anyone who could be bothered to listen that she likes her boyfriends to call her Katy Kitten, the silly cow! The drink had really loosened her tongue, and she was like a deranged man-eater and talking utter rubbish by the time I went home. Dennis wasn't impressed at all. I think everyone expected me to take her in hand, being of the sisterhood and all that but I was loving every cringeworthy minute and let her make a complete arsehole of herself.'

With that revelation, Samantha made Anna laugh for the first time that day.

'When do you think the affair started? That's always bothered me as much as who she is, exactly how long had he actually been cheating on me?'

Anna had finished her tea and Archie was beginning to stir.

'I am almost sure something happened that night because she let slip in the office that Matthew had taken her home, they shared a taxi but like I said, after that dinner, things changed.'

'Did Dennis know? He's never given me any indication that he was aware of what was going on, did he say anything to you?' Anna desperately hoped Dennis hadn't been covering for Matthew.

'If he did, he never mentioned anything or hinted that he knew. People did say stuff but it was just idle gossip based more on rumour than substance.' Samantha took Archie from his rocker and cuddled him, but there was one more thing she had to say.

'I don't know what you're going to do with this information, Anna, but can I give you some advice? Caitlin saw Matthew as a rung on the ladder and the key to the good life, now he's gone she'll need a replacement. She is one cunning woman and won't let anyone stand in her way, and I don't believe for one minute she loves her fiancé, she'd dump him in an instant if someone better came along. What worries me is that Joe is due back in September and Caitlin will see him as one of two things: a threat to her control of the company or, even worse in my opinion, as prey. He's young and may be easily influenced by her blonde hair and seductive ways or manipulated and then hung out to dry. I mean it, Anna. She will stop at nothing to get what she wants. You need to get rid of her quickly, before he comes home.' Samantha gently kissed the top of her son's head, her eyes full of warning and truth.

Anna was horrified at Samantha's wise words. She also knew that they were on the money. There was nothing for it – she had to take action, remove the threat – today!

CHAPTER 39

Anna was driving much too fast but she didn't care. As she sped along the dual carriageway, great chunks of worry, unanswered questions and self-doubt blew away in the wind, dropping onto the road behind her to be trampled and squashed by hundreds of tyres. It was weird that after all this time of feeling too much, Anna felt nothing apart from freedom. A whole year of suffering every negative human emotion possible was finally coming to an end. Paranoia, loss, jealousy, anger, fear, doubt, loneliness, depression and worst of all, seeing her self-esteem wither and vanish, had been replaced at last by knowing she was on top. A survivor. Having answers had set her free and given her the power to take control.

She felt so sorry for Samantha. How could Matthew have treated her so badly? Anna remembered her starting at Harrison's, an eager sixteen-year-old who impressed everyone with her dedication, ability and willingness to get stuck in. They had seen her grow up almost; rewarding all her hard work and the extra training courses she took with the job as his PA. They had even gone to her wedding for heaven's sake! Anna was incredulous. Who was this man she had known for over twenty-five years? He wasn't the husband and father that she remembered, and to throw it all away for someone like Caitlin was just beyond comprehension. Everything she had been told about him was so out of character. Perhaps he'd been body-snatched by aliens, even that was easier to come to terms with than the reality of the situation.

Pulling off the expressway onto the main road, Anna looked for a newsagent. She knew exactly what she was going to do and say. Checking the time on the display she noted it was 11.58. Everyone would be going for lunch soon so she had to hurry, she didn't want Caitlin to leave the office before she got there. After making hasty purchases and with a plan of action rooted in her mind, Anna drove through the front gates of Harrison's. Instead of parking in one of the two directors' spaces at the front she carried on around the back of the main office building to the car park. And there it was for everyone to see, in all its shiny red glory – Caitlin's Audi. If only Anna had parked here in the past she would have seen it and the mystery could've been solved so quickly. Jeannie was right after all. Taking the manila folder she had bought from the newsagent off the passenger seat, Anna locked her car and went inside.

As she pushed open the swing doors that led into the large secretarial area, most of the desks were empty and she could see the backs of people making their way outside to sit in the sun. They were using the rear stairs that led to the loading bay and a small yard that held benches and chairs for the staff to use. Nicki, the receptionist was just getting her things as Anna passed by and looked slightly startled to see her there.

'Hi, Nicki, I'm just popping in to see Caitlin. I found some paperwork at home she might find useful, is she in her office?'

Tapping the folder as proof, Anna smiled cheerily and carried on walking as with a hint of sarcasm, Nicki confirmed that Caitlin was in residence.

Gripping the file to prevent her hands from shaking, not from nerves, just pure, unadulterated rage, Anna pushed open the door without knocking, taking the occupant who was mid-telephone conversation completely by surprise. Anna strode in confidently, unannounced and unafraid. Closing the door firmly behind her she paused for a while and stared, waiting until the phone was placed in its cradle and she had Caitlin's full attention – then she spoke.

'Hello, Kitten, I hope I'm disturbing you. I thought it was time you and I had a nice little chat, don't you think?'

Anna enjoyed watching Caitlin go deathly white before the blood returned to her face and red heat began to creep into her cheeks.

'As you can see, I'm a little bit busy at the moment, Anna, but I can spare you a minute or two if it's urgent. What exactly would you like to talk about, oh, and please take a seat?'

Caitlin gestured grandly to the chair in front of her desk which irritated Anna immensely, along with the speed with which the ice maiden had regained her composure.

'Let's get one thing straight before we start. This is my company and I do not need to be invited to sit in a chair that I happen to own by anyone, and *especially* not by you. Secondly, I'm a little bit busy too as it happens so don't waste my time pretending you have no idea why I'm here. I've come to discuss your sordid little affair with my husband.'

'*Ten-nil to me*,' thought Anna, '*now just hold your nerve.*'

Caitlin seemed momentarily lost for words, or was she just preparing her response?

Then Anna spotted it, an almost unperceivable twitch at the corner of her eye, or was there the start of a smile creeping to her lips? Then it dawned on Anna that the woman seated before her was enjoying this, a moment of triumph, glad at last that her opponent knew about her. After tempting Matthew away from his wife and family the revelation was actually giving her a kick, and this alone unnerved Anna.

'Well, it's taken you long enough to work it out. I can't say I'm surprised though. Matthew always said you were a bit on the dim side but you got there eventually, do you expect a pat on the back or something?' Caitlin smirked openly, calmly twirling her pen around in the air, observing Anna's reaction, gauging how much pain, if any, her words had caused.

They actually hurt a lot but Anna didn't show it, gathering her inner warrior she wore her anger like armour, deflecting cruel words and responding instead with sentences laced with acid.

'You know, Caitlin, or Kitten, or whatever sad, silly name you prefer, I was married to Matthew for a long, long time and don't need you or anyone to tell me what my husband thought of me. On the other hand, we had many conversations regarding your personality traits or should I say lack of them and to sum it up in one word, from the moment he met you he thought you were vile. I always feel that first impressions are usually the most accurate. Still, I accept that somehow you managed to persuade him otherwise because you have no redeeming qualities that I've been told of, so I can only assume it was sex. And if that's all you had to offer it's really quite pathetic.' Anna continued, maintaining control and momentum, not giving Caitlin chance to respond, 'Anyway, back to business. Now everything is in the open we need to decide what to do with you or more to the point, how quickly we can get rid of the stain you have left on my company because don't think for one minute that you'll be keeping your job. I want you out, preferably today.' Anna hadn't raised her voice once and had enjoyed immensely the words 'my company'.

Caitlin didn't blink, no doubt calculating her next move, showing no emotion, then, putting down her pen she leaned forward slightly, resting her arms on the table and attempted to regain the upper hand.

'I think you'll find there are employment laws in this country and correct me if I'm wrong, but I don't think sleeping with the boss is a sackable offence, so sadly for you, Anna dear, I'll be staying put, like it or not.'

Caitlin attempted a confident look but Anna sensed that she was rattled.

'I'm fully aware of your rights, Caitlin, but consider this. It's common knowledge that you're not well liked throughout the company so imagine if I threw some fuel onto the fire and let it be known about your affair. Yes, I really would do that because I'm quite sure that I'd get the sympathy vote, they've already been gossiping so why not go the whole hog and expose you? I could easily play the grieving, cheated on widow, all sad and lost, which is bound to ensure everyone here would despise you even more than they do now. Not exactly the ideal working environment, is it?' Anna waited calmly. She was actually enjoying this.

'Do you really think I give a toss about what those morons think? I can deal with them. They don't worry me in the slightest because I don't want their friendship, never have, and never will. They're nothing to me, so do your worst, Anna. Go humiliate yourself if that's what you want, they're just empty desperate threats.' Caitlin sat back in her seat looking smug.

'Well, that may be so but once the gossip starts in here it will spread to our clients and don't forget that before you even tarnished this company with your existence, Matthew and I were both well liked and familiar with all of our customers. All those company barbeques and intimate dinners weren't just for the fun of it, we built up relationships with them all and I know damn well that they won't take kindly to shaking your hand in the future. No, Caitlin, your reputation and respect will be flushed right down the toilet but if that doesn't convince you, perhaps when I've had a nice long chat with your lovely fiancé, Gavin, I'll be able to tap the last nail deep into your coffin. How does that grab you?' That's when Anna saw the fury light up in Caitlin's eyes.

'Don't you dare speak to Gavin! Leave him out of this. He's got nothing to do with it.'

Caitlin's voice betrayed a hint of panic so leaning forward across the desk Anna smiled savagely, looking straight into her eyes.

'Try me, Caitlin, go on, just try me. I've got absolutely nothing to lose, have I? Whereas in your case, all you have left is poor, pitiful Gavin. The mug who makes do with the dregs of another man's affair and is stuck with an unfaithful, conniving bitch into the bargain. I pity him being married to you so perhaps I'd be doing him a huge favour. I can't believe you are actually going through with this sham wedding but really, that's all you've got to cling on to now. So I'm telling you for the last time, I want you out of Harrison Haulage before our son comes back to take over, got it?' Anna held her breath as she waited for her words to sink in.

Caitlin's eyes narrowed and for a heartbeat her body language said she was beaten, or so Anna thought.

'So, that's what you're scared of is it? Poor, poor Anna. Are you afraid that when Joe gets back I might go for the full set, father and son? Now there's an idea. Can't say I fancy soldier boy, he's not my type, all muscle and probably a half-wit but I suppose I could be persuaded if I was in the mood for a bit of rough. But Joe, now he's more my style. I can see myself seducing the son and heir to all of this. Quite a challenge, don't you think?'

Caitlin laughed in Anna's face and that was it, the fuse was lit.

It had never happened before, but a red mist really did settle over Anna as her blood boiled and her heart raced causing nerves and sinews to twitch as her overloaded brain blew a fuse and took matters into its own hands. Anna snapped. A jolt of untamed fury shot through her body triggering a violent reaction. Without warning, her legs sprang upwards propelling her forwards then, as her outstretched arm flew into action, her flattened palm connected with the side of Caitlin's face, pounding into her cheek, forcing her head to fly back as the sharp clap of skin hitting skin was almost as shocking as the act itself. Anna's hand stung like hell but she relished the pain, knowing Caitlin's face would be hurting much, much worse.

Sucking in a lungful of air, Anna hovered over the desk and placed her hands firmly on its surface, leaning in as close as she could get to Caitlin's face which was now pumping out tears from horrified eyes. She sat there, holding the side of her head with both hands, too stunned to move as Anna spoke slowly and calmly with a voice full of venom and a chilling warning.

'Listen to me very carefully. You will clear your desk and be out of this building by Friday lunchtime. If you are still here after that, then mark my words, Caitlin, I will destroy you. I will leave you penniless, disgraced and alone so perhaps in the meantime you might find a use for this.'

Picking up the folder Anna slammed it hard into Caitlin's chest. A newspaper slid out, unfolded at the Situations Vacant page where Anna had circled the words in red marker, the meaning unmistakably sarcastic and its message quite clear.

Standing straight and tall, locking her eyes on to Caitlin as she hooked her bag onto her shoulder, Anna turned and walked towards the door. Just as she reached for the handle Caitlin spoke, her voice trembling slightly. She had one parting shot to deliver.

'He loved me, not you. Just remember that. We were in love and he was going to leave you all, for me.'

Caitlin, despite the crack in her voice, wanted the last word, stopping Anna dead in her tracks.

For a second she had to overcome the powerful urge to go over and beat Caitlin to death with her two bare hands. Instead, without turning, Anna replied, her own voice clear and devoid of emotion, stating fact not fiction.

'But he didn't leave, did he? On the day he died he was still my husband, on his way home and had he not been killed he would've lain in our bed, next to me. You had no idea where he was which tells me you weren't quite as close as your deluded mind seems to think. You weren't the last thing on his mind minutes before he died, I was. Do you know how I know that, Caitlin? Because he sent me a text, telling me to meet him at home and the last words he ever wrote were, I love you.' Then Anna opened the door and walked through, slamming it loudly behind her.

How she managed to walk down the stairs and make it to her car on legs like jelly that somehow held up a violently shaking body, Anna would never know. It was a good job she didn't have to open the door with a key because her trembling hands would have been incapable of the task. Caitlin's cruel words rang in her ears, but she just couldn't let her have the last word. Registering the verbal onslaught, her brain had risen to the final challenge allowing her lips to speak words which were lies, but it silenced the enemy. Anna had left Caitlin with the image of Matthew's last text firmly imprinted on her brain, an imaginary message to his faithful wife, telling her of his love.

Once inside the car Anna took steadying breaths and waited for her hands to be still before she drove out of the yard and onto the road. The vein on the side of her head pulsed wildly and her heart hammered in her chest, she was so angry. Talking to herself was becoming a habit but Anna didn't care. No one could hear her high-pitched, slightly hysterical voice as she ranted, tears streaming down her face.

'How dare she say that, how dare she ruin my life and rub my nose in it? She's a cold, heartless bitch and as for you, Matthew, you disgust me, being with someone like that. I hate you so much right now, I hate you both! And to bring my sons into it, she's a freak, a vile, sadistic freak. So, she thinks it's okay to shatter someone's dreams, does she? Well, it's time to give her a taste of her own medicine. Come on, Anna. Let's show that bitch exactly how it feels.'

Swinging her car around in a manoeuvre that Jeremy Clarkson would be proud of, Anna sped off in the opposite direction towards a car dealership on the other side of town. It was time she had a chat with good old Gavin.

The waiting room was incredibly dull with almost nothing to read on the walls to take her mind off Caitlin, which in a way was good, Anna needed to feed the anger, keep up the momentum and focus on revenge. The cheerful teenager who was sweeping the forecourt had asked her if she wanted coffee but Anna declined, knowing the state her stomach was in it would come back up quicker than it went down, and then he'd be fetching the mop and bucket. He was obviously a bit bored and in the mood for conversation so Anna indulged him, using the opportunity to find out a little more about Gavin which was a huge mistake.

It turned out that Gavin was a thoroughly decent guy who had met Lee (sweeping boy) at the youth centre where he volunteered and ran a football team. Lee had been getting into trouble with the police so Gavin offered him an apprenticeship in his garage and since then, he'd kept his nose clean. Lee obviously idolised his boss. By the time a smiley faced Gavin appeared at the door to welcome Anna and apologise for keeping her waiting, she had lost any inclination to ruin his life.

Swallowing down her nerves she shook his hand and made up a cock and bull story about wanting to buy a runabout for Melanie, half true so not too bad. As they wandered slowly up and down the lanes of shiny second-hand cars, Anna listened to Gavin describing the merits of each one, punctuated with polite salesman-style conversation. They reached a very presentable white hatchback and stopped to admire it as Gavin reeled off its specifications while Anna wished she'd just gone straight home. Noticing that she wasn't really paying attention, Gavin stopped mid-sentence and leant his arms on the roof of the car, turning his head to look at her.

'You didn't really come here to buy a car, did you, Anna?' Averting his gaze he waited for her reply, focusing on the middle distance.

'No, I didn't. So does that mean you know the real reason I'm here?'

Anna felt small and spiteful as Gavin let out a sigh and when he replied, his voice sounded sad and resigned.

'I think you really came here to tell me that Caitlin was having an affair with your husband so if that's the case you're too late, I already knew.' Gavin removed his hands from the car roof and then suggested they go back to his office and continue where they wouldn't be overheard.

Gavin made them both coffee and after switching off his phone, they exchanged notes on their respective partners. Both had one common aim, to hear the truth and as a result, they forged an unfortunate but common bond.

***

Gavin caught them out by accident, just like Anna had, around two weeks before Matthew died. He was driving the youth club minibus to a football match in Southampton when it broke down midway. Caitlin wouldn't have been expecting him back until at least 11pm that night but by the time they'd tried to fix it, given up, then called out the breakdown truck, the match had to be cancelled and everyone went home. With everything that was going on Gavin didn't inform Caitlin of the change of plan until he was almost home, when he rang her from the car, surprising her with some takeaway food and estimating that he'd be back in five minutes. No doubt a state of panic ensued as she chucked Matthew out of bed and tried desperately to cover her tracks before Gavin arrived home.

As it happened, he pulled into their road just in time to catch a glimpse of Matthew's car driving away, like a bat out of hell. Alarm bells started ringing when he got inside and Caitlin didn't mention that Matthew had been there. Despite the hour, had she said he'd popped in to drop off some paperwork then maybe he wouldn't have been quite so suspicious, but after picking up that she was edgy and looked uncomfortable, instinct told Gavin not to mention that he had seen Matthew leaving.

After that he watched her like a hawk, secretly checking her messages while she slept and listening to her phone calls. They were very careful but hearing her whispering in the bathroom, plus the fact she did her best never to leave her phone unattended made him more paranoid. Even though he had no hard evidence, in his heart he knew what was going on. Her loss of interest in him, in every way possible, the way she dressed up for work but didn't care what she looked like at home, the extra late nights and frequent trips away all began to add up.

Had Matthew not been killed in the crash he was sure that Caitlin was going to leave him because their relationship had all but broken down. Then miraculously, straight after Matthew died, almost overnight, she transformed herself into a loving fiancée who couldn't wait to get on with organising the biggest white wedding known to man. And although Gavin was ashamed to admit it, he was just relieved that he'd got her back.

***

Anna had listened in silence as Gavin poured his heart out.

'I bet you think that I'm a real loser, don't you? Forgiving her like that and brushing everything under the carpet, but I felt like

I'd been given a second chance. I didn't want to lose her so I turned a blind eye and carried on.' Gavin looked down at his clenched fists and waited for Anna's verdict.

'No, Gavin, I don't think that at all. When I found out about them I behaved in a similar way, watching him at the same time as hoping it was just a huge mistake and it would all go away. You got what I didn't though, a second chance. At least you had the opportunity to decide for yourself if you could forgive her, I wasn't so lucky. So no, I don't think any less of you, I actually understand.' Anna smiled at Gavin hoping to reassure him that her words were sincere.

'So, how did you find out? I'd rather know the whole version, not just my side of the story. Don't spare me the gory details, I can handle it.'

Gavin's words were admirable if not a little naive because by the time Anna was finished, he'd probably wished he hadn't asked.

Once Gavin knew everything he was painfully aware, as was Anna, that the two people they lived with had been pulling the wool over their eyes for quite some time and the likelihood was that by now, they'd probably be shacked up in a luxury pad by the marina had fate not played its cruel hand. Anna apologised for hitting his fiancée but from the look on Gavin's face, Matthew probably would have suffered something similar had he still been alive.

Gavin understood completely why Anna wanted Caitlin out of Harrison's and promised not to let on that she had been to see him, agreeing that having a threat hanging over her head that her celebrity-style wedding may be cancelled could just do the trick. Once Caitlin was gone Anna couldn't care less what Gavin did.

It was almost 3pm when Anna made her way home. She was completely drained and all she could think of was her bed and going to sleep for about a month, that's how long she felt it would take to rid her of the exhaustion that had consumed her body. With every minute she drove, the more fatigued she became. The multitude of emotions she had experienced since Enid rang her that morning were taking their toll.

Letting herself into the apartment she made strong coffee and opened the patio doors to allow in the sea breeze, hoping the afternoon sun would revive her. Taking her phone from her bag Anna saw a list of missed calls from Melanie, Enid and Daniel. There were a few rather irate text messages from Jeannie containing swear words and threats so knowing she was in big trouble, Anna rang her first, settling down for what was going to be one very long conversation.

Anna had just finished speaking to Jeannie and was increasingly concerned with regards to her best friend's desire to seek revenge at the earliest opportunity, with explicitly violent tendencies. She sincerely hoped Caitlin never crossed her path otherwise Anna would be prison visiting for the foreseeable future, and she couldn't picture Jeannie sewing mailbags.

Too drained to go over it again, she had texted Daniel telling him she would ring him soon, not alluding to the day's drama. Melanie was due home later, after tea with Enid so she had a bit of peace and quiet, time alone to sit and dissemble the events of the day. Anna was immersed in quiet contemplation, watching the seagulls dipping down onto the sea when she heard the buzz of the intercom. Praying it wasn't Anton as she was in no mood for wine and tales of the nightclub she heaved herself out of the chair and lifted the handset.

'Anna, it's Dennis, can I come up?'

Slightly surprised to hear his voice but knowing full well the nature of his visit, she wearily buzzed him in.

CHAPTER 40

Anna opened the door and invited a serious looking Dennis inside. Closing it behind her she asked him if he'd like coffee and made her way to the kitchen. Saying he would love some, he followed her over and took a seat at the counter. The sounds from the road outside, lucky people with normal lives going about their carefree business, cut through the ominous silence in the room. Anna found it oppressive and decided to break the ice so as she spooned coffee into cups, asked Dennis the obvious question.

'I take it you've spoken to Caitlin, that is why you're here, she came running to you telling tales. Well, I hope she told you exactly why I was there and what I wanted.' Anna could hear the bitterness in her own voice but was way past caring.

'No, she didn't have to. I saw you leaving her office and went in to ask her what you wanted. The bright red hand mark on the side of her face told me all I needed to know. And between hysterics and threats to have you arrested for assault, I got the gist of the conversation.'

Dennis accepted the coffee that Anna slid across the counter before sitting down opposite from where she could look him right in the eye.

'Good, well we all know where we stand then, don't we? That leaves just one burning question and it's for you, Dennis. Did you know about the affair or did Matthew pull the wool over your eyes as well as me and his whole family?' Anna took a sip and waited, she couldn't call it, was he in on it or innocent? Then he dropped the bomb.

'I knew, Anna, and I'm sorry, I really am. That's why I'm here, to explain. God knows I've wanted to for so long but I didn't know if you knew or not, so I kept quiet.'

Dennis looked down into his cup, unable to meet her eyes as Anna felt a knife twist in her heart and the pain of another as it stabbed her right in the back.

'Well, it's been quite a day of revelations, Dennis, one more confession isn't going to kill me so whatever it is you've come here to say, just get it over with. To tell you the truth nothing surprises me anymore, not where Matthew's concerned.'

Hearing the anger in her voice Dennis gave a weary sigh of regret, and then began his story.

***

He had his suspicions after the managerial dinner where, by this time, he was already starting to regret championing Caitlin's cause and going against Matthew's instinct when they hired her. There was an undercurrent of dislike amongst the staff where she was concerned and he also realised there was an unsavoury side to her personality. The dinner clinched it and he was appalled by her behaviour, especially towards Samantha. Her antics at the staff Christmas party were the icing on the cake for which he harshly reprimanded her, but it was clear then that it was water off a duck's back and she was one to be watched, which he did.

He was aware of the rumours circulating the office and tactfully discussed Caitlin with Matthew, hoping he would at least take a hint or be warned off, unfortunately neither occurred. When Mary was sick, Dennis had to put her first and in the meantime Caitlin wreaked havoc at Harrison's. He took his eye off the ball and unfortunately gave her the perfect opportunity to get her own way, with the full support of Matthew. While Anna was experiencing the after-effects of his altered personality at home it hadn't gone unnoticed at work either, especially by Matthew's oldest friend. Finally, Dennis decided he'd observed him for long enough so after being made aware that there had been some kind of argument with Samantha, his patience ran out.

Dennis resolved to confront him and had intended to do so the very next day. So he was relieved when, the next morning, he took a call around 11am from Matthew who sounded irate and on the verge of tears. He asked Dennis to meet him because he needed to talk. He also insisted that their meeting remain a secret and especially didn't want Caitlin to be aware of it.

Dennis made his excuses at work and left as soon as he could, telling no one where he was really going and up until today, nobody knew, not even Mary. They met at a pub on the outskirts of town around midday and sat in the beer garden, well away from prying eyes and where they couldn't be overheard. Dennis suspected that Matthew wanted to confess and on that sunny July morning, he did just that.

'He was in a terrible state, Anna, he looked and felt wretched. I actually thought he was going to have some kind of seizure. The whole affair had taken its toll, the stress of keeping it all hidden and the lies involved were making him ill. He was at the end of his tether and just wanted to get it all off his chest. I'm not defending him at all. I'm just trying to give you an idea of the kind of state he was in. I was so relieved that he'd contacted me and not vice versa so I just listened while he tried to explain.'

When Anna remained silent, Dennis continued.

'It had begun, as I suspected, after the dinner. Matthew had stayed to pay the bill and the rest of us shared cabs home. We all thought that Caitlin had left before us but she must have lingered until we were out of sight then made her move. Matthew admitted he had quite a lot to drink but was no way near as drunk as Caitlin so against his better judgement he did the decent thing and offered to see her home.

'During the taxi ride she became unwell. It was probably all an act but Matthew helped her inside her house, fully expecting Gavin to be there so he could hand responsibility over to him. It turned out he was on a lads' night out and was staying at a hotel. Once the cab was sent away and she got Matthew inside, Caitlin made a gradual and miraculous recovery. That's when the waterworks were turned on and she confessed how unhappy and lonely she was with Gavin, who she made out to be a tyrant. I didn't need to be drawn a sketch and I knew what was coming next, the scene where Matthew comforted a tearful, unloved, misunderstood woman and how one thing led to another and they ended up in bed. The next day, Matthew was mortified and ashamed and desperately regretted what had happened. Naively, he thought that it could be forgotten and put it down to a one-night stand but Caitlin had other ideas.

'From that day forward, she led a full-on assault using a mixture of temptation and good old-fashioned blackmail. Before he knew it he was in too deep, scared to death that she'd tell you whilst allowing flattery, excitement and his ego take over. The way he described it, it was like being on a roller coaster he couldn't get off. I really couldn't believe what I was hearing, Anna. He even admitted that he sometimes felt jealous of Joe and Sam because they were having the adventures he'd missed out on, travelling the world and doing an exciting job. Melanie was due to go to university and he felt life had passed him by. He'd dedicated his youth to the firm and his family and at the beginning the thrill he got from his affair was like a drug that he couldn't get enough of. That's when I really tore a strip off him, making excuses and being envious of his children really disappointed me, and I told him so.

'I pointed out how lucky he was to have a family and children; some people would give their right arm for the charmed life he led and he was throwing it all away on some kind of mid-life crisis. I told him it was pathetic and worst of all he was jeopardising all that for someone like Caitlin. It made my blood boil. To be fair, he'd already come to that conclusion himself and he knew he was behaving badly in every way possible. He was pushing you away because he felt so guilty and the betrayal was eating him up inside. Matthew admitted that sometimes he couldn't bear to look at you because he felt so bad, you didn't deserve any of it and he hated the person he'd become.

'He still loved you, he told me that and I believed him, Anna. When you see your best friend crying over a pint of lager in full view of the waitress, that's when you know they mean it.' Dennis took a sip of his cold coffee, waiting for Anna to speak.

'Well, that's as maybe, Dennis, but he certainly wasn't thinking like that when he went looking around swanky apartments with that bitch. I bet he didn't tell you about that, did he? That he was going to sell our home and move in with her.' Anna was fuming, remembering the shock of that day and the awful realisation that Matthew was going to leave her. This ingrained image was hard to reconcile with the one Dennis painted.

'He did tell me and, yet again, it was more as a result of Caitlin's master plan, her constant pushing for commitment and trying to force his hand. She was ready and willing to leave Gavin, all Matthew had to do was say the word and she would be off. Stupidly, he had gone along with her pie in the sky ideas about getting a place together, saying that one day, when the time was right he would leave when in fact he was fobbing her off, just to shut her up.

'Unfortunately, she believed him so went ahead and arranged the viewing without his knowledge and asked him to meet her at the marina. He turned up presuming it was for a quick lunch, totally unprepared for her big surprise because when he arrived, Caitlin was in the company of an estate agent, who, to make matters worse was a member of Matthew's golf club. To avoid an embarrassing scene he just went along with it. He told me she was beginning to behave like an unhinged bunny boiler and even expected him to sell your house to pay for the apartment. He had absolutely no intention of doing that and assured me he was desperately trying to find a way out of the relationship.' Dennis looked flushed and anxious. Beads of sweat had formed on his head.

He really wanted her to believe what he was saying, Anna could tell from his whole demeanour.

'So what made Matthew ring you, why did he decide then, on that particular day, to confess? Was it the row with Samantha? She said he didn't take kindly to being told a few home truths.' Anna was trying with all her might to remain hard, not allowing the image of her husband crying in a beer garden to soften her feelings towards him.

Dennis gulped as he met Anna's eye.

'No, it wasn't the row with Samantha, even though it did add to the pressure because he thought she was going to tell you what was going on, she was mad as hell with him. Did you know that Jeannie had words with him too? Apparently she saw something at the airport. It rattled his cage but he managed to convince her it was totally innocent.'

Anna confirmed she knew all about that.

'Okay, well that's one good thing, but you're not going to like this, Anna, and it's going to hurt you very much when I tell you. The reason he knew the game was up was because he was caught out by someone very close to home.' Dennis paused, giving a pensive Anna chance to prepare.

After placing her trembling hands on the counter in an attempt to steady her nerves she told him to carry on as a million questions invaded her brain. The most important one was about to be answered.

'The night before he died Matthew was in his office with Caitlin, apparently they were in the middle of something. I didn't care to hear the details, but during that time Melanie walked in and saw them. She turned up unexpectedly and caught them red-handed. That's when he knew it was all over. For whatever reason, Melanie has kept what she saw to herself ever since.' Dennis hadn't a clue what to do or say next so just waited and watched.

Anna was in shock, her eyes were wide and she couldn't catch her breath, her hands were glued to her mouth holding in a scream that was fuelled by sheer temper and rage and disbelief. It began to boil the bile in her swirling stomach that was making its way up her throat. She was going to be sick.

On shaking legs, Anna rushed over to the sink, the cold stainless steel under her palms calmed her slightly as she closed her eyes, willing herself to get a grip and not throw up. Feeling a firm hand on her shoulder she listened to his words, telling her to breathe and take it easy.

Dennis assured Anna that it was going to be okay and they'd sort it out. He filled a glass with cold water and told her to sip it slowly as he guided her back to the stool before sitting back on his, waiting until she was composed.

Anna remained silent for a while, wiping her eyes with a tea towel, sipping her drink, deep in thought, trying to take it all in and when she finally spoke, her voice was hoarse and trembling.

'I can't believe that Mel has known for all this time. Oh my God. What has Matthew done to this family? She's kept it all to herself to protect me, just like I protected her. If only we'd all been honest with each other. I should've had the guts to confide in all three of them but instead I put Matthew's memory first. I've been so stupid. I hate him right now, Dennis, I really hate him for doing this to us, especially Melanie.' Hot, angry tears spilled from her eyes and she couldn't hold in the sobs any longer, but she still wanted to know the rest so told Dennis to ignore her and carry on.

'Matthew said that Melanie flew out of the office before he could to stop her. He chased after her in his car but she refused to get in, screaming at him and calling him all the names under the sun. She ran away and even though he followed her she managed to shake him off. He rang her continually but she refused to answer so he left messages, begging her to ring him back. Panicking, he went home and waited there, fully expecting her to expose his affair. Obviously, when Mel did turn up you were at home and she stormed off to her room, staying there all evening. He didn't dare approach her while you were about so after spending a sleepless night going over everything in his head he woke up to find she had gone to work. That's when he decided to ring me, he needed advice.'

'So what was your advice?' Anna was wrung out and her tears had finally dried up.

'I told him to tell you everything, just the way he'd told me. That none of it was excusable no matter which way he explained it, but he had to speak to you before anyone else did. At least that way he would save you the added humiliation of being told by Caitlin or worse, by Mel, then you could deal with it your own way or together. I said he owed you that at least. I couldn't give him any assurances because I had no idea how you'd react, if you would forgive him or kick him out and divorce him – unfortunately it was a chance he had to take. Either way, nothing could be as bad as the living hell he was in. If he had carried on like that I truly think he would've had a heart attack.' Dennis leant forward and gently held both her hands.

Anna remained silent and processed the information in her head, staring into the distance and feeling strangely detached from the whole situation.

'Listen, Anna. I want you to remember this. These are the last words Matthew said to me, for all I know, to anyone, so please believe what I tell you. He was very emotional but we talked it all through again and he was adamant that it was over with Caitlin. He had finally seen her for what she was, manipulative and calculating. We agreed that we would pay her off and get her as far away from Harrison's as possible, she'd done enough damage all round and had to go. I promised I would stand by him and help him through whatever storm he had to face, I'd even talk to you if need be. Matthew promised to go straight home and speak to you. I said I'd pay the bill at the bar and asked him to ring me later that evening just to let me know how things were.

'Just before I got up to leave he broke down again so I waited for him to pull himself together and then, this is what he said. He told me that no matter what happened or what you decided to do, he would always love you. That despite his stupidity he had never, ever stopped loving you and if he had just one wish it would be to turn the clock back and start again. He sobbed as he told me he would never let you down again, that he would spend the rest of his life making it up to you and putting things right. He was terrified that you wouldn't give him the chance and that he would lose you forever. He couldn't bear the thought of it and wouldn't be able to carry on without you by his side. I told him to go home and tell you exactly that. I shook his hand and said goodbye and that was it, the last time I saw him, our last handshake. He must have gone for a drive and then on his way home, he had the crash.' Dennis's voice cracked with emotion as he valiantly struggled to hold back his own tide of tears.

He lost the battle.

'Oh, Dennis, please don't cry, you did your best and you weren't to know what would happen. I'm just glad you got to speak to him so that he could explain otherwise we would all have gone on forever not knowing and keeping secrets. Thanks to you and your friendship, Matthew still got to tell me how he really felt and now, I know everything. I know he loved me, so thank you, Dennis, thank you so much.'

Anna's voice broke and they both sat there for a while, holding hands and crying. There was nothing more to say.

Later, as they drank tea together, emotionally drained, Dennis had one last thing to say.

'I want you to know that I have been keeping an eye on Melanie for you, albeit from a distance. I looked for signs that she was distressed or needed an ear but she gave nothing away so I thought it best to let her deal with things her own way. Obviously, I couldn't say a word to you, how could I shatter your world twice by telling you that Matthew was having an affair? I decided to leave things as they were and be on hand if ever you found out. So there you have it, the whole sorry tale. Are you not even a bit angry with me, Anna? Please be honest.'

He looked so weary and dejected.

'Dennis, I'm going to tell you exactly what I told Samantha. You are totally blameless in all of this. Almost everyone I know has kept quiet for their own very good reasons, even me. We have borne the guilt of their lies and betrayal and it's got to stop. We all did what we did with the best intentions, so please don't beat yourself up anymore, it's been a long year for all of us.' Anna pulled one her best smiles out of the hat before asking an important question of her own.

'So what are we going to do about Caitlin? I don't want her at Harrison's, Dennis. I'm adamant that she goes and we're not paying her off either, she can go to hell.' Anna was back in control now and meant business.

'Well, thanks to you threatening to tell her fiancé everything I don't think that will be necessary. I took it upon myself to let her know that Matthew was going to end their relationship and ask you to forgive him and most importantly, I told her that he loved you and always had. I didn't want her under any illusions on that score. Anyhow, she's agreed to go with immediate effect plus a month's wages and a glowing reference. Her reasons for leaving will be stress related. I really don't care what she tells her fiancé but that's what our staff will hear. There might be a bit of gossip and rumour but nothing too bad and one thing's for sure though, they'll all be pleased she's gone.' Dennis smiled encouragingly.

Anna hugged the red-eyed man before her, he had been put through the mill but out of everything she was most grateful that he had put Caitlin straight about Matthew's intentions which, unbeknown to Dennis tied in with her parting shot, making it less of a lie.

The noise of a key in the door alerted them to the unexpected return of Melanie so before they had time to prepare themselves she was standing in the hallway, looking nervously from one to the other, their reddened eyes giving the game away. Melanie's voice quavered as she spoke.

'Mum, Dennis, what's wrong, what's going on? It's not Sam is it, or Joe? Please tell me they're okay.'

Instantly comprehending Melanie's train of thought, Anna rushed over to reassure her that both were safe.

'No! I promise. But you have to keep calm because we need to talk and before I begin, I want you to know that you have done nothing wrong, okay?'

Anna was gripping her daughter's hand, willing her to understand but Mel remained silent, looking from her mother to Dennis, fear reflecting in her eyes.

'Melanie, sweetheart, I know about your dad and Caitlin. I have for a while, and so has Dennis, that's why he's here. I know you have too, but it's okay. I understand everything now. It's all in the open so there's no need to worry anymore.' Anna was holding Mel's hands tightly as if to prevent her from running again.

When Anna saw the crestfallen look that washed over Melanie's face before crumpling, all she could do was take her in her arms and let her cry it out, and then wait until the tears subsided.

Over Melanie's shoulder, Dennis indicated quietly that he was going and left them to it, miming he would ring later.

Steering the sobbing, trembling child over to the sofa, Anna made her sit and here, with her head laid on her mother's chest, Melanie sobbed and sobbed whilst being shushed and assured that it was all going to be okay – a gentle hand stroked her face and loving arms held her tight.

Eventually, in a barely audible voice, interjected with hiccups, Melanie told Anna what happened at the office that day. It made her cry even more but she needed to say it, go over it one more time and make her mother understand.

***

Melanie had finished her shift and should've got a lift home with Tania, but Tania had a date straight after work so Melanie suggested she drop her off at Harrison's. Knowing her dad would be working late she planned to catch a lift and maybe talk him into buying her a sneaky burger on the way home. The cleaners let her inside the building on their way out with the bin bags so Melanie had no need to be buzzed in. Consequently, when she burst into her dad's office, shouting 'surprise', that's exactly what she got. And so did Matthew and Caitlin.

You didn't have to be a scientist to work out what was going on. Caitlin was standing behind Matthew, her arms were folded around his shoulders, and she was kissing his neck, whispering and giggling. Melanie saw the look of horror on her dad's face as he flung Caitlin's arms away from his body and jumped out of his chair. Time stood still for a second, then Melanie legged it, bursting through the swing doors and taking the stairs two, three at a time, hearing Matthew calling her name, begging her to come back.

She ran through the industrial estate towards the docks but Matthew caught her up. He stopped the car and got out, trying to force her to get in, pleading with her to listen and let him explain. Melanie told him he was disgusting and she hated him, that he had ruined her life and she was going to tell her mum what she had seen, screaming hysterically as she walked away that Caitlin was a slag and if she ever saw her again she'd kick her head in. Matthew chased after her and grabbed her hand, refusing to let go until she listened, that's when a dock worker spotted them and shouted from a crane to leave her alone so she took her opportunity and ran off again, eventually losing him.

By the time Melanie got home she'd calmed down and knew she didn't have the bottle to tell Anna. Seeing Matthew's car in the drive she feigned a headache and went straight to bed, refusing to speak to her dad when he knocked on her door and setting her alarm for an hour earlier, leaving home the next morning before anyone was up.

Melanie still didn't know what to do with the information she'd stumbled upon but one thing was for sure, she wanted to make him suffer that day and refused to answer any of his calls or texts. When the police came that night to inform them there had been a terrible accident and that Matthew had been killed instantly, in that second and ever since, all Melanie wanted was her dad and to take back the cruel words she'd said. To tell him that she did love him and no matter what he'd done she loved him so much it hurt, but it was too late, he was gone.

Anna was devastated. To know that her daughter had held on to this secret for so long and somehow managed to carry on with her life, protecting her at the same time as bearing this awful burden, broke her heart all over again. Yet she remained calm as Melanie continued, words tumbling out in between trying to catch her breath.

'I wanted to tell you so many times, Mum, but what good would it have done? It was easier to keep quiet and I thought I was the only one that knew. I didn't want to be the one that made everything even worse. Joe was so far away and I didn't want to bother him. Jeannie would've flipped and so would Gran. That's why I rang you when we found those flowers on the grave. I knew exactly who they were from so I listened to your voice, wondering if you'd give me a clue that you knew. I took great pleasure in chucking them in the bin. I wanted to tell Sam there and then but he was going to Afghanistan and I didn't want to upset him before he went away, so I said nothing. I couldn't believe that Dad would go off with someone else but I saw it with my own eyes. He hurt me too, you know? I thought we were the perfect family and you'd always be together but he wrecked all that and most of all he cheated on you. You looked so sad after he died and I was relieved when you started to move on. I just wanted to support you and encourage you. Then, when you met Daniel, I saw you smiling and happy again and I was too because you deserve it, Mum.'

Melanie sniffled and wiped her nose on her sleeve, reminding Anna of when she was little.

Anna squeezed her tightly. There was nothing else to be done after that except relate to Melanie the long, drawn out events of the day. She may as well know the nitty gritty, the time for half stories was over. When Anna had finished, Melanie sided with Jeannie and thought Caitlin should be strung up but they made a pact that there were to be no more scenes at Harrison's and definitely, no more secrets – ever! They sat there for a while, peacefully lost in thought until Anna remembered that Melanie was supposed to have tea with Enid.

'Why did you come back from Gran's early? I wasn't expecting you till later.'

Melanie rolled her eyes and tutted loudly.

'Gran and Gladys were late coming back from bowling because they'd stopped off for a quick rum and coke at the pub and she didn't have time to get tea ready, so she suggested we get a kebab. I didn't really fancy one so said I'd pass and I wanted to check on you.' Melanie chuckled to herself. 'She's a right one our gran. Do you know that she's made friends with someone called Naseem the taxi driver? He's the one who took her home on New Year's Eve. Well, he's her new best mate and runs errands for her. Apparently, if she needs any shopping she rings his cousin who owns a mini-market, puts in her order, and then Naseem collects and delivers it. Gran refers to him as her dedicated driver. We'll have to keep a close eye on her, she might get ideas about getting toy boy, it happens all the time. I've read about it in magazines.'

Melanie was deadly serious and looked at Anna with a knowing expression.

'Please, please do not wish that on us, Melanie, it would just about finish me off.' And as if Enid's psychic powers were working overtime, she chose just that moment to send Anna a message, causing her to let out a huge sigh and flop back onto the sofa.

'Well, I'm in big trouble now. After everything that's gone on today I totally forgot to order the bloody set-top box. She's going to love that.'

Both dissolved into fits of giggles and the tension of the past few hours slipped away as Melanie hugged her mother tightly.

'I love you, Mum.'

'I love you too, Mel… and I fancy some fish and chips, come on, let's go out.'

CHAPTER 41

They walked along the seafront to the chippy then decided to eat their food outside, sitting on a bench looking out to sea. It was the best fish and chips Anna had ever tasted. Having gone a whole day with just tea and coffee to sustain her, she savoured every mouthful and could feel her energy levels gradually rising. Once they'd eaten they made their way back along the promenade before resting in the little green shelter opposite the apartment, breathing in the sea air and going over the day's events.

Melanie opened up, telling Anna how she remembered the funeral like a surreal dream, as though she were an actress in a play and none of it was really happening while at the same time, being on red alert. She was watching for Caitlin the whole time, knowing that she might lose it and everything would have come out, right there in the church or by the grave.

Bringing up their conversation in France when she asked her mother if she was happy in her marriage, Melanie confessed to being on the brink of telling Anna about Caitlin, just so her mum wouldn't feel guilty about Daniel, but lost her nerve. If Melanie had known Dennis and especially Jeannie were in on it then she would've confided in them, but she genuinely thought she was the only one. There had been so many occasions when Mel had wanted to ring Caitlin up or send her a message telling her how much she hated her but somehow, managed to restrain herself.

'The only person out of the loop is Sam and I think if we've learned anything today, it's that he needs to be told everything as soon as possible, don't you, Mum?' Melanie waited expectantly for Anna's response.

'Yes, I know. I will tell him face to face when he comes home next weekend for my birthday but I'm not telling Gran, there's nothing to be gained by it and you know how she would go on and on. I don't want it being brought up every time we mention your dad, either. I can just see her ruining every Christmas dinner or family event. She can be tactless sometimes, especially after a glass of sherry and I'm not giving her any ammunition.' Anna knew she had made a sensible decision, for once.

'I agree, and then there's Joe. You will have to email him and explain all the details, because if you ring him it will cost a bomb, it's far too complicated.'

Standing up, she turned to face Anna offering her hand.

'Come on, no time like the present. You write to Joe and I'll sort Gran's telly out, and you'd better ring Daniel and fill him in. I want you organised and sane before I go back to uni in the morning. I reckon we're in for a very long night, mother dearest.'

With that, Mel hauled Anna off the bench and, arm in arm, they went inside to put the world to rights.

Anna's sleep deprived eyes burned in their sockets. It had been two days since Melanie had gone back to uni and she hadn't slept a wink. Daniel had offered to drive over and keep her company but she put him off, needing time to catch her breath. There wasn't much he could say regarding her revelation apart from assuring Anna that all of her actions were justified, even the slap.

He did find it hard to imagine Anna hitting anybody though, saying he'd have to watch his step in the future and avoid getting on her wrong side.

The email Anna sent to Joe was like a school essay but as Melanie had said, it was much easier than explaining on the phone. She had to wait until the next day before he replied but when he did, Joe was livid. He couldn't get his head around what his father had done and felt that Matthew had tarnished their reputation at the haulage company. He was also glad that Caitlin was gone, saying there was no way he could have worked with her – the situation was unthinkable.

Anna still had to tell Sam but she would do it face to face. As much as she dreaded the conversation, Anna told herself that it would be the final revelation and then they could all get on with rebuilding the future. But there was something else.

No matter how hard she tried to ignore it, Anna knew that despite having laid so much to rest over the past few days there was still something she needed to do, her subconscious was goading her into exorcising a remaining ghost. There was no avoiding it and as she rubbed her tired eyes, Anna gave in to whatever demons lurked in her head and despite the unearthly hour, got out of bed and met the day head on.

Walking towards the cemetery Anna recalled her own naivety in thinking that since Caitlin and Matthew's affair had been unearthed, she would be able to scrape the whole sordid mess up and bury it again, that knowing the truth would put an end to her worries and troubled mind. Instead, something had been keeping her awake at night and finally, in the early hours of that morning, as dawn broke and the sky lit up the waves on the sea, she realised what it was. She hadn't said goodbye properly and there was one more thing she needed to do.

Buying flowers from the stall at the entrance to the cemetery, Anna walked along the tarmac path and retraced the route the funeral cortege took to Matthew's grave. She silently overtook an old lady, walking painstakingly slow as she pulled along her tartan shopping trolley. Her moss green mackintosh was sensible as the forecast threatened rain, and looking up, Anna noticed that the sun was having trouble breaking through the grey clouds. She could feel goosebumps spreading across her arms where her T-shirt left them bare and her toes already felt cold, popping out from her sandals. She had dressed in a hurry, before she chickened out and changed her mind, so hadn't given the tree shaded conditions of the stony-grey graveyard much thought, and today the place looked distinctly unwelcoming and gloomy.

His resting place was set at the bottom of a soft slope, just to the left of the path and as Anna made her way towards the headstone that she had chosen but until now, never seen, the silence of her surroundings unnerved her. Anna imagined him lying on the top of the soil, waiting, eyes closed, still and cold with his arms crossed over his chest, annoyed with her for taking so long to visit him. Approaching the grave slowly she read the words which were engraved deeply into the stone.

Precious are the memories of Matthew Robert Harrison
Beloved husband, father and son.
Always in our hearts.
1965-2016

Anna knelt in front of the grave.

'Hello, Matthew, I thought it was time we had our talk. I'm sorry it's taken so long for me to get here, but I had some things to sort out.' Anna removed the old flowers from the pot in front of the stone and feeling relieved they were the ones that Mel and Sam had left, replaced them with her own.

Reading the inscription again, the words tore at her heart which had grown heavy and a dull pain was developing deep inside, swelling outwards with each beat, consuming her arteries and wreaking havoc throughout her body. The words which were once clear began to swim in pools of tears until she could no longer read them. The pain forced its way upwards, rising from her chest, running like a river, gurgling in her throat.

There was no way she could hold it in any longer, her anguish erupted in huge sobs and gulps, as uncontrollable tears flooded from her tired eyes. Covering her mouth with shaking hands became futile, nothing could tame the despair that tore through Anna's body, so she gave in and allowed a year's worth of hurt to spill onto the grass which covered Matthew's grave.

There was no telling how long she had been there before she gained some form of control and composure, but once the worst was over Anna sat back, at the foot of the stone, crossing her legs and resting her elbows on her knees. She tried hard not to think of the bones that lay below, it freaked her out so instead, she talked to the headstone.

'I found out everything by the way, but I suspect you already know that. I often wonder if you're watching me from the other side, checking up on us all, because I do believe that's where you are, I have faith that you are okay. Dennis eventually came clean and told me about your meeting and your confession. I must admit it had become quite a mystery to me who the other woman was and as usual, I was barking up the wrong tree. It was a huge shock when I found out. I would never have suspected her and to be honest I still can't understand what you saw in her, she's abhorrent.' Anna felt a rant coming on but after making a pact never to allow Caitlin to ruin her day, firmly shut her out. Today was just about Anna and Matthew.

'You know what hurts more than anything, is that we never got our last conversation, did we? Even though it would have been painful and awful, I feel as though we were robbed of the chance to put things right. I don't know if I would have forgiven you, Matthew, or if I would've been able to carry on as before, knowing what you'd done. But deep down, we still loved each other and all those years would have stood for something so maybe we could have found a way to work things out.' Anna could feel the tears coming again; her heart hurt so much that she truly thought it was bruised. Wiping her eyes, she carried on.

'Maybe I have to accept some of the blame. Perhaps I'd taken us for granted, stopped trying in some way and become complacent, but all you had to do was talk to me, tell me how you felt… for God's sake we'd been together long enough to know how to communicate. Why did you stop talking to me, Matthew? It was so unfair. I was there all the time, waiting for you, loving you, I never stopped. I tried so hard to be the best wife. I wish I knew where I went wrong and in the end you made me feel worthless and humiliated. We did so well to build our family and our life yet somewhere along the line you got bored with it.' Anna could feel the anger spreading through her bones, it was so frustrating, the lack of answers or the chance to scream and shout at him, face to face, let him know just how much damage he'd done.

Maybe she'd want to slap him as hard as she slapped the other one, make him feel the pain and realise what he'd ruined in the pursuit of excitement, weakening to lust. Then she reread the words on the stone, 'Precious are the memories', and the anger subsided.

'I'm sorry for getting annoyed, it rips me up inside sometimes, the waste, all those happy times with the kids and those with just me and you. It was within touching distance, wasn't it? The holidays we had planned, remember, you wanted to buy a boat so we could sail at the weekends even though neither of us had a clue how to do it, but it was something to look forward to. All the nights we lay in bed, making plans in the dark, where we would go, exciting city breaks and romantic dinners for two, all smashed to pieces. But I want you to know that the words on the stone are true. I will always have my precious memories. I won't ever forget the good times, I promise. I'm still here with the children and I still have my future with them, you don't. And I'm sorry for that, Matthew, I truly am. Even if we hadn't been able to sort things out you'd still have them and they'd have you in their life. It isn't fair that you won't be part of the memories they make in the future, you didn't deserve that. We all loved you so much, and I miss you. I always will.' Anna's body was consumed by tiredness, every fibre of her being felt heavy and she wanted to lie down so badly, sitting was such an effort now. She lay down on top of the grave, her head resting on her hands as silent tears flowed, sobbing quietly, no fuss – just peaceful, sad rivers of water, flowing along with the memories and pictures that swam in her mind, easing the pain.

Anna was aware of birds singing, traffic in the distance and the sun heating her arms and face when it appeared through a cloud, then she would be cold and she knew the sky was grey, but she didn't care, the quiet was so calming. Then the sound of a lawnmower somewhere close roused her.

Sitting up she brushed bits of grass and soil from her clothes before standing, taking another look at Matthew's headstone.

'I'm glad I came to see you now. I promise I'll come back if I ever need to talk or anything. I won't just leave you here on your own. There'll be loads I need to tell you about the kids, even though I hope you are still keeping your eye on them from up there. I'll see you soon, okay.' Anna picked up her bag and after taking one last glance, she made her way home.

Anna strolled along the seafront that was buffeted by a coastal breeze while above her head, seagulls swooped and screeched, the spring sun warming her face. Despite the world going on around her, as cars zoomed past and people got on with their lives, she had a sense that for her, this was no ordinary day. With every step she took Anna felt her spirits lift. She was unburdened, liberated from all that held her back, had dragged her down or made her sad. There was no turning back the clock, she knew that but oddly enough she didn't wish for it, not anymore. The hand that fate, destiny, life, God or whatever had dealt her was something she would learn to live with, make the most of and, weird as it may seem, accept.

Stopping to look out across the choppy water, Anna held on to the iron rails of the promenade, inhaling deeply, and then smiled. She had three beautiful children, a wonderful man who loved her dearly and she loved back just the same, a crazy old mum, a loyal Jeannie, a family and friends. What more could anyone ask for? She only had one life on this earth and from that day on, Anna Harrison, posh apartment owner, supermum, all-round wonder woman and survivor was going to enjoy every second of it.

Book 2

CHAPTER 1

Despite her promise to live life to the full, when it came to her birthday no amount of playing it down or insisting on there being no fuss was taken any notice of. All Anna's protests fell on belligerent, deaf ears and a party had been organised for the weekend. Jeannie took control and wanted to arrange everything so knowing when she was beaten, Anna gave in and left her to it. The venue was her apartment but caterers were bringing food and Daniel was providing the wine. Anna was secretly looking forward to having everyone there; this was the start of a new year in her life and the end of a truly horrendous one that she couldn't wait to see the back of.

The one sticking point was Enid who at present was blissfully unaware of Daniel's existence. To avoid any confusion or explanations on the night, Anna had decided to grasp the nettle and take her mother for lunch where she intended to tell Enid all about him. Seeing as she'd recently declared an interest in exotic food, Anna had booked a table at a Mongolian restaurant. If she liked a bit of spice then this was just the place, but to be on the safe side, Anna nipped into the chemist and bought a packet of indigestion tablets en route. The last thing she wanted was a midnight call from Enid or A&E saying she was having a heart attack when it was just a bit of wind caused by curried goat.

'So, to what do I owe the pleasure of our little trip out?' Enid asked Anna as she got back into the car.

Anna tensed slightly and assured her mother all would be revealed once they got to the restaurant, saying she had a bit of special news but Enid would just have to be patient.

411

'Really, well I hope it won't be anything bad. I've been having strange dreams lately. My Indian spirit guide has been passing on vibrations where you're concerned and from what I'm channelling at the moment, I think romance may be on its way.'

Anna nearly crashed the car and could feel the heat rising from her neck, spreading its giveaway glow all over her hot cheeks.

'Mother, what on earth are you talking about and since when have you had a spirit guide or been able to channel anything? You are not psychic so stop pretending you are, it gives me the creeps and you know it!'

Enid did one her dramatic huffs and folded her arms. 'Well, Miss Know-it-all, for your information I am psychic but still, if you insist on being cynical, so be it. Gladys believes and I told her I've definitely seen a man on the horizon and the spirits are never wrong.'

Enid turned to look out of the window, lips pursed and fingers tapping, just waiting for Anna to take the bait, which she did.

'Okay then, Mystic Meg, tell me what you've seen. I could do with a good laugh.' Anna had calmed herself down and was looking forward to hearing whatever rubbish Enid came out with.

'Well, it's all a bit floaty but when the mists of time clear, I keep getting the letter D, perhaps David or Donny or it might be Danny, I'm not too sure.' Enid sat with her eyes closed, concentrating on her vision, humming gently just for effect.

To say the smile was wiped off Anna's face was an understatement. The mists of time thing had made her giggle and for a second thought that Enid had remembered Anna's teenage infatuation with Donny Osmond, but now she was getting a bit twitchy as her mum continued in full flow giving a performance to rival Gypsy Rose Lee.

'I can see the sea which he crosses frequently and many green fields with small fruit trees on them. I'm not sure what they mean though. The vibrations suggest he may be a grape farmer, or something to do with wine. The thing that sticks in my mind is blue eyes, lovely blue eyes. Then it all goes misty again. In another dream there are wires, hundreds of them stretching all over in different colours, just like inside a light switch, and then I lose the connection. So that's that, I know you think it's a load of rubbish but it's all about interpreting what the spirits are trying to tell me.' Enid looked quite pleased with her performance and was eyeing up Anna's reaction.

Thankfully they had reached the restaurant, thus ending the conversation and giving a rather shaken Anna a few minutes to come to terms with her mother's shocking, new found ability. Nothing more was said on the matter until they were seated at their table with a mountain of freshly cooked prawns and chicken coated in aromatic spices both lovingly prepared by a friendly chef on a large grill. Enid tucked in and was thoroughly enjoying herself, chattering on about never eating a Mongolian before and having to bring Gladys, until Anna could stand the stress or avoid the inevitable any longer. Throwing caution to the wind just blurted it out.

'Mum, you know when I said I had some good news, well it seems your spirit guide Big Chief Sitting Bull or whatever he's called, is actually right. I've met someone who means the world to me. His name is Daniel and he does in fact have lovely blue eyes and is an electrician. The sea that he travels across is the channel, he visits his daughter in France and that's where I met him. As for the trees with fruit on, I think that may be the vineyards he visits, he's interested in wine you see and will be bringing some to my party on Saturday. I wanted to tell you before you met him, but it looks like you already knew.' Anna couldn't quite believe the words coming out of her mouth but the facts spoke for themselves and somehow, against all odds, Enid had foreseen Daniel.

The look of triumph on Enid's face made Anna want to groan, knowing that the paranormal floodgates were now open for business and they'd never hear the end of it.

'Well, that's lovely, Anna, but there's no need to be sarcastic about my guide who, for your information, is called White Bear. I may have special powers but I still want to hear all about this

Daniel. Tell me everything, we've got ages, and they said we could go back for seconds, so I think I'll have some curried goat next. I wonder if it's chewy, do you think it will play havoc with my teeth? Come on, get on with it, I'm all ears, it's about time you got back into the saddle.' Enid stabbed a large prawn and waited expectantly for Anna to begin.

After she had told her the story from start to finish and Enid had almost single-handedly wiped out the entire contents of the Mongolian buffet, they sat in silence drinking thick coffee. Enid had listened to Anna without interruption and seemed genuinely pleased for her daughter and was looking forward to meeting Daniel and Josh at the weekend. Anna glowed with happiness. Now Daniel's existence was in the open she could truly get on with getting to know him more.

Jeannie was dying to meet him, having annoyingly missed her opportunity the last time he stayed in Portsmouth due to work. Anna was sure Sam would be no trouble and as for everyone else in the world, she was past caring. After Matthew's behaviour she felt entitled to be happy and she really was – at last. She was still shell-shocked at her mother's accurate vision although had no intention of discussing it or encouraging her in any way. All that paranormal stuff gave her the heebie-jeebies. Silence never lasted long where Enid was concerned and after a moment she put down her cup and sighed. Anna prayed another prophecy wasn't on its way.

'You know, love, I've been hoping you'd meet someone and remembered my advice from when I was poorly. I don't want you to be lonely or end up being a batty old biddy like me, don't protest, I know I have my moments but that's my way of coping. Keeping myself occupied and getting out and about, well, it's just making up for lost time. Even though I gad about with Gladys I'm still alone when I turn out the light at bedtime. I don't want that for you. I missed my chance to find someone but I think you'll be okay. Things have worked out for the best now and you have someone to look after you again and have fun with so I'm very, very happy for you. And, Anna, just remember that even though you're an adult, I'm still your mum and I am always here if you need me. You only have to pick up the phone and I'll be straight round.' Enid refilled her coffee and took a sip. Conversation over.

Just for a heartbeat, Anna thought she spotted a chink in Enid's Teflon coated armour and the merest hint of watery eyes, then the moment passed. After Enid's well-meant speech Anna remembered her promise not to keep secrets from family, and after being touched by her mum's words, took the opportunity to explain all about Matthew, despite the risks involved.

Anna dropped Enid off at Gladys's and watched her mum bustle up the path, eager to pass on the news about Daniel and extol the wonders of Mongolian food. Enid had promised to keep the details of Matthew's behaviour private after swearing a tribal oath in the presence of her spirit guide, so Anna drove away quite content, yet still in a state of bemused shock at her mother's accurate predictions regarding Daniel. More annoyingly, while Enid and her iron clad stomach had no after-effects from their meal at all, Anna felt a very bad case of indigestion coming on.

She was just letting herself into the apartment when Daniel rang. It was stuffy inside so Anna headed straight to the patio doors and slid them open. Experiencing the sea air rushing in still hadn't lost its sparkle as she relaxed on one of the chairs, watching the traffic on the Solent and listening to Daniel chatter on.

'So how did lunch with your mum go? She sounded lovely when we had a bit of a chat earlier, she gave me a good grilling but apart from that she seems really nice. Did she pass on my message? I thought she might have forgotten.'

Anna went still and a nerve twitched in her jaw.

'What do you mean a bit of a chat, when did you ring? And no, she didn't pass on a message.'

'I rang a couple of hours ago. Your mum answered your phone and said you'd gone into the chemist so I asked her to tell you I'd called. It was nothing urgent, just about the wine for Saturday. I tried to go but then I couldn't shut her up. She wanted to know who I was so I told her we'd met in France last year. Obviously I kept it vague, no gory details. Then she wanted to know where I was from and what I did for a living, and then why I was bringing the wine, so I told her I was a bit of a collector. I hope I haven't said anything out of turn, what's wrong, you've gone a bit quiet is everything alright… Anna, Anna, are you still there?'

Anna was actually struck dumb. How could she have fallen for all that codswallop about spirit guides and visions? Enid must have answered the phone and saw not only Daniel's name, but his photo on the screen. It was a lovely shot of him from when they stayed at the hotel, that's how she knew he had blue eyes. The rest, Daniel had told her under intense interrogation, giving her all the information she needed for her fake premonition.

'Sorry, Daniel, yes, I'm still here and there's nothing wrong but I swear, one of these days I'm going to swing for my bloody mother!'

Sam came home on the Thursday before the party and Anna was grateful for the time alone with him before everyone arrived at the weekend. As promised, she had cooked him one of his favourites, spaghetti carbonara, and they had eaten it on the patio where the small chimenea gave off a cosy glow, warming the air and wafting heat around their ankles. She was dreading the conversation they were about to have so let him enjoy his food and relax before she told him about Matthew. These were his last few minutes of blissful ignorance and Anna felt dreadful that she was about to burst a bubble. Reminding herself that this wasn't her fault and she had nothing to feel guilty about, she took a breath and got on with it.

'Sam, I'm glad we've got a bit of time together before Mel and Daniel arrive because I need to have a talk about something. I've kept a secret from you but it's time you knew the truth.' Anna swallowed nervously and took a sip of her wine as Sam sighed and tried to lighten the mood.

'I knew it, I'm adopted. I always told you I was the odd one out, now I know why.' Sam was joking but a flicker of worry shot across his face. 'Sorry, Mum, go on, I'm listening. I'll be serious, promise.'

Anna put down her glass and continued.

'Just listen to me all the way through. I'll tell you the basics and then you can ask me whatever you want, okay? Just bear with me while I get it over with.' She saw Sam nod and clasp his hands together which were resting on his chest, he was ready.

Once Anna had finished explaining all about Caitlin, in an attempt to mask his emotions, Sam got up sharply and walked to the edge of the patio, resting his hands on the balcony, staring out to sea. Anna focused on the yellow flames in the fire, silently cursing Matthew for causing the pain that their son was experiencing and truly hoped he was looking down right now into Sam's face, witnessing for himself the result of his selfishness. When Sam turned he was composed but wrapped his arms around his body as if to protect himself.

'I can't believe it, Mum. I honestly can't believe any of this. I know it's true because you wouldn't make this up but I just can't get my head round it.' He walked back over to the table and slumped into his chair taking a long drink from his bottle before dragging his palm wearily across his face.

He looked at Anna and held out his hand which she grasped and held tightly. It was with great self-control that she kept it together, she had no more tears for herself yet they were oceans left for her children and the look of disappointment on Sam's face was hard to bear.

'You'd better tell me the rest, don't leave anything out or spare me the details. I want to know the lot, and then I never have to talk about it again.'

So Anna did just that, she told him everything.

She could tell by the look on his face that Sam was having trouble matching the dad he knew and loved with the one Anna was telling him about. He was also astonished that Melanie had kept it to herself because they were always close and he would have expected her to tell him. Anna explained everything in detail, the sequence of events and how she'd slowly pieced things together, the fact that everyone had been protecting each other's feelings which had resulted in a mammoth lack of communication and a mountain of turmoil for all who kept the secret. What she needed Sam to understand was that they'd only acted out of love and concern for each other, there was no grand conspiracy to keep anyone in the dark, it was simply about damage limitation.

'Well, it's a pity Dad didn't try a bit harder in that department because if he had then we wouldn't be having this conversation, would we?'

Anna could hear anger in his voice, yet still, she could tell he was let down, deflated.

'I know, Sam, but if it gives you any comfort at all he regretted everything. Dennis said that Dad wanted to put it right. If we hold on to that thought maybe it will be easier to remember the Matthew that I knew, the person that was your father. We all make mistakes and I know what he did was beyond bad but at least he realised that, he wasn't going to leave us and wanted to make amends.' Anna had given it her best shot to make him understand and had been quite generous where Matthew was concerned, considering she was royally pissed off with him and sick to death of cleaning up his mess.

Sam shook his head and began to move their plates over to the kitchen. 'Come on, let's clear this lot away and get another drink, my head's ready to explode.'

A deep crease set across his forehead as he silently loaded the dishwasher and helped Anna tidy up. They worked quietly together for a while, cleaning up whilst avoiding the subject of Matthew. Once they were settled on the sofas, Sam rested his head back with his eyes closed as Anna curled up in a corner, watching him and trying to read his mind.

'When I'm away with the lads from work I see all sorts of behaviour, especially on nights out and sometimes even the married blokes misbehave. I've seen it with my own eyes but never paid much attention to it before, you sort of ignore it. I never get involved but maybe now I might just go over and say, hey mate, pack it in, you don't know how many lives you're going to cock up messing about like that. I'll probably get a black eye but if it stops anyone feeling like this it'll be worth it.' Sam took a swig of his beer then looked over to Anna and continued.

'I can't believe that you had to deal with it on your own, Mum. That's what's getting to me the most. I was getting on with my life while you had all that to cope with. Then, without our support and keeping it all inside you've managed to move house and make friends in France, even sorting that cow of a woman out. I was proud of you before but now… well, I think you're something else and Dad's an idiot to risk losing someone like you, he's a fool. I'm so flaming annoyed with him.' Sam shook his head and closed his eyes.

Anna sensed he was holding in his tears and trying hard not to swear or get upset so filled the gap to give him time.

'I promise that from now on there won't be any secrets. If we've learned anything from this, that's the biggie. I'm going to treat you all like real adults from now on, not just miniature versions that I protect from the big bad world. You are all independent and can deal with life, probably a lot better than me. And thanks for the compliment by the way. I'm glad I make you proud.'

Sam opened one eye and looked over at Anna, smirking.

'Get real, Mother. You know very well that you won't be able to resist interfering and as for leaving us to the perils of the world, that's never going to happen, is it? It'd make you ill and drive you mad at the same time. You can't kid me, but nice try.'

Anna launched a cushion at his head, knowing he was pulling himself out of his mood.

Realising that the wine and her confession was catching up, after yawning loudly Anna thought it best to call time. 'Well, if that's how you feel I may as well stay true to form and send you to bed for an early night, you'll need your energy for my mad rave on Saturday. You know what us old people are like when we've had one too many, especially your gran and Gladys.'

'Mum, forty-four isn't that old but take your own advice and get some kip, we don't want you getting overtired and having a tantrum. I'm staying up for a bit. I might watch a film.'

Sam flicked off his trainers and lay down on the sofa, he was surfing the channels and seemed fine.

'Okay, as long as you won't be lying there festering or feeling upset. I'd rather keep you company if that's the case.' Anna wasn't sure if he was bluffing and putting on a brave face.

'See, what did I tell you? You lasted for a whole five minutes. Go on, go to bed.'

Sam obviously wanted to be alone and was trying to get rid of her in the kindest way, so stifling another yawn, Anna took the hint.

Following the night of revelations with Sam, Anna had woken up to find the apartment empty and after a momentary flap, spotted the note on the worktop saying he'd gone for a run with Anton. Flooded with relief, Anna got on with preparing his breakfast, also taking the opportunity to ring Daniel and let him know how it all went. He would be arriving that evening with Josh and there would be no chance to discuss Sam then. The looming boyfriend-meets-family scenario gave her a serious case of monster butterflies that were furiously battering their wings against her stomach. Thank goodness Mel would be home for backup and could be thoroughly relied on to stand in her mum's corner.

'Mother, I'm home, just having a quick shower. Get my breakfast on, woman, I'm starving,' yelled Sam, then the bathroom door slammed shut.

As he sat there a few minutes later, munching on his bagels and bacon, watching the news, Sam looked like he hadn't a care in the world so Anna steadfastly avoided the subject of Matthew when to her surprise, he brought it up first.

'I did a lot of thinking last night and on my run this morning, and I reckon I've sorted things out in my head. The way I see it is this, what Dad did was the pits and I will never ever understand why he was so stupid and I'll always be mad with him for hurting you. But then, I can't rub out all those years when he was the best dad in the world. He never once let us down and was always there for me. I don't want to forget him being like that, how I did in the seconds just before you told me. The only way we can get over this is by putting him into two compartments, Dad before the affair, and then just blanking out what he did with *her*. Otherwise, we'll all be miserable forever and I for one don't want to be talking about it for the rest of my life, there's no point.' Sam picked up the other half of his bagel and tucked in, waiting for Anna to reply.

In truth, she was a little taken aback by the wisdom of her son's words. Whether she liked it or not the 'Before Matthew' as Sam had put it was a wonderful father and husband, so why should six months of lunacy be allowed to wipe out twenty-five years of happiness? They all knew what he had done, vaguely understood some of the reasons why, but it would do absolutely no good banging on and on about it. They all needed to move on so really, despite her wounded heart, she agreed with everything Sam said.

'Sam, you're right, just remember your dad as the one you know and love. I don't want any of you to take sides, there's no need, no point really. You are very wise in your own, down-to-earth sort of way and I admire your honesty and loyalty. Right then, do you fancy an egg or some more bacon?' They had both said enough, it was time to move on.

CHAPTER 2

Despite any misgivings Anna had beforehand, she thoroughly enjoyed her birthday party and everyone she had invited turned up, plus a few more she hadn't anticipated.

Jeannie had come up trumps and the caterers brought a feast of wonderful, summery food. Daniel must have raided his cellar or the local off-licence as there was enough wine and beer to sink most of the ships docked in Port Solent. Melanie had strung twinkly fairy lights around the flat and along the balcony and Philip had taken control of the music, saying he wasn't having any of that thumping, grinding nonsense that got on the nerves of anyone over the age of thirty.

With an hour to go before everyone arrived, Anna smoothed down her dress. She had splashed out on a sleeveless antique lace creation and some very high slingback shoes that came in a box and bag that looked as expensive as the footwear inside. Anna allowed herself a small smile, not at her appearance in the mirror, simply because all the pieces of her life were fitting into place, especially as Daniel and Sam were getting on well and their meeting the previous evening wasn't half as cringeworthy as she had anticipated.

***

Melanie had breezed in that Friday afternoon, full of life and ready to start her summer vacation. Anna was a bundle of nerves and had been the butt of Sam and Mel's relentless teasing all afternoon as she fidgeted and paced and was nicely wound like a bobbin by the time Daniel and Josh arrived. After the handshakes and polite conversation were dispensed with, Josh in his relaxed way said that the apartment was awesome and wanted a grand tour. Before she knew it he had been whisked off to look at the view and the happy banter of young people filled the void of adult stiffness. Then Anna breathed out.

***

Anna was jolted from her thoughts of the previous evening by Daniel coming up the stairs. Sergeant Jeannie had commandeered him but he'd escaped bottle opening duty and left Philip to be bossed around for a while. He stopped when he saw her standing in front of the mirror, the twinkle in his eyes telling her she looked fine. Coming over to stand behind her, Daniel folded his arms around her waist and pulled her close as he rested his head against hers, then looking into the mirror he told her reflection she was beautiful. Anna turned to face him and planted a firm kiss on his lips, their fingers entwined and she thought for the hundredth time how well they fitted together.

In every way they matched, their bodies, their minds and now their lives were merging into one, slowly and surely forming bonds and making memories. He had given her a white gold necklace for her birthday which matched the bracelet from Christmas, the only pieces of jewellery Anna wore as now her hands were bare. The lack of a wedding ring on her left hand had been noticed but not commented on by anyone, apart from Daniel. As they lay in bed under the stars the night before, he'd held up her hand, touching her bare wedding finger and asked if she was okay about it. Anna told him simply that she knew it was the right time to take it off and yes, she was okay, very. When Anna returned from the cemetery she had gone straight upstairs to take a shower and without too much thinking and while her mind and heart were in unison for once, she slipped off the ring and placed it under the shelf of her jewellery box, closing the lid firmly on the past.

The buzzer on the entry system forced them apart and ended their kisses, leaving Anna flustered and slightly puzzled as to who could be at the door. It would be over an hour before she expected people to arrive and the caterers had already done their thing and left. Her first choice would have been Enid, getting there early to bag a seat, or maybe it was Melanie who'd nipped out earlier. Sure enough, when Anna flung open the door her daughter was standing in the hallway holding a wheelie suitcase and promptly shouted, 'Surprise,' to which the smiley face of Rosie and chubby cheeked Sabine appeared.

'Rosie! I don't believe it, come in, come in, give me a hug, I'm so happy. I can't believe you came all this way for me.' Anna was over the moon as she ushered in her first guests.

By the time they'd caught their breath, fed and changed Sabine, the buzzer began to ring with the arrival of the rest of Anna's guests.

First were Dennis and Mary, the former seemed a little on edge, however, Mary threw herself into saying hello to everyone, the shackles of guilty secrets not weighing her down like those of her husband. Next was Samantha and Rob, minus baby Archie and then Tania, Melanie's old school friend who looked the most glamorous Anna had ever seen her, smiling when Mel whispered it was all for Sam who didn't seem to have noticed. Three of Jeannie's friends from work arrived, Maria, Jan and Paula, all dressed to impress, their effort aimed in the direction of Anton whose imminent arrival was eagerly anticipated.

After a lull where Anna mingled, there was a commotion at the door and before she even looked, knew who it would be. Melanie was having words with Enid so Anna went over to investigate and found her mother and loyal sidekick Gladys, plus two old chaps, Neville and Ted, the latter being pushed in a wheelchair by a slightly flustered young man. Both elders were dressed very smartly in varying shades of brown and beige and clutching bottles of pale ale, it was like they blended at the seams, accessorised by their beer. Looking immensely stressed out, Naseem, the taxi-driver-cum-wheelchair-pusher, was introduced by Enid, which is when Anna noticed he was also holding a lead that led to Frank, the very ugly dog. Mel was pink-cheeked and held one hand to her head as she spoke.

'Gran, you cannot expect Naseem to look after Frank all night and anyway it's probably illegal to let a dog sit in the passenger seat of a taxi, and you can't expect him to take him for a wee either, he's got a job to do.'

Melanie was getting nowhere with her gran who had talked Naseem into pushing Ted from the taxi to the apartment. Naseem, however, had drawn the line at dog-sitting and now Frank had been barred entry.

'Well, Neville doesn't like leaving him on his own so we brought him with us but now you're worried about the bloody carpets, what do you expect us to do with poor Frank? You're being very unreasonable, Melanie.'

Enid rolled her eyes then spotted Anna who had overheard and was already reconciled with the fact that Frank would just have to stay.

'Right, Melanie, please take everyone's coat and get them a drink. Sam, stop laughing and take Frank to the balcony, he'll be fine out there. Naseem, please come inside and have a drink and something to eat before you go back to work. I'm sure you could do with something.' Anna welcomed them in and closed the door, listening to Enid mutter as she stomped by.

With the crisis averted but before Enid had a chance to settle into a seat for the whole night, Anna grabbed her mother and steered her towards Daniel.

'I'd like you to meet somebody, Mother. I'm sure there's no need really as White Bear has probably told you all about him, but I thought you might like to put a real face to your vision.'

Enid was oblivious to Anna's sarcasm and folded Daniel into a warm, cuddly hug, telling him that he was exactly as he had appeared to her but even more handsome in the flesh, at which Anna gave in, rolled her eyes and left them to it.

Arriving next was Aunty Elsie with floaty dressed Naomi and her long-haired, goatee-bearded boyfriend. Fergal was from Ireland and a ranger in the National Park and a bit of a hippy, going by his shorts and sandals. The room was filling up and a happy hum of conversation and well chosen background music added to the ambience, even two of Sam's mates from school had called in before heading into town for a big night out.

Anna was taking a moment, happily watching her guests and spying on her mother. Rosie and Jeannie were engrossed in conversation while Sabine sucked quietly on her dummy, sleepy dark eyes surveying the strangers in the room. Josh, Sam, and his friends were laughing loudly on the balcony and Naseem was on the sofa, chuffed to bits to be tucked between the air hostesses. Enid and her gang had bagged the dining table and were tucking into plates loaded with food while Tania (one eye permanently trained on Sam) helped Mel fetch more drinks for the pensioners. She felt Daniel's arm slide around her waist as he pulled her close and kissed her quickly on the cheek.

The front door opened and Anton bounded in, laden with champagne and the biggest bouquet of exotic flowers Anna had ever seen. He was escorted on each arm by two stunning blondes, almost wearing dresses and teetering on the highest, most dangerous heels. Both were tanned to perfection and chemically enhanced in every department possible.

Sam came in to welcome them and morphed into a rather smooth, attentive barman, popping open the champagne and pouring everyone drinks. The two lovelies stood guard around their boss and knowing when they were beaten, the air hostesses decided to get smashed and just enjoy the evening, agreeing that Anton was right up his own bottom, too high maintenance and the wrong shade of orange. Naseem was in nirvana, stuck between the lovely ladies and seemed to have forgotten all about his taxi, which was most likely plastered in parking tickets.

Suddenly the lights were dimmed and Anna sensed activity behind her. Jeannie appeared with Mel and Sam and a birthday cake, set alight with what she really hoped wasn't forty-four candles. Everyone began singing 'Happy Birthday' and she felt

Daniel by her side, his hand on the small of her back, letting her know he was there.

After all the excitement, the party eased down a notch and everyone settled into comfy chairs and ate dessert, but there was one more surprise left for the evening and to Anna's relief, it had nothing to do with her.

The guests were brought to attention by the tapping of glass and all eyes fell on Philip who called for a little quiet as he had a very important task to perform. Holding out his hand to Jeannie, he pulled her towards him and in a very swift, possibly rehearsed movement, whipped a black box from his pocket, and then went down on one knee. Anna was in floods of tears before her brother even got the words out but she managed to hear him tell Jeannie that it had taken him far too long to realise that the love of his life had been right under his nose all the time, so before she got bored of him, wondered if Miss Jeannie Brown would do him the very great honour of being his wife.

Anna knew what the answer would be and the cheers that went around the room left her in no doubt it was a yes. She couldn't see Philip kissing Jeannie because her eyes swam in a mist of happy tears but she could picture them both in her mind, her best friend and her gormless brother, in love, together at last, where they belonged.

Wiping her eyes on the tissue Daniel silently offered her, Anna pulled herself together and fought through the throng who were congratulating the happy couple. The second they clapped eyes on each other, both Anna and Jeannie set off again, crying tears of happiness, totally unrivalled since watching the Bay City Rollers at the Portsmouth Pleasurama in 1978.

After a while the guests started to drift away; some going home, some heading to Anton's club and amidst the farewells the phone rang, making everyone jump, apart from Mel who was sparked out. Lifting the receiver and expecting trouble at this time of night, Anna was kick started into life by the sound of a far-away voice.

'Hello, Mum, sorry it's so late there but Happy Birthday. Did you have a good party? I wish I could have been there, I'm really missing you all.' Joe was at the end of the phone. Anna's day was complete.

CHAPTER 3

No amount of cajoling or showing her photographs and painting idyllic pictures would persuade Enid to visit France so it was with resignation that at the end of July, Anna packed her case, loaded the car and drove towards the ferry terminal, leaving Portsmouth and her mother behind for a month in the sun. She was catching the overnight ferry to St Malo and had booked a cabin on the ship, looking forward to the experience of sailing over instead of flying.

Anna was over the moon that Sam would be staying for a fortnight, and then Philip and Jeannie asked if they could tag along and bring Summer and Ross for a long weekend. Daniel was due to arrive during the last week so hopefully, they would all be together at some point, even if it was just for a few days. The car was now crammed with enough food to feed an army because no matter how wonderful French cuisine was, Anna knew her lot would still want English bacon, Cheddar cheese and brown sauce. Therefore, anything that wasn't available in the Super U was clinking away in the boot.

Once she had negotiated the ramp onto the ferry, and then the very tight squeeze into her parking space on the car deck, Anna felt rather elated and was eager to explore the ship. First, she dumped her bag in her cabin. There was a bunk bed, made up with crisp pink and white sheets, a little bathroom with a shower, tea and coffee making facilities and a TV. Through the small porthole she could see other ferries waiting at the docks and imagined how cosy it would feel later when she looked out at the lights from other ships, sailing to faraway places. Anna then spent a good hour exploring the ship and getting her bearings.

She felt a rumble underneath her feet and realised it was the ship's engine so feeling like a child, Anna made her way to the front of the ferry. She wanted to experience the journey down the Solent and, in particular, was looking forward to spotting her apartment as they cruised by. Having spent many hours watching this very same ferry make its way past her home it gave her a bit of a thrill now she was actually on it.

It was 8.30pm and still light as they passed the grey fleet of battleships which moored along the Solent at the Navy base, then the Spinnaker Tower which she could see from her apartment, lit up at night like a shiny beacon, guiding sailors home to shore. Cameras clicked as they sailed past HMS Warrior, often mistaken for HMS Victory, Lord Nelson's ship at the battle of Trafalgar, then onwards towards open water.

As they neared Southsea, Anna's eyes scanned the shoreline and pinpointed the coastal route towards the apartment. She spotted it easily and felt a rather childish bubble of excitement, observing her lovely home from the ferry. She also resisted the urge to wave and say, 'Hi, it's me', her old habit of talking to four walls still lingered. They glided past Southsea Castle and the circular forts that guarded the mouth of the port and then they were in the Channel. The Isle of Wight ferry chugged past them on the return leg of its voyage and Anna could see the coastline of the island ahead, remembering day trips in the school holidays with the kids and their tingly, sun-kissed faces and shoes full of sand on the way home.

By the time Anna had settled into her cabin and was lying in bed watching TV, she was exhausted from the buzz and exertion of her new experience and knew how all the little kids on board felt. They had passed Jersey and Guernsey and as she had anticipated, it was cosy in her little room watching the twinkling lights of the coastline and the odd glimpse of ships, far away on the horizon. Yawning, she set her alarm for the morning, heeding Daniel's advice that it would be an early start after losing an hour with the time difference, Anna turned out the light and snuggled down under her duvet. She had left the curtains open to let in the glow from the moon and as she lay there listening to the chug of the engines, lulled by the slight rocking of the ship, Anna embraced the happiness she felt inside. Looking forward to a hug from Mel and then being joined by the rest of the clan, her eyes grew heavy and like a seasoned mariner she slept soundly, sailing off into the sunset towards France.

It was a cool morning as Anna drove down the ramp and off the ship. The sun was up there somewhere but couldn't find a chink in the armour of white clouds but assured by a sunny weather forecast, she passed through border control and made her way out of St Malo and towards the autoroute. The view she had seen of the Breton port as she stood on the deck of the ship while it entered the harbour tempted Anna to linger and explore. Now, her only thoughts were of getting to the gîte so she concentrated on Daphne's voice, her old friend calmly talking her through her journey.

This was the first time she had experienced full summer at Rosie's and as Anna sped along the autoroute and then headed inland, she reminisced about her autumn explorations and wintry New Year, comparing the green fields she saw now, that were sprouting with corn and maize, to the ones ready for harvest or covered in December frost. Anna realised that whatever the season, the countryside held on to its beauty and its ever-changing scenery made her feel alive. Witnessing nature doing its thing was quite special and she envied the farmers and country dwellers that were surrounded by it.

Daphne didn't let her down and within fifty minutes, Anna was trundling up the lane and pulling onto the drive. She was eager to get inside but beaten to it by a smiling, waving Rosie who appeared at the door and before she could take a breath, felt herself enfolded in hugs and assailed by barking, giddy dogs. The same feeling of contentment as always welled up inside Anna's heart because being here was just like coming home.

After a warm bear hug from Melanie, Anna was tentatively asked if rather than joining her at the gîte, she kept her room in the attic. Apparently, Melanie loved her little space in the roof and it was more convenient for work. Rosie hinted it was most likely to do with Pascal, as the stairs had been doing a lot of creaking late at night or early in the morning. While Anna didn't want to dwell on secret assignations between her daughter and Pascal, she had promised Melanie that she'd treat her like a grown-up so agreed, as long as Mel popped down to the gîte when she was free, with or without love's young dream.

Anna's first week in France was a mixture of relaxation and preparation. The three other wooden cabins were occupied and she enjoyed sitting on the decking, reading or chatting with her neighbours while the sound of children playing in the small pool or on the play area gave the place vibrancy. The evenings were usually filled with barbeque smoke wafting around the field as muted voices filled the air, eating and drinking in the moonlight until the early hours.

Anna flitted from the gîte to the restaurant or Rosie would push Sabine down in the pram, where she could relax away from the hubbub of the hotel. Zofia called by for coffee or Anna walked up to her house, never coming back empty-handed as there was an abundance of salad and vegetables in Dominique's garden and she relished living off the land and eating truly fresh produce. Anna envied them the outdoor space and tending to the land, it had once been an ambition of hers to have a small vegetable garden and the only real drawback of her apartment.

Other days, Anna would collect Sabine and push her pram down to the village to buy fresh bread or cakes and visit Sebastien who seemed to have forgiven her for choosing Daniel. She had tried to sneak past one day but after spotting her, he invited her inside for coffee where she sat happily, listening to the chatter of farmers and the old villagers who were a permanent fixture at the bar, causing Anna to wish she could converse with them, even a little bit.

Going in and out of shops, the owners were always so polite and she was okay at bonjour and au revoir, but that was her limit. Maybe it was time to learn properly although just the thought made her nervous, knowing she lacked the confidence to go back to college. Stirring her coffee, Anna told herself off, asking which was worse, learning a bit of French or feeling like an alien and unable to communicate? Maybe it was time to go back to school.

It was Saturday night and Anna invited all of her French friends for a get together, eager for her family to meet everyone and after making a huge list, wandered around the Super U with Sam who still had a ten-year-old's knack for filling the shopping trolley with unsuitable sugary food and stuff he really, really needed. These were hidden amongst an assortment of cheeses, cured mountain sausage, scallops which would be cooked in a creamy garlic and wine sauce, artisan bread for dipping and steaks from the butcher's counter. Anna hoped to show her French guests that the English also knew a thing or two about entertaining and wanted to spoil them as they had her in the past.

The evening was a huge success. Anna was basking in the praises from her very full and slightly tipsy friends and family as Sabine nodded in her pram while Summer and Ross slept peacefully on the sofas inside. Wrapped in blankets, they were totally exhausted from non-stop swimming and had worn themselves out running wild and free in the field. The bottle of Baileys she had bought on the boat was almost done for so Michel, who was actually relaxing for once and had turned up after the last diner had left, nipped home for a bottle of eau de vie which he was now sharing amongst the hardier drinkers. Anna tried some and found it far too strong; it was made from fermented fruit which was distilled, its name meaning water of life. Anna was more inclined to believe that too much eau de vie would take the lining off your insides and speed up the day you met your maker, so sensibly stuck to the wine.

Not to be outdone, Dominique produced a bottle of absinthe, lovingly made from the leaves in his garden, which glowed green inside the bottle. Sam, after assuring everyone that he had completed a secret military exercise involving alcohol and was trained in the art of drinking copious amounts of anything, continued to sample both. Anna made a mental note to leave a bowl by his bed. The thought of the huge meal he had just eaten, topped off by Eton mess which was now swirling around in his stomach along with the vibrant green absinthe, didn't bode well. She definitely wouldn't expect to see him at breakfast in the morning.

Pascal was quite merry too. Sam had finally become bored with teasing Melanie, not that she cared. Despite her brother's mickey taking she clung on to her boyfriend's hand while she chatted to Jeannie, who had also embraced country living and transformed herself from permanently glamorous to a make-up free, bare-footed, earth goddess.

Once Philip, Jeannie and the kids had left with sad, sun-kissed faces and made promises to return again one day, the week passed quickly with trips out. There was sightseeing and go-karting with Sam, Pascal and Mel (Anna minded bags and took videos) then they went to the man-made beach next to the lake where they sunbathed and messed about on pedaloes. Today, however, was a rest day and Anna had volunteered to mind Sabine for an hour while Rosie went to the dentist. Melanie and Sam were on an errand for Michel and had taken her car so she was enjoying the peace and a quiet read while the baby slept.

The afternoon sun bobbed in and out of the clouds, warming her face and making her drowsy. She must have nodded off when the sound of children, squealing in the pool wakened her and she noticed her book had slipped to the floor. Bending down to retrieve it, Anna yawned, focusing on the other guests as they went about their day, sunbathing, reading or playing football.

Her attention was then drawn to movement in the copse where a figure was making its way down the path into the field, towards the gîtes. Anna thought nothing of it at first but as she watched some more, noticed something familiar about the way he walked, the pace of his stride and the shape of his body. The glare from the sun made her squint so she had to shield her eyes with her hand to get a better look. When it hid behind a cloud, Anna saw him clearly and in an instant realised who this tall, fair-haired figure was as her heart hammered in her chest. It couldn't be. It wasn't possible. So many thoughts raced through her head as she tried to make sense of what she was seeing.

Anna's throat constricted and her eyes swam with tears as she gave in to reality. 'Oh my God, it's Joe,' she said out loud as her legs began to walk towards the figure who had begun waving, his long arms swaying above his head. Her walk became a run and those swaying arms were soon wrapped around Anna's shoulders, holding her tight as she sobbed tears of pure joy and shock, clinging on to him, afraid to let him go in case she was still sleeping in her deck chair and this was all a cruel dream.

Over his shoulder and through blurry eyes she could see Mel and Sam watching from the path, their arms round each other while bemused guests stared on wondering what the fuss was about. Eventually, Joe eased his hold on her and she looked up into his tear-stained eyes.

'Hello, Mum, I thought I'd surprise you. I hope you're not annoyed?'

Taking Joe's face in her hands she swallowed, Anna could still barely speak but she managed to squeak out a few words.

'Hello, son, of course I'm not. I am so glad to see you. I just can't believe you're here, give me another hug.' Anna rested her head on his chest and closed her eyes, feeling the heat from his body and the strength of his arms, making a memory of him coming home, holding him tightly. It was similar to the memory she made on the day he left, but this time, she wouldn't let him go.

CHAPTER 4

As usual, everyone was in on it. Joe, as it turned out, was homesick and even though he had another month to go before he was due back, was badly missing his family. Stacey, the girl he had been seeing in New Zealand had already gone home so Joe rang his brother for a heart to heart. In his no-nonsense way Sam just told him to book the next flight and come home, so he did. Extremely jet-lagged but eager to get to his family, Joe had literally stepped off the flight from Auckland and waited until he could get on a plane to France. The errand for Michel was a myth but Sam and Mel needed an excuse to take the car. Rosie wasn't really at the dentist either – it was a ruse to pin Anna down at the gîte.

Not sure what time zone he was actually living in at the moment or whether he was supposed to stay up or go to sleep, Joe sat on the deck with Anna and Sam eating hastily prepared sandwiches and filling in the gaps of his trip. Soon though, fatigue took over, the weight of his heavy lids forcing him to give in and get some kip. Later, as Anna quietly closed the door on her sleeping son, she smiled contentedly and still not quite believing that they were all here, together at last, her family.

Joe slept for twelve hours solid and woke up just as the mist was lifting from the fields and the birds were singing their morning songs in the trees around the gîte. Anna heard movement in the kitchen below and went downstairs to find him sitting on the deck, drinking coffee and eating cereal with a blanket round his shoulders.

'Morning, son. It seems strange to come down and see you here. I woke up in the night and had to convince myself that it wasn't a dream. You certainly know how to surprise someone. Did you sleep well?' Anna shivered in the early morning light.

'I slept like a log. And I know what you mean. I woke up and couldn't remember where I was, it took me a while to get my head straight. Shall I get you some coffee?' Joe yawned loudly.

Anna was already turning to go back into the kitchen and ruffled his bed-hair as she passed. 'No, I'm fine I'll do it. I'm going to get my fleece, back in two minutes.'

While Anna warmed herself with coffee they sat together and watched the fields appear through the white mist. They could hear tractors in the distance as farmers started their day but apart from that, it was just the two of them and the birds. Anna filled him in on Philip's visit and what they had been up to in France, then where Dominique lived and so on. She couldn't wait for everyone to meet him and vice versa. Joe explained that once Sam said the words 'just come home' it all seemed so obvious and simple and he couldn't wait to pack his bags and get on the plane. He knew in his heart that time was up and there was no point in prolonging things, plus this way, he got to spend time with his family before starting work. This subject led to the obvious conversation about Matthew.

'I had a long talk about Dad with Sam, and just so we're clear, I don't think I can be as forgiving as him and Mel. No matter how I look at it the whole thing makes my blood boil. He betrayed all of us, most of all you and I don't think I can ever forgive him. For a while it put me off going to work at the firm. I just felt embarrassed and couldn't face everyone gossiping but Sam reckons it will be yesterday's news, plus they're so glad that cow has gone they've forgotten all about it.' Joe's mouth was set in a firm line of determination and his brows furrowed angrily.

'Joe, the last thing I want is for any of this to affect your future. The whole family has been waiting for you to come back and get stuck in. The only thing you ever wanted was to work with your dad and then take over at Harrison's. One of those dreams won't come true but the other will. If you let her spoil this for you she's won, any indication that she's made me unhappy, in any way, will be a victory so please don't give her the satisfaction. As for your feelings towards your dad, maybe as time passes the anger will ease and you'll be able to forgive him. If it makes you feel better, I know exactly how you feel but I want to be happy. And I want all of you to move on and be happy too.' Anna paused and gave Joe time to take in her words before continuing.

'Sometimes, when bad things happen, you can't for the life of you think how any good can ever come out of it, so the only thing left to do is learn from someone else's mistake. Maybe one day in the future, you might be meet temptation, then perhaps all this will make you stop for a second and remember what a mess your dad made of things and you'll resist. Hopefully though, your moral compass is set straight and there'll be no need.' Anna waited. The sun was breaking through the white sky so she watched the clouds and waited for Joe to speak.

'I hope you're right, Mum. I hate feeling like this and I won't let *her* win either. I'll go back and make you all proud, I promise. I'm glad I came home, I missed you like mad you know. Anyway, shall I go and wake lazy bones up? I want to start my French holiday and need my partner in crime by my side.' Joe stood and then shuffled inside, wrapped in his blanket.

Soon, she heard shouts from Sam telling Joe to get lost (or words to that effect) then a lot of thumping around and shoes hitting the doors. Things were getting back to normal at last.

It hadn't occurred to Anna that Joe would have a problem with Daniel; after all, everyone had got on well with him. So it came as quite a shock to notice the sullen look on her eldest son's face when over breakfast, Sam asked what time he would be arriving. Maybe it had been there before and she was so wrapped up in spending time with her three kids that she hadn't picked up on it, but as Anna sipped her coffee it dawned on her that whenever Daniel had been mentioned, Joe kept quiet.

Playing devil's advocate, she hoped it was because he was a little nervous or maybe felt left out and awkward, being the last member of her family to be introduced. Nevertheless, deep down, a gnawing uneasiness settled over Anna as she observed Joe and waited for an opportunity to speak to him alone. As luck had it, Sam decided to go into the village to play tennis with Dominique so without wasting any time, the minute he set off across the field, Anna waded in.

'Joe, do you have a problem with Daniel staying here or just a problem with him in general? Because if you do, I'd rather you get it off your chest right now.'

The old Anna would've felt she had gone too far saying even that, whereas the new Anna was quite prepared to stand her ground. This worm had turned long ago.

'I just think you've rushed into having a relationship, that's all. It's too soon and seems sort of disrespectful. Some might say that you're on the rebound. Anyway, I thought this holiday was for us, special family time, and he's not family.' Joe's arms were crossed over his chest and his mouth had set in a determined, stubborn line.

'Right, let's get one thing clear, straight away. Firstly, I have not rushed into anything. Had I taken up the many offers from Jeannie's friends to go out on the town with them and pick up blokes for whatever purpose, then I would hold my hands up and plead guilty to the charge of being disrespectful. On the other hand, some would say I well and truly deserved to take my mind off my lying, deceitful, unfaithful husband and wish me the best of British.' She saw Joe flinch slightly, hearing the truth obviously stung.

'Secondly, I have been virtually single since the day I found out about the affair, longer if you count back to when it started. I purposely took my time getting to know Daniel, enjoying a purely platonic relationship for months; the rest, quite frankly, is none of your business. Had I not had him to confide in and listen to my endless woes I think I would have gone under. He is the most kind, understanding, supportive human being you could wish to meet who only ever puts me and my feelings first. He is not some gigolo who is out for what he can get and I feel lucky that he has chosen me because I'm sure he's not short of female attention. He is decent, hardworking, and loyal to his family and to me, which is a lot more than can be said for your father.' Anna was surprised at the conviction and passion in her own voice, saying the words to Joe made them so real, and Daniel even more precious than she had realised.

'Okay, I get it, there's no need to rant. I'm just having trouble sorting all this out in my head. I feel it's my responsibility to look out for you all, now that Dad's gone. Maybe it's easier for Mel and Sam because they've been here while stuff was going on. I feel a bit out of the loop, a bit on the outside.'

Anna knew he was making excuses and backtracking but wasn't prepared to let him off just yet. Joe needed to be taught a small lesson and there was no time like the present.

'Let's get this right, Joe. For almost a year, both your sister and brother were in the dark about a lot of things so don't make out that they were privy to stuff that you were left out of, but regardless, they supported me unwaveringly on many issues and their main objective was that I should be happy. And as for you taking responsibility I think that for the time being you should concentrate on your career and let everyone else get on with their own lives. We've all been through a lot and can manage quite well without anyone assuming the role as head of this family and just so that we are clear, if anyone gets the big leather chair at the top of the boardroom table, until otherwise stated, that person is me. Have you got that?' Anna thought that she may have gone too far, more or less telling him to wind his neck in but the last thing she wanted was Joe swanning around like 'the big I am' at work or at home.

He had a lot to learn and maybe clipping his wings now would stop him from making an arse of himself at Harrison's. When he slid back his chair and started to clear the breakfast things in silence, Anna really thought she'd pushed her luck but stood firm, knowing that sometimes, a bit of tough love was called for. After a couple of silent trips back and forth to the kitchen, Joe sat back down and placed his outstretched arms on the table.

'Okay, Mum, I'll try, for your sake. I get what you are saying and I can't expect to just come back and take over, but I really can't get my head round you being with someone other than Dad. It's just too weird. Maybe when I've met him I'll understand. Mel and Sam think he's great so I'll keep an open mind.'

Joe smiled, looking about as unconvincing as he sounded, still, Anna had said her piece and would have to leave the rest to fate and failing that, a dash of Daniel's charm and personality.

Anna had planned a barbeque and a get together later in the evening with Daniel, her friends and family – that's if World War Three hadn't been declared. The edge had been taken of her excitement and replaced by nervous anxiety and a hint of foreboding. She was feeling gloomy now, especially about rowing with Joe so soon after he came home, not to mention the ever-continuing ripples of Matthew's indiscretions which made her so angry. Sometimes she thought the after-effects would never end.

It was obvious that Joe had said something to Melanie and Sam about Daniel as during the evening, they overcompensated and tried a bit too hard to bring them together in conversation. Anna had also caught her daughter watching Joe; as though Mel was on standby, ready to fend off any antagonism should it arise. All in all though, the evening went better than she'd imagined and Joe, in his defence, did make an effort, hiding his scepticism well. Melanie and Pascal sloped off first. They were both up early the next day on breakfast and dairy duty respectively. Anna still hadn't delved into how their romance was developing, leaving the task of moral judgements to Joe.

Taking the bull by the horns, Anna announced that she was shattered and ready for bed. Daniel didn't take the hint and decided he'd have another beer with Sam and Joe then follow her up. She cringed slightly, avoiding eye contact with her eldest son and having had enough of walking on eggshells and feeling embarrassed about sleeping with Daniel, gave up and left them to it.

It was 1.30am when she felt Daniel slide into bed beside her and snuggle up. She knew he was a bit merry and given any encouragement would want to lure her from her comfy pillow and peaceful sleep for a spot of early morning passion, so to punish him, Anna feigned exhaustion.

'Stop pretending you're tired and ask me how it went with Joe. I know you're dying to, so come on, let's get it over with then I'll let you ravish me.'

Daniel was laughing as he kissed her neck as Anna smiled in the dark. He knew her so well.

'Okay then, smart arse, what went on? And just so you know, I have absolutely no intention of ravishing you tonight. I've waited three weeks for a night of passion whereas you would rather drink beer with my sons. Bloody charming.' Anna was curious and in truth, not even slightly annoyed.

Daniel chuckled to himself and assured her that all was well with Joe and a spot of male bonding had taken place. He could of course be persuaded to tell all for a quick kiss and a fumble under the sheets, but otherwise, his lips were sealed. Not one to shy away from a challenge, Anna flipped over to face Daniel, his smiley blue eyes watching mischievously in the moonlight. They were impossible to resist and anyway she was wide awake now. There was no way she was going to cut her nose off to spite her face so without further ado, Anna proceeded with an in depth and relentless interrogation, reminding a rather triumphant Daniel that she didn't do fumbles, they were for wimps.

One week later, on the final day of her holiday, Anna stood in the kitchen garden holding a wicker basket while Rosie filled it with fresh salad. The four of them were having a farewell dinner that evening before Anna caught the morning ferry from Saint Malo with Daniel, which was the only thing that cheered her up. They had planned to sit on the deck in the sun and enjoy the view during the six-hour crossing. Daniel had to drive straight home as he had work and Anna wanted to see what state the apartment was in after Sam and Joe had been left to their own devices for a week. As soon as he arrived in Portsmouth, Joe had rung to say how much he loved the apartment and thought she'd made a good move, leaving Anna relieved that for once he approved of something she'd done. Hallelujah!!

Dennis was as surprised as everyone else at Joe's return, assuring him that all his colleagues were looking forward to having a member of the Harrison family on board again. Melanie had another fortnight in France and Anna knew there would be tears when she had to leave Pascal behind so in an attempt to cheer Mel up, had assured her daughter that he was always welcome in Portsmouth.

They were discussing the young lovers' predicament as Rosie plopped onions and radish into the basket when she remembered some news for Anna. 'You know that family in the gîte next to you, well they've asked to book yours for next year, apparently they want to bring more people. I said I had to check my bookings but in truth I wanted to give you first refusal. Don't feel under any pressure to say you'll come but I don't want you to be disappointed, that's all.' Rosie had to get up so she could stretch her legs and back while Anna pondered.

'Oh no. I do feel as though that's my gîte now, but I may not need something so big next year. Flipping heck. I wish I had a crystal ball right now. It's okay, Rosie, just say they can have it. I suppose I could always sleep on your sofa.' Anna felt even more fed up and that the day was going downhill.

'Okay, if you're sure and the sofa has your name on it, but before you go all gloomy on me, I've had an idea, a bit of a plan, and part of it is purely selfish.'

Rosie sat on one of the iron chairs as she spoke to Anna who was all ears.

'I have lots of acquaintances who pass through the hotel, but apart from Zofia and Ruby, I missed having a best friend. It sounds a bit childish but it's true. I knew from the moment we met that we would be mates and then this place worked its magic and we just clicked. Over the past year I've really enjoyed having you in my life so, if you intend being a frequent visitor to La Belle France, maybe in the long run it would work out better if you bought a place of your own. It'd be an investment as well as a holiday home so I think you should at least consider it.' Rosie waited for her words to sink in, watching and waiting for Anna's reaction.

'That's one of the nicest things anyone has ever said to me, and the feeling is mutual by the way. You've changed my life and I can't imagine not having you in it, this place feels like home and you are part of my family now. But as for buying something here, I've never even thought about it, Rosie. In theory, I may visit about four or five times a year and you're right, if I had my own place I could come over for weekends and the family would be able to stay whenever they felt like it, so I suppose it would be perfect!' Anna's mind was racing with possibilities and plans, picturing an imaginary cottage in the countryside, causing her heart to beat like mad as adrenaline pulsed through her veins.

She could have a little vegetable garden and a dog to keep her company at night (any excuse would do) she would learn to speak French and make new friends. Daniel would love it and so would the kids, and Jeannie and Phil. Anna could hardly contain her excitement and thrust the basket into Rosie's hands, telling her she would see her at dinner but needed to wake Daniel up from his afternoon snooze and run it by him.

Rosie was laughing as Anna shot out of the gate and down the path. She imagined sparks shooting from Anna's brain and a multi-coloured aura surrounding her very giddy friend. Rosie knew it was the hotel, casting a spell and before long, they would all have a lovely new neighbour.

That night, the pros and cons of purchasing a holiday home in France were gone over with a fine toothcomb whilst Anna and

Daniel ate and drank the night away with Rosie and Michel. The pros heavily outweighed the cons, so it was a foregone conclusion and by the time they all said goodnight, a plan had been formulated. Anna would visit her accountant the second she got home and Rosie would keep a look out for suitable properties.

It was really going to happen. Anna Harrison, the widow of the county, ex-boring person and champion ditherer was going to buy herself a home in France, and she couldn't wait.

CHAPTER 5

House hunting in France wasn't as simple as Anna had hoped it would be and after months of trawling the Internet and buying every property magazine she could lay her hands on, the search had drawn zero results. She received regular emails from the local estate agents but nothing had taken her fancy. By the time November arrived with its frosty mornings, Anna had almost given up hope of finding her place in the sun and was resigned to waiting until spring to resume her search. Which is why, the sound of Rosie's excited voice came as a complete surprise as she sat on the floor of the apartment, listening to the howl of the storm that was battering the seafront.

'Anna, it's me. I think I've found it, I think it's the one you've been looking for. It was pure luck to be honest but I just had to ring you straight away and tell you. Zofia's cleaning lady saw her sister in the bread shop and she told her that the English neighbours had decided to sell their house. It is exactly what you've been looking for and they haven't even put it on the market yet so if you're quick, you could snap it up. It's fate, it has to be, don't you think?'

Rosie hadn't taken a breath and was rattling on like a machine gun and Anna was relieved when she eventually came up for air.

'Rosie, slow down, have you actually seen this place and where is it exactly? We don't even know how much it is or what it looks like.'

Anna was laughing as she spoke to Rosie who was soon in full flow.

'Of course I know what it looks like because as soon as Zofia told me we both jumped into the car and nipped over to have a peep. I've taken some photos and will send them as soon as I get

446

off the phone, and I know exactly how much they want because we saw the woman who owns it in the garden and I thought, sod it, and introduced myself. She invited us in for a cuppa and even showed us round, so are you interested? Look, just get off the phone and I'll send the pictures. Then ring me straight back, okay?'

Without giving Anna the chance to respond Rosie hung up, so doing as she was told, waited patiently on the sofa for an email to arrive.

On hearing the ping of her mailbox, Anna dutifully opened the message and downloaded the photos. As soon as she saw the first one her heart began to thump and a huge smile lit up her face. As she flicked through the rest of the images she reached for her phone and rang Rosie. Her friend was right. This was the one she'd been looking for.

It was a cold, late November morning as Anna and Rosie set off to view the house, in truth, not the best day to see for the first time your potential holiday home. The fields and lanes were swathed in a depressing, grey drizzle, the type that clings to your clothes and soaks you through. Despite the weather, Anna was still raring to go and had hardly slept since Rosie rang with the news. Daniel couldn't believe her luck after seeing the photos, wishing he could have gone too but work commitments prevented it, so she booked a flight and flew out the next day.

The house was situated just outside the village of Le Pin which bordered Saint Pierre where Rosie lived, and according to her friend, less than a ten minute walk away. The house had been restored by an English couple who had lived there for almost six years, however, due to family issues they had decided to go home and wanted a quick, no fuss sale.

'That's it over there. You can see the back of the house from the road.' Rosie pointed to her right where plumes of smoke were pouring from the chimney, attracting their attention.

It was nestled behind a large furrowed field which separated the house from the road; the low tiled roof sloped down to small windows that lined the pale, pointed sandstone of its walls. Anna was eager to see more so they turned right into a lane where the white sign which directed them towards the house said '*La Roberdière*'. It made Anna smile because as she drove down the bumpy track, she couldn't ignore the overwhelming sensation that she was coming home.

Rosie pulled into the garden which had a gravel drive and a large, circular grassed area in the centre. '*That's where I will put a table and chairs, with a huge parasol, and I can watch the sun go down over those hills every night.*' Anna was lost in her own world as Rosie turned off the engine, breaking into her daydreams so they got out of the car and stood peering through the drizzle at the view. Neither said anything as they took in the landscape before them.

The fields rolled away as far as the eye could see and through the mist, they could make out the spire of a church and small hamlets tucked between the hills on the horizon, as the graceful arms of wind turbines rotated in the wind. Turning to take in the front of the house it was just as lovely as in the photos, even in the dreadful weather. The double-fronted farmhouse with its creamy walls and original square framed windows looked cosy and inviting. To the left, adjoining the main house was a hay loft which was built on four strong legs. It looked in need of minor repairs but apart from that the structure appeared sound. Rosie turned to Anna and smiled then nodded her head towards the door, indicating it was time to stop gawping and go inside.

The owner, Marge, was waiting to greet them, apologising as she showed them into the kitchen that her husband, Des, was at work. Anna eagerly took in the interior, a central wooden staircase spilt the bottom floor into two large separate rooms, and the back wall of both was open stone and had been pointed to create a feature throughout. The remaining walls had been plastered and painted in a soft cream, giving an open feel to the rooms. Anna's brain whirled as she imagined painting them warm, rustic colours, earthy and traditional. Each room had a fireplace on the gable wall, holding wood burning fires which pumped out heat, leaving the unmistakable aroma of log smoke wafting faintly in the air.

The kitchen in which they were standing was cosy and functional with modern wooden units lining the walls and a long counter separated the cooking and eating area. A door cut into the stone wall led out into the rear utility room and a loo. A large wooden table and chairs sat in the centre of the kitchen in front of the fire and a sofa under the front window looked so inviting, just crying out for one of Anna's blankets. She could see herself in there on cold nights, listening to the radio while she cooked or relaxed on the settee, wrapped in a blanket drinking a glass of wine while she read.

Then, when she saw the lounge she was spoilt for choice. Two large sofas and an armchair were arranged in front of the fire, a dining table to the rear of the room was set against the stone wall and in the summer, she could throw open the French doors that led onto the small back garden. And that was where, at long last, Anna would have her vegetable patch.

Upstairs there were three bedrooms, each with their own small en suite and as Marge explained, the door at the end of the corridor which ran along the back of the house, led into the hayloft outside. They had intended converting this into extra rooms for guests but things hadn't turned out as they'd expected and it was never finished. Anna already had plans for the hayloft. She would make it into a modern pine bunkroom, like in Rosie's gîtes. Outside, she would turn the space under the legs into a terrace with fairy lights, a chimenea and patio chairs, a cosy place to sit in the evenings. The giant cogs in her head were really working overtime now and as they clomped downstairs after Marge, Anna turned round and quickly gave a triumphant Rosie the thumbs up. All that was left now was to do the deal.

Over cake and tea, Anna got straight down to business, 'I absolutely love your house and I'm in a position to make you an offer for it. So if it's alright with you, I'd like to buy *La Roberdière* for the asking price and get the ball rolling as soon as possible. How does that sound?'

Anna looked hopefully across the table and waited for a response which didn't take long because once the reality of her words sunk in, Marge promptly burst into floods of tears.

'I think we can assume that's a yes then,' Rosie piped up and clapped her hands in delight. 'Shall I stick the kettle back on, Marge? I think we all need a strong cup of coffee and then we can make some plans and get cracking.' Getting up, she winked at Anna then tottered off, mission accomplished.

***

It was now Boxing Day and Anna was thinking of her little house. It would be hers by the end of January when she'd be flying over with Daniel to sign the papers and move in.

They'd had a lovely time over the past few days. Daniel and Josh came to stay and for Christmas dinner they were joined by Enid, Gladys and the lovebirds Jeannie and Phil. Christmas Eve had been fun; they ordered a huge Chinese takeaway and pigged out in front of the telly. Afterwards, the kids took themselves off to Anton's club with strict warnings regarding the over-imbibing of alcohol and, if the aforementioned Chinese food was sicked-up on any part of the apartment, severe punishments could be expected.

Once they'd left, Daniel and Anna set about placing piles of gifts under the tree and when everything was to Anna's satisfaction, Daniel suggested they take a bottle upstairs and relax under the stars so after a bit more faffing, she took a last glance at the hideous tree, dimmed the lights and made her way to the bedroom.

Daniel had poured two glasses of champagne and was waiting for her on the small balcony. It was quite mild for December and the night was still so when he beckoned for her to come outside, she slipped on her cardigan and did as he asked. Sliding the door shut behind her she accepted the bubbling glass and leant against the rail, looking out to sea. The sky was blazing with silver stars and the moon was full, casting a bright orb of light onto the gentle waves and the little boats that bobbed about on the Solent.

Daniel stood behind Anna and wrapped his arms around her, then whispered in her ear.

'Are you happy now, Anna, I mean, really happy?' He kissed her cheek gently and waited for her reply.

'You know something, Daniel? Christmas Eve is my favourite night of the year and I used to relish every second of this day, getting things ready and fussing about, it was the best part, all the expectation and excitement. Twelve months ago I never could have dreamed that I would be as happy as I am right at this minute. I thought that the joy of this night had been ruined forever by memories of the past. If someone had told me then, that it would all work out, I'd have thought they were mad but here I am, with you. You are my very special Christmas present, plus, all the kids are here, they're happy and doing God knows what at Anton's. I have my little house in France to look forward to and this place to live in. I have been truly blessed, so to answer your question, yes, I am deliriously happy.'

Anna rested her head on Daniel's chest and gazed out to sea. After a few moments spent in deep thought he loosened his grip and turned her to face him where she was met by his blue eyes, staring into hers, and she sensed he was nervous.

'Well, I hope that what I'm going to say now won't ruin the night and if it does you have my permission to chuck me off the edge, but I've wanted to tell you something for ages and give you this.' He fumbled in his pocket for a second then pulled out a small, dark blue box.

Anna's mind raced wildly along with her galloping heart and sensing her surprise, Daniel sought to reassure her.

'Don't panic, I'm not going to propose, well not right now, but I bought you this because I was wondering if you'd wear it on your right hand, as a symbol of us, our commitment to each other? I need you to know that I love you with all my heart and hope that someday in the future, I don't care if it's fifty years from now, you'll love me enough back to swap the ring to the other hand and be my wife. But until then it's a token of my love and it might just ward off any admirers who fancy their chances, what do you think?' Daniel's words hung in the still night air and dropping pins could've been heard a mile away.

Looking up, Anna couldn't see him anymore because her eyes were blurred by pools of tears that began to trickle down her cheeks.

'Of course I'll wear it, you idiot. I love you too, I have for ages. I just didn't want to scare you off so I didn't say the words, but I wanted to, so many times. I love you, Daniel, I really do, so much.'

Anna heard him breathe a sigh of relief and then he started to laugh, and she began to cry and laugh at the same time.

She also wished she had a tissue because she was getting a bit snotty. 'Well, open it then, let me see,' said Anna.

Fumbling with the lid as he obeyed, Daniel quickly opened the box to reveal a brushed platinum ring, dotted along the flat band with tiny, sparkling diamonds. Anna caught her breath then held out her right hand as he slipped the ring on to her finger.

'It's perfect, just like you. Thank you, Daniel. For waiting and being patient and just for everything really. This is my best Christmas Eve ever.'

And with that they kissed, a kiss full of passion and promise and love.

CHAPTER 6
Present Day

It seems hard to believe that two years have passed since Matthew's death. I've been thinking back to that day in the funeral car when my leaden heart was so full of misery and bitterness that just surviving the next twenty-four hours would have been something of a miracle, so to imagine I'd get over my husband's betrayal and eventually carve out a new life that is happy and full would have bordered on insanity. Well I can assure you that I'm not crazy. I'm standing here on the deck of the ferry, free from the burdens of the past which weighed me down for so long. I have confidence and strength that I deemed beyond my grasp, a future that contains hope and purpose and a fully functioning heart that is light and full of love.

Dusk is approaching but when I cross the Channel, I always stay on deck and watch the sun go down. It's a free pleasure in life and I try to enjoy this spectacle wherever I am, so I shall keep my spot here at the front of the ship until my hands become numb or the wind starts to pinch my face. I'm doing my best to hold back the march of time and avoid more wrinkles so I won't tempt fate and linger for too long. Portsmouth and the Isle of Wight are far behind us now and I will soon be able to pick out the lights of Guernsey in the distance.

Talking of lights, this time, my dear sons managed to behave themselves as I sailed past the apartment. It's become a bit of a tradition now that if anyone is home when I cruise by we ring each other and partake in a spot of frantic waving. People standing on deck or looking down from the restaurant probably think that I'm barking mad but I don't care. Joe bought some binoculars which he insists are for bird watching but all three of them just like to sit and spy on people from the balcony, and now he can spot me a mile off. Anyway, in February, as I neared the point where I can see the apartment, my attention was drawn to a flurry of fireworks and then flashing disco lights. As I got nearer it was quite clear they were coming from my place so in a temper, I rang to give Sam and Joe what for. Parties are banned, full stop. They couldn't hear me at first because of the music so turned it down and after they taped my ranting and raving then posted it on bloody Facebook, they both wet themselves laughing. I'd been had. I still rang Anton and got him to check, just in case, but it was fine, no rave. The little sods.

I'm on my fourth trip over since I finally got the keys to the house. It's coming together nicely now and I've loved every minute of putting my own mark on the place. The first night I stayed there with Daniel we slept on a duvet on the floor and camped out, it was exciting but extremely cold. You have to adhere to a rota of bringing in logs and keeping the fires going otherwise the thick stone walls never warm up. We've got the hang of it now but I assure you, January in France could freeze the marrow in your bones.

My mother finally made it over at Easter once I managed to convince her that I had satellite television and that she could watch all her soaps, and *Foyle's War* and *Heartbeat* and *One Foot in the Grave*... you get the drift. Melanie agreed to bring her on the plane as long as Mum wore normal clothes and didn't show her up by getting drunk. It all went quite smoothly but Melanie was visibly relieved when I collected them at the airport, unceremoniously handing over total responsibility to me the second they arrived.

My mother, after all her humming and hawing, loved France and had a ball with her new best friend, Marie, Rosie's mother-in-law. Despite neither being able to speak one word of the other's language they found a common bond in brandy and coke, chocolate éclairs and card games. Mum tried everything on offer where food is concerned and their friendship was sealed after a night playing bingo down at the *Salle des Fetes*, more commonly known as the village hall, where, with a lot of help from Marie, our Enid won a fondue set. The offending article is still in its box in the kitchen cupboard but Mum loved every minute and the whole experience has given her hours' worth of storytelling down at the community centre.

As for Melanie, her romance with Pascal seems to blossom as the seasons turn. She's already at Rosie's, working through the summer and when it's time for her to do her university placement in France, Henri has promised to fix her up with a post in his department. She will be able to live at my place and knowing it will be cared for and not lonely while I'm away is a bonus. Pascal is becoming interested in politics and wants to try for election to the farmers union. He believes passionately in protecting the land and the rights of his fellow workers and Melanie is constantly in awe of him. Who knows, one day she may be married to a French politician, or *Le President*, you never can tell.

Joe's doing well at Harrison's where he's been working hard and Dennis has taken him under his wing, along with Samantha who agreed to come back on a part-time basis to work with Joe and help him learn the ropes. She's been there so long she knows the firm inside out and was really missing her job. Joe's still not one hundred percent on team Daniel and gets on his high horse now and then where being the boss's son is concerned, but I keep him in check and we are muddling through.

As for Sam, there's no change there, thank God. He's still the same, easy-going lunatic who breaks hearts all over the place and lives life to the full. Despite his job I actually worry about him the least of all my kids as he exudes self-confidence and takes things at his own reliable pace. I still dread him doing another tour in Afghanistan but I'll cross that bridge if and when I come to it.

Oh, I forgot to mention the new addition to our family, my beautiful little Pippa who I adore beyond compare and has brought untold joy to my life. She's downstairs now, asleep in my car and I will have to nip down later and take her for a quick walk. Joe and Daniel travel a lot and even though I'm fine in Portsmouth, I was slightly nervous about being alone in the countryside in France so a dog was the ideal solution. Bulldogs are the perfect apartment companion and once I made up my mind it was full speed ahead. Everyone loves her even though she's a terrible snorer, it's so loud I can hear her upstairs but I find the sound strangely reassuring. She is so happy to see me when I come home and gives me a huge welcome so I never, ever feel lonely. I do admit that Pippa is becoming a bit of a diva and takes a huff if she can't sit on the front seat of the car or you pinch her special spot on the sofa, and will only eat biscuits if you dip them in tea first, but my girl has personality and I love it.

I'm sure it's not just my family that has its ups and downs and I frequently console myself in the knowledge that I wasn't unfortunate enough to be the mother of either the Ice Queen or Pongy Paloma. I rarely give the former any brain time but I bumped into Gavin, not literally, at the petrol station just after New Year and he told me that he split up with Caitlin soon after she left Harrison's. At first he felt sorry for her as she really did have some kind of nervous breakdown so the wedding, fortunately for him, had to be cancelled. He bankrolled her for a time until eventually his patience ran out. He was sick of being used and faced up to the fact that he would always be second best, so kicked her out. Since then, he's been dating the girl who delivers parts to his garage and has never been happier. Last he heard of Caitlin she had moved to London and was spreading her own, special brand of misery at an investment bank.

I can't wait to get to France. I'll be there for two whole months until September. Zofia is trying to convince me to stay until the apple picking season as she will be working in the fields, bringing in the harvest. You can earn around a thousand euros a month and she says it's great fun, you meet lots of new people and I could practice speaking French. I must admit I'm quite tempted so will see how I feel nearer the time.

At long last I've enrolled on a beginner's course in conversational French at the local technical college. I admit that I nearly chickened out on the first night but fate put me in the lift with an equally nervous lady called Mandy who was also contemplating doing a runner. Luckily, by the time we reached the second floor we had recognised in each other kindred spirits and jollied ourselves along sufficiently and found the courage to enter the classroom. Our teacher, the lovely Roland who is French-Mauritian, has the patience of a saint. He's semi-retired and after years of teaching adolescent boys, the strange mixture of students in my class is probably a walk in the park in comparison. Anyway, I shall soldier on and see how it goes, if nothing else I have met a new group of people who are gradually becoming friends and like me, enjoy a few glasses of red in the local pub after lessons.

I'm also looking forward to seeing how Rosie and Michel's barn is progressing. They wanted to get started on renovating their future home but the bank was unwilling to lend. I had funds left over from my French house budget so I offered to loan them what they needed. Once they have put a new roof on and done some basic structural work the bank will more than likely look upon the venture favourably and they will be able to complete their home. It was the least I could do as without their friendship and support I don't think I would be where I am today. Now, when Rosie walks past the barn on her way to the gîtes she can see her dreams becoming a reality and has hope for the future, just like I have.

Two years ago, if you had asked me about my hopes and dreams, I can honestly say that my spirit was so crushed that I had none. I thought my life was over and couldn't see any way through the fog of self doubt and shattered illusions. Now, I have both, nothing fancy or pie in the sky just everyday stuff like the children being happy and my family staying fit and well.

My next challenge is the vegetable garden. Rosie did point out to me that it's quite a lot of hard work keeping it under control but I am undeterred, especially because Pascal has kindly offered to go over once a week and tend it in my absence. He refused to take any payment, so as is the French way I will find something suitable to barter in exchange for his services. Sam suggested I just swap Melanie which wasn't quite what I had in mind.

My other dreams are for me and Daniel. I don't think there is anything I would change about our relationship right now as it works just the way it is. He is still busy and loves his job which takes him away quite a lot. I miss him when he is gone but I know he will be back so wherever our rendezvous takes place, his house or at mine, it keeps things alive and exciting. We are still able to enjoy what's left of our prime and have no intention of settling for pipe and slippers just yet. When that time comes I content myself in knowing without doubt that he will be there, we will embrace that chapter together.

Until then we have lots to do, like exploring France. It will be the second time round for Daniel but he insists that this time will be better with a companion. We plan to use *La Roberdière* as a base and see the sights. I've already bought a travel guide and started marking off the pages but the first destination isn't too far away because Daniel has booked us into the Hotel de la Plage at St Marc sur Mer. The grand seafront hotel fascinated me the first time I saw it and I've even watched the film, *Les Vacances de Monsieur Hulot – Monsieur Hulot's Holiday*. Daniel knew how much I wanted to stay so he reserved a suite with one of the huge iron balconies that look out over the Atlantic. I can't wait. It's just for the weekend but I love it there, it holds special memories and we will make some more together with Pippa because she can come too. Daniel has promised to wine and dine me with haute cuisine and then I'm going to sit and watch the sunset and listen to the tide. After that we are travelling south to see his daughter Louise and her family. I'm extremely nervous about it but I've spoken to her a couple of times on the phone to break the ice and she sounds lovely, just like her dad.

The stars are coming out now and when I see them I think of Matthew and wonder if he's up there, twinkling down on me, keeping watch, checking in now and then to make sure that we are all okay. I know he made mistakes, a huge cock-up if we are being honest, but I am convinced that he would only want the best for his family, for us to be happy. I also wonder what I will say to him when I meet him again because I know I will, just like my mum knows she will meet my dad. I'm also slightly concerned that there may be some kind of protocol to follow when you get up to heaven. Would husband number one get priority over husband number two, is there a pecking order? Or is it all peace, love and harmony? Perhaps you have a group hug and let bygones be bygones. Tricky or what? Still, whether it's politically correct or not I may cause a scene in the arrival lounge because I have a few things I need to get off my chest and some choice words to say to Matthew Harrison when I see him, and that's a fact!

Maybe he won't recognise the Anna I have become. I know without doubt that the last two years have changed me, they've opened my eyes and from now on I will live by a whole new set of rules. Firstly, I will not become complacent in my relationship. The safe haven of marriage and motherhood that I'd inhabited since I was a teenager shielded me in some ways from the harsh realities of life and human nature. I never imagined that someone else would want my husband or that he would stray, but he did. Maybe I was naive or took my eye off the ball, but it won't happen ever again. I will have the courage of my convictions, trust my instincts, and believe in myself, then if someone kicks my legs from under me I will be independent enough to stand back up and carry on.

It's funny how things from the past come back to haunt you now and then but tonight, I keep thinking of that day on the high street, when I was a child. I can't get the sad lady in the funeral cortege out of my mind. I wish I could travel back in time because I would run over to the car, bang on the window and tell her that it's all going to be okay. That I have survived the journey and so can she, and she shouldn't be afraid because the funeral is just a ritual, an ordeal, but afterwards she will get on with her life. I'd tell her to look around and draw courage from the love of her family and friends who will hold her up and when she's ready, she will find her way, just like I did. One step at a time.

It's getting a bit nippy on deck and the sea is quite choppy. The sun has just gone to bed and I think that perhaps I should do the same. Most of the passengers have gone inside now and there's not really much to see out here. I'll go down to the car and check on sleeping beauty and then I think I'll call it a night. That northerly wind has blown all my cobwebs away and cleared my head. I don't want to think about the past anymore. Tonight this ship is ploughing through the waves and taking me into the future so that's what I'm going to focus on.

I've learned quite a few helpful phrases and words in my French class and I have a favourite which I always use whenever one of my lot are going off somewhere, there seems to be rather a lot of coming and going these days. As I look up into the dark, starry sky and speed through the waves towards France, to everyone I love and hold dear, who surround me with friendship and support and especially those who I may not meet for some time, I send you all my love, always and forever. *À bientôt...* I'll see you soon.

THE END

ACKNOWLEDGEMENTS

I would like to thank the following wonderful people. My husband Brian who is the love of my life. Amy, Owen, Harry, Mark and Jess who make me so happy and proud. My precious mum whose faith in me never ever wavered as I wrote this book. Angela, Mandy and Anita for being brilliant friends and so much more. All my friends and loyal readers. My ARC group who are all superstars. Nicki Murphy for her support and friendship. The wonderful team at Bloodhound, Betsy, Sumaira, Alexina, Tara, Abbie, Fred and especially Heather who has worked so hard on this story and the whole series.

Printed in Great Britain
by Amazon